RECOMBINANT

EXPERIENCING TRUE PURPLE
BOOK 1

L. S. SILVERTHORNE

AWARD-WINNING AUTHOR

L.S. SILVERTHORNE

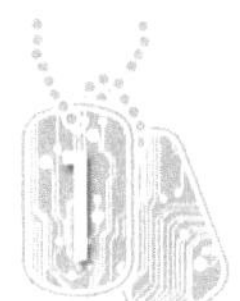

RECOMBINANT

EXPERIENCING TRUE PURPLE

They stole his memories. Controlled his dreams.

Because he was government property.

They gave him a year to live. At an alien war front.

To save a world he'll never see.

Programmed to fight and kill, he's not like other recombinants.

He just wants to live.

An overwhelming alien force moves toward home system as the front line fragments. With most advanced tech destroyed and human armies decimated, recombinants (cloned soldiers) are the last line of defense against the alien surge.

Until one recombinant defies his programming.

A combat medic's investigation reveals a catastrophic failure in the tech, endangering Earth's entire recombinant army. Reporting the defect will destroy hundreds of recombinants, including this enigmatic recombinant defying his programming. But saying nothing risks losing the war—and her home world.

Recombinant

Book 1 of the ***Experiencing True Purple*** series

Lisa Silverthorne

Published by ElusiveBlueFiction.com

Elusive Blue Fiction Logo designed by Samantha Romage

Cover Design by Lost Souls Studio

Additional Cover Elements licensed from Creative Market, DepositPhotos, Shutterstock

ISBN-13: 978-1-955197-00-7 (Hard cover)

ISBN-10: 1-955197-00-8

ISBN-13: 978-1-955197-01-4 (Trade paperback)

ISBN-10: 1-955197-01-6

For my dear friends, RON AND LISA COLLINS.
You helped make this book happen. Thank you. Lisa is one of the most amazing copyeditors I've ever worked with and helped fix my errors in an earlier draft of this story.

And a huge thanks to one of my best friends, PATRICIA DUFFY NOVAK *who lent her stellar copyediting chops to the final version of this novel.*

Novels by L.S. Silverthorne

Experiencing True Purple series:

RECOMBINANT, Book 1

HELIX, Book 2

SPLICE, Book 3

Standalone:

REDISCOVERY

Writing as Lisa Silverthorne

A Game of Lost Souls series:

Contemporary Romantasy

THE CINDERELLA HOUR

THE PRINCE CHARMING HOUR

THE EVER AFTER HOUR

THE FALLEN HEARTS SEASON

THE RISING SPIRITS SEASON

THE ETERNAL SOULS SEASON

THE ROYAL WEDDING HOUR

THE HEAVENLY HONEYMOON HOUR

THE DIVINE NEWLYWEDS SHOW

THE CELESTIAL COUPLES SHOW

THE ENOCHIAN APOCALYPSE SHOW

THE ANGELIC ANNIVERSARY SHOW

THE PERDITION PICTURE SHOW

Complete Series!

Curse and Crown series:

Epic Court Intrigue Romantasy

THORN & BLADE

STORM & STEEL

The Spiral series:

Dark Contemporary Fantasy

BETWEEN

REPRISE

AVENGE

The Resurrectionist Papers

Paranormal Romystery

GRAVE RECKONING

Standalones:

ISABEL'S TEARS

LANDFALL

PACIFIC BLUE TATTOO

Short Story Collections

THE SOUND OF ANGELS

THE MAGIC OF ORDINARY THINGS

TIMELESS

WINTER'S EMBRACE

1

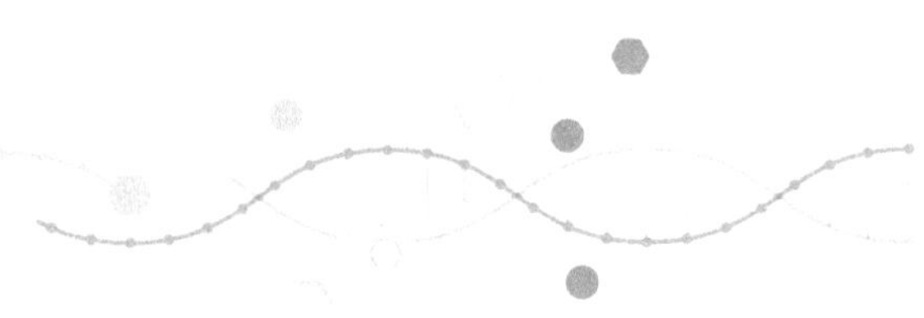

PRIVATE PETER MITCHELL huddled in a trench and hoped the mud would hide his shaking. His gut clenched, the odor of sulfur and sweat making him ill. If only he could sink into the soil and disappear. The other soldiers would be glad to see him gone. One less terrified recombinant to risk washing out the entire unit.

He'd failed enough training sims. He couldn't fail any more.

Gripping the plasma rifle in stiff, aching hands, Peter scanned the swamp. Trees tangled along the banks, blackened trunks trailing skeins of vines and brown moss. The murky water swirled and rippled, lapping softly against grassy patches of mud. Fog settled in pockets of brush, obscuring the distant landscape.

Heat roiled in the trench, the air so thick and raw with sulfur that his throat burned with every breath. It would rain again before the mud hardened. A simulation of summer at the front.

Peter hoped he never saw the real thing.

Three other recombinants crouched in the trench beside him. Their taut, grim faces burned with concentration and a hunger that Peter didn't share. The barrels of their plasma rifles skimmed across the edge of the trench as they scoped for their target. Antarans.

Again, Peter reminded himself that the enemy they faced was only a VR image, but he had no stomach for killing, not even virtually. He wanted no part of it.

Private John Stingley crawled across the trench and flopped down between Peter and Private Steven Drake. Sting ran a muddy hand through his curly blond hair, darker than Peter's straight blond locks, and scanned the horizon. Sting grabbed the small sensor grid hanging around his neck and swung it in a quick arc.

"Nothing's out there. I don't get it," Sting said.

Sting turned his back to the horizon, slumped down in the trench, and sniffed the air.

"Maybe that's part of the sim," Drake muttered. His stringy, chestnut bangs clung to his forehead. He brushed them out of his hard, grey eyes. "I just want to shoot something."

"Whatever," Sting said with an eye roll. "You'll get your chance to hunt at the front, Drake."

"Not if Mitchell fucks up again I won't," Drake muttered.

Peter had already learned to avoid Drake at all costs. Three times in the infirmary had driven that lesson home.

Sting ignored Drake. He nudged Peter, startling him. "Run point. Let me know when you see something."

"Sure," said Peter, his lungs aching from the heat.

He laid a hand to his chest and looked away from Sting.

"And read it right this time, Mitchell or you'll fuckin' regret it!" Drake shouted. A scowl twisted across his angular face.

"Leave him alone," Sting snapped. "You're not exactly a grid expert either."

Drake kicked at the drying mud. "At least I can fucking tell what's coming or going. Mitchell can't tell an Antaran from a stump, much less its direction. By the time he calls incoming, those things'll be sittin' on our chests suckin' out our hearts."

"Just shut up and do your job," Sting snapped with a growl. "I'm tired of your bellyaching."

Peter glanced back at Sting, offering a quick smile of thanks.

Sting was the only recombinant Peter knew who'd been to the front and survived to tell about it. They brought Sting back to the training station to work with a new batch of fresh Antaran bait and accompany them to the front.

Fighting down his fear, Peter hurried ahead to the edge of the swamp and crouched. Glancing around at the stillness, he raised his sensor grid and scanned the perimeter.

He'd long understood that recombinants were expendable.

In the brass' eyes, recombinants were recycled soldiers lucky enough to have air in their lungs. Any breaths he took were gifts as far as UCOE was concerned. Especially since units like Peter's had a life expectancy of one year. Most of them never returned. Not like there was anyone around to miss them.

A faint alarm pulsed from the sensor grid.

Stiffening, Peter studied the terrain grid, searching for a ghost echo signature. For something that marked Antaran presence.

He'd learned in class that Antarans altered their molecular structure to mimic objects around them. They adapted quickly, Lieutenant D'Angelo had warned. Every shift produced a sweet smell, like honey, and somehow, it momentarily confused the sensors.

He searched the treetops for a glint of talons and sniffed for the scent of sweetness.

Not even a trace hung in the air.

Pivoting right, Peter scanned. Swallowed a breath. Nothing.

Swamp sounds died away to a whisper, soft chirp of the grid echoing. Louder now.

Something was in the swamp.

He frowned. *Was it entering or leaving the swamp?*

Slow, agonizing pulse of the alarm made him tremble. He froze, his stomach tightening.

They were close.

Inhaling sharply, he moved behind a rotting tree on the edge of the trench, longing to sink into its soft, crumbling wood.

"Please—just get me out of here alive," he muttered under his breath.

"What was that, Pete?" Sting answered on his comm.

Sting was the only one in the unit who called him Pete. He wrinkled his brow, sliding closer to the tree.

"I'm—uh, I'm picking up movement."

In moments, Sting and Drake were behind him at the trench's edge. He glanced over at Sting whose gaze flitted across the muggy swamp.

Deadly silent. Peter's heart pounded against his chest. Deadly still.

Insects buzzed in the lazy calm. Grass rustled. Birds took flight.

The chirping alarm heightened, now an audible wail.

Peter's muscles went taut like overstressed wires. He sniffed for a trace of honey.

Nothing.

His throat went dry and tight, and he fought to form words.

"Something's in the swamp," he said, his voice slow, barely above a whisper. "But I can't tell what it is."

He closed his eyes, shivering, and hugged the tree with his back. He didn't want to die.

Drake rose on his elbows, muzzle of his plasma rifle jerking toward the swamp. Sting turned his gaze to Drake and the other recombinant behind him. Private Wendy Evans. Short and flame-haired. A new recombinant that Peter didn't know.

"Anything there?"

"Not yet," came Evans' muffled reply. She scrambled around the edge of the trench.

"Keep a close eye on that grid, Pete," said Sting. "The bastards'll sneak up on you. And watch for a bow echo. Sometimes, they double back."

Sting started to turn away from Peter, but something caught his gaze. He squinted. "What is it, kid?"

The kindness in Sting's voice surprised Peter. He tried to answer, but the mounting sound of the alarm, the shuffling in the trench, and his growing terror immobilized him.

He shook his head, unable to answer.

"Look, it's just a sim," said Sting with a smile. He reached out and ruffled Peter's blond hair. "You've spent long hours in the classroom and VR-chamber. You've run hundreds of computer sims. This one's just another sim, Pete. It's not the real thing yet. Tell yourself that."

Nodding, Peter forced a smile.

Sting cast a lingering stare at him. "You're different. Younger looking. I've seen plenty of scared recombinants, but not this bad." He grinned. "Don't worry. It's not like you've got a soul to lose or something."

The alarm whistled louder.

Peter glanced wildly around, fingers white-knuckling the rifle. Drake and Evans stalked the trench's perimeter, peering through the haze for a sign of movement.

Sting motioned at the others, his gaze on the horizon. "We're programmed to live for this stuff, but you—damn kid, you're terrified. You really hate it. Not sure how you slipped through the wash outs." He squeezed Peter's arm. "Look, you're gonna be okay. Just do what you were trained to do."

Peter's arm muscles relaxed. He let out a sigh. "Thanks, Sting."

"Forget Mitchell!" Drake shouted. "He can't read the damned thing!"

Drake planted himself in the mud, the stock of his plasma rifle pressed against his shoulder. "I've got movement in the southern quadrant."

Drake squinted as he clicked on his laser sight. The red beam trailed off into the fog.

"Come and get it, you bastards."

Everyone except Peter shifted toward the southern end of the trench. He wiped the sweat from his bangs and stared at the grid.

Southern quadrant? No, Drake was wrong...or was he?

A small white movement trail boomeranged across Peter's grid. Air displacement.

Antarans moved by air displacement. He remembered that from class. That displacement caused a faint, ghostly trail across the grid. It sounded so easy. *So why couldn't he read it?*

He sucked in a hot breath, sweat pouring into his eyes.

Were the Antarans retreating? Or coming in from the north?

"Drake, you're wrong," said Peter in a low voice, turning.

The alarm quieted, slipping into the silence.

Peter scanned the perimeter again. From the motion on the grid, he knew they were close, but he couldn't pinpoint a location.

"They're retreating," said Evans.

She snapped a hand through her spiky red hair and leaned on her rifle. She was lean and graceful, that glint of hunger in her brown eyes. Like the other recombinants around him.

Why was he so different? Why?

Drake kicked at the drying mud. "Damn! No kills today."

"Hold position," said Sting, his voice ominous in the silence. "They're still out there."

"But the grid says—"

"They won't leave without attacking us!" Sting insisted. "They always attack."

Sting rose to his knees and crawled to the center of the trench. And waited.

"I see nothing out there!" Drake shouted. "You're full of it, Stingley."

"Yeah, they're long gone," said Evans, crouching beside Drake. "No kills. A day wasted."

Sting glared at them. "Don't get stupid now. We can take these bastards if you don't let your guards down. And don't get cocky, Drake."

The alarm whispered, a trail of movement in the northern quadrant.

Peter swallowed hard, trying to hold back his fear. His chest ached at the sensor's pulse throbbing again, the sound rising then quickly fading.

Drake and Evans rushed back and forth in the trench.

"Dammit, Mitchell," Drake snarled. "Do your job! You're on point. Where the hell are they?"

Shaking, Peter held the grid closer to his face. Seeing traces of movement across the grid. A faint bow-shaped echo splashed across the northern quadrant again and then disappeared—closer this time.

A cold heaviness gripped his insides. *Dammit, there was nothing to target! Nothing.*

"Stay with me, Pete," came Sting's calming voice above the soft grid alarm. "Don't fade on me now. We need you."

The sensor's alarm suddenly shrieked in Peter's ears, the pulse turning into a solid, high-pitched whine. A bow echo slithered across the grid, nearly on top of them.

"Sting! They're overrunning us!"

"Hold your positions," Sting said, his voice steady. "Attack on my mark!" He turned toward Peter. "Where are they, kid? I'm not seeing them."

From somewhere inside, Peter felt an Antaran presence. It came swiftly and felt like nothing he'd ever encountered. He sniffed the air. Hanging above the sulfur and sweat was a trace of honey.

Sting whirled, sniffing the air.

His surprised gaze locked with Peter's wide-eyed stare. Peter became aware of the tree against his shoulder again and a sickness trembled in the pit of his stomach. His muscles seized with dread as he turned slowly to look above his head. He gagged, the scent of honey and sulfur overpowering.

They were directly overhead.

"Pete, look out!"

A spiked appendage ripped down from the tree, snapping around Peter's chest. He screamed, firing off a round of shots. He felt his flesh tearing, his intestines wrenching. Everything darkened.

"End training sim!" Lieutenant D'Angelo's sharp voice punched through Peter's agony.

The swampy landscape and the Antarans dissolved into the fading sunlight. Spiked appendages dissipated into the air and Peter found himself lying in a dusty trench staring up at an amber sky. He crawled toward the wall and collapsed, his fingers still gripping unseen talons. His breath still came in gasps.

"You're dead, Mitchell," said D'Angelo, his angry form hanging over the edge of the trench. Short and wiry. Square jawed. Hard dark eyes. "You're all dead!"

Peter groaned, his plasma rifle falling to his side. He glanced at the other recombinants and then averted his eyes from their fury—except for Sting.

Maybe they should wash him out?

But this taste of life, this whiff of what lay beyond this place—his place—burned a fire inside him. And he didn't want to give any of that back.

Sting leaned against the dirt wall of the trench and shook his head as if he'd just lost a poker game. Sting was only twenty-three, but he looked thirty. Not even his curly blond hair and haunted, pale green eyes made him look younger now. The front had aged him. Would that same haunted stare look back at him from the mirror? If he lived that long.

Drake scowled and kicked dirt at Peter. "It's Mitchell's fault, sir! Our first off-site training sim and you get us all killed like fucking noobs! I'm not washing out because of you!"

Drake lunged for Peter, but Sting stepped in, shoving Drake backward. Drake tried to break past Sting, but Sting smashed his fist into Drake's chin. Drake stumbled backward and fell into the dirt.

"Back off, Drake! We were supposed to work as a team and we screwed up—together. We're not here to kill everything that moves."

Drake bared his teeth at Sting and jerked himself out of the dirt. He kicked the wall of the trench and turned his back on Sting.

"All right, fall in," said D'Angelo. "Get your asses back to base, double time! This unit will repeat the sim again next week."

Peter kept his head down as Drake, Sting, and Evans climbed out of the trench. He wanted to kick himself. Drake was right. It was his fault they failed the training sim.

Why couldn't he locate the Antarans before the sensor grid went berserk? Why couldn't he control the fear?

Lieutenant D'Angelo waited with a stony expression as recombinants emerged from other trenches in the barren field. The air smelled of dust and sweat.

Peter looked at the horizon without the presence of the VR swamp filter. Someone once told him that the ID chip in his neck made the sim feel real while the VR filters made everything look like Ku'Tal.

This planet was nothing more than a sandy wasteland. Sand and nothingness stretched endlessly into the distance, broken only by the dark, boxy shuttles sitting on the runway. But to him, it was beautiful with its amber sand and pale sky, the only planet he'd ever seen before. He loved its warm, gritty scent.

He trotted toward the shuttles that would ferry him and his unit back up to the training base that orbited this planet. On the far side of the planet, where the water resources were acceptable, he'd heard there was a small mining town and a shuttle port. A real one, not like this small platform. Out here, there was nothing, yet the vastness and wild expanse excited him. He wanted to walk all of it, feel the warm amber sand against his toes, the hot sun against his face. He'd never seen a town before.

Sighing, Peter moved to stand with his unit and sidestepped a pair of furry rodents scampering through a patch of dry grass. This morning, he'd seen one of those creatures in the launch bay and tossed it some crackers he'd saved from mess. The little creature didn't belong up there. He understood that feeling.

Drake shoved past, his elbow grinding into Peter's back. Peter winced and tried to move away, but Sting slid into formation between them. Drake backed off.

"No worries, Pete," Sting said and popped Peter on the shoulder. "Wasn't your fault. Those Antarans wreak havoc on the grid and sometimes, the computers laying out their movements can't keep up. Drake didn't read it any better."

Peter nodded. "Thanks."

"Attention!"

Peter and the other recombinants snapped to attention, waiting for D'Angelo to dismiss them.

"We're bringing in a new training sergeant and a field sergeant to take over this unit. It's your last hope, boys, or HQ's going to wash out the lot of you. Your unit's sim scores have pulled your ratings way down."

Peter stiffened. *Wash out?* He closed his eyes.

It was painless, they said, that recombinants didn't suffer. They just went to sleep. Sometimes, the wash out's xDNA sequence was even culled from the databases and never replicated again. He'd read that much in the library.

Nevertheless, washing out meant a nothingness that Peter couldn't bear.

"Sergeants Temple and Galloway will work with you guys starting tomorrow. There'll be more classroom, more VR sims, and a few more rounds of off-site drills like this one. Make sure you pass this round. Either way, it'll be your last round. Now, report to your seating assignment on the shuttle. Move it!"

Peter and his unit hustled toward the shuttle. As he reached the ramp, Drake drove his fist into Peter's back. Peter stumbled, his face skidding across the ramp. He fell headfirst into the sand.

From the ramp, Drake pointed at him. "That's a warning, Mitchell. If you fuck up one more time, I'll shoot you myself before I let you wash out the entire unit." He disappeared into the shuttle.

Peter's face and knees burned as he staggered up from the ground and hobbled up the ramp. How could he overcome his fear long enough to pass a training sim that would send him to the front to die?

2

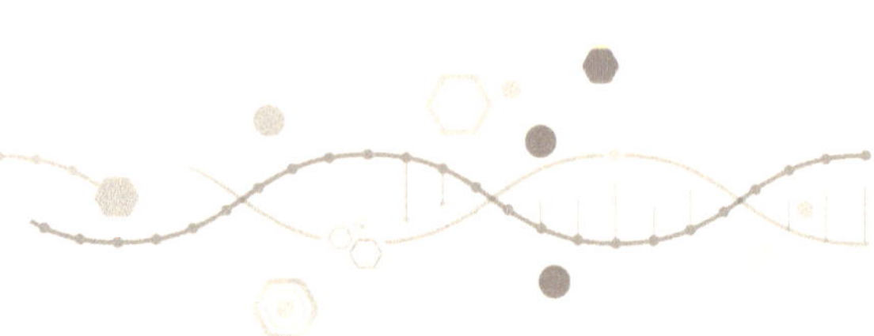

"IT'S the smell I always remember—the stench of dried blood never leaves," said shift coordinator, Dr. Kai Drew.

Nice enough—and easy on the eyes with his jet-black hair and pale blue eyes—when he wasn't being a control freak.

Dr. Jeannette Kingston tried to tune out Kai's voice, concentrating instead on the dead recombinant soldier on her autopsy table. And the grim task ahead of her. But Kai kept talking—as usual.

He made a sour face. "Detox mist smells like minty death. Strong enough to kill germs and anything else healthy that gets in the way."

Like a recombinant, she reminded herself.

Cloned from recombinant xDNA patterns developed and owned by the United Countries of Earth, these soldiers were government property—along with the microtechnology they were required to exhume and return. Four natural nucleobases and four artificial ones, mapped and edited to produce the ultimate soldier, copyrighted and trademarked by UCOE. Along with the secret progression process that brought them an adult soldier in only months.

This recombinant on her table had given his life to push back the

Antaris Nation from home system and he deserved her full attention, even if it was only a few minutes.

"After working here, you never forget the smell of death. God, I miss lunar colony. We had state-of-the-art stations and tech there. Best tools around. Not this archaic crap."

Ruth Becker. Two years as a Reclamation Specialist. Never happy. Bitching about the tech. Again.

Jeannette rolled her eyes. Woman had the compassion of antistatic wrap. Jeannette was sure she'd been a retired department store mannequin before hiring on here. Ruth didn't need an MRC to perform these gristly reclamation tasks. She'd opted out, but to her, cloned soldiers were just cattle. Like the old earth factory breed and butcher farms. Steaks on legs. To her—and many others—recombinants were just mobile meat shields.

Ruth wore an orange-flowered lab coat and hip-hugging green scrubs, dark hair tied back in a ponytail, and dull brown eyes. She found the standard UCOE issue blue scrubs distasteful, and bought her own. Ruth's station was part of a pod of four stations in front of Jeannette's, beside DiFiorio's, and diagonally from Kai's.

Unlike Ruth, Jeanette didn't need to stand out. She wore the standard issue blue scrubs and grey lab coat.

"How about you, Jeannette?" Ruth asked in her antagonistic, prodding way. Sarcastic and condescending, she had a mean smirk on her face, the one she painted on whenever she trash-talked somebody. Which was most of the time. "What gets to a decorated front line medic?

Jeannette cringed. *My coworkers.*

Ruth laughed, the sound like a braying donkey. "This must be like a regular Saturday night to you. Just another day at the front, right, Jeanette?"

Jeannette glared at her.

If her memory replacement chip allowed her any memories at all, Jeanette might bristle at the sharp, ever-present mint tang of germicide. Or the cloying metallic scent of dried blood clinging to her autopsy table and permeating the entire Reclamation Station. No matter how many times it was sanitized and sprayed. Smells that clung to everything until she let the shower—and her MRC—wash it all away. Wash away the massive number of casualties coming through the station. The smell of death that never left.

Yeah, they were only recombinants, but to her, they were still people. With hopes and dreams no matter how short their lives were, they were still human.

Sometimes, the pleasant scent of the lavender oil she daubed under her nose to mask it all floated over the blood and decay smells. Like her MRC parsing most of her past, scrubbing away everything but safe, recycled images. Safe memories that allowed her to keep recovering government hardware from the huge volume of dead soldiers and uploading their MRC data to home system.

That let her do her part for the war effort. No matter how painful.

But, every single day, those scents and images were raw and fresh. And she hated them.

"Red?" Kai stared at her with those intense blue eyes, pressing his mouth into a grimace. "You okay?"

He called her red because of her auburn hair. She didn't mind. It was endearing the way he said it. And it pissed off Ruth, so win-win.

Jeannette cast a quick glance at him, surprised he was asking her (rather than telling her) how she felt, and stepped back from her autopsy table. One of twenty stations in the cavernous room, the flow of red body bags constant—along with the occasional blue bags. Red for recombinants, blue for UCOE citizens/soldiers. The transport personnel had already placed two more red bags on her rack. She glanced at her watch and held in a groan. 1100 hours. Only seven more hours to shift's end.

Today—the bodies, the callus remarks, the smell of germicide and death—it all just felt like too much. She rubbed her sleeve across her forehead, careful not to touch the gloves to her face.

"I guess Jeannette just remembers all the tears she's shed for these recycled soldiers. Boo fucking hoo." Ruth sniffed and pretended to rub her fist underneath her eye, mocking tears.

Her horse laugh cut through Jeanette. Enough already!

Gritting her teeth, Jeannette surged around the edge of her table and into Ruth's station. She glared at the skinny, arachnid-of-a-woman.

"You want to know what *I* remember, Ruth?" Jeannette slammed the shards of a broken MRC onto Ruth's table. "I remember the bits and pieces of these recombinant soldiers' lives from their MRCs! When they were living, breathing, laughing human beings who died without ever living so we could keep our comfortable little lives happy on lunar colony. But to you, they're just cattle bred to die!" She poked Ruth's lab coat with her index finger, smearing blood on her lapel. "That's what this decorated front line medic remembers. And you can shove your boo fucking hoo, Ruth."

Ruth stared at her unblinking, her eyes wide. Along with every Reclamation Specialist within earshot. Including her supervisor, Kai whose mouth was open just slightly.

A cart of red body bags squeaked past, bound for other pods, as Jeannette walked back to her station. She cast a withering look at Ruth who was amazingly silent for once and returned to the dead young man on her table.

She glanced at Kai, expecting to see his face pinched with anger as he wrote her up for disorderly conduct.

Take your best shot, Kai. She didn't care. Her only regret was not remembering this tomorrow. She hid her smile. But Ruth would.

For a moment, Kai's gaze met hers and he smiled. Stone-faced, control-freak Kai Drew was smiling at her. He looked away, back at the body on his table and Jeannette thought she heard him chuckle.

Jeannette stepped behind her L-shaped station and slid into her desk chair. She rolled it over to the processing computer that was perpendicular to the autopsy table. Beside the computer stood an MRC processing unit and sequence capture scanner, ready to capture a soldier's mission data and final moments, uploading them to the solar array for analysis. The overhead lights stabbed crisp white beams at the dark floor as Jeannette recorded the incident in her log file.

Called *my life*, the file loaded every time she logged into any device, mobiles included. Pathed to her personal key ring, she kept it off the solar array. These bits and pieces of her life were safe from her MRC's parsing (which uploaded automatically to the solar) and contained everything she wanted to remember.

Just facts in the third person though—a poor substitute for a real life.

The only thing missing was the phrase, *Dear Diary*, but the log file was the best way she'd found to retain the moments important to her. Like the death of her two-year-old daughter, Rena Diane Kingston, and the memories of her ex-husband. She didn't want a Xanax life, but the MRC had been a requirement back then. She wanted to remember the pain along with the happiness.

Without both, she couldn't tell the difference.

And she didn't want her MRC (or the government) to choose what she'd remember. But removing an MRC wasn't as easy as installing one. The thought of permanent memory damage terrified her.

Ruth started chattering quietly with Angelino DiFiorio or Dr. Di as the women called him. He was dark and handsome, quiet and somewhat caring for a Reclamation Specialist. Like Jeannette, he'd been to the front, but because of an injury, he had his MRC removed.

She worried about him sometimes, when she saw his concern when unzipping bags. Sometimes, he'd stand there, eyes closed, shoulders hunching as if preparing for the remains that lay inside. She saw his watery eyes when he talked about some of his cases. Sometimes, he talked with a haunted expression about some of their last moments, moments captured and played back by the MRC processing. The last forty-eight hours of life.

Rendered in an eerie, first person point of view, those moments haunted Jeannette. She understood his reaction. She'd already seen enough to last her a lifetime this morning. And she'd recorded some of her reactions in her log file.

DiFiorio's eyes seemed glazed over as Ruth chattered away at him. He sighed and cast an understanding look at Jeannette as he unzipped another body bag.

Jeannette turned back to the computer and sent off her report on the sandy-haired young man, Dylan 1201. She always gave them first names. Sounded nicer than John Doe. She usually called the men Dylan.

After zipping up the red bag, she affixed the fluorescent yellow *completion* scan label, and slid the bag onto the narrow conveyor belt that ran between the reclamation pods. When she turned to the rack of body bags, two more red bags had been added.

Daubing more lavender oil underneath her nose, Jeannette slid another body bag onto the table and unzipped it. A young woman, barely twenty (the age RDC was producing right now) lay pristine on the table, stark overhead lights washing out her smooth face and animating her dull brown eyes. Still open.

Turning to the computer, Jeannette created a new record and typed in a name for the dead recombinant. Recombinant #1202, Rena 1202. She always named the women Rena. After her daughter.

There wasn't a mark on the young woman's body, not even a scratch. But her empty brown eyes stared straight ahead. Jeannette reached down and closed the woman's eyes as she scanned the tag affixed to the body bag. She frowned at the reclamation code NALIQ that appeared on her screen. She hadn't seen that code in a while, but knew its meaning well.

Nominal Aggression Level and Intelligence Quotient.

No need for an autopsy on this one, she thought with a sigh. Rena 1202 never reached the war front on Ku'Tal. UCOE labeled her unusable and washed her out with a lethal injection.

Couldn't she have helped the war effort in some way? Why just extinguish her life like this? Why? It made no sense!

Disgusted, Jeannette threw her laser scalpel onto the instrument tray beside the clear workstation panel. The loud clang echoed through the usually quiet room, startling several specialists. DiFiorio and Kai both stared at her, Ruth rolling her eyes.

"What next? Hair too light, eyes too dark!" She stepped away from the young woman. "Why just kill them like this!"

Kai frowned. No doubt ready to supervise her back to her station. God, she was so tired of everything being micromanaged and coordinated and supervised. Sanitized and expunged. Everything from her conduct to what swirled through her dreams at night.

Kai seemed unaffected by the seven-year influx of bodies from a war Earth was losing badly. People were being slaughtered on Ku'Tal's swampy battlefields. But it wasn't so bad. They were just recombinants, right? Most of UCOE's expensive, high-tech weaponry had perished in the war's first three years. By year eight, the war had mutated into something out of the 20th century because the money had simply run out. So, the military merged with bioengineering. Recombinants became inexpensive to produce, but was their presence only perpetuating the inevitable loss?

And at what cost? They were already creating disposable people. What next? There had to be another way.

Kai's attitude toward the recombinants was distant and clinical, not hostile like Ruth's, but disturbing. And it drove her crazy. MRCs had a way of doing that to people. Like her, he'd been a front-line medic. Here six years to her four.

"At least that one had a shot at it," Kai replied, motioning at her with his scalpel, his loud voice carrying through the cavernous room. "Without UCOE, she'd just be bits of xDNA in a test tube somewhere."

Jeannette glared at him. *Two months of training—some shot.* "What's the point of creating them and then destroying them? In case these body bags aren't enough of a reminder, we're losing this war. Badly."

She braced for an acerbic reply, but Kai didn't rise to the occasion. Instead, he calmly set down his laser scalpel. The blue beam was luminous against the anti-contaminants misting the body bag on his exam table. He peeled back the flaps, revealing a badly mangled body.

Jeannette sighed.

Antarans had butchered that one.

"Without them," he said, motioning to the dead recombinant soldier, "this could be you or me in this bag. Home system would have already been overrun and we'd all end up like this. UCOE's damned lucky to have the recombinant technology." His voice had an edge to it. "And we're damned lucky they're fighting for *us*!"

Ah, her words hit a sore spot. She'd made some progress after all.

"Lucky? Lucky to have MRCs and microfeeds and recombinant reclamation? Like they were given a choice to fight."

Their gazes locked and the anger in his eyes was bright.

Finally, he tapped the body bag on his exam table. "Yes. But I'm tired of seeing people mangled to bits like this—even recombinants."

She snapped her glove tighter over her left hand. "So how long are we going use them as human shields?"

"Until there's another way," snapped Kai, his eyes narrowed as he concentrated on his workstation screen.

Jeannette sighed and returned to Rena 1202. No one seemed to be looking very hard into another way. She smoothed a lock of brown hair out of Rena 1202's eyes. As long as the recombinants were produced quickly and in record numbers, it was just some distant war in someone else's backyard back home on Earth.

She slid Rena 1202's body closer to the sequence capture scanner at the far end of the table. Red lights winked on and crosshairs slipped across the recombinant's still face as the scanner gathered streams of data from the MRC in her neck.

The scanner hummed softly, converting the raw data into enhanced viewable format. EVF produced a first-person video effect of the memories parsed and stored in the chip. The MRC held all of this young recombinant's memories and then selectively parsed out everything but the harmless ones for transmission back to the recombinant. It even hijacked her ability to form new memories.

Just like hers.

Jeannette always did the conversion and scan before removing the chip, in case the MRC was damaged during the extraction.

Ruth's horse laugh echoed through the chamber and Jeannette fought down the urge to strangle the woman as she waited for the scan to finish. In another moment, the MRC processing unit flashed a green light, data successfully scanned and transferred. Jeannette ran an authentication procedure on the chip, the AWOL tracker long disabled. AWOL trackers began signaling when their temperature sensors fell below 96 degrees or exceeded a defined perimeter. But usually, only death or extraction set one off.

Picking up the tissue-resin separator, she bent over the recombinant. Using gentle pressure, not that it mattered now, she extracted the MRC from the back of the recombinant's neck. After cleansing the thumbnail-sized black chip with saline, she snapped it in the input slot. The small view screen embedded in the face of the unit lit as the instrument whispered to life, LEDs flickering as the final conversion of data began.

She reached up to the view screen and turned it off, offering this recombinant the only privacy she could. She didn't need to see the young woman's final hours of life.

All through the room, screens flickered, muffled voices and whir of machinery punctuating the hush. She tuned out the sounds, instead opening her login script and typing in a note about Rena 1202 and her reaction to the wash out code. It galled her, but Kai was right. Her MRC would parse out anything that caused an adverse emotional reaction to doing her job.

Without warning, the processing unit powered down and a red light flashed on the panel. She leaned closer. The chip verification light pulsed red—MRC failure.

She cursed under her breath and returned to her control panel display, sliding windows and data across the screen with her index finger. This was the second MRC failure she'd seen today.

"Dammit, not again," said Troy Davies, a Reclamation Specialist in the pod across from hers. "Hey, anybody else gettin' these MRC failure codes? I've had them all week."

"I've had two today," replied Carolyn, another Reclamation Specialist across the room.

"One here," answered DiFiorio.

"I've had two," Jeannette answered. "I'm running diagnostics on the chip and my unit. I'll let you know what I find out."

"Everyone else, run diagnostics," Kai announced and stepped away from his table. He walked down the long aisle, his shoes tapping dully against the grey composite floor. "This has been happening all week," he announced, his voice booming through the chamber. "Probably an array glitch or a hiccup in the solar. Don't move on to your next case until you run diagnostics."

In a few moments, Jeannette's MRC processing unit passed the diagnostics test. It was the chip.

She read through the error messages, memory addresses, and framework codes until the first clue emerged. According to the analyzer log, this MRC had malfunctioned from its first insertion. A parsing failure, no microfeed online. With more and more recombinants needed at the front, RDC was probably rushing through the MRC insertions.

She sighed. There was no way around it. She'd have to talk to Kai again.

"Kai," she called, keeping her tone distant. "Take a look at this."

He hurried toward her workstation. "What'd you find?"

She pointed to the results on the display flickering above her desk. "Chip was bad from insertion and nobody caught it."

While Kai studied the numbers, she removed the chip from the processing unit and enfolded it in antistatic wrap.

Kai frowned and rubbed his clean-shaven chin, coal black hair short and thick. He was more attractive than Dr. Di, tall and leanly muscled with those large blue eyes that made her dizzy if she stared into them too long.

"Okay, send the specs and results to me for this recombinant. I'll make sure RDC's aware of the glitch. A rare mistake, I'm sure."

Did he honestly believe that? "Rare mistake? You heard the room—everyone's had some failures. Look at this one closer, Kai." She pointed at the dead recombinant. "She washed out. Not enough aggression. Most likely because her MRC didn't parse out her human nature."

"Don't go there, Red," he snapped, his blue eyes darkening. "This job just gets harder when you do. They're savin' our asses. Or did your MRC parse out the massive losses of life we had in the first three years of this war?"

She glared at him. Like him, she'd been a medic on the front lines. She saw that slaughter first-hand. That's what sent her backpedaling to this place.

It was the one thing UCOE *didn't* want her to forget.

She poked a finger at his chest. "I remember the colonies destroyed and the men, women, and children who died there. No one who lived through those days could ever forget the genocide in Taus—MRC or not."

His eyes were blue flames. "No, but a lot of us are trying. Day by day we're trying. We're up to our asses in bodies, working twelve-hour shifts at half salary! And who knows when the whole thing's just gonna collapse around us?"

A chill slid down her spine. She hated it, but he was right. "Then why destroy any of them?" she asked, her voice softer. "Use them *somewhere*."

Kai shook his head. "Too much maintenance and training cost—I don't know," he said, the anger fading from his voice, quickly replaced by weariness. "I don't know much about anything anymore, Jeannette."

There was an awkward silence building between them until finally, Jeannette changed the subject. "I'll run diagnostics on my other failed MRC and port those over to a share on the solar."

"Fine." He paused for a moment, his gaze softening, then he moved back to his station.

She watched Ruth ~~flirt~~ joke with Kai until the smile and calm returned to his face. Jeanette sighed. She'd managed to get on Kai's bad side again. Out here, everything was so temporary and sometimes that applied to her judgment. The only thing she and Kai Drew had in common was this station. And the arguments. But Ruth was always there to stroke his ego and throw herself at him.

It didn't matter, she told herself as she turned away from him to sort her reclamation tray. He and arachnid woman belonged together.

She looked through the wrapped and tagged MRCs and microfeeds she'd removed today until she found 1189, the other MRC failure, and ran diagnostics on it.

There had to be a pattern to these failures.

AT THE END of her twelve-hour shift, Jeannette dumped her blue scrubs and grey lab coat in a bin and left the autopsy floor for detox. She pulled on a green sweat-suit from a small locker by the doorway and moved toward the lift.

"Red, wait up!"

Kai. She stiffened, her mood darkening. She was too tired to argue with him again today. Tomorrow. After she'd forgotten today.

She kept her back to him as she stepped into the lift, pretending not to have heard him. The smell of lavender lingered above the cloying copper stink of dried blood. She was just too tired for another argument with him—coordinator or not.

"I've got the Specialists' diagnostic reports," he called. "Over two weeks' worth."

Damn him! She wanted that data. She scowled. *And he knew it.*

She resisted until the lift door was almost closed. Unable to restrain her curiosity, she stuck her hand over the sensor and the door slid back open.

She kept her hand over the sensor until he'd run down the long, grey corridor and bounded into the lift. He leaned against the back wall and waited until the doors closed. He smelled like soap and coffee. The lift whined and slowly began its climb out of the Reclamation Station's belly and into the upper decks.

"What do you have, Kai?" she asked in a weary, annoyed voice, staring at him with crossed arms.

"In the past twenty-four hours, forty-two MRCs failed processing across the station," he said, his blue gaze intense.

Jeannette raised an eyebrow. "Forty-two? That's a lot."

He nodded and continued. "Yeah, but the number goes up considerably for the month. It looks like there may be a problem with firmware production at the Recombinant Development Center. I traced the batch numbers on the chips—four batches so far."

Batches of MRCs may be affected? She held back a gasp.

Thousands of recombinants could be needlessly destroyed because of this malfunction, delaying training and troop deployment. And if they made it to the front, would the defect affect battle outcomes?

She slumped against the lift's sidewall. "This is bad," she mumbled. "How many MRCs are we talking about?"

His gaze fell to the floor. "Thousands...and who knows how many other batches may be affected." Finally, he glanced up at her. "We've got to alert RDC about the problem. It all looks cut and dried to me."

Cut and dried? Her stomach knotted. On Kai's say, batches of recombinants would be labeled defective and destroyed. Living human beings, artificial produced nucleobases aside. She couldn't live with that—with or without her MRC.

The lift doors slid open and Kai moved toward them.

"Wait," said Jeannette and grabbed his arm. "Let's get some coffee and talk about this."

"What's to talk about?" he said, his eyes narrowing. "They have to know about the problem. You know Colonel Stanton's position on recombinants: zero defect tolerance."

Jeannette sighed. Colonel Stanton demanded that any and all defects be investigated and reported to UCOE immediately. The woman was obsessed with conspiracy theories and activist sabotage. She likened them to tree huggers and those early save-the-whales movements. To her, they were dangerous to the war effort.

And if things continued, trees and whales might be the only survivors of this war. Besides the Antarans.

Her grip tightened on his arm. He didn't pull away. "Hear me out first, okay? As my supervisor, you owe me that much."

He stared at her a moment and then finally nodded. "All right, Red."

"Hey, you guys campin' in there or what?"

Four tired technicians in rust-colored uniforms stood in front of the lift doors, waiting impatiently to enter.

"Sorry," said Jeannette. Quickly, she dragged Kai out of the lift and down the crowded corridor toward one of the break rooms.

At the end of the grey corridor that smelled like reheated chicken was a small blue room. She led him past a beige pleather couch and over to several chairs that huddled in a semi-circle beside a cooling unit and sink. A thin portal gave only a glimpse of the stark coldness of space, the stars pale and faint. The room smelled of stale coffee and germicide.

Jeannette moved to a small coffeemaker perched beside the cooling unit. The carafe was half-full of coffee. She picked it up and sniffed. Cold and stale. She made a sour face and dumped the coffee into the sink. She put in fresh grounds.

Kai glanced at his watch and frowned. "It's gettin' late. I've got to start on this report."

Wasn't he even going to investigate those numbers?

Jeannette motioned him toward a faux wood table. Reluctantly, he sat down, his arms crossed and his posture stiff. He'd already made up his mind.

She sat down across from him, hands on the table top that smelled like lemon cleanser. A nice change from the mint-scented germicide that misted the reclamation stations. And everything else in the room.

"I'm not going to falsify anything, if that's what you're about to ask me," he said.

"Don't be ridiculous," she snapped, slapping her hands against the table top. "So, what happens when you report that four MRC batches *may* be affected."

Kai thought for a moment, his gaze traveling toward the coffeemaker and then the floor. "You know Stanton's SOP," he said finally, "She'll recommend to RDC that they recall all affected recombinants."

She nodded. "And then what?"

He pressed a hand to his chin, his brow furrowing. Blue eyes so bright. God, they were hypnotic. She looked down at his hands.

"End of the line."

A cold chill touched her skin. "Exactly. We both know RDC would destroy every single one rather than risk a contamination of already well-conditioned soldiers."

He sighed. "I don't care. I won't cover this up, Red. It could impact the war's outcome."

"And so could *reporting* it," said Jeannette, her voice rising. "The destruction of thousands of recombinants would cause severe troop shortages. That tenuous front line could fall, Kai."

Not to mention the senseless loss of life.

She leaned toward him. "As a colleague, I'm asking you to hold off sending that report to Stanton until we've investigated the malfunction further. Deeper."

She needed to observe the defective MRCs in use. Then she'd know more about the problem.

He waved her off. "What's the point? The data's clear, Jeannette."

Uh oh, he called her Jeannette. He was serious now, falling back to protocol. She was losing him.

"Besides," he continued, "it'd take months to gather enough defective MRCs for study and we don't have that kind of time."

"Not the chips, Kai. The recombinants."

Kai's mouth fell open, his eyes wide. "What? Recombinants?" He rose from the chair and started toward the door. "No way, Jeannette! No way!"

"Kai, please," she said, rising from the chair. She rushed in front of him, blocking his path. "Let me study some of the recombinants from those MRC batches, see how they perform in training. If most of them are washing out, then there's no point in waiting. But if they're functioning according to protocol, then why have thousands destroyed and risk troop shortages on Ku'Tal?"

"But if their chips are malfunctioning, RDC needs to know," Kai insisted. "It's their decision, not ours."

She waved her hands in the air. "We don't even know the scope of the problem yet! If Ku'Tal falls, the entire Taus system will be overrun, so none of this would matter anyway. Kai—all I'm asking for is more information." She held out her hands. "A little time, that's all."

The gurgle of brewing coffee drew Kai's attention. He moved toward the coffeemaker and grabbed two mugs. "Coffee?" he asked, holding up a mug.

"Stop changing the subject," she said and moved toward him. "I want an answer."

He filled two mugs with coffee and handed one to Jeannette. He took a long, slow sip.

She slammed her mug down on the countertop, spilling it. "Dammit, Kai, you're stalling! I want an answer from you."

Kai set down his mug. "All right. I'll try to get you three weeks to investigate the MRC situation."

"Six," said Jeannette.

"Three!" he shouted, frowning.

"Six, Kai," she said and crossed her arms. "Three weeks isn't enough time."

His intense blue gaze studied her for a long time. Softening. She held her breath.

"Okay, Red," he said finally, sighing. He pointed a finger at her. "Six weeks, but if this goes through, I want weekly reports from you. Otherwise, Stanton'll climb my ass every week about it. I'll try to get you aboard the nearest training base, probably the one orbiting Civilization. It's the shortest hop from here and they always need medics."

Jeannette smiled and squeezed his arm. "Thanks, Kai."

"Don't thank me yet," he said, holding up a hand. "I haven't gotten clearance yet." Then he made a sour face. "You're not turnin' into one of those rabid activists, are you? UCOE had to do something...the technology was there."

She waved him off. "No, I just want to do the right thing for everyone."

At last, Kai smiled. "You'll have six weeks to figure out what that is. I'll keep you informed." He turned and left her in the break room.

Jeannette took a sip of coffee. Six weeks wasn't very long. She'd have to work quickly to gather data. The first thing she needed was a list of recombinants with affected MRCs that were aboard the Civilization base.

She grimaced at the bitter coffee. Kai was right; it was terrible. She dumped it and headed back to the lift. After a good night's sleep, she'd decide what to do with that list of recombinants once she got it.

Before Stanton found out she was studying recombinants.

JEANNETTE THOUGHT the government created MRCs just to cover up their glacially long wait times. Two weeks had already passed. She feared it would take months for her leave to be approved.

The cloying smell of dried blood and minty germicide, ever-present in the Reclamation Center, was overpowering today. She'd already opened at least thirty body bags, all of them from Ku'Tal. The endless procession of half-faced, burned bodies made her ill.

A constant reminder that the Antarans were winning.

She'd just closed out her last autopsy record when a tall, quiet medtech in orange scrubs laid three red body bags on her rack. Sighing, she reached into a drawer beneath her work table and retrieved a small vial of lavender oil. Removing her gloves and protective face visor, she quickly smeared the strong oil under her nose and slipped on gloves and visor again, grey lab coat dingy against her blue scrubs.

Taking a deep breath of lavender, Jeannette opened the body bag.

She scanned the reclamation tag for Dylan 1388: a recombinant male. Nineteen-maybe? So young. Jeannette peeled back the body bag flaps, blood and germicide misting her visor. Inside were only partial remains. The scan entry scrolled across a virtual display that hung above the body. The last line read: CoD—cascade mine.

She turned away from the body. Didn't need a tag to tell her the cause of death. Her chest tightened and her hands began to shake. She couldn't turn around and look into this recombinant's eyes.

"I can't do this," she said with a groan, squeezing her eyes shut.

"What do you have, Red?" Kai asked from his station, concern in his voice.

"Cascade mine. My sixteenth today." She glanced up at Kai and slid the blood-spattered visor off her face. "I'm sorry," she said in a half-whisper and dropped her visor on the floor. It clattered against the grey composite floor. "I just can't do this."

She knew all these emotions would be gone tomorrow, but right now, they were raw. She couldn't deal with them anymore.

Jeannette walked away from her station, the composite floor amplifying every step down the long aisle to the exit. The room turned deathly silent and she felt her co-workers staring at her. Ruth was probably trash-talking the decorated front line medic falling apart on the job. But she didn't care what they thought anymore.

She had to get out of here.

In moments, footsteps clacked behind her, echoing her steps as she hurried into the hallway. She knew it was Kai before his hand ever touched her sleeve.

"Write me up, kick me out, Kai," she snapped, not looking him in the eye. "I just don't care anymore."

He moved in front of her, both hands on her arms. "It's okay, Red," he said in a soft, concerned voice. "These past few months have been rough for everyone." His expression was kind, sympathetic. Not at all the Kai she knew. She'd expected him to order her back to her post, but for the first time, his eyes mirrored the weariness she felt in her soul.

Jeannette bit her lip. "I've been doing this for four years and I'm good at my job, but I'm tired, Kai. I'm so tired of the constant loss of life that comes through here—citizens...recombinants. I'm tired of the front line slipping closer and closer to home system. It's all coming down around us, Kai. All of it!"

"It's okay," he said, his voice comforting.

"What happens when we run out of recombinants, Kai?"

His grip on her arms tightened and she grabbed hold of his wrists, wanting to feel the warmth of someone else's skin, the pulse of a heart through living veins. She'd felt so many cold limbs and hands today that her hands felt numb.

God, the feel of warm skin! She'd almost forgotten how it felt.

He stared at her hands a moment then his intense blue gaze met hers. After hours of handling the dead through rubber gloves, the numbness was overwhelming. He must feel this way, too. Shouldn't they all feel this way?

"The Antarans haven't won yet, okay," he said. "Okay?"

Finally, she nodded, letting go.

"Until then, we're not giving up. That's why you're gonna investigate this MRC anomaly."

"Leave approval will take months and you know it," she said, frowning. She wanted to make a difference, not just clean up someone else's mess.

Or process the overwhelming number of deaths that home system didn't see. Didn't feel.

He smiled. "That'll give you several weeks to write up the results after you get back."

Jeannette's eyes widened. "You're not going to wait for approval? What about Stanton?" Stanton would be furious when she found out.

He shook his head. "Civilization training base needs a medic—I checked last night. I'll temporarily assign you there until a replacement's found." He let go of her arms and pulled a small datapad out of his grey lab coat. Quickly, he scribbled down several lines of information with his index finger. "Give me three days to get you aboard. Until then, I'm putting you on light duty. You can use that time to assemble your gear."

She reached out and squeezed his hand. Warm and vibrant. Full of life. "Thank you, Kai. This means a lot to me."

"I know," he said. "Go get some rest, shake it off, let your MRC do something good for a change."

His hand brushed across her cheek, so warm and pulsing with life. The light touch of his hand surprised her as she stared at him.

He'd never done that before. But it felt so good, that connection, however brief.

An awkward silence built between them until he stiffened, his gaze darting from hers. Abruptly, he turned toward Reclamation. She watched him disappear through the double doors before she turned toward the lift. Thoughts of being away from reclamation duty sent waves of relief through her.

Maybe she could finally save some lives—maybe even her own?

3

DIANA TEMPLE FLUNG the green-tailed dart with an assassin's accuracy. It clipped two others on the outer edge of the bull's-eye, scattering them on the floor as her dart slammed home.

Four soot-smeared miners groaned, smelling rank with ore and sweat, and complained, throwing grubby betting stubs onto the dusty pub floor. Three military shuttle pilots, clean cut in olive green launch suits and smelling like dust and beer, tossed their stubs on the nearest table.

"Dammit, Temple," shouted one of the shuttle pilots. "I had you on that last shot. How'd you drop that dart just right?"

Diana grinned at him as she scooped up the pile of credits under the dart board. He was slim and handsome with dark brown hair and light eyes. In his sleek, olive drab launch suit, Jimmy Callahan was hot, but he played darts like he played women: anything was a target and he threw himself at every single one. Hoping to score. Today, that was her.

"Skill," she snapped. "Because every week, you tell me I can't make that shot and every week, I do." She propped a hand on her hip. "Guess I just like proving you wrong."

Callahan's buddies laughed at him as they retrieved their pint glasses of watery ale from the nearby tables scattered around the dart board. She slipped her dart winnings into a small pouch at her side and jangled it at Callahan who scowled.

Next month's rent and a few nice meals.

A playful smile slid onto Callahan's tanned, clean-shaven face as he walked toward her, boots clicking against the sticky, pale wood floor. He laid his hands on her shoulders. His hands were warm through her gauzy white blouse. He smelled like heat and oil.

"Then prove me wrong again and go out with me." His voice was buttery smooth, his hand sliding down her arm. Gently, he nudged a lock of warm brown hair out of her eyes. The rest was tied back in a thin purple scarf.

She laid her hands on his chest. "For dinner and dancing."

"Yeah," he said, slipping his arms around her waist.

Pulling her against his chest.

"Champagne and chocolate mousse," she asked softly, leaning forward.

"Anything you want," he said, his smile turning to a grin as her hand slid up his neck to his chin.

"And a quick roll in the glitter district," Diana purred in a throaty voice.

"Yeah," said Callahan through hooded lids. Then his eyes widened. "I mean, no!"

Still smiling, Diana grabbed hold of his chin and shoved him backwards. "That's what I thought," she said with a laugh, moving to the dart board. She picked up a fallen dart and flung it at the board. "Sorry, not my game, Jimmy."

"Aw, Diana..." said Callahan, walking toward her with a frown, holding out his arms. "It wouldn't be like that."

One of Callahan's buddies, Pearson, took him by the arm. "Give it up, Jimmy, let's go," he said with a laugh. "You're not her type."

"Yeah, but there's always next week," said Callahan with a wink at Diana as he turned to his other buddy. "C'mon. It's almost time to pick up the refurbs." Callahan and his buddies walked past the bar toward the front door.

"The what?" Diana called.

"Recombinants," Pearson answered as he shoved open the heavy, carved door. "They're training in sims planet-side today."

"Thought you guys flew combat," she said, frowning.

Shrugging, Pearson paused in the threshold. "Gotta start somewhere," he replied. "Seeya next week."

"Bye, guys. It was a pleasure taking your credits."

Pearson followed the others outside. They walked past the pub's front window and its green neon letters spelling out The Treehouse.

Gotta start somewhere. Pearson had a good point.

Diana sat down in a wooden booth against the far vine-draped wall. Her glass of watered down ale was still cool as she pressed it to her lips.

Would bussing around trainees get her a shot at being a combat pilot?

She set down the glass, her gaze traveling to the dart board across the room. It probably paid better than occasional contract work and dart board winnings.

She leaned back against the polished, honey-colored wood and stared up at the insect netting covering the ceiling. On the exposed rafters, pink and red birds chattered. Today, the pub was quiet enough that she could hear the little birds sing.

The room smelled almost like cedar, reminding her a little of Earth. Civilization was a long, long way from the place she grew up, but she felt at home here, enough to defend home system against the Antarans. They had to be stopped here. Mom and Dad wanted her safe on lunar colony studying biomorphic design, but that had been Mom's dream, not hers. She hadn't found her dream yet, but she was still searching.

The sound of wind chimes echoed through the pub. Her com unit. From a lace pocket on her left sleeve, she slid out a flexible, business card screen. Her mother's oval face appeared.

"Hi, Mother," she answered, laying the card screen on the table and switching to a virtual display that hovered above it. "How are—"

"Diana, good! Glad I caught you!" Mother's hazel eyes glistened, her voice filled with excitement. Diana braced herself. Another one of Mother's intuitive inspirations was coming. She felt it. "Your cousin Phoebe chimed me about a wonderful new position for you! It's a wonderful career, you'll love the work!"

Diana held up her hand. "Whoa, resister check, Mother. Let's start over. Hi, Mother, how are you? You're terrific? That's wonderful." She laid her hand against her chest. "How am I? Well, I'm just great. Thanks for asking."

Her mother sighed. "Dear, I realize you're fine, but I didn't want you to miss another opportunity." She shook her head. "It hurts me just thinking about you on that awful mining planet. And flying shuttles? Honey, isn't it time you grew out of that phase?"

Diana gritted her teeth, biting back an acerbic reply.

"Your father offered to send you enough credits to—"

"Mother. Let's go through this once more." She'd gone through the shouting and anger too many times. Today was a good day. She wouldn't rise to the occasion. "I'm not moving back to lunar colony and I'm not interested in anything you or Phoebe cook up for me."

Her mother threw up her hands, eyes teary, that exaggerated hurt expression on her face. "Diana—we're just worried about you, all right? Dear God, you're so close to the war front. Aren't you terrified?"

Only of going home again. "No, Mother. I'm fine, I—I just want to..." *Want to what? What did she want?* To do something that mattered, to make an effort, contribute...to find herself in the process. "I want to—take a hot shower and pay my bills. I've gotta go. I'll ring you and Dad next week, okay?"

"Okay, dear," said her mother, nodding. "Please be careful. We love you."

"Love you, too," said Diana, leaning toward the virtual display. "Tell Dad for me."

"Give David a kiss for us."

Diana frowned. "David? Mother—David's on Io, remember? Training officers. New contract." God knew how often Mother bragged about David's new post, telling Diana she should be looking for something similar.

Her mother shook her head. "No, Diana. He took a new job. Love you!"

The card screen blanked and the virtual display dissolved. Stunned, Diana stared at the grey screen. *David took a new job? Out here?* She groaned and picked up her glass of ale, taking a long, watery drink. Why couldn't Mother ever finish a story? She always jumped lanes in mid-conversation, leaving Diana with bits and pieces she had to connect on her own.

Setting down the ale, she leaned over the card screen again. "Call home," she said as the screen wavered and flashed.

But the pub's front door opened and a uniformed man stepped inside. His dark hair, cropped short and feathered, was slightly disheveled and his face was shadowed with stubble. The charcoal grey jacket and pants looked almost crisp. He was travel-weary, thinner than she remembered, but always that good-looking, guy-next-door appeal. Her heart skipped a beat. David!

"David!" she cried, shuffling out of the booth and running toward him.

"Diana!" He wrapped his arms around her in a hard embrace.

Finally, he let her go, holding her out at an arm's length, a grin on his face. "God, it's great to see you! You look a little thin—you getting enough to eat?" He reached for his wallet. "Do you need some money? I just got paid and—"

She waved him off. "David, no—I'm doing fine."

"But Mother said—"

"Mother doesn't know!" she shouted, unable to keep the edge out of her voice. "Why won't anyone in this family accept the fact that I'm doing fine?" She stormed over to the booth and plopped onto the seat. She slid her mobile back into her sleeve pocket.

David wandered over to the table.

"Diana, I—"

"Mother sent you out here, didn't she?" Diana snapped, crossing her arms.

He smirked. "In a way. She and Phoebe found me a lovely job at lunar colony. So, I enlisted."

Diana burst out laughing as David slid into the opposite side of the booth.

"I got my military trainer's cert a few months ago and I've been training officers on Io." He held out his sleeve, showing a UCOE insignia and some braided coils. "I'm now Training Sergeant David Temple."

"Congratulations," said Diana, picking up her glass of ale. "Maybe you'll make Colonel before you're thirty?"

David ran his fingers through his short brown hair. "It doesn't work that way, kiddo. Besides, thirty's less than two years away. Maybe by then this war will be over?"

David ordered an ale and drank it slowly.

"So, David, tell me about this new job?" Diana asked.

"Not job, post," he answered. "Because of my training experience and sensor grid expertise, I got offered this sweet position at Civilization's training base. It's a great, long-term opportunity." He glanced around, shaking his head. "You guys really call this place Civilization?"

She set down her glass. "Have you seen what's beyond this planet?"

"No, and I don't plan to, either," he said with a smile. "I'm permanently assigned to the base and won't see combat."

He'd learn soon enough that no one out here planned very far into the future. "Sounds like a great job. What kind of training is it?"

"I'm supposed to turn a bunch of misfits into soldiers."

"Misfits?" Diana frowned. "What are you talking about?"

David shrugged and laid his head against the wall. His eyes closed to slits. "This base is where they send new guys and misfits.

My job is to make sure they all reach the front, so they'll do some good." His voice softened. "The brass said it'd be a big help to the war effort." He smiled. "I'm still not sure if I'm a new guy or a misfit."

"Some of the base personnel were downside today running their boys through some VR training sims," said Diana. "Their shuttle pilots spent most of the day here." She patted her credits pouch. "And I relieved them of a few credits before they had to pick up their units."

"Did you talk to the pilots?" he asked, sitting up.

Diana nodded. "They call the recombinants *refurbs.*"

David was silent for a moment. "Those are the misfits I'll be training. Training guys genetically designed to kill the enemy can be difficult. They don't have an original thought in their heads—just conditioned responses. That's what they say anyway. I'd prefer to train officers or even office personnel. They volunteered, like me."

Conditioned responses? Diana bristled at the phrase. *Was that really true? Did recombinants only think about killing? Were they more like androids than people?* "You say that like they're animals."

David took another sip of his ale. "They're difficult to handle on purpose, Diana, so their environment's carefully controlled. That's why they aren't allowed off base without military escort. The military controls all input they receive. Even their memories are controlled."

A cold chill shivered through Diana. "Their memories? That's horrible!"

He looked away. "Maybe. Maybe that's the only way they can be controlled, I don't know. They don't seem to care, even when they wash out." He rubbed thumb and forefinger against the bridge of his nose. "Listen, I didn't come here to argue about recombinants. I was hoping you'd put me up for the night."

Relieved David had changed the subject, Diana let her uneasiness about the recombinants fade. She knew that good or bad, David would live with it. "My place is small, but you'll fit." She glanced around. "Where are your bags?"

"At the shuttle port in a locker. I'll stop by and pick them up."

When they finished their ales, Diana motioned him up from the booth. "C'mon, let's get your bags and go home."

"Lead the way, little sis."

She hurried toward the door.

Outside, the breeze had died, holding in the oily scent of machinery and the burnt smell of laser drills. The amber sky was dull, endless sand stretching away from the city. Behind the industrial section was a quaint little village that had grown up beside the planet's only river. In the village, a visitor could get a hot bath, a good meal, and a cool place beside the river. She wanted to take David down to the river and show him the colored lights and the skimmers rushing past. There was something intense about sitting on the calm edge of chaos, but she longed to fall off into the excitement and swim for once.

She led David down the blistering ribbon of pavement, past throngs of miners on break or hurrying to their shifts. The sun glared down on them as they reached the shuttle stop into the village. She and David ascended the platform and waited in silence.

Diana wondered about the recombinants and how they'd managed to survive. Why would they even want to survive? They probably felt as temporary as Civilization's makeshift buildings. She had never known much about recombinants, but hearing David talk about how they were treated suddenly made her feel uncomfortable. What would it feel like to have no past, no family, and no future? A lot of people hated the program and wanted it stopped. It was always a hot topic.

The thought slipped away as the sleek silver transit pod glided up to the shuttle stop. It was shaped like a bullet and super fast, rushing along the ruddy sand like an arrow. She clambered aboard, David in tow.

DAVID SEEMED MORE relaxed after a hot shower. Dressed in a blue sweatpants and white t-shirt, he collapsed onto her overstuffed teal sofa that faced the window. The bright sunlight drenched it and made him cover his eyes. Diana moved to the window, quickly drawing the beige shade to block the intense sunlight.

"Thanks," he said.

The room was small but cozy. All she had was a sofa, a chair, and a desk in the room. An area rug of muted teals and purples spread over the wood floor. A print of misty hydrangeas hung on the cream-colored wall above her desk. On the far wall (that she'd painted amethyst last month) hung a holo print shuffler that changed every few minutes from one Pacific Coast lighthouse to another. In the far corner of the room stood a large black trunk. She'd carried it from home system with everything she cared about inside. So far, everything still fit.

David pointed at the trunk. "You going somewhere?"

She sat down in the beige chair beside the couch and leaned toward him. "David...*are* you sure you're ready for this assignment?"

He frowned. "Of course, I am. I've already served at three training bases in home system—"

"What about in Taus?" she asked.

"No," he answered, sitting up. "But I expect there to be a learning curve."

Diana shook her head. "It's a lot different here than home system, David. In a month, if we're all still here, ask me again about the trunk."

The expression in his eyes was sober and she saw a glimmer of fear. The war was real here and he seemed to be realizing it for the first time. "I'm glad you're here, Diana," he said. His mouth pressed into a faint smile. "I've really missed you. You were always the one with the spark in the family."

She reached out and squeezed his arm. "I've missed you, too, David. Can I give you a little advice?"

David's posture stiffened, but finally he nodded.

"Civilization is constantly on edge. There's never enough supplies or work or time and the war is just a stone's throw away. Things change fast here. Be aware of that and you'll be fine."

"Good advice," he said and sat up on the couch. "So, what sort of contract work are you doing?"

"I was hired to shuttle a doctor from a Reclamation Station to the base tomorrow. She's your new medic."

"What's she like?"

Diana rose from the chair. "Haven't talked to her yet. I'll tell you about her tomorrow over supper." She grabbed hold of his arm and pulled him to his feet. "C'mon, let's make spaghetti and talk about the old neighborhood."

"Spaghetti," he said, "just like old times—without the noodle flinging."

"That's what you think," she said with a grin and hustled him into the small u-shaped kitchen. "You handle the beer and I'll handle the spaghetti."

"I'm on it," he said, moving to the silver cooling unit against the wall of the sunny yellow kitchen. Took a while to get hold of some paint out here, but she paid a little extra for the pale buttery yellow.

In a short time, Diana had spaghetti and garlic bread on the little table in the corner of her sunny yellow kitchen, cobalt blue and white dishes bright. She and David ate and laughed about their childhood until it was almost ten. After David helped with the dishes, Diana setup the sofa bed. He hugged her again and said good night. He had to be on base early and would be gone before she got up.

Feeling exhausted, Diana went to her room and read for a while until she fell asleep. She'd forgotten how comforting David's presence felt. Out here, comfort was fleeting and until now, she hadn't realized how much she'd missed it.

4

JEANNETTE PACKED, double-checked, and repacked all of her mobile equipment, anything to fill the long hours before going off-station. She needed to observe the recombinants in training. Field data would be invaluable against the grim statistics she'd already gathered in the autopsy room. What better way to observe them as station medic? Sometimes, Kai was brilliant.

Out in Taus' cold emptiness, it was evening. Mess was long over and many of the station personnel were asleep. Her quarters aboard station were small, but comfortable. One room and the latrine. Somber shades of charcoal and cream enfolded the walls and floors, accented only by the handful of her impersonal belongings: two glass red roses; teal-framed, revolving images of desert sunsets on the walls, lavender pillows on the portal window-seat and loveseat. The scent of recycled air overpowered the warm vanilla air freshener she'd just misted.

Sometimes, she wondered if these things had ever been hers. It bothered her not to have images of family and friends setting on her desk or adorning her walls like normal people. Her MRC had parsed out most of the people she once cared about, but that only managed to push the death of her young daughter deeper into memory. She'd preserved a small essence of her daughter's memory and her past in a log file.

It was all she had.

She sighed, unable to recall the events for herself. She'd recorded them the night her ex-husband's body came through the station. In the parsed memories of his MRC lay the memories of Rena Diane Kingston, their little girl who drowned in the backyard pool when she was two. Before the war.

That devastating event had ended Jeannette's marriage and her contact with her husband, Dylan. She'd recorded all of those parsed memories into a file. The pain came not from the absence of memory, but the absence of feeling. She couldn't find closure in those events, just interruption.

Where had she worked afterward? After Rena died. After the divorce. She only had shadowy images of laboratories and figures. What had she done with her life? She knew she'd gone into research. Contract work most of it. And then there was a job with security clearance. The rest was hazy. All of it buried in the depths of her memory replacement chip. Her MRC.

So much of her life was embedded in her login file that opened every morning when she logged into the solar array, but so much more of it was just—missing.

She was living in the third person, if this could even be called living.

The com unit on the wall chimed and Jeannette rushed toward it. "Dr. Kingston."

"Red? Kai. Listen, I've got everything arranged. They couldn't spare a shuttle pilot, so I hired one from Civilization."

"Military or civilian?" Jeannette asked.

"Civvie. She'll be here tomorrow at 1300 hours. Is that enough time?"

Jeannette smiled. She'd been packed for days. "I'm all set, Kai. Thanks for everything, okay? This means a lot to me."

"Sure thing. I'll see you off tomorrow. Get some sleep, huh?"

"I will."

She cleared the connection, feeling excited for the first time in years. She was doing something that mattered again. She sat down on the window-seat and cradled a pillow as she stared out into the ubiquitous sea of darkness surrounding the station and its flicker of distant stars. Was there anything beyond the Antarans? For the first time in a long while, she was prepared to find out.

BY THE NEXT MORNING, Kai had assembled a list of recombinants with MRCs from the suspected batch numbers. The list was in her share when she rose half-asleep to the scent of fresh coffee and the steady glimmer of her message alert. With cup in hand, she sat down and said, "open new message from Kai Drew."

The virtual display appeared above the table. She double tapped a flashing box with Kai's name and the message opened into a virtual display.

"Scroll at my reading speed," said Jeannette and a list of names slowly worked its way down her virtual screen.

She stared at the screen. Recombinants had names?

Surprised, she could only stare at the names for a moment as they slipped past. She never knew recombinants had assigned names. Why weren't the bodies tagged with their names? Their MRCs only held an ID number encoded into the chip, no name included. A simple scan read the ID number and determined a recombinant's home base. There were over two hundred names on this list, each one representing a potential defect. She read through some of the names as they scrolled past: JarrettJ, Jones...KellyD, KincaidR...LewisH, LindleyC...MarshD... MitchellP...

She looked away, staring instead at the rich black coffee swirling in her cup. These young men and women could be the next recombinants to wash out of Earth's armed forces. She hoped to find them adjusting well to their training rather than succumbing to flaws in their MRCs. She'd find out soon enough though.

"Send this list to my private solar space," she said and rose from the chair. "Transfer locally to all my devices."

IT WAS ALMOST 1300 hours when Jeannette reached the launch bay in the belly of the Reclamation Station. Her equipment, tagged with her name, sat on a large, flatbed cart that had been sent down a few hours ago. She flicked on her wrist display and the small screen winked on, paging slowly through a text file.

Her log file. A backup in case there was a system glitch. She'd already lost too much of her life. She wouldn't lose these surviving bits, too.

Good, everything was intact. Even the list of recombinants was there.

She rattled off an assessment of equipment on the cart as her display device recorded the inventory. After she'd finished, she flicked off the display and looked around for her pilot.

The tall, drafty launch bay smelled of exhaust and polymers, the walls and floors a dull grey except for the cream-colored maintenance area. Red and blue lines cut across the floor in abstract patterns that made no sense to Jeannette, but they seemed to lead to specific areas. On each side of the docking and maintenance zone stood two, huge launch chutes. All around the perimeter of the maintenance zone stood several wire cages containing tools and parts. Techs in rust-colored coveralls swarmed the area and a handful of olive-suited pilots walked the bay with datapads.

With all the uniforms swarming the bay, Jeannette's pilot stood out. The brown-haired young woman leaned against the nearest tool cage talking to some military pilots. She wore a brown leather jacket, white t-shirt and pale blue pants. A vivid purple scarf loosely circled her neck. Slim with bright eyes and a warm smile, she joked with some of the other pilots. Jeannette moved with hurried steps across the bay toward the young woman.

Two UCOE pilots in tan uniforms stepped out of Jeannette's way as she approached.

"I'm Dr. Jeannette Kingston," she said, extending her hand to the young woman. "You must be my pilot from Civilization."

The young woman's smile brightened as she shook Jeannette's hand. "That's me! Diana Temple. Nice to meet you."

"And you. How long before we're ready to leave?"

Diana shrugged. "I'm ready whenever you are. They've already cleared my launch. Do you need help with your gear?"

"Yes, that would be nice. Thank you."

Jeannette led her over to the cart and Diana took charge, pushing the cart across the blue lined floor toward the left-hand chute.

"I'm over here in blue chute," said Diana, her voice sweet and pleasant. "It'll just take me a moment to load these into the hold and we'll be off."

Her laid-back, friendly manner put Jeannette at ease. "Thank you," said Jeannette.

With her slight build, Diana didn't look strong enough to load those crates, but she seemed to manage without much difficulty.

"Red!"

Jeannette turned at the sound of Kai's voice.

He rushed across the bay. "I was afraid I was too late to see you off."

She motioned toward the sleek, olive drab shuttle that perched on the launch trace. A standard UCOE shuttle. Diana was lifting polymer crates into the rear hold.

"You're just in time," she said. "Diana was kind enough to load my equipment. Then we'll be away."

He reached out for Jeannette's hand and pressed a small silver disc into her palm. "More data," he said with a wink. "I broke into one of the databases and ganked some additional MRC data. It seems that one other Reclamation Station has reported MRC failures. Thought it might help."

"You're a gem, Kai, thank you," she said, her hand lingering against his for a moment. His warmth was intoxicating.

He smiled and started to reply, but Diana walked up.

"We're ready, Dr. Kingston." She turned her gaze to Kai and extended her hand. "Hi, I'm Diana Temple—we spoke on com. Thanks for the job. I appreciate the work."

"Kai Drew. Nice to meet you, Diana," he replied, shaking her hand. "I've already transferred the credits for this job to your account."

"Thanks...my landlord will appreciate that," she said with a smile.

"I'll contact you by the end of the week, Kai," said Jeannette.

"Be careful, Red," said Kai. He turned back toward the lift as Jeannette turned toward the shuttle. Diana took her cue, leading her to the hatch.

Diana tapped a few keys on the door keypad and the door slid open. Jeannette climbed inside the dark shuttle that smelled like dust and oil, slipping into the co-pilot's seat. Diana closed the door and bounded into the pilot's seat. She flicked on the instruments and went through a verbal flight check. The onboard computer engaged and verified each system, the red and green glow casting a strange patina throughout the cabin. The shuttle had that familiar, recycled smell with a hint of vanilla. The scent of aging polymer clung to the seats.

"Strap yourself in, doctor, and we'll be on our way," said Diana, her attention still on the instrument panel.

Jeannette reached over to the restraint harness and clicked it into place across her body. Diana strapped into a harness and after a few adjustments to the controls, she taxied the shuttle down the awaiting launch trace.

In moments, the automated launch sequence engaged and the shuttle careened out of the chute. There was a rush of darkness and that familiar heaviness against Jeannette's chest and then the darkness lit with stars.

She stared out at the russet glow of Civilization thin on the horizon and twinkle of distant lights beyond. In those distant lights, the war raged with its fear and raw fury. Somewhere out there, hundreds of recombinants were dying as a shuttle dropped in hundreds more. And the Antarans pushed deeper in system. She thought back to her list: Lewis...Marsh...Mitchell—was there a place out there for these recombinants? Beyond the front? She sighed, leaning back against the seat.

Or did a UCOE body bag, tagged wash out, await them?

5

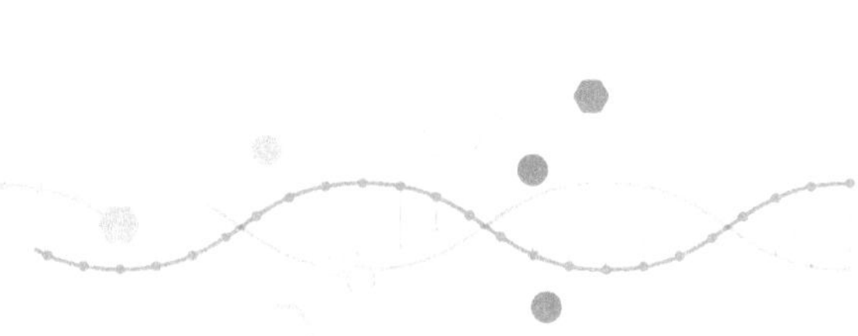

PETER MITCHELL ROSE to his feet with the rest of his unit and saluted Lieutenant D'Angelo as he bustled into the brightly lit classroom, two younger sergeants in tow. Chairs scraped across the dusty floor, desks creaking, the air smelling of aftershave and mouthwash. Peter glanced down at his dull green uniform and boots that needed polishing and hoped this wasn't a surprise inspection.

D'Angelo and the two sergeants moved to the front of the white classroom with its three rows of white polymer desks and chairs. They stood beside the white boards and computer screen lining the front wall.

"At ease," said D'Angelo, his voice gruff and hurried. His hair was cut high and tight, greying at the temples, and his hook nose looked sharp like a hawk's beak. "The man standing to my right is Sergeant David Temple, your new training sergeant. He just shipped in from Io colony to work on this Taus base station. While you're on this base and doing sims on Civilization, Training Sergeant Temple will manage your unit's basic training under my direction."

The Lieutenant let his words settle through the room.

"The man to my left is Field Sergeant Anthony Galloway. When you ship out for the front, Field Sergeant Galloway will be in charge of your unit. Galloway, under my direction, will manage your tactical and weaponry training here."

D'Angelo's prominent chin pressed his thin lips into a grimace. His average height and stocky build made him look pudgy against Sergeant Temple's tall, sleek frame and Sergeant Galloway's shorter, thinner build. D'Angelo's hard, dark brown eyes were shadowed into deep sockets as if he hadn't slept in days. Temple, his short-cropped brown hair neatly combed, looked well rested and content, a few years older than his trainees. Galloway's short, black locks were slicked stiff against his scalp. He seemed quiet and restrained, his grey eyes dull. He looked older than Temple.

D'Angelo looked through Peter and the other recombinants as if they were just another VR simulation. There were times when Peter felt like one.

Peter and the rest of the unit, fifteen soldiers in all, shifted nervously, their hands resting behind their backs. Most of the sergeants he'd encountered were severe and treated recombinants badly. Would Sergeant Temple and Sergeant Galloway be that way, too?

"Good morning," said Temple, smiling. "Looks like we're all going to be spending a lot of time together." He took a step forward and cast a nervous glance at Lieutenant D'Angelo. "My job is to help you become efficient soldiers. I'm going to work you hard, but together, we'll get through your required sims." Temple stepped back and took his position beside D'Angelo.

Sting, two rows across from Peter, shifted uncomfortably and whispered something to one of the recombinants.

"We need you at the front to make sure the Antarans don't threaten Earth," Temple added. "We're fighting for our freedom and our lives. The only way we'll succeed is through commitment and training."

Peter cringed. Citizen things. He wasn't really from anywhere. He had no home world and he'd never seen this place called Earth.

This space station was all he'd ever known for the few months he'd been alive. Freedom? Life? He'd never known those things. And what was this *we* about? Temple wasn't going to the front.

Galloway stepped forward. "I spent four months at the front. My specialty is tactics and weaponry." His voice was tight. "By the time I'm finished with you, you'll either be specialists or washed out. There is nothing in-between."

The words *washed out* gave Peter a sick feeling. He let out a heavy breath.

"Attention!" D'Angelo shouted.

Peter snapped to attention.

"Report to your next class. Dismissed."

Peter filed out behind the others, passing the sharp-edged Galloway and the intense, young Sergeant Temple who also stood at attention. For a moment, they held eye contact. Temple nodded toward him and Peter awkwardly returned the gesture.

After the unit was out of the sergeants' and D'Angelo's sight, several of the recombinants burst out laughing.

"Get a load of the recruitment poster boy," Sting said with a snicker. "And that burn-out leading us at the front. He looks like an addict to me." His laughter pealed through the hallway. "So, Temple and Galloway are gonna teach me something about the front."

Drake cackled. "I know all I need to know. Shoot first. Kill anything that moves."

Peter pulled back from the group, sickened. He desperately wanted someone to teach him how not to be afraid. How to die with dignity. But most of all, he wanted someone to explain to him why he had no choices and no future. Sighing, he cast his gaze to the floor and plodded to his next class. As he slipped into another white desk in another white classroom, he wondered which death would be worse: washing out because he failed or being slaughtered at the front because he succeeded.

FOR THE REST of the week, Peter saw little of Sergeant Temple. The recombinants spent most of their time in Sergeant Galloway's tiresome weapons, tactics, and hardware classes. Because of their low team scores, the entire unit underwent remedial courses on reading sensor grids, which Sergeant Temple taught.

The following week, Temple drilled them daily, and Peter did his best to read the grid. The sim readings, he was told, were based on actual scans from the front. The Antarans seemed to manipulate the grid to reflect what they wanted. Peter doubted that any classroom instruction would help him guess an Antaran's next move.

Throughout the drills, Drake cast angry glances at him. Whenever he encountered Peter, Drake bumped into him or shoved him. Peter did his best to stay away from Drake, but they were in the same unit—Peter couldn't avoid him forever.

After today's classes ended, Peter headed to the bunkroom. He turned a corner and a fist struck him in the chest. Peter wheezed for breath as someone dragged him into an empty classroom. Still dazed, Peter fought to clear his vision until he was looking into Drake's fierce, hungry eyes. Two recombinants who Peter didn't know waited behind Drake, their fists clenched, and looking just as eager to pummel him.

Peter staggered to his feet.

"Thanks for the extra class time, *buddy*." Drake shoved him backward. Peter stumbled, breaking his fall by grabbing hold of a desk. "Appreciate your dedication."

Drake moved forward, the other recombinants following. He pushed Peter again. Peter stumbled backward, taking a step away from him.

"Well, I've got a message for you, Mitchell. You'd better pay close attention to it or you'll wake up with your brains spilling all over your bunk."

Peter backed away. Any message Drake delivered would involve pain.

"You don't know shit, Mitchell and I'm sick of your fuck ups!"

Drake lunged at Peter, his fist connecting with Peter's jaw. He pounded Peter in the face and head until Peter fell. Peter tried to shove him away, but Drake sat on his chest, pinning him to the floor. The other recombinants kicked him in the side and legs.

Peter's lip split, blood rushing down his chin. His eye swelled. His nose throbbed and his sides ached as they continued to kick him.

"Fight back!" Drake shouted. "What the hell's wrong with you? You're a soldier! Act like one!"

Peter closed his eyes, unable to dislodge Drake, and hoped Drake would just tire of beating him.

Someone jerked Drake off him. Peter's eyes snapped open. Sergeant Temple stood over Drake, shouting at him and gesturing furiously. Two MPs entered the classroom.

"Take these two to a holding room until I can get to the bottom of this," ordered Temple. "Take this one to my office. And get a medic down here." Then he turned to Peter. "Soldier, are you all right?"

Soldier? No one on base called him that. Ever. "I—I think so, sir."

Temple smiled. "Thanks for the compliment, private, but I'm a not a commissioned officer. I'm a sergeant. A noncom. You don't call sergeants *sir*."

"Yes, si—Sergeant Temple."

Temple checked him for broken bones. "Just call me Sarge, Mitchell." He held out two fingers. "How many fingers?"

"Two, Sarge."

"You'll live," said Temple, patting him on the shoulder.

In moments, a medic hurried into the classroom. She dropped down to examine Peter. Temple knelt on the floor beside him.

"What started the fight, private?" the medic asked as she opened her bag. Her thick, auburn hair was cut short around her thin face and over her ears. She had large, kind eyes.

Peter's gaze drifted toward the doorway.

"Come on, private," said Temple, his voice rising. "I caught them in the act of beating you senseless. Talk to me now or talk to me after a week in the brig."

Temple crossed his arms and waited, but Peter couldn't bring himself to tell him anything.

"Patch up Mitchell and bring him to my office. I'll talk to him and Drake together."

"Mitchell?" asked the medic.

Temple nodded. "Yes. Mitchell." He turned and left the room, leaving Peter alone with the medic.

"That gash over your eye needs to be sealed," said the medic.

"Thank you," Peter said in a quiet voice.

"I'm Dr. Kingston," she replied with a smile. "I'm new to the station."

"Me, too," said Peter.

Gently, Dr. Kingston cleaned the wound with some sort of cold solution and a swab. Her fingers were warm and soft against his brow. Another medic treated him once. He took care of the injury, but Peter still remembered how the man had treated him like a piece of furniture.

"So, what happened in here?" she asked. "Just between you and me, okay?"

Peter sighed. "Just some of the guys blowing off steam," he answered, looking away.

Dr. Kingston pressed a small device to the gash and warmth spread through the wound as the device passed over it. Peter closed his eyes.

"At you?" she asked.

He shrugged. "It's okay—I brought it on myself. They're just better at this stuff than me."

A worried look spread across her face as she put away the device and began applying a bandage. "You mean the training?"

"Yeah, I guess. It doesn't bother them like it bothers me."

Dr. Kingston seemed distracted as she closed some of the deeper cuts on his face with little thin strips that pulled at his skin.

"You're all set, private, but I'll need you to come to the infirmary in a week. I'll notify your training sergeant. Who was it—Galloway?"

"No, Temple."

"Temple, right," said Dr. Kingston.

Peter rose unsteadily from the floor. "Thanks, Doc," he said and hobbled into the hallway where an MP detail awaited him.

The detail led him down a brightly lit, narrow corridor on the base station's upper decks. They passed several offices until the detail halted at a door at the end of the hall. They opened the door and escorted him into Sergeant Temple's office. He cautiously sat in a hard metal chair in front of Temple's desk. Drake sat in the other one. He scowled at Peter and then looked away.

"If this happens again, you'll both do brig time. Do you understand me?"

Peter and Drake nodded.

"Now, I want to know who started the fight."

"Drake," said Peter.

Temple turned his stern gaze to Drake. Drake's steel grey eyes darkened and he glared at Peter.

"He should be washed out!" Drake shouted, pointing. "He can't stomach combat, so why's he still here? If he wants to wash out, let him, but don't let him take all of us with him."

Temple frowned, his gaze shifting to Peter. Peter squirmed under the scrutiny.

"Are you afraid of combat, private?"

"No, Sarge," Peter answered in a quiet voice. "I'm just afraid of dying."

"Well, that's normal for a—" Temple stopped.

"For a real person?" Peter asked softly. "For a citizen? Is that what you were going to say, Sarge?"

Temple's face flushed. "Yes. But I thought recombinants were created without that fear. Any deviation is considered unusable."

Peter sighed. "Aren't you afraid of combat, Sarge? Doesn't your heart hammer in your throat at the thought of confronting an Antaran?"

"Of course. But I'm not—"

"A recombinant, I know. I can only guess how it feels to live like you do. To walk through grass with your bare feet, to smell rain. Touch snow."

Temple shook his head.

"See, Sarge," Drake shouted, "He's crazy! Wash him out!"

"I've read about all these things," said Peter. "I've seen videos and images. I've heard the sound of rain, but I've never felt it." Peter didn't look at Drake but concentrated on Temple. For once, someone was listening. It didn't matter that the sergeant couldn't change a thing. He cared enough to listen. "They tell us when we first achieve consciousness that if we're lucky, we'll live as long as a year when we reach the front. Recombinants have to cram a lifetime into that one year. Sarge, if you had a year to live, would you spend it at a war front?"

Temple tried to speak, but all that came out was silence. He was quiet for a long time. Then finally he spoke.

"It's not my job to decide the morality of the Recombinant Defense Program. I'm sorry, but it's not. The fact remains that if this unit doesn't successfully complete its training, it will be washed out. Do both of you understand that?"

Peter nodded. Scowling, Drake nodded.

The meeting was interrupted by a beep from Temple's mobile.

"Excuse me a moment," he said and turned to his handheld.

From his chair, Peter saw part of a message. Something about needing to hire a new shuttle pilot.

Temple smiled. "All right, gentlemen," he said, turning back to them. "This better not happen again. I need to make a call. You're dismissed."

Peter struggled against his injuries to rise from the chair and hobble out ahead of Drake.

6

DIANA HAD JUST COME BACK from town and was fumbling with her door lock when her mobile rang. She flung open the door and rushed into her dark apartment, fumbling it out of her front pants pocket. Tripping over a boot in the entryway, she fell into the kitchen floor, yellow tile hard against her knees.

Her mobile chimed again as she struggled to press her hand against the light pad on the kitchen wall. Lights flicked on throughout the three-room apartment. She scurried to her feet and flicked receive on her mobile, David's picture on the screen.

"David?" she cried, out of breath.

David's weary face hung in the view screen. Something was wrong. She slid the *conceal face* slider to *view face*, allowing David to see hers.

"David? What's the matter?"

He rubbed his eyes. "Just some personnel problems. I won't bore you with those. Look, there's a job notice going out tomorrow. The base station needs a new shuttle pilot. They're accepting civilians. Interested?"

Diana grabbed a straight-backed cane chair from the corner and tossed her purse on the dining table. Across the room near the sink, the cooling unit buzzed as new ice fell into the ice tray. After four months of unemployment, she craved another chance to fly. But working as a shuttle pilot again? The job paid well though—that steady paycheck David was so fond of—and it was with UCOE. Her dartboard winnings would take care of this month's rent, but what about next month?

She smiled. "Yes, I'm interested." She leaned forward. "What do I have to do?"

"Show up at the shuttle port tomorrow morning—early. They're processing apps in the port. If they like your experience, they'll bring you up to the station and interview you. Then they'll submit all the qualified applicants to D'Angelo who'll make the final choice. We need a shuttle pilot right away. Fair enough?"

"Fair enough, David." She studied the lines around his mouth. "Look, I know something's bothering you. Wanna tell me about it or should I keep pestering you until your head explodes?"

David sighed and gave a forced-sounding laugh. "Not yet. I need to sort some things out first, okay?"

"Is it about the recombinants?"

A look of surprise washed across his face. "Yeah. Why do you say that?"

She shrugged. "They seem to challenge your traditional reality a bit, David. You've always liked everything in its place. Recombinants don't seem to fit. Are you surprised by that?"

"No. What I am surprised by is why I've never heard a recombinant object to his circumstances before tonight."

Object? Diana frowned. *Would it do a recombinant any good or just make things worse for them?* "What do you mean *object?*"

He sighed and ran his hand across his face. "Diana, I can't put him out of my mind. He asked me tonight why he had no chance to live and no future. Why it was okay for us to be afraid to die, but not him? It was chilling."

"Wow, David—that must have been tough." She was silent for a few moments. "What did you tell him?"

David grimaced and Diana saw the guilt in his eyes. He pinched the bridge of his nose with thumb and forefinger. "I gave him one of those stupid, bureaucratic answers." He sighed. "I told him it wasn't my job to debate the morality of the Recombinant Defense Program." He tapped his fingers on his desktop, the sound hollow through the comm. "He wasn't combative or angry. God, Diana, he was just sad. So sad it made my chest hurt."

"What are you going to do about it?"

"I don't know." He looked away from the screen. "If I talk about it, they'll wash him out. I've got to make him into a soldier somehow. Anyway, will I see you tomorrow after the interview?"

She nodded. "I'll be at the port by nine."

"Oh nine hundred. Sleep well, sis."

"Right. You, too, David."

She reached out to close the connection.

"Diana?"

"Uh-huh?"

"If you had a year to live, what would you do?"

She wrinkled her brow. Everything. She was only twenty-one. Why would he ask such a thing? "I'd cram as much as I could into that year, living, feeling, experiencing. Why?"

"Never mind," he muttered. "It's not important. See you tomorrow."

THE NEXT MORNING, Diana woke up before the alarm screeched in her ear. After a quick shower, she dressed in a metallic silver suit and the purple scarf Grandma Temple had given her. It still smelled like the lilac cachet Grandma had packaged with it.

Diana hurried down the short hallway and veered right into the kitchen. It was a small, u-shaped kitchen, appliances and cabinets on all three walls, dining table in the corner nook. A glass-topped table rested against the wall by the doorway. Her boots clicked against the tile as she moved to the heating unit. She filled the old blue tea kettle with water from the sink and set it on the smallest heating grid. It warmed quickly at the presence of the kettle. By the time she'd dropped bread into the toaster and set out butter and jelly, her kettle was singing.

She carried the kettle to the table, pouring hot water into her teacup. Fragrant cinnamon and spices wafted up from the cup as the tea bag steeped. Returning the kettle to the heating unit, she retrieved her toast.

As she drank cinnamon tea and ate toast, her thoughts went back to David. He had talked so strangely last night. Secure, orderly David already bothered over the plight of one recombinant—all in a week's time. David had never been one for causes. Why was he suddenly so concerned about recombinants? The new UCOE Constitution excluded recombinants, defining citizens as only those with naturally combined DNA—copyrighted xDNA classified as other. All part of the wartime effort, the UCOE Council had announced to surprisingly little protest from most special interest groups. That ruling had always bothered her, but David had never mentioned it.

She took a bite of the buttered toast with grape jelly. Because of their copyrighted xDNA, recombinants were property of the government. They could discard them and use them at will. Recombinants kept the war out in deep space, on alien soil, and far away from Earth and the minds of its voters. It also kept young men and women home safe while recombinants lived and died to keep them that way. She didn't know what to think. She'd never met a recombinant.

Diana finished her breakfast and hurried down to the shuttle port. The small, drafty port was nothing more than a large hangar with a ticket counter, a coffee house, and harsh lighting. She hurried past the ticket counter toward UCOE's shuttle bay. Her boots clicked sharply against the polymer flooring as she rushed down to the makeshift recruiting stand.

A sleepy-looking clerk sat up straight when she approached and requested an application. She filled it out quickly on the datapad and waited while a stiff-shouldered sergeant perused the information.

"Ever worked with the Armed Forces, Ms. Temple?"

"No, but I can fly anything you throw at me."

"It's just a shuttle ferrying trainees back and forth."

"Should be easy then," she answered.

He pointed to the shuttle bay across from the table and handed her an ID badge that read guest. "Take that to the gate. You'll need it to get into the base for an interview."

She accepted the badge and went to wait at the gate for the shuttle.

After several, grueling interviews, Diana escaped with a shred of patience and a promised call by the end of the week. She called David from her mobile and he came down to meet her.

"How'd it go?" he asked, guiding her toward a lift.

She crossed her arms. "Fine, if you like being interrogated. I was afraid they'd waterboard me."

David rode with her in the lift and walked her to the main shuttle entrance. A smaller version of the Civilization coffeehouse was tucked into a corner of the brightly lit bay. The smell of bacon and fresh coffee warmed the air.

They sat a table near the door and drank coffee as they talked about being kids and the old house in Washington State.

"Have you decided what to do about your personnel problem?" Diana asked, stirring more sugar into her coffee.

David set down his cup. "Not yet. I'll just let it alone, forget about it."

"David, it's not going to go away."

His face paled. "Why do you say that?"

"If you were a recombinant, would you forget about your situation?"

He shook his head, a sick look on his face. "For now, I'll let it alone."

After two cups of coffee, Diana climbed aboard a shuttle and David went back to work.

The call to report to duty came Friday morning at eight a.m. Diana danced around the living room in her green robe. She was a pilot again. For UCOE. She grinned. Mother and Dad would be horrified.

Diana didn't care. She lived to fly, even if it was only to shuttle recombinants back and forth to training. It counted as hours toward a fighter pilot certification. All that mattered was she was flying again.

7

DR. KINGSTON TOSSED her med kit onto the nearest counter. The infirmary only had a handful of patients today. The artificial smell of citrus mixed with germicide, stinging her nose. Only three other medics were on duty in the over-bright chamber, tending the handful of patients. She made the fourth. She leaned against an exam table, trying to collect her thoughts.

Without even checking her list of affected recombinants, she knew she'd find Peter Mitchell's name there. The training bothered him. And he was performing poorly. She shook her head, sighing. This young man was headed for a wash out. How many more of the recombinants on her list were careening toward wash out, too?

Her stomach clenched and she folded her arms against her torso. Was the MRC malfunction much worse than she'd originally thought?

One of the nurses in crisp grey scrubs looked up from his datapad. "You okay, Dr. Kingston?"

She nodded. "I'm fine." She glanced toward the short hallway off the central exam room. "If you need me, I'll be in the research room doing the write up on the patient I treated."

The hum of equipment was steady in the room. Turning abruptly, she walked across the infirmary's central hub of exam tables and testing facilities. Four hallways branched off the hub, leading to patient beds, operating room, diagnostics, and medics' offices.

She veered into the far right hallway and slipped into the research room. With only the thin light of a desk lamp and glow of a virtual screen and keyboard, she collapsed into a chair and rubbed her eyes. She had to examine enough recombinants on her list to gauge the extent of the MRC malfunction. But how? She leaned on the armrest and rested her forehead in her palm. How to examine that many recombinants without drawing suspicion? She needed a plan.

For a long time, she sat with her eyes closed in the cool half-light. She turned every possibility over in her mind, but came up blank. She'd have to swallow her pride and call Kai for some advice. He'd gloat for weeks after this was over, she knew, but she had no choice.

With reluctance, Jeannette tapped in Kai's code. She waited through several buzzing rings until finally, his voice echoed from the virtual display. She enabled the video feed. He looked a little haggard, like he'd worked a few too many double shifts, but his tired eyes quickly brightened.

"Hey, Red. How are things going there?"

"It doesn't look good, Kai. I think the malfunction is worse than we suspected."

His eyes widened. "What? Worse?"

Jeannette nodded. "I had to treat a recombinant today. He got into a fight with another recombinant. Kai, he told me how bothered he was by his training. And that he wasn't doing well at the exercises."

Kai rubbed his jaw. "Bothered by his training, huh? Not enough killing?"

"No, too much."

"Too much?" His gaze fell to the floor. "And you think his behavior is caused by a malfunctioning chip?"

"Yes, I do." Jeannette logged into the computer and opened the list of recombinants from the affected MRC batches. She quickly found Mitchell in the list. "The recombinant's name is on the list you gave me."

For several moments, Kai was silent.

"I need to get closer to the affected recombinants, Kai. As a medic, how can I do that?"

"Good question," he mumbled, pacing in front of his screen. "Let's think about this for a moment."

"I only have a few weeks before they get a permanent medic to take my place.

"I know, I know," he said, holding up a hand as he paced. "Let me think."

She leaned back in her chair and sorted through possibilities—physicals, blood tests. All of that had already been done before the recombinants started training. What about the front would require a medic's intervention? She propped her chin in her palm.

"Kai, what about vaccinations? I could insist that all of the recombinants on my list be checked—and the proper vaccinations be verified for Ku'Tal."

Kai stopped pacing and hurried back to his chair. "That might work. You could do quick checks on each recombinant."

Jeannette frowned. "Think it will work?"

"Why wouldn't it?" he asked, shrugging. "Just go talk to the training sergeants. They're good people. They'll cooperate." He smirked at her. "In the meantime, I'll uh—review the vaccine records for your list. Any sort of you know, clerical error could require that those codes be verified."

Jeannette smiled. "You're awesome, Kai! Thanks."

She thought back to her conversation with Mitchell. His training sergeant had been there. What was his name? She'd heard it before, but where? Temple—his last name was Temple.

"Do you know anyone by the name of Temple?" she asked.

He nodded. "That shuttle pilot I hired was named Temple. Remember?"

She thought back, trying to remember, but drew a blank on the name. Damned MRC must have parsed out her name, but not the event. She longed for the day when she'd be free from this MRC's little prison. Sometimes, the parsing was so illogical that it seemed almost random.

"Was that her name? I don't remember." She searched on the name Temple and came up with one match. David Temple, Training Sergeant. She frowned. But who was her shuttle pilot? Surely, they were related somehow.

"There's a training sergeant called David Temple here at the base. Think he's related to your shuttle pilot?"

"Maybe," Kai said and sat down in his desk chair. "Her name was Diana. I just sent her mobile code to you. Call her and see if they're related."

Jeannette ignored his snicker. Kai's attempt at humor was actually a good idea. She'd call Diana Temple and see if the young woman might be interested in a few hours as a research assistant. With the training sergeant's sister nearby, she might get more information on the recombinants than she would in an interview.

"Go to bed, Kai. You look lousy."

He rolled his eyes. "Thanks, Doc. Too much coffee. G'night, Red."

The screen turned grey as the connection cleared. Jeannette leaned back in her chair and closed her eyes, thinking through her options. But after a few minutes, she came back to her original conclusion. Diana Temple could provide a lot of information she'd never obtain elsewhere. Yawning, she sat up and faced the virtual display. She retrieved the mobile code from Kai's message and then called Diana.

The connection was fast, but it took a few moments for Diana to answer. A soft, waiting chime trilled several times before she appeared on the screen. She wore a purple t-shirt and grey sweat pants. Her brown hair pulled back in a ponytail. A datapad and a handful of papers lay scattered across the small desk. Diana set down her glass of water.

"Dr. Kingston?" she said with a smile. "From the Reclamation Station, right?"

"Yes," said Jeannette with a nod. If only she could retrieve the details of her life that easily.

Diana leaned against the table, propping an elbow. "What can I do for you, Doc?"

This felt so awkward. She barely remembered this young woman. Much of that day had been parsed out. Sometimes, she never knew what would remain the next day. She'd take careful notes tonight before she went to bed. "I'm new at this station and I don't really know anyone." Jeannette cringed. The more she talked, the worse this sounded.

"I'll bet," said Diana, still smiling. "Moving around so much can be tough."

Only when she couldn't remember anything but what was happening right now. "Yes, it is. See, you're the only person I know around here. Could I ask you a few questions about the base?"

"Of course," Diana replied. "I just got a job at the base, so maybe we could trade information?" She twirled a pen around on the desk, her gaze falling. "It's not full time yet, but it could be if I do well."

"I'll happily share what little I know," Jeannette said with a chuckle.

Diana looked up and leaned closer to her mobile screen. "Just how bad are the physicals?" she asked in a low voice.

Jeannette turned her gaze to her workstation and called up the week's list of appointments. She quickly found Diana's name and added the appointment to her own schedule. "They're not life-threatening," she said. "You'll be fine. You're scheduled with me."

"That's a relief." Diana took a drink of water as she settled into the chair, folding her arms in her lap. "Okay, what would you like to know?"

"Are you related to Training Sergeant Temple?"

"He's my brother," she answered with a grin.

"Terrific," Jeannette said in relief. "We haven't formally met yet, but I think I'm going to be working with him soon."

"David's by the book, so I'm sure you won't have any problems working with him. David listens."

"I'm glad to hear that," Jeannette said, trying to hold in a sigh. By the book. That could mean trouble if she didn't follow the strictest protocol with the recombinants. She stared at Diana for a moment. "Another question for you. Where planetside would someone post civilian employment requests? Is there a central job kiosk somewhere?"

Diana's eyes widened. "There's a kiosk at the shuttle port." She was quiet for a moment. "What kind of job?"

"I need a part-time assistant to help me with some research I'm conducting." Having Diana involved might ease some of the training sergeant's scrutiny. "About five to ten hours on base every week."

"What are the requirements?" Diana asked, sitting up.

Jeannette smiled. "Just data gathering and interviewing recombinants. Nothing overly specialized."

Another pause.

"How much does the job pay?"

"Twenty-eight credits an hour." Paid out of her own pocket, but no one needed to know that. She watched Diana's eyes brighten.

"How do I apply?"

Jeannette laughed. "You just did and you're hired."

"Awesome!" she cried. "Thanks so much. When do I start?"

She tried to hold back her smile. "Stop by the infirmary next time you're on base and we'll set up a schedule. Sound good?"

"Sounds wonderful. Maybe I'll even make next month's rent?"

"Talk to you soon," said Jeannette and she cleared the connection.

Jeannette slid her chair over to the desk and doubled-tapped her list of links until she located her log file. She scrolled through the document page by page, watching all the words rush past. Her whole life flickered by in black and white. Her marriage. Her divorce. Names and dates and places that she had no memory of, no resonance with. It read like someone else's life, yet she knew it was hers. Only through the hazy afterimages that touched the edges of thought.

Jeannette stopped paging through when the name Rena scrolled onto her screen. A distant remembrance chilled her. She swiveled away from the screen, her hands shaking. A case she handled in her ER rotation during her residency. She clutched the arm of the chair, remembering a little girl brought into ER.

Cyanotic. Pupils fixed, fading pulse.

The little girl had drowned in a swimming pool when her father left her alone in the backyard. She winced. Cyanotic. The paramedics had revived her en route, but the little girl died before Jeannette could even tube her. Jeannette's eyes stung. Rena. That was the little girl's name.

Taking a deep breath, Jeannette moved to her screen again. She hesitated then scrolled down the page. Tears rolled down her cheeks when she found the little girl's full name further down in the file. Rena Diane Kingston—her daughter. She began to shake.

For a moment, she couldn't breathe. The words glared back at her, the whole gut-wrenching ordeal, yet she remembered nothing. All of it had been parsed out of her memory. All of it! It read like a news article. Anger rose hot on her cheeks and she pounded the desk.

"Where are her images? And the memories?"

Why had they taken the only part of Rena that still remained? There was nothing tangible left of her daughter. Nothing at all. Even those memories were locked away, out of her reach. She gripped the hair at her nape, wanting to claw out the horrible chip that had stolen everything from her.

Someone rapped on her door.

"Yes?" she answered, wiping the tears from her face.

The door creaked open and scalding light seared the cool darkness. A nurse stuck her head in the door.

"Doctor, we've got a tech on his way in. Severed the tip of his index finger."

She sighed and rubbed the bridge of her nose. "I'll be right out."

The door closed and she turned to the screen again. She'd update the file before she went to bed. Otherwise, there was no telling what she'd lose come morning.

8

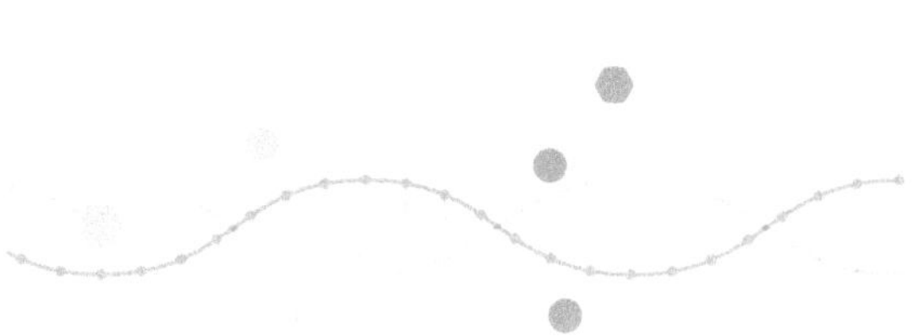

DIANA PACED OUTSIDE the shuttle port coffeehouse. The port was cool and drafty, a welcome change from Civilization's steamy streets. She shoved her hands into the pockets of her grey flight suit, wondering how long she'd have to wait to pick up the recombinants from the sim site. Her mobile hadn't gone off yet. The site was a huge patch of barren land twenty minutes south of the city. Nothing but dust and rock. UCOE had invested a lot of money in that stretch of land, developing VR simulation equipment that portrayed a painfully realistic war front. David said it felt like the real thing and it was as close as he'd ever want to get to Ku'Tal.

For over a week now, Diana had spent only a few hours jumping atmosphere and cruising into the base station. The rest of the time, she stalked the port hangar and this coffeehouse. If things didn't change by the time she made rent, she'd resign. She hadn't gone to see Dr. Kingston yet. Her physical was scheduled for day after tomorrow. She'd talk to Dr. Kingston afterward.

Diana entered the dimly lit coffeehouse and sat down at a corner table. Supper was a few hours away, so she only ordered coffee and a cheese Danish. She fiddled with the purple scarf tied in her hair as a herd of people passed by the coffeehouse, just arriving on an off-world shuttle. Two families shuffled children down the long walkway toward the exit, and traveling merchants wheeled cases of goods away. Who would bring their families out this close to the war front, she wondered?

Three people entered the coffeehouse and moved toward a booth beside Diana's table. A blonde, her hair braided down her back, sat beside a short man with dark hair and a Van Dyke beard that circled his mouth. A tall, gangly man with a nervous gaze wedged himself into the booth across from the other two.

Diana sipped her coffee and glanced at her watch: 14:50. She groaned. Would this day ever end?

"So, can we land on Ku'Tal without detection?"

The voice was so quiet she almost didn't hear it. Then the words hit her. Land on Ku'Tal? Diana set down her cup and listened. Who in their right mind would choose to go the front?

"They're working on the problem. Be patient, Kev." The woman's voice. "We'll wait for Ron like he asked. Do this wrong and we'll blow everything."

"How many this time?"

A pause. "Three, maybe four. We'll skim them outside the city and be out of here in two days."

"Linda and I'll go to Mimi's for the cargo and meet you at the river tomorrow night."

The conversation fell silent, leaving Diana hungry for more. *What cargo?_Were they gunrunners? Data pirates*? She knew Mimi Constantine, a friendly, divorced woman who ran the nicest restaurant in Civilization. Called End of the Line. And it was. The restaurant hugged the river and was the southernmost point on Civilization. Beyond the river was desert and nothingness. She'd talked with Mimi on slow nights over a glass of merlot. Mimi wasn't the type to run guns.

Diana checked her credits pouch and smiled. Enough to dine at End of the Line tonight.

Her mobile vibrated. She gulped the last of her lukewarm coffee, leaving remnant crusts of the cheese Danish on the plate. Time to pick up the kids. She paid her check and raced down the hangar to the shuttle.

THE ASCENT to the station was rocky, the g-forces making her stomach twist. The stick fought her every maneuver, but she held onto it. When the winking lights of the launch bay swung into view, Diana squinted, pretending the small pinpoint was the bull's-eye of a dartboard. She aimed the nose of the shuttle toward it and kicked her thrusters.

When she docked with the station, she quickly completed her shutdown procedure and climbed out of the cockpit. She turned in her duty sheet to a maintenance engineer and watched the recombinants hustled out of the passenger cabin by a drill sergeant. They looked like young men and women about her age, but from what they'd said in the vid streams, recombinants were incapable of independent thought. Trained only to seek and destroy the enemy. More like androids than humans.

She'd never actually spoken to one, but they looked as human as she did. That made her uncomfortable.

The recombinants shouted and caroused, pretending to shoot aliens. They jabbered away about how many biodrones they'd shot during the sim. Some went into great detail and Diana tuned them out, disgusted by their fixation on killing. Maybe the vid streams were right after all?

Another shuttle landed after hers and more recombinants filed out. It looked like David's unit.

Several recombinants surged out of the shuttle, screaming and shoving each other.

"I shot every bastard that moved!" one shouted, grinning as he hurried to the lift.

"They splatter real good, don't they?" another one replied with a snort and followed the first recombinant.

Two more recombinants trickled out, more behind them.

"Get out of my way, wash out," shouted one of the recombinants with a growl. The name on his jacket was Drake.

The other recombinant, tousled blond hair, soft pale blue eyes, was on his knees by a stack of crates, watching something. She hadn't noticed him until now. The loud private kicked at his leg.

Something small and dark scurried out from the behind the crate. The private called Drake leered at the creature, raising his boot to stomp it.

"No!" the blond private shouted. He broadsided Drake who tumbled into the crates. The little creature froze, terrified by the noise. The blond private reached down to it.

"I won't hurt you, little guy," he said in a half-whisper and bent down. He laid his hand, palm up, on the ground.

To Diana's amazement, the fuzzy creature scampered into his hand. He scooped it off the floor and for a moment, his gaze locked with hers. The kindest, bluest eyes she'd ever seen, a shy smile on his handsome oval face. For a moment, he took her breath away.

He surged toward her as Drake came after him.

"Ma'am," he said, holding out his hand, "could you please take this shuttle stowaway back down when you go? Please?"

The desperation in his eyes touched her, and she held out her hands. He stared at her as if mesmerized for a moment, and then he gently laid the trembling little mouse-like creature in her hands. Private Drake seized him by the shoulders and spun him around.

Angry, Diana stepped between them. "Private, don't you have someplace to be?" she demanded.

Surprised, Drake stared at her for a moment, his anger diffusing. "Yes, ma'am." He glanced around the launch bay and then slunk away toward the lift.

The blond private turned around and grinned at her, but his gaze fell quickly to the deck. "Thanks," he said, not looking her in the eye.

Then he reached down and petted the little creature in her hands. He didn't look at her as he talked. "I've seen this one hiding behind the crates for a day or so. Today, I was finally able to coax him out. Thanks for setting him free." He smiled and glanced up at her as he hurried away toward the lift.

Diana found a small transport container in the office and poked some holes in it. Then she placed the rodent inside and hurried across the launch bay with the container. She caught a lift to the station's main floor and called David.

"Hey, big brother, got a date tonight?" she asked. He stared at her through an exhausted mask of worry. "David, are you sick?"

He shook his head and offered a weary smile. "No, I just need to get out of here for a few days." His voice softened. "It's really gettin' to me, Diana. I can't recommend a guy like that for wash out. I know it's my job, but I just can't do it."

"Get a pass and come down to Civilization with me. I'll take you out to dinner and we can talk about it."

He smiled weakly again. "I'll do that, sis. Let me clear it with D'Angelo first."

Diana bought a cola from the vending machine and waited for David's message. She bought a small package of trail mix and shared it with Mitchell's fuzzy brown mouse-creature. A long time later, her mobile vibrated. David's message scrolled across the screen. "Meet you at your shuttle." She tossed the empty cola container into the recycle bin and hurried down to launch bay with the rodent.

IN THE DIM amber light of the cockpit, David looked ill. He sat with lids half closed, arms folded against his chest, and eyes sunken into their sockets.

Diana adjusted her angle of descent and rode out the drop into atmosphere. David leaned back and squeezed his eyes shut, his lips turning white as he pressed them together.

"David, I'm really worried about you," she said, casting quick glances at him. This wasn't like David.

"I confess, I don't know why I'm letting this one recombinant get to me. I've washed out soldiers before."

She didn't know exactly what happened to recombinants after they washed out. She knew they were sent back to the Recombinant Development Center. Maybe they were retrained? Still, the concept was unsettling.

"How is he getting to you?" she asked.

"I've never seen any recombinant want to live as badly as he does. When I talk to him, I'm talking to a real person, not some cloned, mindless soldier-bot with an unalterable path of instructions."

The ship jerked and pitched, skipping through the atmosphere, and then dropped again. Diana held her vector, making minor adjustments until she broke through the gravity well. The ruddy landscape filled the cockpit view as the shuttle stopped shimmying and leveled out.

He rubbed his eyes. "He's just a scared kid, Diana, who knows there's more out there than dying at the front. And he has no chance to escape his fate. He's going to die—and no amount of training and preparation will change that. Drake, Mitchell, Stingley—the entire unit will be dead by this time next year." He shook his head, staring out at the dismal stretch of rocky desert surrounding Civilization. "And we'll just make more and send them to their deaths, too."

"That's how the program was designed, David."

"I know and it never bothered me until I met this private, Diana. He's different and he's affecting his entire unit. And me. I'm doing everything I can to keep him from washing out, but, Diana, he's so different from the others."

Diana shrugged. "Maybe it would be best to let him wash out?"

"Diana!" He glared at her.

"Well, if he's as different as you say, then it'll only be harder on him out there. Wouldn't it be better not to send him to the front instead of making him suffer?"

His face pinched with anger. "We're not talking about a sewer rat here! He's as human as you and me. He should be allowed to decide for himself and not be led around by the nose like some animal. They're people and we're treating them like cattle! It makes me sick." Sullen, he turned away.

"I saw your unit return from Civilization today. They had one thing on their minds. Killing. That's all they talked about." She dropped her speed and veered toward the shuttle port runway. "Well, except this one private. He rescued a rodent from the launch bay today. The one called Drake was going to stomp it. He asked me if I'd take it back here and release it."

David sat up, the anger slipping from his face. "Mitchell rescued a mouse?" He groaned. "See what I mean, Diana?"

She shook her head. "What do you mean?"

"That was Mitchell. He's the recombinant failing his training sims."

Her eyes widened. No! That young man couldn't be Mitchell. She hadn't been able to stop thinking about him and how he'd risked getting beaten up for a mouse. He had such a boyish look about him, thick blond hair, tousled, and sad, pale blue eyes pleading with her to save a mouse. She stared over at David who pensively gazed out the portal. Now, she understood his dilemma.

She requested clearance into the port and touched down. The shuttle screamed down the runway. She kicked in the resistors until the shuttle slowed and glided toward the hangar bay. She taxied over to the bay and shut down. David stepped out of the shuttle in silence, duffle bag in hand. Diana walked beside him, carrying the container with Mitchell's mouse inside. She'd release it near her apartment, by the river.

David didn't say another word on the city shuttle or up the stairs to Diana's apartment. He plopped down on her couch and leaned against the arm until his eyes closed. She covered him with a blanket. She needed to clean up for supper, but first, she had a mouse to release.

DAVID AWOKE AROUND 1920 HOURS. He staggered into the bathroom and cleaned up. When he emerged clean-shaven, hair combed, and eyes more rested, he looked like David again. He managed a smile.

"Sorry I snapped at you earlier," he said and sat down at Diana's kitchen table.

"It's okay," she said, handing him a cup of coffee. She sat down across from him and sipped cinnamon tea. "I haven't seen you this concerned about something since they set traps for stray dogs in our old neighborhood."

He laughed and took a long sip from his coffee. "You weren't concerned until Cordy got out. Then you were ready to have the entire neighborhood arrested."

Diana thought about Private Mitchell again, wondering if that other recombinant had cornered him and beaten him up. He'd been trained to fight though, she reminded herself. Private Mitchell could take care of himself.

"While you were sleeping, I made reservations at End of the Line," she said.

"End of the Line?" He made a sour face. "What's that?"

"It's a nice restaurant in Civilization. Their food's very good. Stop fretting and relax. You'll have a good time."

When David finished his coffee, Diana grabbed her purse and they left for the restaurant. She almost told him about the odd conversation she'd overheard in the shuttle port, but decided against it. David worried enough for the both of them. He was already upset. He didn't need any more stimulus.

The transit ride at dusk was a short one through Civilization's darkening streets. The transit tubes rose above the buildings, giving them a panoramic view of the city. Colored lights lit rooftops and lampposts throughout the barren place. The air cooled as they neared the river, the tart ore scent fading. Across from the transit stop was the simple river stone facade of End of the Line. Inside, tapestries of sultans and desert palaces adorned the walls and ornate pillows with gold piping and tassels lay strewn across the backs of booths. Mimi Constantine had a fondness for Middle Eastern culture.

Mimi stood at the reservations desk, her strawberry hair tied up in a tangle of piled curls. She wore an iridescent green sari on her athletic frame. Mimi was old enough to be Diana's mother and there were times when Diana wished she were.

"Diana Temple!" Mimi rushed over and hugged her.

When Mimi let her go, Diana motioned toward her brother. "Mimi, this is my brother, David. He's stationed at the base."

"Pleased to meet you, David." Mimi put on a mock frown and put her hand on her hip. "Girl, how've you been? Haven't seen you for weeks. Is everything okay with you?"

"Everything's fine. I have a job now, working as a shuttle pilot for the base. Making my rent on time and everything."

Mimi picked up a couple of menus. "Let's get you a table overlooking the river, kids." She led them through the main room where a Sitar player strummed a bittersweet song. She passed the player and moved toward the windows. The table was low, only pillows for chairs. David grimaced.

"Would you prefer a more conservative table, David?" Diana asked, pointing toward the tables with chairs.

Sighing, David shook his head. "You're always too flamboyant for me, little sister." He bent down and collapsed onto one of the pillows, bobbing back and forth until he found his balance point. With lithe grace, Diana sat on top of her pillow and scanned the menu. Mimi left them alone.

"Order whatever you like," said Diana. "My treat."

"It's all so expensive, Diana. We should have gone to the pub. You've got rent to pay and probably other bills—"

"Would you stop? I'm using the rest of my dartboard winnings. My paycheck will cover rent and utilities. Relax! Stop trying to take care of everyone, okay?"

He laughed. "I'm sorry. I'm used to being in charge, I guess."

Diana leaned across the table. "You did an excellent job of taking care of me when Mother and Dad were at work. But I'm an adult now. I need you as my brother, not my father. Be my friend now, okay?"

"Only if you'll let me buy the wine."

"Deal."

Mimi returned to the table. "You kids want something to drink?"

"A bottle of your best merlot, please," said David.

"Ah, a nice meal tonight." Mimi winked at Diana. "Your brother is a good man. A little confused, but he means well."

She flitted off toward a wine cabinet near the kitchen.

"I think I was just insulted," said David with a laugh. "What did she mean by that?"

Diana giggled. "Mimi is a bit of a psychic. She reads palms and auras, stuff you'd find silly and ridiculous."

"No one can tell my fortune from lines on my hands," he insisted, crossing his arms. "It's not possible."

Soon, Mimi returned with a bottle of merlot and two glasses. She plucked the cork from the bottle and filled their glasses with wine. The oak-scented merlot sparkled as Mimi lit the candle on their table and left.

AFTER A GLASS OF WINE, David relaxed. The taut expression on his face loosened. His whole body seemed to let go of its tension. He was more animated, talking about things beyond work. He laughed and joked, being more like the David she remembered. It was good to see him relax.

Soon after their entrees arrived, the two men and woman from the shuttle port entered the restaurant. Diana ate her pasta slowly, her concentration divided between David's conversation and what was happening at the reservations desk. Mimi seated the trio at a table right beside the kitchen.

"Diana, are you listening to me?"

"Huh? I'm sorry, what did you say?"

"I was talking about the time you messaged me, begging me to convince Mother and Dad that you should go to Mars colony for computer certification." David took a sip of wine. "Mars—what a crazy notion that was."

"But I wanted to be on my own, that's why I chose Mars."

"You were thirteen. Way too young to go off to Mars like that."

"No, I wasn't," Diana said with a frown. She'd wanted to study on Mars, but she let David talk her out of going. Where would she be now if she'd gone? Lots of her friends had gone and every one of them had good jobs. None of them were part time space taxis. "You went at sixteen."

"But back then, there wasn't a war going on," said David, his voice somber.

Diana shifted her gaze back to the table by the kitchen, finding it empty. They were gone! She'd let the wine and conversation distract her.

LATER, Diana and David ate chocolate cake and drank coffee. She gazed out at the lights twinkling off the river, wondering how Mimi was involved with those people. How could she even ask? *Excuse me, Mimi, but are you running guns through the Taus system?*

When the check came, she and David scanned it with their mobiles, transferring funds to the bill. Mimi walked them to the door.

"How was your meal, kids?"

"Best food I've had in months," said David, patting his stomach.

She squeezed his shoulder. "Good. You need more meat on your bones. And you!" She patted Diana's arm. "You take care of yourself and your brother. His aura's pretty battered right now."

She and David strolled outside. They walked silently through the well-lit street toward the transit stop. Finally, David broke the silence.

"My aura's pretty battered? What the hell does that mean?"

Diana laughed. "She just tells you what she sees, David. She picked right up on your confusion."

"A blind monkey could have picked that up," he said with a laugh.

"So, what are you going to do about it?"

"Be patient," he said, looking off into the distance. "I'll help him as much as I can. That's all I can do."

She wanted David to help Mitchell, too, but she kept it to herself. She started to mention the people in the shuttle port this afternoon, but the rush of the transit filled the evening stillness. She let their faces and conversations slip into the night as she boarded the transit behind David. Like David, she would be patient. Right now, all she had was time.

9

COLD RAIN POUNDED the VR chamber, simulating autumn and the latest developments at the front. The smell of moldy leaves hung in the air. Chilled to the bone, Peter shivered as he crawled across frozen ground, sensor grid in hand. His plasma rifle, strung across his back, dragged the ground. If the temperature dropped any lower, the rain would freeze.

He glanced back at Sting, who struggled behind him. Peter's teeth chattered, the cold unbearable. Drake slithered up beside Sting.

"Anything yet, Pete?" Sting asked in a soft voice.

Peter studied the grid for any movement, any trace of Antaran presence. None. He shook his head.

"Why the hell do they put this stupid fucknut on point every time?" Drake.

"Shut up and keep watch on our flank," said Sting. "We'd never even hear him call out with you runnin' off at the mouth."

A whine filtered out from Peter's sensor grid. A bow signature, but he didn't know how to read it. Did they double back east or west?

"I've got something," Peter mumbled. "Bearing east." He sniffed the air. A sweetness clung to it despite the cold rain.

"Take up positions on my mark," said Sting. He turned east and raised his rifle. Drake flopped down on one side of Sting, his laser sight activated.

"Still bearing east," Peter said, and gripped his rifle. He turned to the east, but something nagged at him. He stared at the grid again. "No, wait! West. West!"

They all three turned, rifles raised, but seconds too late to ward off the swarm of Antarans that rolled over them from the west.

"All right, kill the sim!" shouted Sergeant Temple from the observation booth.

"Damn you, Mitchell!"

Drake leaped at Peter, his fist exploding into Peter's mouth. The stock of his plasma rifle cracked against the side of Peter's face. Peter staggered then dropped to the floor of the grey-walled VR chamber.

The freezing rain and Ku'Tal swamps had long disappeared, but he was still shaking. Drake tried to hit him again, but Sting jumped him, slamming his fist into Drake's gut. Drake doubled over, the rage knocked out of him.

Dazed and hurting, Peter writhed on the floor, clutching his jaw.

"You okay, kid?" Sting asked, helping him up from the floor.

Peter nodded. "Fine."

Sting made a sour face. "Sure you are. You look like hell. Let's get you back to your bunk."

Sergeant Temple met them at the VR chamber exit. He squinted at Peter. "Mitchell, are you all right?"

"Fine, Sarge," he muttered, his lip already swelling.

Sting stared at Temple. "This sim isn't going to determine our final ranking, is it?"

"There's still time to pass, private."

"We'll get it under control then, Sarge," Sting said, and hurried into the hall.

"Get him to a medic," Temple ordered the sim detail.

"Not without your permission, Sarge," said Peter. "D'Angelo's orders."

Temple's mouth gaped. It took a moment to find his voice. "Get him to his bunk then. He's excused from exercises for the rest of the day. I'll arrange for the medic. Dismissed."

PETER WAS grateful to have his bunk under him because the room kept spinning. His head ached. He was so tired of fighting with Drake and the Antarans.

Sting sat down on the edge of Peter's bunk, twisting his hands nervously. Peter's bunk was nearest the door and the bathroom. Rows of bunk beds filled the room, allowing only small walkways between the bunks. Light from the latrine filtered into the gloomy chamber, traces of chlorine and soap in the air. The door into the main hallway stood open.

"Pete, you've got to pull it together, man. You don't want to wash out."

"Why?"

Shocked, Sting whirled around, his face contorted. "Washing out is the end! They strap you down to a table and dump a lethal dose of drugs into your system. You go to sleep and never wake up."

"It'd be better than having an Antaran string my guts across the swamp."

"But there's a chance you'll survive!" Sting grabbed him by the shoulders. "Look at me. I came back! Don't you want to live, Pete?"

Peter laughed bitterly. "Live?"

More than anything in this world, Peter wanted to live—but not like this. He gazed up at the data transfer headgear hanging above his bunk. Every night, he and the others strapped themselves in and let UCOE create their hopes and dreams for them. He couldn't even dream on his own. His eyes welled with tears.

"I want to walk out of this place and never come back, Sting. I want to live like real citizens. I'm tired of being a recombinant."

Sting slapped his hand over Peter's mouth, the force burning his swollen lip and bruised chin.

"Don't ever say that out loud again!" Sting's voice was a sharp whisper. "They'll wash you out for sure if they hear that kind of talk. Stow it, kid."

Peter stared into Sting's intense green eyes as Sting pulled his hand away from Peter's mouth. "Why do you care, Sting? I'm a misfit. The whole unit wants me out. Drake wants to shoot me."

Sting sank back against the wall, letting his head rest against it. He stared at the ceiling. "When I achieved consciousness, I only knew what I'd been programmed to know. I went through the training sims, the courses, the headgear, and I passed everything they threw at me. They told me I'd survive six months at the front... because of that, I'd be a hero."

"A hero?" Peter remembered one of the techs telling him how it would be an honor to die at the front. Easy for them to say from their safe, backwater base.

"Yeah, can you believe I bought into that? A hero." He laughed. "They're all so full of shit. Back then, I believed anything they told me. Let them fill my head with idealism and all these lies." He tapped the headgear. "I went to the front expecting to be a hero, to die for my home world. Hell, I wanted to die, Pete. I expected it."

Expected to die...Peter cringed at those words. That part of being a recombinant had always terrified him. He was expected to die.

Sting smiled. "But, Pete, I didn't die out there. I went through a year of hell, watching my buddies fall in droves, getting ripped up by Antarans, but I survived. Now, all I really think about is killing any Antaran that moves." His voice trailed off to a whisper. He stared down at his hands clutching at the faded green blanket. "Sometimes, though, I wonder what it'd be like to walk away from here. To be more than a dead hero." He caught Peter's gaze and held it. In Sting's eyes, Peter saw the things he could barely articulate.

Fighting stiff, aching joints, Peter sat up. With a hand supporting his ribs, he pointed to the headgear. "I used to want to be the people in the data dumps, live what they'd lived," he whispered. "Now, I want to have my own dreams."

He thought of that stunning shuttle pilot who took that little mouse down to the surface. She'd been on his mind ever since then and he longed to just touch her hair. And that brightly colored scarf around her neck. He'd never seen that color before. Her presence made him feel warm and comfortable, like a hot shower or drinking hot coffee on a cold night.

Sting's jaw tightened. He nodded and looked away. "Stick with me then, kid," he said, his voice returning to normal. "Our best chance is to survive the front. But we can't do that unless we pass the training. Get through that first, okay?"

"I'll do my best," said Peter.

Patting Peter on the shoulder, Sting rose from the bunk. "Get some sleep. I'll give you some grid instruction after mess."

"Thanks, Sting."

"And I'll check with Sarge about that medic."

Sting left him in the silent bunkroom. Peter rolled over, grateful not to be in transfer headgear, and thought of that shuttle pilot's thick, dark hair and sweet smile before he went to sleep. He chuckled at her getting in Drake's face and telling him to get lost. Something he wanted desperately to do.

EARLY THE NEXT MORNING, a guard shook Peter awake. He carried orders per Sergeant Temple stating Peter was to report to the infirmary. Peter showered and dressed in his drab green uniform, his head still aching from Drake's rifle. His ribs throbbed with every twist of his torso. He glanced over at Sting, who slept in the bunk across from him. Sting was sound asleep, headgear pressed against his head. With effort, Peter pulled on his boots and followed the guard into the hallway.

The network of hallways, beige on beige, curved around the rim of the station and he followed it out of the recombinants' wing and into the main hallway. The base layout confused him with all its hallways and rooms. He'd never been above level six before, but the lift was taking him all the way up to level three. Excitement mixed with apprehension as the lift stopped and he stepped off. Only officers entered the infirmary.

Two guards, dressed in royal blue, met him at the lift. With crisp turns, the guards led him left. He glanced behind him. The first guard remained behind in the elevator. The hallways seemed wider up here and a calm blue covered the walls, the floors a few shades darker.

Officers shuffled past in their royal blue coats and trousers, colored medals and commendations sparkling on their lapels and shoulders. They looked regal and confident, but stiff as they walked past, footsteps echoing. They took no notice of Peter and his escort. Abruptly, the guards stopped just past a set of double doors to Peter's right. The doors slid open, startling him. With reluctance, he entered the infirmary.

The room was deep and mostly oval in shape. Another section to his right curved into a hallway with small, private rooms. Three other hallways connected to the big oval room. Calm blue permeated the walls, gentle blue blankets covering stark white sheets on two rows of sick beds. At the foot of each bed was some sort of sensor grid, much larger than the small, handheld grids he'd been training to read. The floor was glossy, speckled blue and squeaky as he stepped toward the desk. A thick, antiseptic smell hung in the air, smelling bitter and reminding him of his time at RDC. It smelled like that awful, bitter-smelling brown liquid they used to disinfect the floors and walls. The muscles in his neck and jaw tightened, the old fear rising in his throat.

"Is there something you need?" asked a clear voice to Peter's right. He turned slowly, his head hurting. A woman with short auburn hair stepped out of the far hallway and moved toward him. She wore thin, gold wire glasses and white scrubs, like the ones he'd seen at RDC.

Then he recognized her as Dr. Kingston, the medic who had treated him before. He liked her.

"I was told to report here, ma'am," said Peter, standing at attention.

"Mitchell, right?" she asked.

He nodded, still at attention.

"No need for that stance, private," she said and frowned. "Another fight?"

He nodded again.

"Come over here and let me see what I can do," Dr. Kingston said with a reassuring smile and motioned to him.

Relaxing a bit, he followed her deeper into the infirmary.

He passed a tall, glass cabinet containing all sorts of little bottles. Pausing by the cabinet, he peered inside, marveling at all the colored spheres and liquids. All of these medicines—and so many! He ran his index finger across the glass.

"I never knew they made so many kinds of medicines," he said with a smile.

He glanced around at all the equipment, the blinking lights, the soft whirring of some machine in the far corner. There was so much to see here. He loved to see new things.

Dr. Kingston motioned him toward the nearest bed. "There's a medication for just about every ailment these days."

When he finally sat down, she frowned at the bruises on his face.

"Except for an old-fashioned fist fight. Please tell me the other soldier looks worse."

Peter laughed. He'd expected a medic like the ones at RDC, but Dr. Kingston seemed so different. "Just in my imagination."

Her frown dissipated, replaced by a smile again as she pressed silver disks to his neck, wrist, and chest. He ran his fingers across the disks, wondering what they did. The sensor at the foot of the bed began ticking and beeping. Recording his vital signs, Peter realized. He leaned over, watching the lines pulse across the grid.

"My body makes this grid do all that?" he said with wide eyes.

"It sure does. So, what happened this time, Mitchell?" Dr. Kingston asked.

He shrugged. "Same story. I screwed up and Drake pummeled me for it." His mouth fell open. The last thing he wanted was to stir up Drake again. "Please, forget I said that."

"Okay, done." She moved to the sensor grid and pressed several keys, her gaze focused on the display.

He watched her every movement. "What does that do?" He pointed at a large grey button. "And that?"

"Those are for analyzing injuries."

He smiled. Most of the time, when he asked questions, they were ignored. But Dr. Kingston didn't seem to mind answering.

"You seem very different from this other recombinant, Drake," she said, "I mean, the one whose name I've forgotten."

Peter sighed. "I'm not exactly UCOE's definition of a model recombinant."

"You're certainly a model patient." She typed some more, and then looked up. "Well, soldier, it looks like you've cracked a rib and have one heck of a headache." She reached out a hand to his face, tilting his chin up toward the light. "That cut on your lip needs sealing, too."

Her touch was so gentle against his face. He wasn't used to gentle.

Peter watched in fascination as Dr. Kingston assembled her equipment from the cabinet at the bed's end. There were bottles and sprays, bandages—all sorts of things he'd never seen before. He reached out and ran a finger over the implements. So many things he never knew existed. He could only imagine the wonders that lay beyond this training base.

"You must know so much," Peter said in a half-whisper as he turned a bottle over and over in his palm.

"The more I learn, the less I know," she said with a chuckle and picked up a small can.

"The less you know?" he said in surprise. "How is that possible?"

He was already struggling with the grid. Would he actually get worse at it?

"Before your first fight with Drake, you'd never met me before, right?"

He nodded.

She adjusted the nozzle on the can. "When I told you my name, you learned something about me. So even though you learned my name, you knew absolutely nothing about me."

Peter's brow wrinkled as he thought about her words. After a moment or two, it made sense. "It's like one little thing opens up a whole world of other things."

"Yes, exactly right, Mitchell. You're very bright."

He smiled until it hurt his lip.

She held the can to his face and carefully applied a thin stream of some clear liquid. With a small wooden tool, she spread the liquid across his puffy lower lip. The liquid seemed to dry quickly, forming a layer over the cut. The sore pain dissipated.

"That will numb the pain a bit as it heals the gash," she explained. She motioned toward his shirt. "I need you to remove your shirt now, please."

Struggling with the movements, Peter slowly unfastened his shirt and slipped it off. When he'd finished, she moved close, a roll of thick, almost spongy bandage in her hand.

The infirmary door opened and a brown-haired woman with a scarf around her neck walked into the room. Peter sucked in a breath of air, his heart racing. That was her—the shuttle pilot!

She walked with such graceful movements and so much confidence. Then she turned and her gaze met his. For a moment, he held his breath as the room grew brighter. He couldn't look away from her. She was the most beautiful thing he'd ever seen.

"Hello," she said.

"Hi," he said in a soft voice.

Dr. Kingston raised an eyebrow. "Hello, Diana. I'll be with you in a moment. Just finishing up with Private Mitchell."

Diana's eyes widened and she moved over to him. "Oh, no—what happened, Mitchell? You look really hurt." She laid her hand on his bare shoulder and his skin sizzled with her touch. He couldn't speak for a moment.

"It's okay," he said with a shrug, not wanting her to let go of his shoulder.

Diana gently touched his chin and turned his face into the light. Her warm vanilla scent, silky locks of dark hair, and haunting brown eyes. She was so beautiful it made his chest hurt.

"That looks awful." Diana turned her gaze to Dr. Kingston and a hint of vanilla touched him again. He drank it in. "Is he going to be all right?"

"He'll be fine," said Dr. Kingston. "The injuries are minor."

When her hand fell away from his face, he felt cold again, but her enveloping gaze quickly warmed him. "Mitchell," she said, grimacing, "this fight wasn't about that mouse, was it?"

He shook his head. "No, something I did in sim. Or didn't do."

She stared at him, as if waiting for him to continue. He couldn't believe it. She wanted to know more.

His gaze fell to his hands. "I caused the unit to fail another sim, so they let me know it."

"It doesn't matter, okay? You'll get the hang of the training. I know you will. Anybody who goes out of his way to save a life—no matter how small—has a lot going for him. That took a lot of guts, Mitchell."

"Thanks," he said. "I appreciate that."

Dr. Kingston picked up the roll of spongy material. "Raise your arms, please."

"Take care, Mitchell," she said with a wink and moved back to the waiting room.

Carefully, Dr. Kingston unrolled the material, wrapping it around Peter's rib cage. The material was soft and supporting and his chest felt better as she affixed the end in place.

"How's that feel, private?"

"Much better, thank you."

She handed him his uniform shirt and a bottle of pills. "Take one or two of those every four hours for the pain. All right, private, report to mess. Dismissed."

"Thank you, ma'am," he answered and put on his shirt. He rose from the bed and moved toward the waiting room.

"I really enjoyed talking with you, ma'am," he said to Diana. "Hope we meet again sometime."

"I'd like that, Mitchell," she said with a smirk, "but it's just Diana."

"Diana," he said with a smile, nodding. He waved at her and stepped into the hallway. Even the swollen lip couldn't hold back his grin.

The guard detail was waiting for him and led him to the lift. They rode down with him, delivering him to the recombinant mess hall on level seven.

Peter went into the mess hall, but decided to go up to level six and thank Sergeant Temple for sending him to infirmary. It was the best day of his life.

He hobbled down the hallway and into the lift. After requesting level six, the lift whirred up, leaving the stink of fried fish behind. He stepped into the hallway and navigated the maze of corridors until he found Sergeant Temple's office. Peter raised his hand to knock when he heard Sarge's voice.

"Yes, sir...I know, sir." His voice was agitated, as if someone was yelling at him.

The muffled, angry voice of Lieutenant D'Angelo crackled through Sarge's small office. He must have been on the comunit.

"Dammit, Temple, stop stalling! I want that inventory for reclamation orders on my desk pronto, do you understand me?"

"Yes, sir, I understand, but the final rankings are two weeks or more away. The current scores—"

"To hell with more scores!" D'Angelo roared. "You're with those soldiers every day! You know which ones can cut it and which ones can't. Use the sim data you have and rank them! If they're not passing by now, they'll never pass. By the end of the week, Temple."

"But, sir, the scores—"

"By the end of the week, sergeant."

A sudden quiet hit the room. In a few moments, something slammed against the desk.

Peter backed away from the door. Was he about to be washed out? Terrified, Peter ran down the hallway and into the lift.

AROUND 1400 HOURS, Peter and the other recombinants reported to the station's eighth level classrooms. He sat through a grid course led by Sergeant Temple. The entire unit studied maps of Ku'Tal, the planet where the transport would eventually drop them—if he didn't wash them out. Ku'Tal was one of five planets perched on a line drawn between UCOE Forces and the Antaris system. Peter and his unit would spend at least six months at the front trying to find and destroy a principal munitions depot. If he lived through that, he'd return to this base station in the middle of nowhere.

He smiled. With Diana.

When the unit had gotten through the last of the maps, Temple dismissed them but stopped Peter as he followed the others out of the classroom.

"Mitchell, report to my office in five minutes."

Peter choked back a breath. "Why, Sarge?" Was this it? Were they washing him out?

"We need to discuss the situation in your unit."

Nodding, Peter slipped out of the room. He walked down the hallway and waited outside Sergeant Temple's office. His stomach ached with dread. Finally, Temple hurried down the hall toward his office. Peter swallowed hard and came to attention, saluting.

"At ease, private," said Temple, unlocking the door. "You don't salute your sergeant."

"Yes, Sarge," Peter said, dropping his hand to his side.

"Come in and have a seat."

The office was small and grey, the light softer than the glaring hall lights. A long, thin portal cut the far wall in half, showing only a glimpse of stars. Sergeant Temple's l-shaped desk rested against the portal. It was a plain desk, grey polymer to match the neutral colors. An array of small images floated above his desk. A black paper organizer with two full slots set on one edge of the desk, two stacks of papers lay next to it. Beside the images, on the shorter part of the desk, stood the sergeant's computer and burgundy desk chair. A door to Peter's right led, most likely, to Sarge's sleeping quarters. The room smelled of a woody aftershave and onions.

Temple dropped into his chair, sliding a half-full cup of coffee out of his way. A sandwich lay untouched on a plate. Peter sat down in the metal chair in front of the desk and clasped his hands together, staring silently at the pale man. Temple's eyes were circled and puffy as if he hadn't slept. His face seemed drawn and flat, the animation and enthusiasm absent. With his forefingers, Temple rubbed the corners of his eyes and then gazed at Peter.

"How you feeling, Mitchell?"

"Feeling, Sarge?"

"After the last training sim?" Temple shifted in his chair, unable to look Peter in the eye.

"I'm not sure," he answered, almost afraid to say anything. "Better, I suppose."

Temple snapped out of his chair, his patience gone. "Look, Mitchell, I'll be straight with you! Your attitude unnerves me. I'm here to do a job and so are you. Now, I need to know how to motivate you to do your best."

"Yes, Sarge."

Temple grabbed hold of the chair arms and turned Peter toward him. Unflinching, Peter stared into the man's eyes, seeing sadness and confusion. Temple's jaw tightened.

"You were created for this task," said Temple, his words softer. "Without this program, you wouldn't have life at all."

Peter cringed. How many times had he heard that speech? "So, I should be grateful for the moments I have? I am, Sarge—I am." But he wanted so many more.

Temple didn't break his gaze. "I used to believe that," he said, "but now—I'm not so sure anymore." His gaze slipped away. He turned and moved back to his chair.

"Are you going to wash me out, Sarge?" Peter asked finally. "Is that why I'm here?" He had to know. He couldn't take the wait.

Sarge turned around and his gaze softened. "No, private. At least not yet."

The tension drained out of Peter's body and he slumped in the chair.

Sarge shook his head. "I've never encountered a soldier like you. I've got to find a way to turn you around—or it could lead to a unit wash out. But you've got to help me." He sighed. "I'm trying to save your life."

Peter bowed his head. For what? A horrible death on Ku'Tal? No, so he could return here—he had to believe that, somehow. "I'm trying to read the grid, Sarge, I really am. But the bow echo confuses me. I can't tell if they're coming or going."

Temple seemed to relax at his mention of the grid. "Sensor grids are my specialty, Mitchell," he said with a smile. "I'll give you some printouts that detail the different signatures and how to read them. Every afternoon, after mess, you'll report to my office and we'll go through grid reading step by step. At the end of the week, I'll test your comprehension. Understood?"

Peter nodded.

Temple pulled a folder out of his desk drawer and handed it to Peter. Inside, Peter found a stack of sensor grid screens taken at the front. On the left side of each printout was a description of the terrain, the positions of the soldiers and the course of the Antarans. The echo signatures were described and explained in extensive detail.

"All right, Mitchell, get to work. Dismissed."

"Thanks, Sarge. I appreciate your help." He smiled. "And you sending me to the infirmary. I'd never seen inside it before. It was amazing."

Peter hurried out of Temple's office. He slipped into the lift and headed back down to the ninth level, the recombinant's wing. He had a few minutes before mess. As the lift whirred down to the bottom level, he couldn't help but wonder why Sergeant Temple had taken an interest in him. The man didn't seem like he'd ever worked with recombinants before. He made statements that seemed to be facts he'd read or been taught, but his eyes betrayed his lack of understanding—and belief. Like he'd spent a lot of evenings locked into data dump headgear, learning things one way, but finding out they were another.

The lift door slid open. There stood Drake leering at him.

"Hey, washout, is it fucking official yet? Are they putting your ass to sleep today?"

Peter shoved past him, clutching the folder to his chest. Drake sneered at him.

"Be warned, Mitchell!" he shouted down the hallway. "If they don't wash you out, I will. My first chance."

Drake's words cut a chill through Peter as he stumbled to his bunk. He slipped the file under his mattress.

He wouldn't wash out! He wouldn't.

He'd learn to read that damned grid and he'd learn to be a better soldier through Sting. But he refused to go willingly to his death with the stab of a needle.

Peter gritted his teeth. He would not wash out.

10

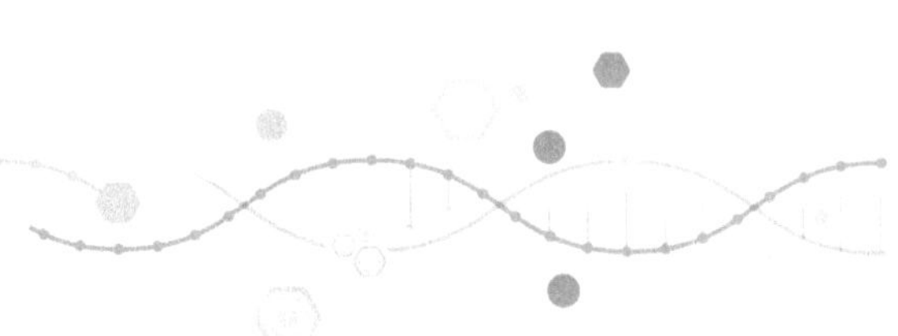

DODGING A MEDIC AND TWO NURSES, Jeannette motioned Diana down the infirmary's middle hallway and into one of the exam rooms. It was a small blue-on-blue room with only a desk and sterilizer, an exam table, and two chairs. Diana sat down in the chair beside the desk while Jeannette flicked on the small datapad in her hand.

"Display records for Diana Temple."

The datapad blanked for a moment and then opened a screen of data. Jeannette read over Diana's chart. Chickenpox at eight, broken wrist at eleven. "Are you still interested in those extra hours?" Jeannette asked, glancing up from the screen.

"Definitely. What kind of data are you gathering, doctor?"

"Page two," said Jeannette as she continued reading. "Page three."

Diana had all the required vaccinations for the Taus system. Last blood workup a year ago. Diana had her whole life ahead of her. Jeannette wondered what brought her out to this lower circle of hell. Then she realized she hadn't answered Diana's question.

"I'm verifying vaccination records for some of the recombinants. Most likely, I'll have to re-vaccinate."

"I see," Diana said, leaning forward. "And you need me to record information?"

"Close pages." She turned toward Diana, trying to remember what she'd been like at this age, but couldn't. "There will be a lot of recombinants to vaccinate, so having someone scan their IDs would be a big help to me. After we've collected all the data, we'll need to compare it to the Base records."

"Then what?" Diana asked, an uneasy look in her eyes.

"Then all the recombinants on my list will be certified for Ku'Tal."

Finally, Diana nodded, a stern expression pinching her face. "Okay, I can do that. I just wanted to make sure there was no experimenting on them because I'll tell you up front, I want no part of that."

"Fair enough. There won't be any experimentation on recombinants. It will be a quick interview and an MRC scan. That's it."

"Great," Diana said with a smile. "Then I'll take the job."

Jeannette extended her hand and Diana shook it. "Welcome aboard, Diana. I look forward to working with you."

"You, too, doctor."

Jeannette returned her gaze to the datapad. "Open input form for Diana Temple with today's date." She cast a sideways glance at Diana.

"Do you and Private Mitchell know each other?" she asked, trying to sound nonchalant as she keyed in codes. But she'd seen Diana's face when she saw Mitchell. Diana seemed quite taken with the young recombinant. But with Mitchell's boyish charm and blond good looks, she wasn't surprised.

Diana studied her fingernails. "I've talked with him in the launch bay."

Jeannette kept her gaze on the screen. "He's very intelligent, seems to learn things quickly. Except how to pass his training sims." He was so inquisitive and even-tempered. It would be a shame to lose such restraint. "Rankings come out soon. I sure hope he passes."

"Me, too," said Diana, looking up. A hint of fear lingered in her eyes.

"Print vaccination list in alphabetical order." In a little slot in the desk, printed pages slithered into a small basket. "He's on this list. We'll have to check his MRC."

She watched as Diana tried to hide her smile. "Oh, good. He seems nice."

"Okay," said Jeannette, clapping her hands against her legs. She rose from the chair. "Let's get some blood drawn and we'll get you certified, too."

Jeannette led Diana out of the room and into a nearby lab.

11

PETER WAITED in the launch bay with Sting and the other recombinants from his unit. The brass had scheduled them for another off-site training sim. Peter dreaded the shuttle's arrival, but at the same time, he felt anxious to test out his improved sensor grid skills. He'd been practicing for a while now. He needed to prove himself somehow to these people. This was his last chance.

Drake laughed and scuffled with another recombinant. Sting cleaned his plasma rifle and joked with Peter.

"So, Pete," he said, wiping down the barrel with a blue cloth, "you gonna help the Antarans today or us?"

"Not funny, Sting." Peter adjusted his rifle on his shoulder. "I've been practicing. Sergeant Temple's been working with me." He paused. "I'm getting better."

Sting locked his holo plasma charge into the chamber and slung the rifle over his shoulder. "I hear D'Angelo's watching us today," Sting said, moving closer to Peter. "Galloway will be rating us, too, so stay sharp."

The roar of a landing shuttle filled the bay, the acrid smell of exhaust permeating the air. In a few moments, the pilot stepped out, and Peter's jaw dropped.

It was her—Diana.

He hadn't been able to keep her out of his thoughts since the infirmary. He kept hoping he'd run into her again somewhere—anywhere. Her hair and eyes were the color of rich chocolate. She was shapely and cheerful, her smile filling the bay with light. She wore a brilliantly colored scarf (in a color he'd never seen before) in her thick hair. Her bright eyes and soft features made him feel calm. And warm all over.

Sting cackled. "What's the matter, Pete? Never seen a girl before?"

"Not like her," he muttered as she approached.

"Hi, guys," she said with a warm smile. "I'm your shuttle pilot today. Bring your gear over to bay two and I'll take you down to the surface." Her gaze flitted toward Peter and she stared at him for a moment or two. "Hey, Mitchell. Looks like those bruises have healed nicely."

"Yeah, thanks. I'm ready to pass this sim," he said unable to look away from her.

He moved closer and her warm, vanilla scent enveloped him. He longed to reach out and touch her hair. Just for a moment. It reminded him of an image from his headgear: a dark-haired woman in a blue dress waving to him as he left for the front. The image was always the same. She dabbed her eyes with a white handkerchief and then hugged him. The sensations were all so real, her arms against his shoulders, the soft lips against his, the smell of soap and flowers. He longed to linger in this memory, even though he knew it wasn't real.

Diana noticed he was staring at her.

"Are you all right, Mitchell?"

Her brown eyes and rosy lips looked so soft in the bay's glaring lighting.

"Is something wrong?"

Slowly, he shook his head. "I've—uh, never seen, um—"

She smiled at him again. "You've never seen what, Mitchell?"

Peter inhaled sharply, pinching his eyes closed for a moment. "Such brightness in someone's face before." Before he could see the reproof he knew must be in her eyes, Peter whirled around and stumbled into the shuttle. "I'd better get aboard."

Sting rushed up behind him and smooched him on the cheek. "Pete's got a girlfriend," he said with a cackle and mussed Peter's blond hair.

"Stop foolin' around, Sting! It's not funny." Peter swiped at his cheek, his face burning.

EVEN AFTER SERGEANT Temple stepped aboard the shuttle and strapped into a restraint harness, Sting continued to tease and annoy Peter. Finally, Peter turned away from Sting, sitting closer to the cockpit, and listened for the sound of her voice.

Every once in a while, a wisp of vanilla touched his nose.

He cast an uncertain look at Sergeant Temple. There was some connection between him and this beautiful woman.

The shuttle dropped through the atmosphere and Peter grabbed hold of his restraint harness. He swallowed and closed his eyes, hoping the nausea passed quickly. Finally, the shuttle touched down and Sergeant Temple started issuing orders in his calm, authoritative voice. Shadowing Temple was Galloway who stood with a datapad, recording who only knew what kind of information. Peter respected Sergeant Temple. No one had ever offered to help him before—except Sting.

"All right, grab your gear and fall in. Move it! Move it!" Temple.

Peter rushed out behind Sting and fell in step with the others. The heat from the desert-like terrain was crushing as Peter stood in single file formation. The air felt thick and heavy. Wisps of brush dotted the flat, barren horizon, sky and ground layered shades of amber and red. Everything smelled of grit and some tart chemical Peter didn't recognize.

"All right, guys, my superior's here, so don't make me look bad," said Sergeant Temple as he paced down the row. Galloway stood a few paces behind him, his face poised above his datapad. D'Angelo stood off to the side, looking distant and unapproachable.

"We're testing for sensor grid precision today," Sergeant Temple continued. "Do me proud."

"If Mitchell's runnin' point, we're fucked," Drake blurted out.

Laughter rippled through the line. Peter hung his head.

Sergeant Temple stopped in front of Drake and glared at him until Drake snapped to attention. "Stow that babble, Drake!" Sergeant Temple shouted. "I'd better see perfect marks from you or you'll be on head detail for the next month."

Snickers arose from the unit.

Drake shut his mouth.

"Anyone else want to be a smart guy?" Sarge cast a withering gaze down the line.

No one uttered a sound.

"All right, break into your subunits and run patrol."

Peter sighed. Just his luck to have Drake in his subunit.

Sullen, Drake moved toward Peter and Sting. He glared at Peter and started toward him, an angry glint in his eye, but Sting stepped in front of Peter.

"Don't even think about it, Drake."

"Whatever, Stingley," he said, shaking his head, and turned away.

Sarge moved through the groupings, assigning point and flank to each subunit. When he reached Peter's subunit, he hesitated. "Sting, you'll run flank." He gazed from Drake to Peter. "Drake, you run point. Mitchell, you run backup."

"Aw, tough luck, Mitchell," Drake said with a sneer. "We'll finally pass a sim this time!"

Sarge caught Peter's hurt gaze and held it. "Trust me, Mitchell."

Trust him? Why? Sarge gave him grids to study and extra

instruction, but he didn't think he was smart enough to apply it. Now, Drake would be intolerable. He hated worrying about Drake beating him senseless when he stepped out of the shower or fell asleep at night. Sarge just gave Drake all the validation he needed.

"Trust me," Sarge repeated, a hand on Peter's shoulder. Then he moved away, rejoining the brass at the end of the field.

Sighing, Peter clutched his rifle and waited for the sim matrix to assemble around him.

With a spark, the scene engulfed him with a blast of cold. Winter on Ku'Tal. Snow raged across the wild landscape, blotting out the skyline. Peter slogged through the knee-deep snow as he, Sting, and Drake patrolled the woods for Antaran presence. With grim determination, Sting swung his rifle in a steady arc back and forth in front of him.

Drake rushed ahead, grid in hand, leaving Peter equidistant between the two as they trolled for monsters.

Frigid blasts ripped across the terrain. Peter gritted his teeth against the cold, his rifle icy against his unprotected fingers.

"Drake, report," said Sting, his voice sharp.

No answer.

"Drake, report!"

Nothing.

Peter pivoted his body to the northwest, the haunting chirp of the grid ahead of him. He listened for Drake's voice.

"Sting, I hear Drake's grid."

"Dammit, Drake! Report!"

Drake's grid alarm grew louder, more intense. Fear swelled inside Peter, rising bitterly in his throat as he rushed ahead, the snow blinding, and tried to follow the pulsing whine of Drake's grid. As the sound grew louder, Peter ran faster. Trees raked across his arms and face, nearly knocking him into the snow. He weaved down the path, his concentration narrowed on the sound of Drake's grid.

He slipped, plunging headlong into a snow bank, but he

scrambled to his feet and kept running. Rounding a curve in the trail, he stumbled again and fell.

Lying half-buried in the snow was Drake's sensor grid. He glanced around for Drake. No sign. Peter recoiled for a moment, his body shaking, but forced himself to retrieve the grid.

"Drake!" He scanned the horizon, rifle raised to his shoulder. "Drake!"

Only the whisper of falling snow and the staccato beat of Drake's sensor grid filled Peter's ears. He gazed at the grid. A bow echo, three of them. Antarans rushing toward him and Sting.

"Sting, incoming! Incoming north!"

Frantic, Peter dashed down the path toward Sting.

He found Sting crouched in the snow, rifle pointing northwest. Sting's face was contorted, anger in his eyes and tightening his jaw line. The corners of his mouth quivered, a bit of fear creeping into Sting's expression as the grid alarm grew louder. Peter fell down beside him and thrust Drake's grid in his face.

"Sting, they've swerved. From the north. Look! The signature says it."

"You're right, Pete. Get ready."

Peter raised his rifle, his heart pounding, and pointed it north.

The wail of the alarm was unbearable.

Peter glanced left and then ahead at the trees. He sniffed the air. Sugary sweetness scrubbed past his face as the wind sliced through him.

From the west.

He turned his body into the wind. He didn't care what the grid showed. They were coming due west.

"Pete, what are you doing? Help me watch."

"They've turned again, Sting. To the west."

Suddenly, the grid fell silent. Sting rose on his haunches. Treetops swayed in the icy silence. Wind whipped. Snow crunched. He turned his confused gaze to Peter.

"What happened? Where are they?"

Peter shrugged, but a feeling of dread pressed against his shoulders. The hair on his neck stood on end.

He gazed up at the trees again. There. They'd come from there.

In a blur of grey, something leaped out of a tree and rolled west toward them in the snow.

Sting whirled, squeezing off shots. Peter fired five rounds until he'd smoked the Antaran. It lay charred and quivering. Ash mixed with clean snow, smelling like burnt sugar.

Another Antaran! A blur of darkness and snow, lunging for Sting.

Sting pivoted and fired. The creature exploded.

Two more sprang from the trees, spiked appendages whipping toward Peter.

Peter squeezed off two shots. One of the Antarans screeched and fell, blackened, into the snow. The other Antaran fell to Sting's plasma fire.

When it was finally over, Sting and Peter had killed eight Antarans.

Sting laughed hysterically and collapsed in the snow, Peter falling down beside him.

"We did it, Pete! You and me!" Sting threw an arm around Peter and hugged him.

"I read the grid correctly this time," Peter announced.

"Read it, hell. Pete! You found those bastards without the grid! I've never seen anything like it!" He shoved icy blond curls out of his eyes.

Grinning, Peter rose to his knees as the sim landscape faded into amber sand. The warmth returned, the burnt sugary smell dissipating. As Peter and Sting got to their feet, Sergeant Temple rushed over to them. They snapped to attention.

"That was one of the best performances of the day, boys. Congratulations, you impressed the hell out of D'Angelo. And me." He moved down to Peter, his face lit with excitement. "Mitchell, you have exceeded all my expectations."

"Thanks, Sarge," he said with a smile.

"What I couldn't tell you before was that the point man was going to be pulled out of the scenario without warning. That's why I made you backup. You read that grid better than a two-year veteran. Let's get back to base." He pointed to the shuttle. "My sister will take you guys back to the station. Move out."

"Your sister?" Peter blurted out without thinking.

Temple smiled. "That's my little sister, Diana. She's a good pilot. Treat her right, boys."

"Pete will, Sarge. He's in love."

"Dammit, Sting, shut up!" He turned his burning face toward Temple. "He doesn't know what he's talking about, Sarge. Ignore him."

"Move out, guys."

Peter hurried toward the shuttle, Sting beside him. When Temple turned his back, Peter slammed his fist into Sting's arm.

"Ow! Pete! Can't you take a joke?"

Peter ignored him. He stopped running when he neared the shuttle. Smoothing his blond bangs out of his eyes, he walked over to the shuttle ramp. Diana Temple stood there, all smiles and charm.

He gazed at her, trying to come up with something to say. Why would she want to hear anything a recombinant had to say? He'd never been to school, had never even seen a city. He'd lived only six months of life and most of it aboard this station.

"Very impressive simulation, Mitchell," said Diana. "David was so excited."

He smiled, his gaze falling to the sand. "Thanks. I didn't know you were Sarge's sister."

"Yep, David's my big brother."

"Sarge is a great guy," said Peter. "We're lucky to have someone like him. And you."

Diana gestured toward a line of rocks. "By the way, your mouse is safe."

He looked up from the sand. This time, his gaze met hers.

"I let it go near the river. That's about twenty minutes south of here, so he won't slip aboard any more shuttles."

"I really appreciated your help. I couldn't stand to watch Drake brutalize that little guy." He paused for a moment. Her scarf caught his attention. "I've never seen that color before."

"You've never seen purple?" Diana laid a hand against the scarf. "This was a birthday gift from my grandmother."

"A birthday gift?" he said, puzzled by the concept. "It's beautiful."

He counted the generations in his head. From a third-generation citizen. Peter wondered how it must feel to celebrate a birth anniversary, but he couldn't grasp a third generation. His xDNA recombination had been programmed to be twenty-two. What would it have been like to live each one of those twenty-two years? Or a lifetime? He stared at Diana in reverence. She had lived so many years already. At least twenty, he was certain.

"Don't you have birthdays where you come from?" Diana's face contorted. "Oh, God—I'm so sorry! That was a terrible thing for me to say. I—I forgot you were a recombinant." Her embarrassment faded and a troubled look spread across her face. "You'd better get aboard and get strapped in, Mitchell. We're lifting off in a few minutes."

Diana hurried around the nose of the shuttle. Feeling foolish, Peter climbed aboard and slid into his restraint harness. Sting climbed in after him, collapsing into a seat. Leaning his head against the wall, Peter closed his eyes. For now, he'd imagine himself talking intelligently to Diana, since he couldn't seem to do it in-person.

Besides, she didn't want to talk to a recombinant. What could he possibly know about anything after only six months of life? His thoughts shifted to his beginnings and the day he achieved consciousness.

PETER OPENS HIS EYES, but quickly closes them as a torrent of sounds and faces rush at him. Words wash over him in booming echoes, meanings and tones colliding in his brain. The words are familiar but jumbled. He tries to cry out, but his dry throat rasps muffled, ill-formed words. His tongue sticks to the roof of his mouth as images touch him, fuzzy, out-of-focus moments like the final flicker of a blown-out candle. Germicide tangs the air with bitterness.

Slowly, resolutely, he opens his eyes again. White light glares down from the ceiling, up from the tiled floor. His eyes water as he looks away. Machines wink amber and green throughout the room, chrome sparkling, white walls pristine.

"Recombination was successful, Dr. Cline," says a voice nearby.

"Scan the batch and make sure the combined genetic structures are free of defects. Make sure the nucleobases are correct. Can't have corrupted nucleotides."

A light whirs across his body.

He sits up, the chill of metal against his new skin, and stares blankly at the white coats bustling around him. His naked flesh pales in the white numbness of the room. His senses rage like a switch flipped on, yet he feels nothing. Confusion brushes against the edges of his memory.

Who is he? Why is he here? Why doesn't he know these answers?

Someone in a mask and white coat drapes a gown around him, the worn, printed blue cotton exposing his arms and legs.

Shutting out the swell of voices, he turns his palms over and up and studies his twenty-two-year-old hands and then his feet.

How does he know he's twenty-two? How does he know the names of things he sees, of sounds, of smells, yet he remembers nothing?

He reaches for memories or thoughts again, but they go no further than moments ago when he opened his eyes. Squinting, he fights to remember beyond this room, beyond this pale skin and roar of voices, but can't. At last he realizes it. There's nothing to recall. His memory is a clean slate.

"Get them in recovery and we'll prepare for the next grouping."

The white coats grab him by the arms, dragging him off the table and into a hallway.

Crack! Doors slam open, spilling into a churning river of people.

He struggles against the sounds. The fear. Antiseptic scent mixes with soap and sour breath. Voices roar, the syllables lost in the droning pulse that vibrates through his bones and into his chest. It's all overwhelming.

"Get out of the way!" someone shouts.

He turns, staring at the man shuffling him through the teeming hallways. People are everywhere! The man—tall, thin, lined face and greying hair—glares at him.

"Move, I said!"

Bodies press against his, writhing and aching, as he fights to get through. Young men and women like him. Soured smells of fear and sweat make him gag. He pulls away from the throng of people shoving him forward, but one of them (the grey-haired one) grabs his arm and shakes him.

A sharp slap to the head makes him stumble. He collapses into the wave of people. Knees gouge his sides. Feet smash his fingers. He grits his teeth, clutching his clumsy, aching hand against the soft gown, and crawls underneath boots.

Someone rips him out of the crowded hallway of white coats and their disoriented charges in printed blue gowns.

"Don't try that again, boy," the voice threatens. The man with greying hair.

A hand rakes across his cheek, cutting it diagonally to his chin. He yelps, clutching the stinging ache, feeling warm stickiness, but they drag him forward, down another hallway thick with people.

A fight erupts nearby, three white coats cornering an enraged man in a blue gown. Screaming, the man punches and kicks at them, but they subdue him. With a whimper through bared teeth, the enraged man hugs the floor, body limp and unresponsive. As he screams and screams.

Finally, Peter is shoved into a small office and the door slams behind him. Two white coats move toward him.

Beneath the white coats are crisp, royal blue uniforms shiny with gold buttons and colored disks across the left breast. He draws his knees against his chest, arms clasped around them, and stares at the uniformed men.

"God, this one's terrified." The mask shakes and points at him. "Why didn't they wash him out?" asks one of the white coats over his mask, through his glasses.

"None of them gets scrubbed unless they're completely unmanageable or have physical deformities," says a woman with pale hair and large gold eyes. "We're way over budget this year. They'll weed out the problems in training. Stanton's orders."

"Better have a jacket ready, in case he bolts or attacks someone. The techs said this batch has a high aggression quotient." His look is wary through the glasses, over the mask.

The man steps forward. Peter tenses.

The woman shakes her head, her white coat rustling. "This one is really docile. Must have gotten a recessive combination. Sometimes, that happens. Don't be so rough with him, huh?"

Peter looks from the man in glasses to the woman. His head aches. His mind is hungry. His heart hurts. His face bleeds. So much is missing.

"You!"

Peter jumps, turning his gaze to the man as he slowly lowers the white mask.

"Yes, you, soldier. You'll be with us for a month or so, learning UCOE regs and anything else we decide to teach you."

The woman offers a stiff smile and bends down. Her comfort is stale, her words empty, canned. "You are a very lucky young man," she says. "If it wasn't for the Recombinant Defense Program, you wouldn't have the gift of life. Soldiers donated their DNA to this program, so you owe your life to UCOE Forces."

"You belong to UCOE," snaps one of the uniformed men behind her. "Don't forget that. And you will defend it with your life. After you're trained, you'll go to the front where you'll help hold the line against Antaran invaders. Last year's recombinants lasted nearly six months, but this year, we've pushed the envelope. We're expecting as much as a year from you."

"In time, we'll move you into the recombinant barracks. For now, you'll stay in the recovery ward."

Peter stares into their eyes, saddened by this realization. He is their property. They made him. They own him. He wonders about the man who once lived this DNA pattern they mentioned. How is this possible? His stomach twists into knots as he swallows back his fear, and his lips fight again to form words.

"What's with this one?"

"I don't know. His scans check out."

"Who am I?" he asks, his voice hoarse and quivering.

"This recombination has been labeled Peter Mitchell," says a mask behind him.

He doesn't like it when they talk about him like he isn't really here. The name means so little to him, but he clings to it. It's all he has as his own now. That and his thoughts.

He stares quizzically at the woman. *Why does she talk to him like he isn't here?*

The woman moves toward him, a white jacket in her hands. The ends of the arms are sewn together. "Hold out your arms, Mitchell," she says in a flat, authoritative voice.

His face contorts. He can't put his arms into sleeves with no openings. Why do they want to confine him like this? What has he done to earn this punishment?

"Why do I need to be confined?" he asks.

She's surprised by his question. "That's an order, mister," she says finally, her tone hardening. "Now." She sighs. "It's only until you're settled. All of you wear them the first day or two." She snaps the jacket at him, her face twisting with impatience.

His chest tightens as he holds out his arms. She slides the white coat up and over his hands. He closes his eyes, fighting the water welling there.

Twisting the straps, she folds his arms against his sides and ties the sleeves behind him.

Frustration shakes his body. He can't belong here. He can't!

She leads him through more doors, more bright lights, and past more beds. Young men and women lie in the beds, their bodies draped in white jackets like his. The woman drops him into an empty bed, tightening the jacket straps before she leaves him in the painful silence of white.

He sees his blond reflection in the chrome light beside the bed and longs to knock the lamp into the floor. Whatever he dreams won't be his, he knows that now, and whatever he lives will be on a battlefield.

He cries out, his voice raw and hot against the moans and sighs in the recovery ward. His chest aches, the reality finally sinking into his brain.

He's a recombinant. A recycled soldier with no rights and no future. Bound for some war front and a brutal death.

12

WHEN DIANA LANDED the shuttle back on the station, she lingered outside the cockpit, watching the recombinants file off. The acrid smell of exhaust clung to her boots and mixed with the stench of burnt polymer. She wrinkled her nose.

Finally, Private Mitchell stepped off. The others looked like grungy soldiers who'd killed too many people and spent too many nights sleeping in muddy trenches, but Mitchell's quiet demeanor was hopeful and filled with longing. For what, she wasn't sure, but he fascinated her.

His sad-eyed gaze met hers for an instant and she smiled warmly at him. Nodding shyly, his handsome, boyish face warmed, but then he turned his blue gaze to his feet and shuffled after the others. David was right. Peter Mitchell wasn't like the other recombinants.

"Good flying today, sis," said David, emerging from the cabin.

"Thanks, David," she answered, distracted. She waited until the last recombinant had raced into the lift. "David, Mitchell was the one that was bothering you so much?"

"Yeah, Mitchell. The quiet one."

"I see that now," she said, turning back to the cockpit to retrieve her datapad.

David followed her. "What do you mean, *I see that now*?" he demanded in his most forceful, older-brother tone.

Hoisting her duffle bag onto her shoulder, she moved around the shuttle and turned toward the lift. "Just what I said."

She started across the grimy bay floor, dodging two techs rushing toward a landing shuttle. David ran after her and blocked her path.

"Diana, tell me what you mean by that."

She let her bag slide off her shoulder. "He's different, David. He's not the wolf they train recombinants to be. He's a lamb and I'm surprised he's made it as far as he has." She gestured toward the lift. "Didn't you see how he recoiled from the shots he fired? The others hungered for more. Peter Mitchell just wanted to survive the encounter."

David sighed and turned away. "I just hope it doesn't get him killed."

"Me, too," she said, grabbing his arm. "But that's your job, to keep him alive."

David's eyes burned. He glared at her. "For what? A tour of duty at the front. Wouldn't he be better off washing out?"

Her mouth fell open.

"You said it yourself, Diana. Why should I save him? He's only got a year at the most. The Antaris Nation's too large. We're just buying time with the lives of these recombinants."

She turned away from him. "But I was wrong, David! I was talking like the news stories I'd read. He deserves the same chance as you and I. They all do."

David laughed bitterly. "Tell that to the government. To D'Angelo. They made him and they own him. It's that simple."

"It's never that simple, David. Don't let them convince you it is."

She left David standing in the middle of the launch bay.

AFTER TURNING in her log in the eighth level operations office, Diana picked up next week's flight schedule and returned to the launch bay. She hopped into a passenger shuttle bound for Civilization and strapped herself into the harness. At times, it felt strange being a passenger. The drop-through was short this time, the nausea mild.

She couldn't get Peter out of her thoughts. When the shuttle docked, she stepped out and wandered down to the coffeehouse for tea and a Danish.

Inside the drab little coffeehouse, the scent of burnt coffee blended with grease. Brittle plates clanked against paper-thin silverware. Stiff paper napkins rustled against the soft buzz of conversation. She started toward the counter when she saw those people she'd overheard a few days ago. The man with the Van Dyke beard and the woman with the braid.

Diana searched for a name from the snippets of conversation she'd overheard. Linda.

She and the man hunched over a pile of ketchup-encrusted plates and half-empty water glasses, the ice long melted. Diana picked up her tea and Danish at the counter and slid into a booth behind Linda and the man. She sat motionless, hoping to pick up something concrete from their conversation.

"Did Kev ever call?"

"This morning. Said he could meet us tomorrow night at Mimi's."

"Why tomorrow?" the man's voice was heavy with suspicion.

"Things are getting complicated, so chill. He'll bring whatever he can as soon as he can. Just relax."

Her steady voice commanded calm.

"They're watching the lanes carefully out there, especially for small crafts. What if he gets caught?"

"Then Kev'll forget he knows us. It's that simple."

They rose abruptly from the booth and left the coffeehouse.

Diana took a slow sip from her tea. *Just what was Mimi involved in?*

THE NEXT DAY, Diana made reservations at End of the Line. Mimi was warm and charming on the comunit, delighted that Diana was coming back so soon.

"Will you be bringing that handsome brother back with you?"

Diana laughed. "No, David's stuck on base this week."

"A shame. He could use time with family, to sort out his confusion."

"Why do you say that?"

Mimi laughed. "It's all there to see. His aura betrays him. He has a long way to go in this cycle."

"Cycle?"

Sometimes, Mimi talked about things Diana didn't understand. Auras and mystics were part of Mimi's beliefs, and Diana respected that, even if she didn't understand it.

"Cycle of the soul on its journey. I will see you at seven-thirty, my dear."

"Thanks, Mimi."

Diana chuckled as she closed the connection. Cycle of the soul. David would have cringed.

She spent the rest of the day catching up on her reading and trying to fill the hours before dinner. She was too anxious to concentrate on much. Tonight, she'd find out what Mimi was involved in or why she allowed criminals to do business in her restaurant.

END of the Line's dinner crowd was at capacity and beginning its slow wind down when Diana arrived. Mimi greeted her with warm smiles and a hug. She wore a silky blue jump suit imprinted with black petroglyphs. The clingy material hugged Mimi's aging curves, but she wore the jump suit well, still turning heads. Her hair was loose and curly around her shoulders, her eyelids sparkling with pale gold shadows and kohl liner.

"You look tired," she said, leading Diana past the tables. "I'll bring you a glass of cranberry juice." She set a menu down on the low tabletop as Diana flopped down on a pillow.

"Thanks, Mimi," she replied and picked up the menu.

When Mimi returned with the cranberry juice, Diana set down the menu.

"You should order the fish special," said Mimi. "Sautéed jepis and shallots in a calosaberry-saffron wine sauce with a touch of t'ysh oil and garlic and served over grains. Very healthy. Cleanses the soul."

"Sounds delicious. My soul will try it."

Mimi leaned down, her voice barely above a whisper.

"Your aura has many moments of purple in it, Diana. Spiritual growth and life lessons. There are more ahead for you. Now, drink your juice."

With the poise of a cat, Mimi slipped away to the kitchen, leaving Diana with her cranberry juice. She stared dismally at the glass. She hated cranberry juice.

THE FISH WAS flaky with a buttery flavor, the grains steamed and plump. Diana ate as slowly as she could without her dinner getting cold. Linda and her accomplice hadn't shown up yet. Diana glanced at her watch: 19:55. She strained under the massive helping of fish and grains. How long could she eat on this before her stomach exploded? She sipped the juice and ate tinier bites. Mimi walked by once and gave her a quizzical look, but said nothing.

Diana kept at the fish until well after 20:00. At last, Mimi appeared at the table.

"I'd ask if you'd like dessert, but I don't think we'll be open that long tonight."

Diana laughed. "I would like a piece of fruit pie and some coffee."

"I'll let you know when we're closing," said Mimi and headed toward the kitchen.

Drumming her fingers on the table, Diana fidgeted on her pillow. Below, the yellow lamplight misted the streets and walkways. Colored lights lining rooftops splashed the streets with fuchsias, greens, and blues. She longed to go down to the river and watch the skimmers, but not tonight. She had to find out about gun-runners.

Mimi brought pie and coffee and Diana made a valiant effort to finish it. When she could eat no more, she shoved the pie away. As she picked up her coffee cup, Linda and the man with the Van Dyke beard entered the restaurant.

Thank God. She'd run out of things to order.

The woman's gaze shifted from table to table as if assessing each person's potential to harm her.

Diana sat with her back to the wall and didn't speak until Mimi had taken their drink order. Beyond full, Diana picked at the pie again, pretending to be eating it while she shuffled cherries and crust around the plate.

As she lifted her coffee cup to her lips, Linda and the man rose from their seats. They slipped into the kitchen. Diana got up from the table and strolled over to the kitchen door. If someone stopped her, she'd pretend to be hunting for Mimi.

Standing on her toes, she peered through the swinging doors. Linda and the man stood behind one of the stoves talking to Mimi, who listened intently. Then a third man, the lanky one she saw at the shuttle port, entered the kitchen from a back door. He led two dazed men in civilian clothes into the kitchen. He cast a glance at Mimi, who nodded at him.

"I'll have new IDs for them in the morning," said Mimi. "Any problems with the chip removals this time?"

"None," said the man.

He returned her nod and led the men into a back room off the kitchen.

Startled, Diana pulled away from the doors and stumbled back to her table. Those men had to be soldiers. No. Recombinants. She was certain. She'd read something about chip IDs implanted into recombinants' necks.

As she sat down and brought the coffee cup to her lips, everything became clear. Laughing, she set down the cup.

Mimi Constantine wasn't a gun-runner. She and the others were rescuing recombinants. This was the best news ever.

13

ALL THROUGH THE MAPPING EXERCISE, Peter couldn't concentrate on anything except Diana Temple. He thought about her bright eyes and wavy brown hair held back by that brilliant purple scarf. A color he'd never seen before, but to him, purple was Diana. He leaned back in his chair, trying desperately to concentrate on the coordinate system, but her face kept entering his thoughts. Her clean scent against the grimy smells of the launch bay.

When Sergeant Temple finally released them, Peter grabbed a quick meal at mess and hurried to the library. He was allowed only an hour, so he accessed as many resources as they allowed him.

Peter enjoyed looking up things he'd seen in his headgear data dumps, places he'd supposedly vacationed, towns he'd supposedly lived in, and people he supposedly knew. He turned away from the screen and glanced at the door. The room was small, holding only five tables with an array of different-sized datapads scattered across the table tops. A lieutenant sat at a table beside the door, monitoring processes on his datapad.

Hunching over a book-sized datapad, Peter tapped out his name and searched the nets for anything that matched. The search produced hundreds of hits, so he scrolled through them until he located a familiar but *inaccessible* database he'd been able to access. UCOE blocked connections to lots of sites and data. They controlled as much as they could, but they couldn't control everything. Peter had already spent four months in this library. He'd learned ways to get around the stops.

Using scripts he'd cobbled together, Peter got access to the database and found a vital statistics entry containing death certificates. There were twenty-three Peter Mitchells listed and he scrolled through every one until he found one who'd died eight months ago. Was he the one? The original from which Peter's xDNA had been cultivated? Or maybe he was still alive? Living a real life, something Peter would never have. Or maybe his name was just a name they'd given him? No connection to the man that donated his DNA?

He glanced at the clock. His hour was half gone. The file came up, but the face staring back looked nothing like his.

Closing out of the database, Peter searched for images until he found one of a riverbank. Mist hung over the gurgling water and the grass was so green it almost hurt his eyes. A delicate willow tree swayed at the river's edge, the sunlit banks warm and inviting. The image reminded him of how he felt when he looked at Diana Temple. Quickly, he sent it to the color printer.

He changed gears and poked around in another blocked database for articles and information on the Antaris war. Hundreds and hundreds of hits came up. He opened an article about a planet called Ballese.

Again, Peter glanced over at the lieutenant, expecting him to kill the session. The man made no move. He'd never gone this deep into the blocked databases before.

Encouraged, he accessed a long article detailing the history of an ill-fated Earth colony. Ballese had been labeled Earth's deep-space jewel. It was Earth's most far-reaching colony. Top agriculturists, climatologists, astrophysicists, and engineers brought their families to

Ballese, eager to found the new colony. According to the report, Antaran forces landed on Ballese and leveled the colony. What was hoped to become the largest shipping route in the quadrant became the most famous disaster in Earth's history. Antarans swept over the planet, killing every colonist and claimed Ballese for the Antaris Nation.

Peter sat back in his chair, a chill settling over him as he thought about those taloned creatures attacking unarmed, peaceful citizens. He gritted his teeth. Like Diana.

There were several articles about a planet once called Naharra. UCOE Forces had detonated a nuclear bomb there, hoping to destroy the Antarans along with the planet. Nuking Naharra didn't stop the Antaran advance and they soon moved deeper into the system—closer to Earth—to a small, hostile world called Ku'Tal. He shivered.

He read on, discovering that the colony on Ku'Tal met with the same fate as Ballese, but UCOE Forces managed to hold the Antarans at Ku'Tal. Peter read about the ineffectiveness of orbital and air strikes on Ku'Tal, strikes hampered by jamming devices, swamplands, and poor visibility.

What kind of hell was Ku'Tal? Where they'd send him soon. If he passed his training.

He pulled up another article, but the lieutenant rose to his feet and moved toward Peter. Peter quickly tagged the article and exited so the soldier wouldn't see what he'd been doing.

"Let's go, private. Your hour's up. Move it!"

Peter snapped up from the chair and fell in behind the lieutenant who escorted him to the door. On the way out, he snatched his printout from the printer and entered the hallway.

Next time, he told himself. Next time, he'd search for more Peter Mitchells and more about the war. He wanted to understand where they were sending him and why. Folding the color picture carefully, he slid it in his shirt pocket. All he wanted was to understand.

From the computer room, he hurried to his tactical courses that filled the rest of the afternoon and part of the evening. After evening mess, he returned to the recombinants' quarters. He dropped down on his bunk and glanced over at the bed across from his, but Sting wasn't there. He was probably in the gym with the others. Peter didn't much care for extra calisthenics or ball games.

Exhausted, he slipped into the shower and enjoyed the feel of warm water against his skin. After drying off, Peter dressed in an undershirt and boxers and started out of the bathroom.

Something hammered into the back of his neck. The room darkened, twisting into shadowy proportions of pain and voices.

Dazed, Peter fell forward into the bathroom. His head smacked against the tile, sending a wrenching pain down his spine. Warm liquid trickled from his throbbing nose, tears from his watering eyes mixing with what he soon realized was his own blood.

He squinted, trying to make out the forms oozing through the room.

A sharp pain gouged his gut. He crumpled into a fetal position, but someone grabbed him by the hair and yanked him up from the tile.

"All right, you little bastard! Let's see how you do without Temple around to protect you."

Drake.

His breath smelled of onions and alcohol. A delirious, uncaged look hovered in Drake's grey eyes. Peter recoiled. Drake punched him in the chest and Peter went down again. The world smashed against his skull, light spiraling to darkness and back again.

Groaning, he rolled onto his back.

Drake and two other recombinants swam in and out of focus. He coughed, his mouth thick with blood and spit. With his left hand, he clutched his ribs.

"What did...I ever do...to you," Peter gurgled, rolling his gaze toward Drake. Drake seemed unaffected by Peter's condition. He laughed and kicked him in the side.

Peter tried to hold back the cry of pain, but it twisted through his teeth and spilled into the bathroom. He curled up again and lay groaning against the wet tile.

Another scuffle echoed through the bathroom.

"I'll kill you, Drake!"

Peter glanced toward the doorway. Sting, sweaty and in shorts, slammed Drake against the wall, his hands around Drake's neck. The other two recombinants lunged at Sting, but Peter managed to shove his foot in one man's path. The man crashed against the tile and lay there without moving. The other recombinant grabbed Sting's arm, but Sting slammed his foot into the man's gut. The man crumpled under the blow as Sting shoved Drake's head back as far as he could.

"If you touch Mitchell again, Drake, I swear, I'll rip your head off and shove it up your ass. You got me?"

Drake was silent.

"You got me?" Sting shouted.

"I got you," Drake mumbled through gritted teeth.

Sting let go of him and Drake slid down the wall. With a pained expression, Sting knelt beside Peter.

"Pete, you all right?" His mouth twisted into a frown. "Man, they did a number on you, didn't they, kid?"

"I'm okay," Peter said, spitting out blood.

Gently, Sting lifted Peter off the floor and carried him to his bunk. He disappeared for a moment and then returned with a wet cloth. It turned red immediately with Peter's blood as Sting mopped at his nose and mouth. Sting moved to his bunk, slid a first-aid kit out of his footlocker, and sat down beside Peter.

"I borrowed this from one of the shuttles," Sting said with a grin.

Peter flinched and groaned as Sting cleaned cuts and gashes on his face and then closed them tightly with small butterfly bandages.

"Hold still," he said, gripping Peter's face with one hand and applying bandages with another.

"Thanks, Sting. Drake would have killed me if you hadn't come along when you did."

Sting waved him off. "Forget it, Pete."

Peter struggled up on his elbows. "I can't. No one's ever stuck up for me before."

"Anything I can do to piss off Drake is worth the effort," Sting said with a snort. His eyes turned serious and his green gaze met Peter's. "Besides, I'm tired of eating and exercising alone." He pushed Peter back down on the bunk. "Now, you lay still and let those wounds heal."

In a few minutes, Sting had Peter's wounds cleaned, bandaged, and comfortable. Sting continued to sit with him, a grin on his face.

"What's so damned funny?" Peter asked, his face throbbing.

"I've been aching for the chance to pound Drake. Glad it was sooner than later."

Peter sighed. "I've been expecting him to attack me, but I guess I was preoccupied tonight."

"I'll say," Sting said. "I'd wager it was about a certain female shuttle pilot."

"Diana Temple."

"Temple?" Sting raised an eyebrow. "Sarge's wife?"

"No, his sister, remember?" Peter was quiet for a moment. "Sting, how do you know if you're in love?"

He laughed and shrugged. "I couldn't tell ya, Pete. I've been with a few women near the front. They're desperate for resources in some of those makeshift tent towns and will trade damned near anything for a lighter or MREs. I loved 'em at the time, but it never lasted beyond a day or so." He sighed. "Never had the chance at anything longer than that."

Never had the chance. *Would it always be like that?*

Peter thought of the headgear images, the dark-haired woman in the blue dress who always hugged him as he went off to war. Even in those images, there was no time to touch her, to explore her—to love her. She was just a comfort image, there to remind him of what might have been—had he not been a recombinant.

"I want that chance, Sting."

Sting's gaze flitted nervously across the room. "Shut up, Pete. I've told you not to talk like that."

"Why the hell not? What gives them ownership? Because their DNA doesn't have an X in front? Because it's original— unaltered? It's all natural human DNA. What's the difference?"

Sting hung his head, a heavy sigh escaping through his gritted teeth. He rubbed a hand through his curly hair, pushing a lock out of his eyes. "I've asked that question once or twice but got slapped down each time."

"Why do they care if we ask questions?"

Sting shrugged. "They say we're livin' lives already lived, some just cut short. Taking over identities—and DNA—from someone else. So, we're just finishing 'em out to some sort of conclusion. Finishing something we didn't start, I guess."

"They say we should be grateful for the short time we have, but Sting, I'm not." Peter's eyes clouded. "It's too short. They taunt us with things we'll never have and then expect us to go die for them."

"I know," said Sting, his head in his hands. "I don't want it to end. Even the grittiest, scariest, bloodiest day at the front I don't want to end, because for those few moments, I'm still living and breathing."

Peter turned his gaze to the sound of boots in the hallway. He didn't want it to end either. There was so much he hadn't done, so much he wanted to experience. So much he didn't even know about yet.

"Lights out in ten minutes," the duty officer shouted.

Recombinants scrambled into the bunkroom and hopped into their bunks. Drake and the other recombinants staggered out of the bathroom and over to their bunks. Sting returned to his bunk. He shucked off his clothes until he was down to his boxers. He moved back to Peter's bunk and pulled the headgear down from the hook on the wall. Gently, he pressed the headgear into Peter's hands.

"Try to dream past the headgear, Pete. Sometimes, if I try hard enough, I break past the info dumps and dream something that pleases me."

Peter smiled and squeezed his arm. "Thanks for everything, Sting. I owe you my life."

"Nah, just a small piece of it. Sleep well, kid."

Sting collapsed into his bunk and yanked his headgear off the wall. Peter struggled to seat the gear right and strap himself into it. It fit like a helmet with earphones, but it was light and pliable. He glanced over at Sting who had settled into his bunk with a stretch. How had he managed to befriend John Stingley, the only recombinant he knew who'd survived the front?

Tonight, the base didn't feel quite so lonely.

Finally, the lights snapped off and the whir of the headgear spinning up filled his ears. His head throbbed and he felt dizzy, but he closed his eyes, immersing himself in the stream of images.

Yawning, he sank quickly into the whispers of data and regulations seeping into his brain. Through the orders and tactical plans reaching him, he saw the dark-haired woman in her blue dress opening a wicker basket. Sun glittered through swaying trees, gold light drenching the hillside and the blanket she'd spread in the grass. Her smile matched the sunlight as she set out iced tea and sandwiches on gold ceramic plates food he'd never tasted.

Peter let the images flow untouched, but as he felt himself lapsing into sleep, he slipped past the woman's image until he was sitting with Diana Temple on that hillside. She laughed and sipped iced tea, her purple dress brilliant in the noonday sun.

14

THE WORDS from her login file glared back, mocking her with details she couldn't remember.

Jeannette set down her coffee cup, pale glow of the virtual screen hazy in the darkness, and wiped tears from her face. She closed the file, but the afterimage of her daughter's name still lingered. Every morning, the grief was new again, but it was better than the numbness of not remembering.

It was still early, but mornings on the training base were hectic. Today would be no different. Especially since she'd created a lot of work for herself by revaccinating over a hundred recombinants. Thank God Diana Temple had taken the job or she'd be swamped. Diana would be here soon.

"Open data from R42 Project."

On the screen, another window opened and her data filled it. Lists of names and MRC batch numbers. Some of the numbers looked off, standing out against the others, but she was no expert in how the numbers were coded. She had shadowy images of a time she'd been familiar with these numbers somehow. But there were no notes in her log file about it. Was it more of her past that she'd lost?

She let the hazy images go, returning her attention to the list again. A quick diagnostic scan of the recombinants' MRCs would alert her to any parsing failures or offline microfeeds. She needed to get through this list as quickly as possible. In a weak moment, Kai had let her investigate, but she couldn't stall his report much longer. Within the week, he'd be demanding results. She had to have something concrete by then or he'd recall her to the station.

Why had he gone to bat for her like that? She admitted there was an attraction to him, a spark that occasionally lit up her thoughts, but nothing had ever happened between them.

After a second cup of coffee, Jeannette made her infirmary rounds, releasing an officer to the duty roster and checking on two cases of food poisoning. She was relieved they got sick planetside and not in the base mess. Although it wouldn't have surprised her.

At 0900, Diana arrived at the infirmary wearing a tan flight suit and white t-shirt. Her hair was tied back by a gauzy purple scarf. Jeannette met her in the waiting room.

"Am I glad to see you," said Jeannette with a smile. "Ready to get started?"

"Sure thing," said Diana. "I have to report to the launch bay at 1600, but I can work until then."

"Terrific, follow me." Jeannette led her through the infirmary's central hub and down the far corridor. "We'll be working in the research room, so look for me here first."

At the end of the hall was a small half-moon room. Jeannette opened the door and flicked on the lights. A bitter citrus smell permeated the room as she stepped inside, Diana behind her. Diana wrinkled her nose.

"Don't worry," said Jeannette with a smile, "you get acclimated to the smell."

"What is it?" Diana asked, walking between exam tables.

"Germicide. They special order the most obnoxious scents just for us."

The room was a self-contained, four-bed clinic, used for backup in case it was needed. White locked cabinets containing supplies and medications lined the far wall and two grey workstations sat at opposite ends of the room, two, small datapads lying on top of the spartan desks. Except for the raceway of blue curtains separating each bed and the desks, everything was white. The temperature was cooler than Jeannette preferred, but she made sure to wear long sleeves.

Diana wandered down to the nearest workstation, looking at all the hardware. "Will I be using any of this?" she asked with wide eyes.

"Only a datapad and MRC scanner," said Jeannette, walking toward her. She picked up a hand-sized datapad with a small, egg-shaped scanner. "This is what you'll use to record information."

"I can handle that," she said with a smile.

There was a long silence as Jeannette sat down at the desk and opened a virtual screen above the workstation. It flickered for a moment and then her data appeared. She'd already cleared her list with the training sergeants, including Diana's brother. Their first recombinant would arrive at 0930. She synced the datapad against her solar array data and called up an input form for Diana. When she looked up, she noticed Diana had her arms folded against her chest as she wandered through the room.

"You look cold. Lab coats in that cabinet by the door."

Diana hurried over to the cabinet. "Got any lab parkas in there?" she asked, pulling out a grey lab coat.

"'Fraid not," said Jeannette with a chuckle.

When all the equipment was ready to go, Jeannette handed the datapad and scanner to Diana. "Take a few minutes to review this input form. You'll have to do two scans. One of their ID chips and another of the vaccine. After that, there are ten questions at the bottom of the form you'll need to ask each recombinant."

"Questions?"

Jeannette nodded. "Observational data. Gives me another source of information. Questions like, how well are you performing in your training exercises, what is the most difficult part of training." She pointed to a little red button beside each question on the form. "Touch this square after you ask each question to capture the recombinants' response. Touch it again to turn off the data capture. Why don't you enter some test records and get a feel for how everything works?"

Diana sat down in one of the workstation chairs and huddled over the datapad. Jeannette stepped away to prepare the vaccines. They'd need about ten every day for a week or so.

FOR THE FIRST TWO RECOMBINANTS, Jeannette watched Diana input the data, making sure she was comfortable with the process. Diana was a quick learner. By the fourth recombinant, Diana had mastered the MRC scan. After Diana recorded the information, Jeannette administered the vaccine and released the recombinant to his escort outside the infirmary.

"Dr. Kingston, what exactly does this ID chip in their necks do?" Diana asked, leaning against the wall as Jeannette disinfected the table for the next recombinant.

Jeannette pressed the disinfect button on the edge of the table. A cover slid across the table, bathing the surface in ultraviolet light. In seconds, the cover retracted and the exam table was ready for another patient.

"It identifies the bearer's unit, date of creation, xDNA nucleobases and batch number, medical information, etc."

"What else?" Diana asked, frowning.

"Are you sure you want to know any more?" She leaned against the cabinet.

"Why do you say that?"

Jeannette sighed. She might as well know all of it up front. "It tracks escaped recombinants and controls their memories—even their behavior."

Diana looked horrified. "Controls their memories?"

"Yes, UCOE doesn't want recombinants to experience anything that might hinder them from killing Antarans." She stepped away from the table and retrieved another vial of vaccine for the next recombinant.

"You mean their memories get erased?"

"Sometimes, yes," she answered, setting the vial onto a tray with four disposable syringes. "When they're working properly."

"I had no idea. What horrible lives they must live." Diana's voice trailed off.

"They aren't the only ones with MRCs."

Diana frowned. "MRC? What's that?"

"It stands for memory replacement chip. It removes memories that adversely affect performance, Diana." She laid her hand against her neck. "Sometimes, it's a godsend when you work at the front or a reclamation station." She sighed. "But most of the time, it just reeks."

"You have one?" She stared at Jeannette.

Jeannette nodded. "When you process dead soldiers all day long, you don't always mind a little memory deletion." She sighed. Only when your life gets deleted without your permission.

"Glad I'm a civilian," said Diana, offering a smile.

A recombinant from Sergeant Temple's unit arrived and Diana sat him down on the exam table while Jeannette filled a syringe. There were three more after this one, so the day was far from over.

ABOUT 1400, Peter Mitchell entered the research room. Despite his bruised face and a deep cut curving across his left cheek, he was a handsome young man—blond hair and wideset blue eyes—especially to Diana Temple.

"Private Mitchell, come in," Diana called. Jeannette watched Diana try to contain her grin, but she couldn't.

Mitchell's face lit the moment he saw her, his eyes filling with stars. He was crazy about Diana. Anyone could see it.

"Diana, hi...I–I didn't expect to see you here again," he said, his gaze not quite meeting hers. "But I'm really glad to see you."

Diana took him by the arm and led him to the exam table.

Mitchell looked from Diana to Jeannette, his brow furrowed. "Sarge said I had to come here and have my vaccines checked." He looked a little unnerved.

"But first," said Diana, "I get to ask you some questions and do a quick scan."

"Does it hurt?" he asked.

Diana shook her head. "Not a bit."

"Roll up your sleeve, please," Jeannette said and picked up a syringe.

She started to fill it when Mitchell saw the needle. He started, his face turning pale, his eyes widening.

"It's painless," said Jeannette.

When Mitchell recoiled, Diana gently laid her hand against his shoulder and kneaded it. "It's okay—it's not what you're thinking." He stared fearfully at the syringe until Diana turned his face toward her. "Peter, it's not going to harm you, I promise."

Immediately, Jeannette threw a towel over the syringe. None of the other recombinants had reacted this way. Mitchell's reaction was odd by comparison.

"Do you trust me?" Diana asked him, taking him by the shoulders.

Slowly, he nodded.

"This vaccine will protect you from illnesses. It won't kill you."

"All right," he answered in a quiet voice, unable to look away from her face as he rolled up his sleeve.

Jeannette swabbed his arm with alcohol.

"Peter, how did your last training sim go?" Diana asked.

Good, she was distracting him.

"Better, I think," he answered, his nervous gaze flicking from Jeannette to Diana.

"David thinks you're very smart."

"He does?" Mitchell replied.

Diana nodded. "He just thinks you need a little more time with the grid and you'll be fine."

Jeannette pressed the needle into Mitchell's shoulder. He flinched, squeezing his eyes closed, and then it was all over. In a moment or two, he opened his eyes, relieved.

"See, it's all over," she said, giving his arm a reassuring squeeze. "Think you can answer some questions now?"

"For you, sure," he answered, the corners of his mouth lifting.

Jeannette stepped away from Mitchell. "Diana, scan his chip and I'll get started looking at the data. Mitchell's our last appointment for the day."

Easy to do when she was the scheduler. Smiling, she sat down at the workstation, pretending to be engrossed in data as she left Diana and Peter alone.

DIANA TURNED down Mitchell's collar and slid the scanner across his neck. His blond hair was so incredibly soft against her hand. It smelled soapy clean, his skin soft and buttery. He was so sweet. And so hot. It almost took her breath.

"What questions did you want to ask me?"

Hundreds, Diana thought. She wanted to know everything about him.

She sat down beside him on the exam table and his attention was drawn to the datapad and scanner. His eyes filled with wonder as he gently picked up the scanner, turning it over in his palm. Nothing was mundane or ordinary to Peter Mitchell and he never hesitated to express that. She found that mesmerizing. And so damned attractive.

"Lots of things," she said with a wink. "You've already answered my first question, about your training."

"So, this thing reads my ID chip?" he asked, holding it up.

"Yes, watch—" said Diana as the scanner beeped, indicating it found Peter's ID chip. She pointed to a box at the top of the little screen. "The information is recorded here."

Several lines of information flashed across the screen, including the words, "property of Unified Countries of Earth." She flinched at the word *property*, but Peter didn't seem phased by it.

"Doesn't that bother you?" she asked.

His gaze fell to his feet. "It does. But I try not to think about it much." He looked up then reached out to her hair, touching her scarf. "This color—purple—is so unusual." He smiled, his blue eyes alight. "Whenever I see it, I think of you."

"That's sweet," she answered, looking into the deep pools of his blue eyes. She didn't see that killer instinct in their soft, sad expression. Only wonder. And that made him so attractive. She glanced down at the datapad. "Okay, next question." She leaned forward and spoke softly. "What's your most secret dream?"

"That's not on the list," Peter said with a smirk.

"How do you know?" she asked playfully.

"Because they already know what recombinants dream." He lowered his voice. "At least they think they do."

"So, tell me then what is your dream?"

His gaze turned far away. "I know all the words: picnic, lemonade, beach, city." He held out his hands. "But I want to feel them. Touch them. What does lemonade taste like? How does sand feel between my toes? What does the rain smell like? I want to know it all, not just read about it."

She sighed. The things she took for granted were the things he dreamed of.

"It's silly, I know," said Peter, swinging his legs. "I've never told anyone that before. If I did, they'd wash me out." He gestured at the room. "But just look in here—so many things I never even knew existed. There's so much I could learn, so much I could do. If I weren't a recombinant."

His eyes burned with intensity.

"Do you know what my secret dream is?" she asked.

He shook his head.

"Neither do I—but all my life I've tried to find one." She always moved from one thing to the next, never spending much time at anything. Always moving to the next thing so fast that the world became a blur sometimes.

He laid his hand against hers. "Maybe a dream will find you?"

JEANNETTE SCROLLED through the data they'd gathered today until she found Peter Mitchell's MRC data. Four of the recombinants on her list had come from Mitchell's unit, their MRCs all from the same batch. Except that Peter's batch number had an extra O in it. Was it a typo? His chip didn't show measurable signs of malfunction, but the three other recombinants in his unit registered various stages of malfunction. One recombinant's microfeed was already offline. She glanced over at Diana and Mitchell when she heard their laughter.

There was a high probability that Mitchell's MRC was affected like the others she'd observed.

She watched his animated expression as he talked, Diana riveted to his every word. What would happen to him and the others if she reported these failures? She feared the answer was all too obvious. *Would RDC really recall the entire batch and destroy them, including Mitchell?*

The risk of their behavior contaminating other recombinants was too high—and so was the cost of feeding, clothing, and housing them. She needed to know how RDC would handle the information before she reported it.

Mitchell and Diana laughed again.

If she reported it.

"My friend, Sting has already been to the front," Mitchell told Diana, his voice loud enough to hear. "This will be his second tour."

Sting? Quickly, Jeannette called up the names of recombinants in

Mitchell's unit. Near the end of the list, she located John Stingley's name and MRC batch number. An older MRC. She needed to scan his and see how an older chip was holding up.

While Diana worked through the questions with Mitchell, Jeannette put Stingley on her list. Once he'd been added, she fired off a quick email to Kai, asking him to check the archives for previous MRC malfunctions and how they were handled. She wouldn't let him know that she'd found malfunctions in living recombinants.

At least not until she knew what future those recombinants faced.

15

THE NEXT DAY, Sergeant Temple assembled Peter's unit outside the recombinant quarters. Peter and the others stood in a nervous line, waiting for what would most likely be their combat orders.

Peter tried to stop his hands from shaking. The last training sims were approaching. He'd known all along they'd be assigned a mission objective and their final sims revolved around that task. If he didn't pass this last set of sims, they'd wash out him. And the unit. He sucked in a breath and stared at the numb faces around him. Some of them—probably him—would wash out today.

He cast a frightened glance at Sting, who nodded reassuringly at him. Sting never seemed to be bothered by problems and procedures. He sat back and let them happen, unconcerned about a bad outcome.

Temple strode down the line, hands behind his back. His clean-shaven jaw was taut, dark hair cut short, pale lips pressed together, and hands clenched. Field Sergeant Galloway stood off to the side, a datapad in his slightly shaking hands. His eyes were rimmed red and his face was haggard. He looked sick. Finally, Temple stopped pacing and came to stand in front of them.

"All right, this is the way it is. We're approaching the final phase of your training. Those who pass will head to the front very soon. Those who don't..." His voice trailed off into a nervous sigh.

Temple said no more on the subject and he didn't have to. Every recombinant in that line understood perfectly what it meant to return to the Recombinant Development Center.

Peter stiffened at the thought.

Temple started to pace again. "You will remain in your subunits to run this last mission sim. It's the culmination of your tour at the front. When you pass this last mission sim, I'll turn you over to Field Sergeant Galloway." He motioned at the half-dazed man behind him and Peter groaned. Galloway looked like he'd been drinking heavily for days.

Temple gazed at the floor. He seemed to be gathering his courage. Finally, he looked up and his gaze fell to Peter. Temple frowned. Peter knew how badly his face was bruised and Sarge noticed. He said nothing but continued his restless pacing.

"At this point, some of you have already washed out. Those with reclamation orders will find a yellow slip inside their footlockers. Those without ROs will report to tactical classroom twenty-one at 0900. Dismissed."

Dread spread through Peter's hands in cold, numbing waves as he turned toward the hallway. His heart hammered against his rib cage as he traversed the dusty corridor. When he reached the bunkroom, he hung outside the door as the others rushed inside. Sweat beaded across his forehead and clung to his upper lip. He wiped it away with the back of his hand and tried to muster enough courage to approach his footlocker.

Sting raced past him and tore open his footlocker. Laughing maniacally, he cheered and held up empty hands. Peter knew they wouldn't wash out Sting. He was too valuable. He'd survived the front.

Peter thought about his own worth and felt sick. What use would they have for an oversensitive, gun-shy recombinant that could barely read a sensor grid?

"C'mon, Pete," he called, motioning him inside. "Just get it over with. They won't wash you out. You got potential."

Peter resisted.

Finally, Sting moved to the door and yanked him inside. Sting gripped Peter by the shoulders and forced Peter to look at him.

"Even if you never look inside that locker, that slip will still be there. You can't wish it away by never opening it again. Trust yourself, Pete and open the damned thing or I'll do it for you."

Glancing from the footlocker to Sting, Peter fought against his fear. He couldn't wash out. He couldn't.

With slow, reticent steps, he approached the footlocker.

He stared at it for a moment and then laid his hand on the dented metal box, its lock laid open. He sucked in a sharp breath and tried to control his shaking hands. And slowly, he raised the lid.

He turned his head away, terrified he'd find a yellow slip lying on top of his uniforms and dress boots.

"Oh, shit!" Sting screeched. "They can't do this!"

Terrified, Peter jerked his gaze to the open footlocker.

Empty.

Only uniforms and a pair of dress boots.

He grinned. He'd made it a little further. He shoved Sting backward.

Sting fell over the edge of the footlocker, cackling as he hit the floor, holding his stomach. "Got ya, Pete!"

"Shut up, Sting," Peter snapped, but Sting's infectious laugh made him smile until finally he was laughing, too.

That evening, after three, grueling tactical courses with hungover Galloway and a short trip to mess, Peter walked down to the launch bay, an ache in his stomach. Four recombinants in his unit washed out. They were shipping out for RDC tonight. Their last shuttle trip.

His stomach twisted into a knot, eyes watery, as he watched them walk that long path across the launch bay. They carried no bags with them. They wouldn't need anything where they were going.

He watched the other personnel hurry back and forth. Did their god hear a recombinant's prayers, he wondered? So many had told him that recombinants didn't have souls. Peter bowed his head and said a prayer for the four, grim-faced men plodding into a shuttle. Just in case.

He walked down the stairs to the launch bay, haunting the washed out recombinants' path toward the shuttle. When he reached the shuttle's closed doors, he saw the pilot rounding the nose. A flash of purple. His chest fluttered.

"Diana?"

She jerked her head up and smiled shyly. "Peter—hello!"

He returned her smile, his heart racing. She remembered his name! He moved closer.

"Are you part of this night drop?" she asked.

"Thankfully no."

"Is it another one of those training sims?" She leaned against the shuttle.

His gaze lowered to the launch bay floor. "No. Didn't anyone tell you? They washed out."

Diana made a clicking sound with her tongue. "Too bad. Will they send them to another base to do something else?"

"When a recombinant washes out, it's permanent, Diana." He sighed.

"What do you mean permanent?" she asked, her brow furrowing into delicate wrinkles that gave her beautiful face such depth.

He tried to look her in the eye and tell her the horrible truth, but he couldn't. He turned his gaze toward a group of techs repairing a shuttle and the words spilled out.

"They say it isn't painful. It's just a shot. You go to sleep and never wake up. They only achieved consciousness five months ago." He felt sick and his knees trembled. He held his stomach.

Her hand pressed against his in a comforting squeeze. Electric current careened through his body at her touch. It was a strange mix of nervousness and pleasure that he'd never felt before.

"I'm so sorry. God, how awful! And how that must make you feel." She turned him around.

He gazed into her eyes, wonder mixing with shock. Slowly, he reached his hand toward her face. She didn't pull away. His fingers brushed across the softness of her cheek, around the curve of her chin, the silkiness of her neck. Embarrassed, he pulled his hand away.

"Forgive me," he gasped. "I just wanted to know how your skin felt. I...I've never been this close to a woman before."

She chuckled, taking his hand in hers again. "Relax, I won't report you." Then she frowned at the gashes and bruises on his face. "What happened—those bruises look fresh."

"Got into another fight...and lost."

"I can see that." She ran her fingers across the bandage on his forehead and around a puffy bruise on his cheek.

He closed his eyes, losing himself in the scent of warm vanilla and the warm whisper of her gentle fingers against his skin. Her hand left his face.

"Temple!" One of the techs moved some equipment away from her shuttle. "You're ready to launch."

She gave the tech a thumbs-up and returned her gaze to Peter. With her right hand, she brushed his bangs off his forehead. "Take care of yourself, Peter. Maybe we can talk again sometime?"

"I'd like that," he answered.

He watched her climb into the shuttle. In moments, the engines fired and she taxied into the launch tube. Peter stared at the shuttle portals, his gut twisting. That was the last thing those poor recombinants would ever see. His mood fell and as he stalked the launch bay, he remembered his first night in RDC. As his memories spiraled backward, he wondered if everyone was right. Did recombinants not have souls?

PETER WAKES from his first night's sleep in the Recombinant Development Center. His arms are stiff from the jacket wrapping them around his body and his throat burns with dryness. It's been twenty-four hours since he's achieved consciousness. His head hurts thinking about it. He imagines this xDNA suddenly retrieved from a pool of genetic material, molded and changed, and then assembled like puzzle pieces into a man.

They gave him knowledge, but his memory is a clean slate. His memories go back only to yesterday. He strains for something deeper, older, but only bright lights and fear return to him in stale waves.

He raises his head from the pillow, freeing his nose from the mildewed bleach scent clinging to the faded white fabric. Nearby, the urine smell is strong. He rolls away from it and the soiled recombinant in the bed next to his.

The two facing rows of beds are filled with sleeping recombinants, all draped in jackets like his. Most of them toss and turn, some groaning, others mumbling.

Where is this place?

In the back of his brain, where they placed basic understanding, he has a shadowy grasp, but he can't bear to dwell on it. Thin, grey light sags through a dirty window above his bed. It's too high for him to reach, much less see out. Grimy smears shadow dusty tile, creating flecks and swirls on the smooth floor.

A woman in white scrubs squeaks down the aisle and stops at his bed. She looks above his head and he traces her gaze to a set of vital-signs monitors. His chart hangs on a hook at the foot of the bed. She picks it up, points it at the monitors, and captures the numbers. Then she hangs the datapad back on its hook.

"You seem calm enough," she says with a faint smile. "Much better adjusted than the rest. I think we can take that off now."

She moves toward him, behind him, and the jacket arms hugging him loosen. He stretches. The need to relieve himself is strong. The woman leads him down the aisle, away from the beds. At the end is a small, poorly lit room. "The latrine's in there."

She's still waiting for him when he comes out. "Better?"

He nods.

"You're a quiet one. Gentler than the rest. Must be a new combination they're trying."

Shyly, he averts his gaze. "Why am I here?"

She leads him back to the bed and sits him down. "I'm sure they told you all of this yesterday, but I'll explain again."

She doesn't seem angry at having to tell him and he's relieved. He doesn't want to stand out in this place.

"This is the Recombinant Development Center and we've called up your xDNA code because you're needed at the front." Her voice has no emotion and the words sound canned, like the woman from yesterday. She picks up his chart again. "When we have you conditioned properly, we'll send you off to a training station. If you pass muster there, you'll go to the front. If not, you'll return here."

"And do what?" The chill of fear blows across his shoulders.

"Your xDNA combination will be returned to the system," she says without blinking.

He frowns. "Returned to the system?"

"It's quite painless," she says casually, adding something to his chart. "They give you a shot and you go to sleep again."

"Only, you don't wake up," he says matter-of-factly, matching her unconcerned tone.

"Exactly." Her smile is cheery.

Peter is horrified. He shrinks back from her. She doesn't understand how her words cut through him. She doesn't realize that she's talking about putting people to death, not recycling aluminum cans or reusing trash bags. Things he knows about but has never seen or touched.

"Make the best of the time you have and try very hard to pass your training. You'll live a lot longer. Some of you may even live a whole year. That's so much better than last year's recombinants. Most of them only survived six months."

Peter shakes his head. To her, he is new and improved equipment, better than last year's model. His stomach burns.

He curls up inside himself, shaking at the thought of war. Killing, explosions, death. He knows about death. He could never learn to kill. Whatever genetic combination they assembled is useless in him, but he won't tell them that.

She leaves him to his misery.

Pulling his knees to his chest, he watches other recombinants awaken to this nightmare. They struggle against the woman, forcing her to summon medics to subdue them. They kick and scream and bite like wild animals.

Why is he so different?

Peter doesn't have their rage, only that sick, sinking feeling of being trapped. He can't even summon enough anger to shout at her, to tell her how unfair this is.

He glances at the sterile white walls and old, worn furniture. Faded white plastic and scuffed metal. It's all he knows, it's all he remembers. He hangs his head, feeling lost. He knows nothing beyond this place. He knows only what they've programmed into his twenty-two-year-old body, born just yesterday.

One of the recombinants shrieks and breaks free. He dashes across the room, running down the aisle, his arms flailing. One of the medics cuts off his escape into whatever lies beyond this area. He circles around a desk, tossing papers at them and overturning a chair. The window catches his attention as he runs down the aisle. His huffing breaths fill the room, his face brightening in the greyness as he leaps onto Peter's bed and claws at a window too high to reach.

Peter stares at him with wide eyes, fascinated and horrified by the raw anger and wildness in the man's face and gritted teeth, all of that glossed by a sheen of perspiration and hope. His black hair is damp and tousled, his face shadowed, stretched, and desperate.

The woman and two medics smash him into Peter's mattress.

"No! No! I can't stay here! Let me go!" His urgent gaze catches Peter's and holds it. "Don't let them do this. Please! Help me!" He twists his face toward them, tears flooding his cheeks. "I don't want to die!"

Peter reaches out and grabs hold of the man's hand. And grips it hard, feeling the warmth and life. The feeling is intoxicating, comforting, and he can't let go.

Peter recoils as the woman pulls a needle from a case and presses it into the young man's shoulder. The young man's body goes slack, his hand falling away from Peter's.

Horrified, Peter watches them carry the young man to his bunk. They lay him on his back as the woman removes a second needle from her case. The young man mumbles unintelligibly and weakly clutches her sleeve as she plunges the second needle into the young man's arm. Peter's guts clench, his whole body lurching.

Slowly, the hand slides away from her sleeve, wilting like a flower in the sun too long, falling limp against the mattress. The young man's chest no longer heaves, the rising and falling ebbing with the departure of the medics. The young man's gaze is fixed on the ceiling.

She takes away the needles, returning to take his pulse. At the wrist. The neck. Reaching down, she grasps the white sheet on his bed and pulls it over his face.

Gone.

Shaking, Peter buries his face in his pillow, trying to block out the images, hide his tears. He wants to scream, his insides heaving, but he holds it back, shoving it down where they can't see. The memory of the man's warm, desperate embrace burns against his hand. He wants to rage at them, at how unfair it all is!

Shoes clomp against the floor and sheets rustle. Someone grunts. Beds creak.

Through his fingers, Peter glances as the medics carry away the young man's body. Trembling, he gags and hides his face again, unwilling to look at the empty cot and remember the warmth of his hand, the memory of the living, breathing young man who had just been there cherishing each breath.

Peter would come to know this later as being washed out.

PETER RETURNED TO THE BUNKROOM, plopping down on his bunk. Sting and the others sat four bunks down playing cards. He watched them laugh and cavort and felt annoyed. Didn't they care that four people just went to their deaths at RDC? The thought made him sick. He hugged himself, longing to be away from this place. Sting cast a glance over at him and quickly excused himself from the game.

"Hey, Pete, you wanna play? Frank'll let you bluff him out of a credit or two."

Peter shook his head and sat up.

Sting plopped down beside him on the bunk and ruffled his hair.

"C'mon, private, shake it off. We lost four today, but you're still alive. Celebrate that."

When Peter didn't respond, Sting slid his arm around Peter's shoulder. "Your life is way too short to mope around about washouts, Pete. They didn't make the grade. It's over for them. It happens. But you've still got time, another chance."

"But they were expecting a year, Sting. They only got five months."

"I know. Recombinants die much too soon, but a lot of them go on." He patted his chest. "Like me. They gave me six months and I'm at eighteen." He pointed to the others playing poker and having fun. "I'm celebrating the fact that we're all still alive and that we still have a chance to live. Come on, celebrate with us."

Nodding, Peter rose from his bunk, Sting beside him. He sat with the others and picked up a handful of greyed, earmarked cards. Soon, he found himself enjoying their company and the fact that he was still alive.

And he'd seen Diana again. Tonight, he had something to live for.

16

AFTER DIANA TRANSFERRED the four recombinants to an outbound shuttle, she felt herself trembling, Peter's words haunting her. "They say it isn't painful. It's just a shot. You go to sleep and never wake up."

What had she just done?

Her legs felt stringy and weak as she walked away from the shuttle gate.

The look on Peter's face burned into her brain. She'd wanted to take him in her arms tonight. That could have been him and it could still happen. The fear had been dark and cold in his eyes, face pasty white, hands trembling. He'd faced his own death tonight and come up on the high side. But his relief was so brief, overshadowed by anxiety that had corded his muscles and tightened his face into a painful mask. He had seen himself in that shuttle.

How horrible it must feel to be a recombinant? Now, she understood David's anguish.

Diana was awake all night until the sun rose, but she wasn't tired.

She hurried out of Civilization's shuttle port and ran to the city transit stop. Grey clouds swirled on the horizon, darkening the amber and red landscape to a deep umber. Everything had gone still, even the murmurs of the city beneath the grey blanket of calm. She missed the sunny amber shades.

For a moment, wind rushed over her, cool and heavy, and she smelled rain and pavement as she waited for the transit.

In the calm rush of air, whispering, the transit lurched slowly, quietly to a stop and she stepped aboard, riding it all the way to Mimi's. Ignoring the time, she stepped into the restaurant.

"We're not open yet," someone called from the dining area. "We begin serving at eleven."

"Mimi?"

Mimi stepped into the foyer. Her copper red hair, drawn up by silvery cords, was pulled away from her face. She wore a flowered tunic and black leggings.

"Diana?" She peered curiously at Diana. A soft wine blush colored Mimi's smooth cheeks, her lips flushed with a hint of mauve lipstick. Faint sable eyeshadow outlined her bright eyes. "What's the matter, dear? It's terribly early. You look troubled."

"I am," she said, leaning against the reservations stand. She bunched her hands together. "I had to do something awful last night."

Mimi took her by the arm and led her into the dining area. She motioned her into a booth and left her, returning with hot jasmine tea and a sugary, iced pastry. Diana wrapped her hands around the cup and stared into it as Mimi slid into the booth. She folded her hands on the tabletop, bracelets jangling, her eyes filled with concern. Diana talked to Mimi a lot, but never about something so dark and troubling. Mimi seemed the sort to offer comfort whenever she could.

"Tell me what happened," Mimi said, focusing her attention away from her servers setting up tables. They flitted past in green, Middle-Eastern-styled tunics, sleeves trimmed in black braid, and carried silverware and burgundy napkins.

Diana drew the white cup to her lips. The tea was warm and sweet, easing the tightness in her throat. When her shaking subsided, she set down her cup.

"Mimi...I didn't know where they were going. I just did my job and transported them back here to another shuttle. If I'd just done something, I—" She sighed and ran a hand through her bangs, finally gripping the warm cup again.

Mimi's brow furrowed. "Where who was going?"

"Recombinants from the base. I didn't know until Private Mitchell told me. God– I feel like a murderer."

"You had to transport the washouts, didn't you?" Mimi shook her head.

Diana nodded. "When a pilot washes out, she can't fly anymore. Has to do something else. When David talked about them washing out, I thought—" She sighed. "I don't know what I thought."

Mimi's face pinched into a frown. "UCOE treats them like dirt and destroys them if they don't perform to exact specification," said Mimi, her tone acidic. "It's all so inhumane. Makes me sick."

Diana gazed into Mimi's eyes. "That's why you do it then. It makes sense now." Mimi rescued them, gave them lives beyond UCOE Forces.

Mimi frowned. "Do what, dear?"

"Get them out."

Her lips pursed, her body stiffening slightly. "Where did you get that idea?"

"I saw some of your cohorts in the shuttle port and then eating supper here. I even saw the two recombinants they helped escape."

Diana glanced around the empty restaurant. In less than two hours, this place would have a line out the door and people eating and chattering at one another while Mimi probably shipped out another recombinant under their noses.

Mimi opened her mouth to respond, but Diana cut her off.

"It's okay. I'm glad!" She laid her hand on Mimi's arm. "I never knew any of this before. Back on Earth, it all sounded so neat and clean. Recycling soldiers to reduce heavy losses. People I knew stopped dying, the lists of the dead started disappearing from websites. Like everyone else, I found it easy to forget people were still out here fighting and dying." She sighed. "That's why I came out here. To understand it all. Except they aren't considered people. My God, Mimi—they're property!"

"It's an atrocity what they're doing," said Mimi, her voice low and drawn. She kept flicking her gaze from Diana to the restaurant now, afraid someone would hear. "They treat them worse than lab animals."

Diana took another sip of her tea. "What do you mean?"

Mimi laughed bitterly. "Couldn't have one of those recombinants escaping and living a real life, could they? That would be criminal." Her words were fast and caustic.

"I want to help."

Mimi was silent for some time.

"Why?"

"Why?" Diana shoved the pastry away. "Because they're just as human as we are. Peter deserves better than that."

A knowing smile spread across Mimi's face. "Peter, is it? Is there a certain young recombinant you've taken a special liking to?"

Diana started to deny it, but stopped. "How can they lawfully be UCOE property?" she asked, changing the subject.

"Because they're made from copyrighted xDNA, sequences and artificial nucleobases that pair to natural ones. They start with UCOE personnel's DNA and the artificial nucleobases that make up the xDNA sequence make the whole chain unique. Copyrightable, that's how. They're inventoried and everything. Have little microchips in their necks in case they wander off. There has to be a better way than recombinants."

Diana made a sour face. "It's sickening."

"You're a shuttle pilot, aren't you," came Mimi's wary reply. "If you're serious, we might be able to work with you. We'll talk about that part later. Now, finish your tea."

DIANA FINISHED her tea and wandered the charged, colorful streets of Civilization until it was late. Then she walked home.

Rain came down in sheets, drenching her flight suit and dark hair. When she got to her apartment, she peeled off her wet clothes and took a long, hot shower. But even the tea and the shower couldn't erase the look in Peter Mitchell's eyes. What bothered her most was that look had been strangely absent from the four recombinants. They all seemed sad, but Peter just ached for them.

She twisted her hair in a towel and sat down on the couch. Rain drummed against the window, thunder a low growl in the distance. Lightning charged the evening sky with a burst of yellow then indigo.

Peter had such a sweet expression, the kind of chiseled good looks that always turned her head in her certification courses. His blond hair feathered softly across his forehead, and his blue eyes shimmered with a newness and fascination with the world. Lots of boyish charm that never got to develop. Everything he experienced was so new to him and he seemed to savor it all.

She laughed and imagined him experiencing the first big drops of rain against his face and the cold, sweet taste of ice cream.

Thunder shook the windows, rain pattering against the glass. The fiery rake of plasma fire, dirty ooze of swamplands against his boots—that's what Peter soon faced. She pressed her cheek against the window, feeling the cold pane against her nose and chin.

How would it feel to have a year to live? Peter Mitchell lived with that every. Single. Day. How could he bear it? How could any of them bear it?

She pulled the mobile out of her pocket and called David.

A sleepy, shadowed face slid onto her screen, his brown hair disheveled and standing out at his right ear. He sat up, a blanket around his bare shoulders, and straightened his posture into a half-slump against the desk.

"Sergeant Temple here," he said, his voice soft and disoriented. He squinted. "Diana? What's wrong?" He rubbed his eyes.

"I didn't mean to wake you, David."

His eyes were fearful. "What's the matter? Are Mother and Dad okay?"

She nodded. "Yes, everyone's fine. I...I shouldn't have called so late. I'm sorry for waking you. I'll talk to you later." She reached down to end the call, but he called out.

"Diana, wait!"

His urgency and concern made her stop. Her eyes filled with tears.

"Kiddo, what is it? Tell me what's the matter."

"I don't know why this is bothering me so much, but it is."

She looked away, knowing if she looked into David's paternal gaze, she'd start sobbing like the high-strung nine-year-old who'd had a nightmare. Most of the time, Mother and Dad traveled, enjoying each other's company or working on their many businesses, so David had been in charge. Diana wondered why they even bothered to have children, but she thanked God that David came first.

Back then, she'd hated them, but now, she understood they had dreams just like hers, dreams that hadn't shriveled and died when their kids arrived. After school, David had been there to greet her with a cookie and a hug. He mooned over her finger paintings and cheered at her gold stars. He was the one who sent her to her room when she refused to eat the overdone macaroni and cheese and he was the one who held her when the thunder got too loud or the wind too shrill. David had been more of a parent to her than anyone.

"Diana, it's okay. Tell me what's wrong." His voice was soft and his eyes held concern. He liked to be needed.

She swallowed back a sob and faced him. "I thought it was a routine run until Peter told me the truth. My God, David...I took them away to be killed." Tears slipped down her face and she brushed them away.

"You talked to Mitchell?"

"He was sick about it. He stalked the bay for a long time. I watched him as I launched. The other recombinants didn't seem to care, but he was nearly paralyzed. I felt so sorry for him. He won't wash out, will he?" She couldn't stop the cold shaking that enveloped her. "Please, David, tell me he won't wash out."

David shook his head. "For now, he's safe, but if he doesn't pass this last set of sims..."

He didn't need to finish the rest of the sentence. Diana recoiled from the words.

"Look, I like him, too. I've been working with him. He's gotten a lot better with the grid and he even managed to impress D'Angelo. He's okay for now." He laid a hand against the screen and smiled at her. "Come on, sis, show me that stubborn resolve of yours. I'll do everything I can, okay?"

At last, she smiled. "All right, David. And I'll do what I can."

"There's nothing in the regs that says a civvie shuttle pilot can't talk to her passengers—even recombinants. He seems quite taken with you. Talk to him. See if you can bolster his confidence."

"All right," she said with a sniff. "Get some sleep now."

"G'night, sis."

"Sleep well, David, and thanks for being there."

Reaching over, she cleared the connection.

17

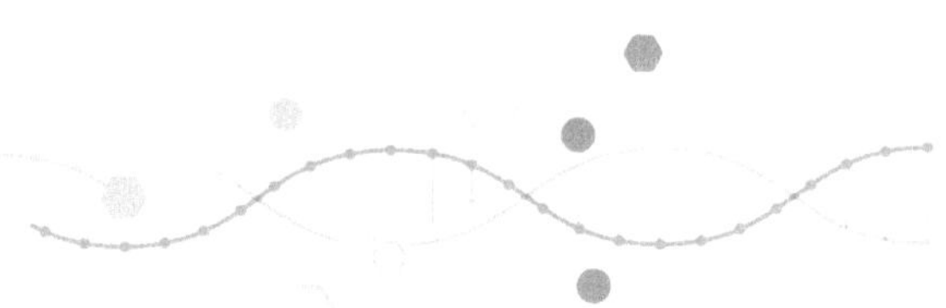

IN THE CLASSROOM, Peter sat beside Sting as Sergeant Galloway went over the mission details. Again and again and again.

Sergeant Temple sat in a chair near the podium and took notes on a datapad. The glaring lights washed out Galloway's gaunt features and ruddy hair as he pointed out landmarks on a computer map, flicking his laser pointer from map location to map location. His face was pinched and he talked so fast Peter could barely keep up with him. The gentle whir of a computer hung just underneath his words.

He outlined everything from where the transport would land on Ku'Tal to how the entire company would be broken into units and finally subunits. He displayed images of the explosives they'd carry and the munitions depot they'd destroy.

Peter tried not to think about Diana, but she invaded his thoughts. If he closed his eyes, he still felt her touch against his face and how smooth her skin was against his fingers. For days, he'd walked around with a hollowness that almost hurt and he longed to hear her voice again. At night, just before he locked into his data transfer headgear, he thought about her until the preprogrammed images and memories intertwined with Diana's image.

It was only alone in his bunk, when the lights were out and the whir of the data dump had begun that he realized how lonely he felt and how much he missed her.

Finally, Sergeant Galloway turned, laser pointer falling to his side. A fine sheen of sweat clung to his angry face. The air smelled of body odor and over-warm equipment. Sting, unconcerned by all the planning, yawned and leaned back in his desk.

"All right, are there any questions?" Galloway asked in a slightly nasal voice.

Drake raised his hand.

"Will we get holos or live charges for the next sim?"

Sergeant Galloway frowned and waved him off. "That's a stupid question, Drake and it has nothing to do with this briefing."

Another hand waved and Galloway nodded him to speak. Someone asked if they'd have bunks or bedrolls at the front. Galloway clenched his hands into fists and gritted his teeth.

Sergeant Temple's face darkened as he rose from his chair and stood in front of the map. "Don't you people understand what Sergeant Galloway is showing you here? Being prepared and knowing the terrain could mean the difference between living and dying out there! Stop worrying about what you'll sleep in and what you shove into your rifles!" His fist slammed against the table. "Dammit! Galloway and I are trying to keep all of you alive for as long as we can!"

Peter raised his hand. "Sarge?"

Biting his lip, Temple cast an angry stare at the room and motioned for Peter to speak.

"Why can't we locate this munitions depot with radar or motion sensors?"

Looking puzzled, Galloway turned his gaze to Temple and bowed to his expertise.

A smile brightened Temple's face. Drake cast a glare at Peter. "An excellent question, Mitchell." He accepted the pointer from Galloway and thrust it to the map, to a section marked swamplands.

"The reason we can't find this depot is because of some new Antaran technology. They've protected the depot with some sort of bioshielded jamming device. We've detected Antaran troop movements transporting serious weapons and explosives into this area, but around this point in the swamps, they disappear off radar and we can't track them. Your objective is to search this area on foot, locate the depot, clear a path to it, and then destroy it."

Peter sank back in his chair. Sounded impossible.

"We can't let them get a foothold on Ku'Tal," said Temple. "If we do, then Naharra was sacrificed for nothing. And Ballese fell for no reason."

Sergeant Temple went over a few more training details and demanded answers to questions as he quizzed them. Finally, exasperated, he slammed the pointer against the table.

"Don't you guys get it? If you don't pass this next off-site sim, you wash out. It's all over for you! Got it? This isn't new stuff. It should be review for you guys! We leave tomorrow at sixteen hundred hours, so you'd better listen carefully." He frowned at Sting. "Sit up, Stingley! You've been there, I know, but if your buddies in your subunit don't do their jobs, you could fail the sim, too."

Sighing, Sting sat up.

"All right, let's go over the depot strike again."

Sergeant Temple handed the pointer back to Galloway and sat down. With a frown, Galloway poked the map with the pointer and went through the mission again. And again.

AFTER A RESTLESS NIGHT'S SLEEP, Peter awoke. Slipping out of his headgear, he tucked it back on its hook and padded into the latrine. He showered and shaved quickly, then slipped into his dull green uniform. When he was dressed, he ate a quick morning meal of cereal and orange juice and tried to savor each sweet bite of sugar against the cereal flakes. His classes dragged through the morning. At noon mess, he picked at his food. Some sort of meat and beans dish that was tasteless but filling. He was too nervous to eat though. This sim was the last one.

He had to pass it.

The rest of the afternoon, he worked with the grid until it was time for the sim. With Sting beside him, they rode the lift and walked silently down to the launch bay. Sergeant Temple issued them plasma rifles with holo charges when they reached the shuttle.

A shiver shot through Peter at the sight of Diana standing near the shuttle, her hair tied back with that familiar purple scarf that made his heart spin circles. He longed to rush over and talk to her, to blurt out everything he felt, but he held fast to the line and stood in formation a short distance from the open shuttle door.

Sergeant Temple went through the roster. Every time he called a name, he motioned them into the shuttle. Drake and Evans were late to formation and Temple gave them hell. When Peter's name was called, he rushed toward the shuttle. Diana smiled when she saw him approach.

"Hello, Peter. Hope you're feeling better."

He nodded, his gaze taking in every curve of her face and every warm highlight in her hair. Her eyes were a sunny brown, like a sun-drenched riverbed. Warmth spread through his stomach and he fought the urge to touch her.

"I've never met anyone like you," he said in a half whisper, not wanting the others to hear him.

"You're sweet," she replied.

He reached into his pocket and pulled out a folded color printout of a lazy brook, the sun shining brilliantly, willow tree branches dragging the bank. He handed it to her. "This picture is how I feel when I talk to you."

She unfolded it and her eyes brightened. "Thank you, Peter...it's beautiful." Her grin filled him with relief.

A hand fell against his shoulder. He turned. Sting.

"Come on, Pete. Stop flirting and get aboard. Let's get this test over with."

"This is the big test, isn't it?" Diana asked.

"If any of us fails this one, it'll really hurt our overall scores. They're scoring on subunit performance today." Peter's voice was tight.

She squeezed his arm. "You'll do fine. I know you will."

He laid his hand on hers and caressed her fingers. For an electric moment, her gaze met his and he saw a flicker of attraction.

"Pete, come on!"

Reluctantly, he let go of her hand. She let hers linger against his arm a moment then she turned away. He watched her touch a small gold heart that hung on a chain around her neck as she moved around the shuttle toward the techs.

His heart beat faster. A god symbol! He'd seen lots of people wear them.

Sting called his name again and he shuffled aboard, rifle slung over his shoulder. He smiled. Had she asked her god for help? For him?

SINCE HE'S ACHIEVED CONSCIOUSNESS, Peter has spent a lot of time connected to data transfer headgear. He's restless, wondering what comes next—a needle or a shuttle? Three people have been injected so far and at every waking moment, he fears he's next. Peter has been at the Recombinant Development Center for nearly three weeks.

He keeps to himself, afraid of the vicious recombinants that stalk the RDC ward. They'd kill him without the slightest provocation. The recombinant in the bunk next to his is cheerful though, his disposition closer to Peter's than the hungry, kill-minded soldiers roaming about the chamber. He's the only civilized one in the room.

Three of the recombinants collide in the aisle, snarling and clawing at each other. Someone shouts. Medics pour inside, beating them back from each other.

"They're animals," says the recombinant beside Peter.

Peter turns. The recombinant's reddish-blond hair is cropped short and wild, hair sticking up over his ears. His brown eyes are soft, the color like the wooden chairs up front in the medic's breakroom.

"Why don't they keep those kind in jackets until they've calmed down enough to manage?"

Two more recombinants, one of them a wild-eyed woman, leap into the fray and pound on the medics. An alarm shrills outside the door. Guards rush into the chamber.

Peter sits down on his bunk. "Why don't they just send them to the front? Don't they want killing machines?"

The young man smirks. "They have to be a little more manageable first, be capable of following orders. What's your name?"

"Peter Mitchell. And you?"

"Charles Conner."

"How long have you been here, Charles?"

He twists the edge of his greyed sheet around his index finger. "A month longer than you." He nods toward the turmoil of recombinants fending off medics. "I used to be like that, fighting and kicking, but I got tired of wearing those jackets. I've learned that if I don't go for the jugular, even if I want to, they don't put those damned things on me."

A team of medics files in, carrying jackets and shouting about a lock down. It takes several minutes to force jackets onto the wild-eyed, screaming recombinants and immobilize them. A medic presses a needle to each one's shoulder until they slump.

Peter gasps, afraid they'll all be destroyed, but the medics carry the recombinants, one by one, to their bunks and leave them. One of the medics walks down the aisle, a pile of jackets in his arm. He stops at Peter's bunk.

"Hold out your arms, Mitchell."

"But I didn't have anything to do with the fighting."

"Can't take any chances. We're locking down the ward until the fighting stops."

Sadly, Peter relents, allowing the medic to drape him in the jacket. He lies angrily back on his bunk, his arms immobile now, wrapped around his middle. The medic fastens Charles into a jacket, too. Peter notices the charm around the medic's neck. The charm is a man, his arms stretched out, his feet crossed. Behind him are two crossed beams, one tall, the other horizontal.

"What is that?" he asks Charles.

"It's some symbol of their god. He suffered for them so they could be free."

"A god freed them?"

"Yep, so their souls would live on with him."

"What about us?" Peter asks. "Could we pray to this god? Would he help us like he helps them?"

Charles cackles, the sound grating. Peter wants to hold his ears.

"Are you kidding me? Recombinants don't have souls. You can't save what you haven't got."

Charles' words cut through him.

"What do you mean we don't have souls? Betty, that social coordinator, comes in and prays for us every week. She says—"

"Exactly what you want to hear. She tells you about your soul not knowing any better. Peter, we're recycled. When the original guy moved out, he took his soul with him. When we die, it's all over. That's why even the religious freaks don't care about us. They don't earn any bonus points trying to save souls that don't exist."

Peter sinks back against his pillow. No soul. The words sting. He balls his fists inside the jacket. Not even their god will listen to him.

AFTER THE SHUTTLE touched down at the practice field, Sarge directed Peter and the others off the shuttle and into formation. The tart smell of ever-present ore dust (that's what Sarge called it) carried across the barren, amber and red landscape, mixing with the dry scent of dirt. Heat roiled around him.

Sarge divided them into their subunits. Sting stood between Drake and Peter and listened as Sarge gave them last-minute instructions. Out the corner of his eye, Peter saw Lieutenant D'Angelo and some other officers striding toward the command booth at the edge of the field.

"Any questions?" Sarge asked, his nervous gaze panning the groups.

No one said a word.

"All right then, do me proud. Show Galloway he's got one helluva unit to lead." Sarge turned on his heel and hurried toward the command booth.

Peter sighed. Sarge would turn them over to Galloway. Peter didn't like Galloway. The man didn't care about anything, including himself.

Abruptly, swampland appeared around them. Sting crouched behind some brush, pulling Peter down beside him. Drake fell to his knees, rifle held firmly in front of him.

"Okay, this is how it's gonna be," Sting said, teeth gritted. "We're all gonna watch our grids and the first person to see a bow echo sings out. Got it?"

Peter and Drake nodded.

"Okay." He turned his gaze to Drake and poked him in the chest. "Drake, you'd better not screw this up."

Drake's mouth fell open. "Me? Talk to your sweetheart about fucking up!"

Sting backhanded him. "Leave the kid alone. I won't tell you again."

A thin trickle of blood appeared at the corner of Drake's mouth. He glared at Sting, wiping it away, but he didn't say a word.

"If we do this right," Sting continued, his gaze moving from Peter to Drake, "we'll be on the fast track to the front. Keep your eye on those grids or I'll rip out your lungs."

Peter nodded, then Drake.

"All right, let's do this. We've got a munitions depot to torch."

Sting dropped to his stomach beside the swampy bank, plasma rifle poised. Drake crawled beside him and Peter on flank. He tugged on the grid slung around his neck and studied the surroundings.

"See anything, Pete?"

"No," he answered calmly. "Everything's clear."

"Drake?"

"Nuthin'."

In moments, the haunting, all-too-familiar whine of the sensor grid echoed like a lonely birdcall across the swamp.

"They're in the area," Drake said, his voice steady.

"Watch my six, Pete. We're crossing over. You're on flank."

"Your six?" Peter asked, frowning.

Sting laughed. "My six-o'clock. My back. That clearer?"

Peter nodded and held back as Sting then Drake moved through the foliage into swampy water. He scanned behind them as he followed them deeper into the swamp.

A flock of birds took flight as they passed a fruit tree.

Shriveled, blackened fruit husks littered the nearest bank. The cloying scent of rotten fruit fermenting in the sun startled him. He sniffed again, realizing the sweet smell was different from the Antaran scent. Fermented. Almost like alcohol.

Drake sniffed the air. "Antarans!" he shrieked, whirling around, rifle barrel drifting toward him and Sting's back.

"No!" Peter grabbed the rifle barrel and tried to shove it skyward as Drake squeezed the trigger.

Light blinded him. Something scraped his face and slammed into his shoulder. Skin burned. The world shifted. He was falling.

Sting's voice slithered toward him as if through swamp water. Hands beat against his shoulder and the burning stopped.

Through an orange haze behind his eyelids, Peter saw the outlines of two people hanging over him.

"Pete, answer me! Pete!"

Finally, he opened his eyes. His head throbbed. He grabbed Drake's sleeve.

"Tried to stop you...from shooting Sting. We'd fail the sim." He swallowed, his tongue thick. Fire raged across his shoulder. "It wasn't Antarans." With his left hand, he pointed shakily at the fruit tree. "Fruit. Rotting fruit."

"Dammit, Drake!" Sting punched him in the gut. "That wasn't a holo charge!"

Drake's face looked pale and guilty. "Me and Evans saw the munitions locker open on our way to launch bay. We swapped our holos for real charges." He couldn't look Sting in the eye.

"Congratulations, asshole," came Sting's caustic reply. "You probably just washed out all three of us."

Peter shook his head. "No, just give me...minute. Catch my breath."

He sat up in the swamp water, his body anchored against Sting's chest. Throughout the swamp, he heard plasma blasts and the bleating of sensor grids.

He'd shove back the pain and do his job. He'd run flank while Drake and Sting went for the depot. It lay somewhere ahead.

"We'll tell Temple holos...got mixed...with real charges," said Peter.

Slowly, he struggled to stand, Sting helping him to his feet.

"I'm all right," he muttered, his knees weak, his shoulder raw. "You two go after the depot. I'll run flank and scan for Antarans, cover your back."

He felt Sting's arm slide around his waist and realized he was sinking again.

"Pete, you can't do it, man."

"I have to!" He gritted his teeth against the pain. "If I don't, we all...wash out. I want to live, Sting." He glared at Sting, clutching his sleeve. "I want to live...and you're not takin' that away from me."

A smile curved across Sting's face. "Okay, Pete. We'll run it your way."

He half carried, half dragged Peter through the water and to a solid finger of land that jutted into the darkening swamp. He propped Peter against a fallen tree and bent down.

"Watch our six, Pete. We're going across to our objective." Sting pointed out the strange, stationary bow echo winking on his grid.

Peter nodded, his breath ragged now. Weakly, he raised the muzzle of his rifle and stared across the swamp. The munitions depot lay ahead in the sprawling swampland.

Fighting his dizziness, he panned the horizon with his grid, looking for signs of Antaran presence as he waited for Sting and Drake to cross.

Sting reached into a pouch at his side and armed a mock detonation device.

Peter squinted at the horizon and thought about Diana. How warm her brown eyes were against that purple scarf. How soft and silky her skin felt. Her warm, vanilla scent. That's when he smelled a trace—almost imperceptible—of honey in the air. He turned toward the brush, to where Sting had started to cross.

It was a trap. The Antarans were waiting for them.

He rose up on his knees. "Sting! Drake!"

His guts wrenched as fire snaked down his side and into his legs. He cried out. "Pull back!"

Drawing his rifle to his throbbing shoulder, Peter fired across the swamp. Something screeched.

Sting armed the device and heaved it toward the depot. Then he and Drake stampeded through the brush back toward Peter.

The ground trembled with movement.

As Drake stumbled past, Peter set himself in the mud and waited for the first sign of the patrol—and for the depot to explode.

His whole body burned. Ached.

Biodrones rushed across the swamp, dirt and mud spattering up from the land, cutting a deep furrow toward him.

Peter swung the rifle toward the sound as the ground erupted in front of him.

He froze, bracing himself for the snap of spiked appendages against his flesh. Recovering quickly, he pointed the rifle barrel at the ground and emptied it.

Plasma fire flashed. The air raged with shouts and shrieks and the stench of burnt honey.

Peter's stomach lurched as he locked another charge into the chamber.

A spiked appendage tore up through the mud. He burned it off with a blast of plasma and kept firing.

A massive explosion rocked the swamp as Sting's bomb detonated. Rock and shrapnel rained down on them. Peter buried his face in his arm, shielding it from debris that ripped past.

When the smoke cleared, Peter had taken out the entire Antaran patrol. He collapsed in the brush, his stomach heaving.

Sting slung his rifle over his shoulder and fell down beside Peter, a hand on his neck.

"Pete! Helluva job! You saved our asses back there! Now, let's get you out of here."

Peter nodded.

Gently, Sting put Peter's arm around his neck, and he slid his arm around Peter's waist. Then he rose from the ground, helping Peter out of the swamp.

Ku'Tal's swamps dissolved around them.

Sting paused for a moment then turned his course across the barren field, toward the command booth where the other recombinants were heading. Sergeant Temple rushed toward them.

"Stingley, what the hell happened?"

Sting cast a disgusted look at Drake who shifted his weight nervously. "Someone mixed up the charges, Sarge. Drake here got a live one and Pete got hit."

Sarge peered underneath the torn, burned shoulder of Peter's uniform and made a sour face. "That needs attending. Come with me." He moved with swift steps toward the command booth. After saluting Lieutenant D'Angelo, Sarge recounted Sting's story. With a grunt, D'Angelo nodded and Sarge returned to them.

"D'Angelo okayed having Mitchell looked at. I'll have Diana take him into town and get him patched up. She'll have him back by the time the sim results come out."

He motioned to Diana who rushed across the sandy landscape. When she saw that Peter was hurt, she gasped.

"Peter, what happened?" Her brow wrinkled. "How could this happen? Wasn't this just a sim?"

"It was an accident," said Sarge. "But I need you to take Mitchell into town and get this wound tended."

She gently brushed a finger across the throbbing crease on Peter's forehead.

"Sure, let me get my gear."

Despite his pain, a shiver of excitement crossed his spine. He wanted to shout. He couldn't stop the faint smile spreading across his face. He was about to spend the day with Diana Temple. He turned his gaze to Drake.

"Thanks, Drake," he said with a grin.

Sting laughed. "Looks like you did Pete a favor, Drake."

Drake frowned. "Dammit. If I'd known it woulda gotten me into town, I'd have turned the fucking rifle on myself."

In a few moments, the whir of a skimmer brushed across the landscape, scattering sand. It slid to a gentle stop a short distance from Peter. Diana hopped out, rushing back to them.

"Okay, someone help me get him into the skimmer." She hooked her hands under his arms and he closed his eyes, fighting back a cry of pain. He gritted his teeth until she and Sting had him anchored into the front seat.

"I'll call you later and give you a full report, David," she said. She turned her gaze to Sting. "Thanks for your help, Stingley. I appreciate it."

Sting smiled his most charming smile. "My pleasure, ma'am. I know you'll take good care of my buddy there."

"Count on it." Diana slid back into the skimmer and set off across the sandy landscape toward Civilization.

THE HOSPITAL STOOD on the edge of Civilization, a tall ivory building surrounded by an amber sea of sand. The sun had already slipped low on the horizon. It would be dark in a couple of hours. Diana stepped down the skimmer's speed and stopped at the emergency entrance, a red door on the side of a brick building with two windows.

An orderly met her there with a gurney. Peter lurched at the sight of the orderly, remembering his days at RDC.

"Diana, please don't leave me alone here," he said in a low voice.

Her gaze softened. She reached out and smoothed the hair out of his eyes. "Don't worry, I'll be right here with you. I won't leave unless you tell me to."

The orderly laid him on the gurney and wheeled him inside, Diana at his shoulder, holding his hand. When she could go no farther, she stood outside the pale blue curtain where he could see her the whole time they worked on his shoulder and forehead.

Finally, the doctor packed and dressed the wound and came out to talk with her. She was an older woman, older than Mimi. Thick blonde hair swept back from her face, strands of grey whitening her hairline. Her brown eyes were kind.

"Private Mitchell will be just fine. There's no sign of shock or internal bleeding. Fortunately, the plasma charge wasn't a direct hit to the shoulder. We'll have him ready in a few minutes." She turned toward the next cubicle but paused. "Some of his blood counts are low. He's a little undernourished. You might tell his superiors to start feeding these boys better."

"I will. Thanks for taking care of him."

Nodding, the doctor moved down to the next emergency room cubicle.

In a short while, the orderly wheeled Peter out to the skimmer, Diana hovering behind them. The orderly helped Peter into the seat and Diana whisked him away, toward Civilization.

"Are we going to the shuttle port?" Peter asked, groggy from painkiller.

She smiled. "Not exactly. I'm taking you to my apartment so you can get some decent sleep. Then, I'm going to get a good meal into you."

He straightened up in the seat, his eyes wide. "Are we going into the city?"

She nodded.

He couldn't hold back his grin.

"Haven't you ever been to the city before?"

"Never. Not any city."

His answer seemed to surprise her. She started to speak, but her gaze fell back to the landscape and she had to make a sharp turn. Sand kicked up on all sides as she swerved to miss a rock. She leveled out her course, the skimmer racing across the sand toward the buildings perched on an island of green ahead.

When she turned around, he was laughing, enjoying the ride.

"Are you ready?" she asked, nodding toward the buildings that rose on the horizon.

He was transfixed as he stared at all the different structures. "I've been ready all my life," he answered.

All six months of it.

18

WITH ALL THE recombinants off base and in sims, Jeannette made use of the downtime to file paperwork and analyze data. She had three days of recombinant data to study and tomorrow John Stingley's MRC would be scanned. That data might be very telling.

Carrying a file folder and her datapad, Jeannette stepped through the quiet infirmary and down the hall to the half-moon room. The bitter citrus scent was softer today as she sat down at a table and swiping her fingers across the virtual display floating above the grey desk, she opened the share with her collected data. She worked through the scan values of the thirty or so recombinants, making note of the recombinants that had officially washed out. Four of them were from Peter Mitchell's unit—same MRC batch numbers. Except for that strange trailing O in Peter's batch number. It made no sense. Probably just an old typo no one bothered to correct.

She frowned. Four washouts seemed a high percentage for one unit.

She'd been immersed in the data for over an hour when her datapad chimed. A vid call from Kai.

"What's up, Kai?"

"Got your email, Red," said Kai, his face taut as he stared back at her.

"Good," she replied. "Did you find out anything?"

His expression didn't change. "Why do you need to know this information?"

She sighed. "So, I'll have all the facts. Is there a problem?"

For a few moments, he was quiet. "Just got chewed out for sending you off-base."

He was going to recall her. For days, she'd been afraid that was coming. "I'm sorry, Kai."

He waved her off. "Forget it. I told them if they had a problem with it, they could write me up." He chuckled. "They did. This morning, I was officially reprimanded."

"I never meant for this to happen," said Jeannette. "I'll get my gear together—"

He held up a hand. "Whoa, Red—I said I got reprimanded, not discharged. All I'm asking is that maybe you speed things along, that's all. You're not coming back until you get what you came for, Jeannette."

She hadn't expected him to stand up for her like that. "Thanks, Kai."

There was an uneasy silence between them. Finally, Jeannette broke it.

"So, what did you find out?" she asked. "Anything interesting in the archives?"

He nodded. "I found a case where a batch of recombinants received MRCs with catastrophic programming errors. They found the errors before the recombinants left RDC, so the chips were replaced."

"That's good!" Replacing chips not recombinants. That was promising!

He shook his head. "Not so good. There was another incident where thirty recombinants received MRCs that failed after they'd left RDC for training. All thirty were washed out." He leaned on his right elbow. "It would appear that if errors are found at RDC, the chips are fixed or replaced. Once they leave RDC though—recombinants are washed out if updates can't fix the errors during the nightly data dumps."

Stunned, she sat back in her chair, her gaze tracking toward the data on her screen. If she reported this error (it was a catastrophic error), then Mitchell and the others with the defective batch numbers would wash out. She needed time to consider everything.

"I know that complicates things, Red, but I thought you should know."

"Yes, it does," she said, staring at the recombinant files she'd laid on the table. "That complicates things quite a bit. But I have five more days of data to collect before I can make a recommendation."

"You do what you have to do," he replied. "I'll stall my report until you're finished there."

"Will you consider my evidence before making a recommendation?" Would he just discount her data or refuse to even consider it?

"Why do you think I sent you out there?" he said, an edge in his voice. He looked away. "You were right. I was wrong not to investigate further, Jeannette. I know that now. There, I said it."

Had she heard that right? Kai Drew had just confessed to being wrong. That must have been some reprimand. "I appreciate you sticking your neck out for me."

"Let me know if you need anything else," said Kai and cleared the connection.

What would she do now? If she found this MRC catastrophic malfunction to be the norm in certain recombinant batches, those batches would be destroyed. But final training sims were today with assignments to RDC or Ku'Tal looming. Nothing would be gained by pointing out the defect at this stage. She'd wait to see who passed their training. Maybe the affected recombinants would be able to function despite the odds stacked against them?

Either way, they deserved the chance to try.

19

A NEW WORLD—THE city of Civilization—stretched before Peter. Dusty gold and red landscapes wrapped around jagged, rust-colored hills, darkening as the pale sun slipped over the horizon. The air smelled dry and gritty, gnarled brush clogging the rocky hillsides. Peter noticed that the closer they got to the city, the faster the amber and red colors receded with the sand. The ground hardened, losing its amber sheen until finally, he saw thin green grass ahead. He turned his gaze to Diana.

"It's the most amazing place I've ever seen," he said, unable to contain his grin.

Diana laughed. "It's just some back world planet, Peter."

"It's wonderful," he muttered, mesmerized by how it all changed so quickly. Like the holos on the datapads.

She parked the skimmer in back of her apartment building. People—citizens—milled past, one leading a child, others carrying brown sacks.

His eyes widened. All of them free to go wherever they chose.

A brown-haired child stared at him as she passed. A white-haired man glared at him. Peter couldn't help but smile at them. They were both beautiful! The little girl with her porcelain face and large doe eyes and the old man, his face liked cracked soil, with his decades of life flashing across his skin and hands. Decades!

Supporting him, her hands around his waist, Diana steered Peter into the building and then the lift. She pressed a button with a four on it. When the lift stopped, she eased Peter into the hallway. She pressed her thumb against the lock on door 414 and helped him inside. She turned right and led him into her bedroom. Carefully, she laid him on the bed. Leaning down, she removed his boots and pulled her pastel-striped comforter over him. Pale blues, greens, and purples!

He smiled. It smelled like warm vanilla, like Diana.

"Can I get you some water?"

"If it isn't any trouble."

She waved him away and left, returning in a moment with a glass of cold water. He drained it. His head bobbed and he let it sink into the soft pillows that smelled like her hair. His mind raced, his body tingling. He was lying in Diana Temple's bed.

"Sleep well, Peter."

She sat with him, stroking his hair until he fell asleep.

HE SLEPT SOUNDLY, free from the data-dump headgear for the first time, free to dream about Diana and anything else he dared to imagine. His dreams were intense, but pleasant, all of them centering on Diana and this strange but beautiful new place. When he awoke, he felt better. Charged.

He rose unsteadily from the bed, his wound hurting, and plodded out into the front room. Diana sat on the couch. Suddenly dizzy, he wavered, reaching for the wall. She leaped to her feet and rushed over to him.

"Peter, careful!" She caught him as he stumbled. Her chest was pressed against his, her arms around him.

For a moment, all he could do was stare into her eyes, but he saw his own sense of wonder reflected back in her haunting brown eyes.

"I'm all right," he said, still gazing into her eyes. "Just a little dizzy. I got out of bed too fast."

He looked away. What would she ever see in a recombinant?

Diana helped him over to the couch. She went into the kitchen and returned with two cups.

"I made us some tea." She handed him a cup of cinnamon tea already sweetened with milk and honey.

At first, the scent of honey unsettled him, but he accepted the cup. If Diana drank it, it must be all right. The warm liquid was thick with honey and cinnamon. He drank deeply, the warmth sliding down his throat and into his growling stomach.

"It's very good," he said, setting the cup on the table beside the couch. "So sweet. Thank you."

She sat down beside him and he reached for her hand, giving it an affectionate squeeze. To his surprise, she slid closer and leaned her face against his good shoulder. He let go of her hand, sliding his arm around her shoulders. She felt so good against his body. He was glad that she didn't mind his touch.

He wasn't used to this kind of closeness, but his body reacted to it as if it was familiar.

The scent of her hair was clean and soft as he laid his face against her neck. Her lips found his, brushing across them. He imitated her gesture, his lips pressing against hers. It was a warm breeze across his bare skin.

She sat up and gazed at him. "That was nice, Peter. I've wanted to do that for a long time. Ever since you dropped that mouse into my hands."

"I never thought I'd be this close to you," said Peter. He ran his fingers through her hair, thick and soft against his fingertips.

She closed her eyes a moment. Then she slid off the couch, pointing to a beige stuffed chair near the window. A pair of dark pants and a burgundy shirt lay in the chair.

"Those clothes are some that David left. I don't think he'd mind if you wore them tonight."

Peter frowned. "Why?"

"I'm taking you to dinner, Peter Mitchell. There's someone I'd like you to meet. Some things I'd like to show you."

His heart raced. Eat dinner? In a restaurant? He'd read about restaurants on the nets. How had he fallen into such good fortune?

"The shower's in the back. Take those clothes and use anything you need in the bathroom."

"I will. Thank you for your kindness, Diana." He rose unsteadily and reached for the clothes. "I didn't know how it felt to be treated like a real person until I met Sergeant Temple—and you."

Turning, he hobbled down the hall to the bathroom.

PETER SHOWERED AND DRESSED. The clothes were a little big, but he managed. He moved unsteadily down the hallway and found Diana in the front room. She had changed clothes, wearing a metallic purple skirt that clung to her thighs and hugged her slim hips. Everything about Diana was warm and purple. Her printed silk blouse was airy, white with purple squiggles around her shoulders, occasionally revealing the curve of her breasts. He watched her walk to the door, transfixed by the fluid motion of her legs and the swish of her skirt.

"You're so beautiful," he said in a soft voice.

"Thank you," she said and held out her arm. "Ready?"

He nodded as Diana took hold of his hand and put it on her arm. Then he walked outside with her into the night. For the moment, the pain medicine the doctor gave him shoved his pain into the distance. He just hoped it lasted until this night was over. A night he didn't want to end.

Diana held his arm as she led him toward a sign that read, Civilization transit stop eight.

Night settled a dark blanket over this quiet, little section of Civilization. Through half-closed lids, Peter marveled at the solitude and safety he felt here, the coolness of the air, how the colored lights blurred into streaks of movement and sound, and smelling Diana's warm vanilla scent against the river's loamy smell that hung in the air. Before him, the city unfolded in bright, colorful magic.

Fluid strands of blue, green, red, and purple outlined stair-stepped buildings and pulsed across rooftops. Gold light misted across the transit conduit as a cart approached. His skin tingled.

Diana reached for the summons button that stopped the transit at this stop, but Peter laid his hand on hers.

"Let it go by," he said with a grin.

She stared at him in mild surprise. "Why?"

"I want to feel it surge past as fast as it can go," he said, his voice intense.

"All right," she said, smiling. "We have all night."

He hurried onto the platform, Diana remaining on the stairs.

The ground rumbled with the transit's approach, vibrating up through the platform and into his feet. He felt its power, its speed reverberate through his body. He raised his arms into the air, ignoring the pain, and flung his head back.

Trembling, he laughed when the warm air rushed across his face as the transit roared past and disappeared around a curve, the sound still whispering in his ears.

He wanted to lean out and brush his fingers across the hull, to connect himself with that dramatic surge if only for a moment, to feel his entire body course with energy, and those fleeting seconds of freedom.

The platform stopped vibrating, leaving behind a trace of mist and a cool backwash of wind. He closed his eyes and inhaled the night, spicy with the smell of food and fuel and sweet with Diana's warm vanilla perfume. His knees quivered.

Diana stepped onto the platform, thrusting her arms around his waist as he began to sink.

"Are you all right, Peter?" Her eyes shined with worry.

"I'm so wonderful," he said with a laugh.

She laughed and propped him against her on a bench as they waited for the next shuttle.

"Are you hungry?"

"Starving," he answered.

She grinned when the rush of another cart blurred past the distant colored lights. She pressed the summons button and the transit came to a slow stop at the platform. He gripped her arm and pulled her aboard.

THE RIVER WOUND through the southwestern sector of the city where Diana took him for supper. He read the elegant sign lit in burgundy and blue, flowing letters spelling End of the Line as they approached the door. An older woman with red hair stood just inside the softly lit entryway. She wore a long, tight-fitting silver dress that shimmered with her every graceful movement. Her smile broadened when she saw Peter, but then her mouth fell open.

"Diana...who is this?" She reached out a hand to his face, cupping his chin with a gasp. "Orlando?"

"Mimi, this is Peter Mitchell. Private Peter Mitchell."

Peter stiffened, his hand falling to the back of his neck. He feared someone would scan him at any moment and toss him into the street.

"Stars in heaven," she said with an airy sigh and let go of Peter's chin. "You look so much like my brother. A much younger version, but so much like him." She pulled in a breath and a smile touched her face as she extended her hand to him. "Mimi Constantine, nice to meet you, Peter."

Reluctantly, Peter shook it.

Did she know what he was yet?

"Private Mitchell?" she whispered to Diana. "How'd you managed that?"

"It's a long story. It's legit. He's got clearance to be in Civilization until tomorrow."

"Well, supper's on me then," said Mimi, sweeping her arm in a grand fashion toward the restaurant. "Follow me."

She seated them at her best booth by the window overlooking the river. Mimi lit candles on the table and served glasses of deep red wine. She studied him for several long moments then turned away.

Peter gazed around cautiously. Would someone object to his presence? He couldn't forget how they'd treated him at RDC. He shivered. They'd taught him his place well.

Diana picked up her glass and nodded to him to pick up his, too. He pressed the glass to his lips, smelling an aged scent hinting of spice and fruit. The liquid rolled over his tongue, spreading warmth through his mouth and down his throat, into his belly. It tasted rich and a touch dry, but it calmed him.

He relaxed. No one would bother him tonight.

He savored his plate of sautéed fruits and meats and sipped wine until he felt dizzy. Diana told him stories about what it was like to grow up as a child and the crazy things she and her brother did. Peter gazed at her across the candlelight that flickered gold across her smooth face and animated eyes. His heart felt light, his admiration and attraction to this amazing woman almost overwhelming. She mesmerized him.

Her smile filled him with peace—like the wine—and sparked his spirit. And something more. An ache in his heart. He longed to feel the softness of her skin against his.

When the meal was finished, Mimi brought out two layered chocolate desserts, each stacked high with frothy whipped cream, thick chocolate sauce and a cherry. Peter stared in awe at his dessert while Diana slid her spoon into the peaks of whipped cream and took a big bite.

He reached out to her, laughing. "You've got whipped cream on your nose."

"No, I don't," said Diana.

He dipped his finger into her whipped cream and dotted her nose with a dollop.

"Do now."

Grinning, she reached out and smeared chocolate sauce across his bottom lip. He kissed her fingers lightly as she slowly drew them back, her eyes burning in the candlelight. Wanting him, he realized.

"There, that's much better," she said, wiping the whipped cream away from her chin and nose.

Peter laughed and reached for his napkin. His hand fell against hers. The heat of her skin spiked through him, replaced by a soft aching need when he pulled his hand away.

"It's all right, Peter," she whispered and turned her palm up toward him, inviting him to touch her.

"But I'm a recombinant," he said, looking away, the words feeling like a death sentence.

"Stop that! You're a human being."

Mimi returned to the table, bringing over a chair and seating herself at the end. Peter quickly wiped the chocolate from his chin.

"So, how was dinner?"

"Absolutely incredible," Peter replied. "I've never even imagined food so good."

Mimi laughed. "You're sweet." She reached out to Diana and took her hand, staring at it a moment. "Fuchsia," she said, and let go.

"What?" Diana replied.

"Your aura. You're relaxed and energized." She nodded toward Peter. "He is good for your soul. Brings out your vitality and spirit."

"Recombinants don't have souls," said Peter sadly.

Mimi frowned, turning her gaze to Peter. "Don't ever let them make you believe that, Peter. That's what they want you to think, so they can take away your hope, make you not care if you live or die. You have a soul and I'll prove it." She took his hand in hers for a moment. "Lavender."

"What?" His eyes widened.

"Lavender," Mimi repeated, her voice louder and more certain. "See, you've got a soul and it's reflecting lavender."

"You're just saying that," he said.

Mimi's face pinched. "I'd never lie about something like that."

Peter smiled.

"Lavender is a young person's color, a pale version of purple, someone just beginning to awaken. You haven't lived much."

"Not at all," he muttered.

"You have a lot ahead of you, Peter. Many cycles of joy and sorrow to endure that will intensify this pale lavender to a true purple. Dark and intense and rich. I hope you get to go through all of those cycles. And experience true purple."

He stared at Mimi, not quite understanding.

"Those with true purple auras have experienced a full life. Perhaps I can help you achieve that?"

"I don't understand," he said, shaking his head, glancing at Diana.

"There's a safe house on Ku'Tal. A simple scan will get you in. From there, I can help you escape."

Safe house? Escape?

His body lurched at the word, chills spreading across his body. He was afraid to speak, afraid he hadn't heard her right.

Could she help him get out of the military? Forever?

Diana cast a strange look at Mimi. "Peter and I will talk about that later, Mimi."

"You know where to find me, then," said Mimi. She patted Peter on the hand. "She's good for you, too, Peter. And I see so much of Orlando in your eyes. It's amazing." Then she flitted away, her silvery dress glittering in the candlelight.

"What did she mean by that?" Peter asked. "And who's Orlando?"

Diana leaned forward. "Don't know. We'll talk about that later. Now, there's someplace I'd like to take you. Trust me, okay?"

Peter nodded and reached across the table for her hand. He'd follow Diana Temple anywhere.

She slid her hand into his and they walked out of the restaurant together.

DIANA LED him through the neon-washed streets of Civilization toward the river. He followed as she weaved through brush and trees, emerging onto a secluded riverbank. She sat on the sandy bank and he sank beside her in the cool sand. The smell of fish and moss hung in the air as the river washed gently against the slick rocks on the bank. City lights illuminated the glassy black water with watercolor glimmers undulating in the darkness.

Skimmers buzzed past on the river, leaving blue and purple wakes. Red and green lights rippled across the water from the opposite bank.

"It's...it's—incredible," Peter said in a half whisper. "The lights, the sounds—the smell of it all."

Her brow wrinkled. "A junky, old skimmer?"

"Yeah, the skimmer, the water, the lights—all of it. How they froth blue and purple and then shimmer with the reflection of the city and the moon." He grinned, glancing up into the sky. "Diana, I can see the moon! It's incredible." His words were breathless.

"Something I take for granted." She sighed. "I never knew what any of you would be like." She looked across the river, into the distance. "Recombinants, I mean."

Peter stretched and sat up, a distant ache returning to his shoulder. "There's not much to us."

"That's not true," she said, insistent as she turned toward him. She grabbed his arm, reawakening his need for her. "Don't say that. I've already learned so much from you."

"From me?" His eyes widened.

"Yes, you cherish every moment, every experience, and you find beauty in things I don't even see until you point them out. It's all new to you and I've forgotten it all. It shouldn't matter that your

DNA is recombined from someone else's. That it's xDNA or whatever."

"But it does," he said, unable to hide his pain. "It means I have no say in what happens to me. No choices. They might be dumping a yellow slip into my footlocker right now. All I've ever wanted was to live, Diana. To walk out of that station and live out my life to its natural end, not some last drugged moments in a broken cot at RDC because I don't hunger to kill."

Her hands went to his, squeezing.

"But look at this!" He held out an arm to the night. "I've never seen anything like it. I've never felt anything like this before, Diana." He returned her squeeze, wanting only to touch her. He moved close enough to drink in her warm vanilla scent. "This is what living feels like and I want to see and hear and taste and feel as much as I can."

"Maybe you can?"

Her words unsettled him. For a moment, he held his breath. Afraid she'd said something else.

Diana's gaze fell to the river bank. "The reason I brought you to supper tonight was to talk to Mimi about the safe house." She picked up a handful of sand and let it cascade slowly from her hand. "Mimi runs an underground group that gets recombinants out of UCOE units."

Underground? Was there something so wonderful out there?

A skimmer whispered past the bank, red and blue light glittering in its wake as it left the city behind.

He'd never even considered escape from UCOE.

"How would that even be possible?" He rubbed his neck, almost expecting to feel the ridge of his ID chip. "A simple scan will tell them exactly where I am. What I am."

Even if they found him right now, he didn't care. To spend these few hours with Diana was worth anything.

"Somehow, Mimi gets recombinants out after they reach the front. I don't know all the details, but I'll find out. I promise."

Another skimmer whisked past, its motor humming.

How could anyone do anything to help?

"For now, just think about it. I'll find out more, I promise. I want to help you."

Think about it? He'd dreamed about freedom for months—forever. He leaned back in the sand and watched the lights flicker against the water.

Diana's vanilla cologne wafted toward him, the loamy scent of river rich and alive against the bank, the quiet rush of skimmers a whisper in the night. Her hand was still wrapped in his as he slid closer. He brought her hand to his mouth and brushed his lips across in gentle kisses. Her skin tasted smooth and buttery.

She rolled toward him. Colored lights danced across her face, cheeks glowing, lips parting as she leaned forward. His lips urgently met hers, need aching, blood pumping. He'd never felt this way before.

Legs intertwined, kisses deepened. He slid his hands under her blouse, around the satin curve of her breasts. She moaned softly, her breath quickening as he caressed and explored.

She pressed closer, her hands gliding down his chest, into his shirt, unbuttoning it, pushing it over his shoulders. He wanted to melt into her kneading hands. Her hot breath pulsed against his neck as she sipped his skin.

"God, I want you, Peter Mitchell," Diana whispered in his ear.

"I—I've never...done this before," he said, breathless.

She led his hands as he stroked her stomach and then fumbled under her skirt, exploring lower and deeper—gently rounded hips, silken thighs. He felt satin panties at his fingertips as she helped him slide them down.

Her breath grew thick and husky, body arching as his hand slipped between her legs. He could barely breathe, afraid if he blinked, it would just be a fleeting data transfer image in his head.

Her mouth found his again, chewing and nibbling his lips then his ear, hands moving to his pants, working feverishly to loosen them.

His body was on fire, hard with instinct and need as his pants slid off into the sand.

Her heart pulsed against his chest as he rolled on top of her, his body throbbing as he cupped her breasts. More fumbling as she gently helped guide him inside her.

She gasped as their hips met and he shuddered, rocking in tandem to her rhythm then his, quickly becoming theirs.

Sensations rushed, their uncontrollable rhythm harder and faster, building, surging. She trembled beneath him, breathless as she whispered his name.

His breath heaved as he buried his face against her neck, urgency pounding through him until he pulled in a breath, his body exploding with fire and euphoria, and then gasped. Diana shuddered, a moan escaping her lips.

At last, he collapsed against her, his body slick with sweat. A skimmer whispered past on the horizon.

Wrapping her in his arms, he nuzzled her chin, her buttery vanilla scent warming him again. Shifting onto his side beside her, he stroked her face and hair. She laid her head in the crook of his good arm, her hands against his chest. She held him as they watched the stars appear in the night sky.

THE SUN WAS COMING up when they arrived back at Diana's apartment. He fell into bed beside her and they kissed until sleep claimed them. It was well past noon when his eyes fluttered open.

When he awoke, she wasn't there. For a moment, he felt empty. Did she already regret last night?

He showered quickly, put on a shirt over his boxers, and went out to the kitchen for a glimpse of Diana.

She sat at the table in a short, silky, green robe, her rich, brown hair wet and slicked back. His heart ached and he went to her, putting his arms around her, his heart overflowing with emotion, his eyes stinging.

Did she still want to be near him or did the sight of him repulse her?

She rose from the chair and slid her arms around his waist, kissing him.

"Good morning," she whispered in his ear.

Warmth settled in the pit of his stomach. She still wanted to be with him. All he could do was hold her, not wanting to be far from her, knowing in a short time, he may never see her again. Sighing, he finally let her go and reached for a coffee cup on the counter.

"Peter?"

He carried his coffee into the living room and sat down on the couch. He set the cup on the table.

"Peter?" She sat down beside him. "What is it?"

He bit his lip and pulled her against him, holding on for dear life, sorrow welling in his throat. "I wish I could stay with you," he said. *Forever*, he said in his head.

"Me, too," she replied.

Her kisses burned through him and he smashed his lips against hers, urgently, desperately. He pushed open her robe, his hands sliding across her body.

They made love again.

Toward late afternoon, Sergeant Temple commed. From the couch, Peter heard his insistent voice. Still in her robe, Diana stood by the desk, mobile against her ear. But Sarge's voice carried.

"Dammit, Diana, he's got to be back on base before mess or we're both in deep debris!"

"I know, I know." Her voice had an edge to it. "I said I'd take care of it, didn't I? He'll be there. Good-bye, David."

IT TOOK every shred of Peter's will to put on his UCOE uniform and become a recombinant again.

He couldn't bear the thought of returning to drills and plans and the killing that would come. But he had this memory to keep, one that he'd made, one the headgear and his MRC couldn't take away. It was his and he cradled it. Protected it. He thought about Mimi and the safe house.

Maybe his one chance to live was to go to the front after all?

Teary-eyed, Diana held his hand in the skimmer and through the shuttle port. He couldn't have let go of her anyway. She was silent at liftoff, her eyes still wet when the base came into view.

He sat beside her in the copilot's seat, a hand on her knee. He couldn't bear to leave her. What if he returned to a yellow slip? A one-way trip back to RDC? Even if he got a transport notice, he was leaving her and he couldn't stand it.

He chewed his lip, fighting back the moisture in his eyes as the shuttle shimmied to a stop in the launch bay.

With a deep, heavy sigh, he and Diana exited the shuttle. He felt a coldness against his skin and an aching emptiness inside as she moved away from him to file paperwork. He leaned against the shuttle, closing his eyes and waiting for her return. Finally, she came back.

"God, I'm going to miss you, Peter," she whispered, her voice cracking. "I've never felt this way before." She started to reach for him but caught herself.

He couldn't touch her now. He felt the distance building. "I don't want to leave you," he said. "I'd give anything to have stayed by that river."

"Me too," she said with a sigh. "Take good care of yourself, Peter. I'm going to talk to Mimi again. We'll figure out a way."

He couldn't help himself. He mouthed, "I love you."

For only a moment, she reached out to his hand and squeezed. With her index finger, she drew a heart in his palm and then closed his fingers around it.

"I'm giving you my heart, Peter," she whispered, giving his hand one last squeeze. Then she let go.

It took his last reserve of strength to turn away from her and walk that long, lonely path through the launch bay. His resolve melted when he reached the lift. He turned, but all he caught was the flip of brown hair and flash of purple scarf as she settled back into the shuttle. His chest pinched as he pressed the lift button and descended to the recombinant quarters.

EXHAUSTED AND SHOULDER ACHING, Peter reported in and went straight to mess. He picked at his lukewarm mashed potatoes and synthmeat, aching for Diana's touch and remembering their incredible meal at Mimi's. He'd never thought much about mess food until now. It was bland and tasteless. Finally, he tossed the tray onto the conveyor and wandered back to the bunkroom. He collapsed on his bunk.

Stripped down to his boxers, Sting sat on his bunk with a towel around his shoulders and a mirror propped against his pillow. He held out his bangs and cut them with a pair of dull scissors. "Damn bangs grow like weeds."

Peter sighed and Sting glanced over at him.

"Pete, you're back! How's the shoulder? Sarge was afraid you went AWOL." He brushed loose curls off his face with a snort. "As if you'd have gotten far."

Peter didn't respond, his gaze lost in the memories of last night.

"What's the matter, Pete?"

Peter rubbed a hand across his neck. "Why am I still in this place?"

"Because we don't have a choice," said Sting, his voice curt. "We sure as hell can't just walk out."

Peter snorted. "One scan would flash *property of UCOE* all over their grids. Within minutes, we'd be shipped off to RDC."

"So, they could take us apart protein by protein first—to figure out why we stepped around our conditioning."

"And then wash us out. I hate the service," Peter said, his voice thin and his eyes watery. He missed Diana and he missed Civilization. He missed being alive, now that he'd tasted life. His chest ached. "Do you know what's out there, Sting? Do you have any idea what we're missing?"

Sting shook his head. Of course, he didn't know. How could he? He'd spent his eighteen months of life here and at the front. How could he know what it felt like to live? None of them really knew, but Peter had felt the moments. And he craved more.

So much more.

Peter rose from his bunk and plopped down beside Sting. Sting set down the scissors. Peter's voice fell to a whisper.

"Man, Diana took me to her apartment...and into the city. Just her and me."

"You went into the city?" Sting's eyes widened. "Weren't you scanned?"

Peter grinned. "No! See, as long as I was with Diana—and not wearing my uniform—everyone treated me like a real citizen. Like a real citizen! I ate at their tables and drank their wine."

"That must have been something," Sting said in a soft voice, almost sounding envious.

"Afterward, we went down to the river and watched the skimmers rush by. The colored lights reflecting off the water were the most beautiful things I'd ever seen, Sting."

"Wish I could have been there with you."

Peter poked him with his elbow. "If we survive this tour, I'll take you there myself. We'll eat and drink and watch the skimmers until sunrise."

"Deal, man," said Sting, smacking him on the back.

"But, Sting, there's more." He lowered his voice. "Diana and I made love last night by the river." His body began to shake, the ache burning his eyes. "And now, she's all I can think about. I need her, Sting. I need her."

His eyes welled with moisture, the ache and emptiness unbearable. His shoulders heaved and he sucked back the pain. Sting put an arm around his shoulders.

"Hang in there, Pete. You'll get through it. First night's the hardest."

"How do you know?"

Sting smiled a crooked smile. "I spent a year at the front. There were women who slipped into camp. They made me feel good for a while, made the death and misery a little more bearable." His eyes turned wistful. "You ache all over after they leave you, because you miss that closeness, even if you're paying for it."

"Paying for it?"

"Yeah, with cigarettes or drugs, even food smuggled out of mess—something to ease the fear. And for that short time, they did care. I loved every one of them and I missed each one after she left. We don't get much gentleness in our lives. I knew it was fleeting, but if that's all I could have, I still wanted it."

"Lights out in five minutes," shouted the duty officer as he stuck his head into the bunkroom. "Stingley, Mitchell, if you're not in transfer headgear in three minutes, I'm putting you on report."

"Yes sir," they answered in sharp voices. Sting reached for his headgear, but Peter grabbed his arm.

"Remember what I told you, Sting. There's a whole life out there, so much more than the crap they're filling our heads with." Peter took hold of Sting's headgear and pulled it toward him. "They want us to believe we've already lived these things."

Sting nodded. "Digitals are sorry attempts at memories. They'll never let us have those things, but they'll sure as hell let us watch them."

"If I don't wash out and make it through Ku'Tal, I'm gettin' out of this place for good."

"What?" Sting's face paled. "But the ID chip! How can you—"

"Lights out in one minute! Mitchell, this is your last warning!"

Quickly, Sting took back his headgear, thrust it on, and fastened the chinstrap.

"There's a safe house on Ku'Tal," said Peter, his words fast and furious. "One scan and we're in. They'll get us away from the service for good, Sting. Forever. Think about that."

Peter stumbled over to his bunk, jerked his headgear off the wall, and shoved it onto his head. Just as he reached for the chin strap, the lights flicked off.

"Remember what I said, Sting," he called. "Forever."

That word hung at the edge of Peter's thoughts as flashes of a summer vacation to the Caribbean Sea he'd never taken oozed through his tired brain. Buildings washed in pastel shades hung at the edge of a glimmering white beach and brilliant blue surf. That woman with black hair lay beside him on the beach in a blue swimsuit. The data dump would soon follow.

As he felt himself sinking into sleep, he transposed the woman into Diana. He held her in his arms, bright sun blotting to night, surf falling away to the hush of river and whisper of skimmers. Pastels turned to vivid lights and swimsuits fell away.

As he made love to Diana, he thought about how it would feel to escape with her—and disappear. Forever.

20

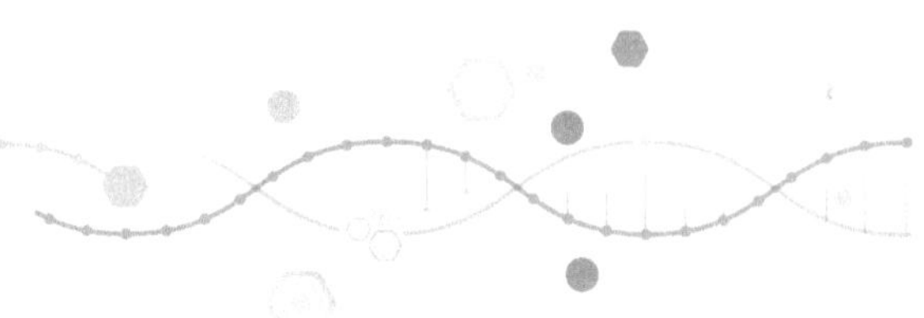

THE NEXT MORNING, Peter showered, dressed, and hustled off to his morning courses and drills. Throughout the day, anxiety trembled in his stomach, and dread hung cold and tight against his shoulders. By nightfall, he'd return to his bunk and open his footlocker. To find either a transport notice or a reclamation order.

There was nothing in between.

He hurried down the hallways and tried to keep his mind off his footlocker and Diana—but failed. He felt sick. What if he never saw her again? He thought of the night at the river and how beautiful her body had been, the sweet, playful sound of her voice, the warm brown eyes seeing past his recombinant status.

The recombinant level was unusually quiet, the impending decisions weighing on everyone. Galloway seemed to have vanished. Recombinants passed each other in silence. No fights broke out. Not even a whispered joke or fidgeting during classes. Everyone seemed preoccupied with what was to come.

Even Sergeant Temple was distant. Peter passed him on the way to mess. Something seemed to be bothering Sarge on a deeper level than the fate of his unit. It permeated his downcast eyes and slow steps. Did Sarge know about his night with Diana?

Peter's last course of the day took him to Sergeant Temple's classroom. Temple's tone was soft, far away, and his lecture on tracking wandered. Finally, distracted, he released them, but Peter lingered as the others filed out.

"Sarge?"

Temple's eyes were bloodshot, eyelids drooping. There was a sort of quiet despair Peter had never seen in this man's usually concerned, caring expression.

"What is it, Private Mitchell?"

"You seem—distraught. Is there something I can do to help?"

Temple's smile erupted into a quick laugh. "Mitchell, you're unique. With reclamation orders pending or a trip to the front, you want to help me." He looked down at his feet and then his gaze met Peter's. "I got the transport roster this morning." His voice was tight.

Peter stiffened, a chill rushing through him.

Sarge sucked in a breath. "*My* name was on it."

Peter gaped. "What? But you're a training sergeant! We were told Galloway would lead us at the front. Of course, we'd all rather have you, Sarge, but you weren't supposed to go."

Temple rubbed a hand across his face. Terror hovered in the Sarge's eyes and Peter felt sorry for the man.

"I *was* a training sergeant, but I've been promoted to field sergeant. Galloway got drunk last night and fell down four flights of stairs. Broke both legs." He gritted his teeth. "I'd like to break his neck."

Peter knew it was considered improper conduct to touch a superior, but he understood this man's fear. It was a cold, sharp image of his own. Peter reached out and squeezed Temple's shoulder. Peter knew his own best hope lay in going to the front, but he had to survive long enough to escape.

"It'll be okay, Sarge. You've shown all of us respect and concern. We'll—watch your six. We'll get you through."

Sadly, Temple shook his head. "We have no choice but to do our best. Do our jobs." He sighed. "I've got my whole life ahead of me, I—"

Peter wilted.

"God, I'm so sorry, Mitchell."

"It's okay. I understand that fear better than anyone, Sarge, but I have the advantage."

Temple frowned. "Advantage?"

"I achieved consciousness with the knowledge that I had, at most, a year to live. So, I live day by day. Citizens live like they'll be here forever. We never know when we'll wash out or die at the front."

Or be lucky enough to reach a safe house.

"That must be a terrible thing to live with."

Peter shrugged. "One day, I hope to say the words, I've got my whole life ahead of me, and mean them." He glanced at the wall clock. Evening mess would start soon. "I've got to go, Sarge. It's nearly time for mess."

Temple nodded as Peter moved toward the door, but Sarge called out his name. Peter turned.

"Sarge?"

"For what it's worth," he said in a low voice, "I don't believe in the Recombinant Defense Program."

Peter smiled. "Neither do I, Sarge," he said and hurried into the hallway.

THAT EVENING, Peter and the others returned from mess, knowing the notifications had been delivered. He moved to his footlocker and stood in front of it, hands quivering when he laid them against the cold metal.

What lay before him? A quick death at RDC or a chance to escape the military at the front?

He heard the snap and creak of footlockers being flung open. Someone gasped, another cried out. Nearby, someone cheered.

He glanced over. Sting was dancing in the aisle, waving his transport notice in the air. Dropping down on his knees, Peter slowly raised the lid.

Lying on his dress uniform was a white sheet of paper. White!

Excitement shivered through him. He leaped up from the floor. He was going to the front.

"Pete!" Sting called from across the room. "How'd you do?"

He hesitated then grinned as he held up a white sheet of paper. Sting whooped and rushed over. He pounded Peter on the back.

"Congratulations, man! Now, we can kick Antaran ass together in Ku'Tal!"

A thousand thoughts flooded Peter's head. Live ammunition, real spiked appendages to shred him, soldiers dying. So many ways to die out there and only one chance to live.

He let out a whoop. It was the best odds he'd had in his whole life.

21

DIANA RETURNED to End of the Line on a mission. If Mimi got recombinants out of UCOE Armed Forces, then Diana would do everything in her power to get Mimi to help Peter. Everything.

The day was oppressively hot. Sunlight scorched walkways and baked shuttle platforms. Diana, wearing shorts, green tank top, sandals and change purse, kicked up amber sand as she ran to the shuttle stop. She stood on the platform, a handful of people around her. The stench of sweat and sunscreen was cloying as the platform vibrated from the approaching shuttle. She thought of Peter standing here with his arms outstretched and head tilted back, laughing as the shuttle raced past the platform. He overflowed with childlike wonder and excitement, intrigued by everything. He didn't hide it. And she loved him for that.

She glanced up at the schedule grid flashing Shuttle Port in green above the platform. The one into Civilization would arrive in a few minutes.

All this time, she'd been running from her parents' wishes and David's ideas of how she should live her life. She'd spent so much time repelling their control that she'd stopped living her own life. There were moments of living. Sparks. The scent of peppermint tea simmering on a stormy Saturday morning, glitter of sunlight on a summer afternoon, the brush of lips in a quiet kiss. She sighed. The heat of Peter's body against hers.

The platform thrummed, the shuttle rushing closer. She moved toward the edge of the platform.

Peter understood these little experiences, these sparks, all of them shades of purple. It was time that she did, too.

Diana thrust her arms into the air and tilted her head back, feeling the wind and the rush as the shuttle surged past. Wind whipped her hair into ringlets and swept over her body. Her skin tingled as she laughed. She felt alive with the movement!

Finally, the track stopped vibrating and Diana drew her arms to her side. Her blood pounded. She ran a hand through her wind-tangled hair and stepped back as the next shuttle, the shuttle into Civilization approached. When it stopped, she piled behind the others and watched the landscape until the shuttle lurched to a stop near Mimi's restaurant.

She hurried across the street and into the dimly lit foyer. No one stood at the front desk, so she walked into the dining room, calling for Mimi. The lights were out, but intense sunlight filled the room. The tables were bare. A pile of burgundy napkins and white tablecloths, pressed and folded, stood tall and stiff on a center table. Trays of silverware were scattered about the room. In the far room, a vacuum cleaner whined as it whisked across carpet.

"Mimi! Mimi, it's Diana!"

Dressed in black leggings and a red tunic, Mimi bustled out of the kitchen, green dish gloves on each hand. Her hair was slightly tousled, her makeup light. Mimi still looked ten years younger than her age.

"Diana, what's the matter? Is the place on fire? I could hear you in the dish room."

Abruptly, the vacuum cleaner cut out, drenching the room in sudden, unnatural silence. Diana shifted her weight.

"I'm sorry," she said, leaning against a table. "I was afraid you weren't here."

Mimi propped a gloved hand on her hip. "Now, where else would I be? I eat, sleep, and breathe this place." She snapped off one glove and motioned Diana toward a chair. "Sit down. I'll make us some tea and we can have a chat."

Diana grabbed her arm. "Mimi, please. I don't want to have tea and chat."

"No tea?" she gasped, a hand to her chest. "This is serious." Mimi, her eyes wide, slid a chair out and sat down. She propped her elbows on the table and stared at Diana.

Diana sat down beside her. "It's about Peter." She lowered her gaze to the table, but Mimi pressed her chin up, the rubber glove wet against her chin.

"What about Peter? Oh, no." She pulled back, surprised. "You've fallen hard for him, haven't you?"

"I couldn't help it," said Diana. "I tried not to." She bit her lip. "I didn't even expect to talk to the recombinants, but Peter was so nice, so gentle—so genuine. I found myself intrigued. And last night...Peter reminded me what it felt like to be alive. I'm young, but Mimi, I'd forgotten." She sighed and leaned back in the chair. "I've been running from my parents, trying to show David and my family that I could take care of myself, but I forgot to live my life."

"I'm glad you figured that out so young, Diana, but what's that got to do with Peter?" Mimi slipped off the other glove and laid it on the table.

Diana gripped Mimi's arm. "I want Peter to have a chance, too. A chance to live his life."

"I know that look, girl. You want me to get Peter out of Ku'Tal?"

Diana grinned. "Will you do it?"

"I don't know, Diana," she said, rising from the chair. "It's not that simple. These things take time to set up. His unit's shipping out at the end of the week."

"What?" Her heart plummeted. "That's too soon!"

"I can't make any promises. We only go in when a unit pulls out and strands soldiers. It takes a long time and lots of resources to get even one recombinant out. And lots of personnel. There are ID chips to remove, new identities to create."

Diana frowned. She remembered Mimi mentioning them. "What about the ID chips?"

"That's how UCOE keeps track of their recombinants. Those chips have to be removed quickly by trained personnel."

"Will you at least try to get Peter out?"

Mimi hesitated.

"Please, Mimi. I'll do whatever you ask."

"Please understand I can't make any promises. It might take his entire tour to get him out—if it's even possible. By then, he could already be dead. This isn't an exact science here."

Diana nodded, trying to shove Mimi's statement away from her thoughts. She couldn't think about that right now.

"Whatever it takes, Mimi. I haven't got much money, but I'll pay you a portion of my UCOE check every week and work here for free in the evenings—"

Mimi waved her away. "I'm not in this for money. It's true, I've got sizable operating expenses, but it's way too early to talk about funding."

"Will you do it?"

"I confess, I was startled by Peter's appearance. He's the spitting image of my younger brother, Orlando. Back when he was that age." Mimi sighed. "All I can promise is that I'll try."

Relieved, Diana sank back in the chair. It was Peter's only chance to live. She just hoped that it hadn't come too late.

THAT NIGHT, Diana, in her green silky robe, sat on the couch with a mystery novel on her datapad. The window was open, letting in the night. The air smelled cool and clean, like it had been washed with rain. In the distance, shuttles whooshed past. A handful of people passed under her window, chattering brightly, laughter pealing, feet shuffling.

She'd skimmed the first chapter when her datapad chimed with a video call. She slid the book aside on the screen and answered the video call. David's tired face peered back at her, his smile weak and his eyes glassy.

"David?"

"Hi, sis," he said, his voice slurred. He smiled grimly.

"David, are you all right?"

David rarely drank. And she'd *never* seen him drunk before.

"I've got...some news to tell you. I haven't even told Mother and Dad yet."

Her heart wrenched at the desperate sound of his voice as he tried to maintain his composure.

"What is it, David? What's the matter?"

"I'm shippin' out—Friday," he said, forcing a smile, his face ghostly white. "Oh, God, Diana...I'm going to the front."

A sharp chill raked her spine. "No! How, David? You're a trainer!"

His image wavered for a moment as he pressed a bottle to his lips. "Damned Galloway! He was supposed to be their field sergeant. In a drunken stupor, he fell down the stairs, broke both legs. D'Angelo promoted me to field sergeant." He looked away for a moment, his eyes rimmed red. "I've filed a will. I want you to have my skimmer and pension. It's all I own."

She turned away. "David, don't! Don't you dare talk like that." Her eyes brimmed with tears as she turned back, fury in her voice. "All my life, you've taken care of me. You've advised me, directed me —even prodded me to take charge of my life. Now, in your first real moment of crisis, you just give up. Was all of that a load of crap?"

"I don't know anymore, Diana. I don't know." He collapsed into a chair, his head in his hands.

"You listen to me, David Temple, and you listen good." She fought to keep her voice from cracking. "You are going to survive this tour because you're smart. You aren't gonna give up either. You're gonna lead those recombinants through those battles and keep them alive. They depend on you. They need you. Especially Peter. You go out there and you take care of those boys. Do you hear me?"

"Mitchell won't survive the front without me to help him," said David, his expression changing to worry. "He's afraid to kill. They don't know that, but it's there subtly in his scores. Maybe I should have acknowledged that fact to the brass, but I didn't. I couldn't."

Diana bit her lip, fighting to hold back her tears. "That's right, David, he needs you and I need you to still be there for me when you come back. You mean so much to me. You were always there when Mother and Dad weren't. I still need you around, okay?"

David smiled. "Thanks, sis. I always knew you got all the brains in this family. Do me proud, okay? Show Mother and Dad who you are, not who they want you to be. No matter what."

"When do you leave again?" she asked, knowing it was much too soon.

"The whole unit ships out Friday."

"And Peter," she mumbled with a sigh.

"What's with you and Mitchell, sis?"

"He means very much to me," she answered. "I wish..." Her voice trailed off. Why did he have to be a recombinant? No. She clenched her fists. Why did they get treated this way?

"I can see it by the look on your face. What happened that night Mitchell got hurt?"

She smiled.

"You're not going to tell me, are you?"

She shook her head. "Meet me for lunch tomorrow?"

He nodded. "Good night, Diana."

"You, too, David."

She swallowed her heart when the connection cut out. The room went silent, David's voice no longer reverberating through it. She hugged herself, fearing that silence, and curled up on the couch. She clutched a pillow to her chest, the room suddenly stuffy, the walls closing in on her.

What if she never heard David's voice again? What if he never came back?

22

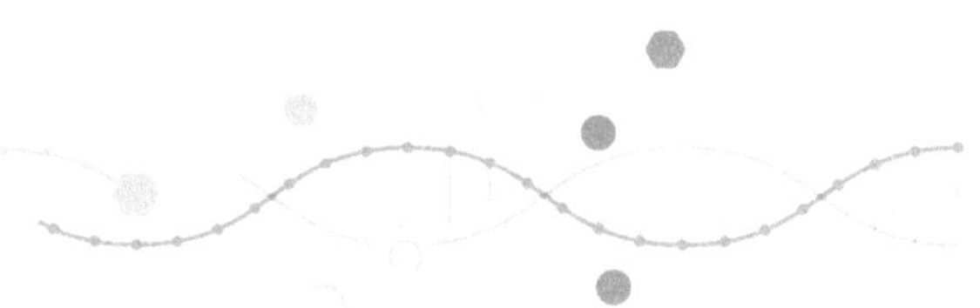

PETER WAVERED on the edge of last-minute lectures, preparation courses, and final instructions. His thoughts drifted away from the front and the training base to Diana Temple and what might have been. Even now, his chest ached with emptiness.

He thought about Mimi and how she insisted he had a soul. How could Mimi see his soul—if he had one—its color or what lay ahead for him?

He wanted desperately to believe that something beyond this confusion awaited him. Was a recombinant's soul worth much—purple or otherwise? He'd read things in the library about psychics, but the articles never mentioned auras. He'd even read about the human soul and how some believed it traveled to a better place after death. At first, Peter had been excited by those words, but that excitement faded quickly when he realized he didn't know enough about this world to judge another. Besides, he'd still be a recombinant soul among citizen souls. How could that be any better?

When he finished his last class of the day, Peter filed toward the hallway. Sting bounded into the hallway ahead of him, his expression hungry and his steps anxious. He nearly ran over Sergeant Temple who stood outside the classroom.

"Sorry, Sarge," Sting called and raced through the hallway toward mess.

Peter eyed Temple strangely, noting the quieter demeanor and solemn expression. Sergeant Temple had curled up inside himself, the fear imprisoning him. Peter understood that crippling fear and for the first time, he looked forward to the nightly data dumps. The gentle whir and the flood of images distracted his mind from the black chill that coiled inside him. Peter noticed the god symbol around Sarge's neck now, glittering silver and gold. It hadn't been there until today. Temple held a long white envelope in his hand.

"Mitchell, you got a minute?"

"Sure, Sarge. What can I do for you?"

"I need you to deliver a report for me."

"I'd be happy to, Sarge."

Temple handed him the envelope.

"Where do I take it?"

Temple pointed to a door at the end of the hallway. "The testing center."

Peter started down the hallway but turned back to him. "Sarge, who do I give it to?"

"To whoever's minding the TC. Carry on, private." Temple turned away, hands in his pockets, and moved toward the lift.

The light dimmed as Peter approached the end of the hallway. Etched in black letters on the door were the words, Testing Center. Peter cautiously turned the door handle and slipped inside. He glanced around for a CO then stopped in mid-stride.

Diana stood in the glare of classroom lights. His heart pounded and he sucked in a quick breath. She wore that shiny purple skirt and a gauzy white blouse, a small black purse on her shoulder. Her purple scarf, tied snugly, held back her waves of rich brown hair. She turned. Her face looked drawn, tears clinging to her lids, but her eyes widened when she saw him.

"Peter!"

"Diana?"

He rushed toward her, wrapping her in his arms. Her warmth made his chest stop aching. He ran his hands down her arms, through her hair, longing for her touch. She slid her hands into his as he leaned down and kissed her urgently, afraid that if he held her too tightly, she'd disappear. She let go of his hands and slipped hers around his waist, pressing her lips hard against his mouth.

They held each other for some time until finally Peter pulled back, remembering the report Temple had sent him to deliver. He stared down at the envelope in his hand and opened it. Inside was a plain white piece of paper. He held it up to her.

Why had Sarge done this for him?

"Sergeant Temple sent me to deliver this report," he said.

She grinned. "I love you, David."

"I've missed you so much, Diana." Peter held her hands again and sat down with her on the table.

"You're shipping out tomorrow," she said, the words hanging as she spoke.

He nodded.

She rubbed her hand against his arm. "You look so tired, Peter."

"I am tired. Training...and thoughts of what's to come have taken a lot out of me."

"I thought your genetic makeup eased some of that."

"Not mine," he muttered. "It's all stressful to me, the killing, the plasma fire, trying to stay alive." He shivered and she pulled him close. Her vanilla scent wrapped around him in warm waves.

"The others," she said, "they enjoy the fighting."

He pulled away again. "If we don't fight, we'll die."

He'd met so many people during his eight months of life. Only a few seemed real to him—Sergeant Temple, Sting...Diana. Diana cared and even though UCOE tried to suppress those emotions in recombinants, Sting cared, too. But Sting hadn't seen what Peter had, hadn't experienced skimmers and a wine-filled sunset with a woman like Diana. Peter's chest ached at the thought of what lay beyond the fighting. He didn't want to risk losing that feeling forever.

He gazed into Diana's eyes, feeling groggy and confused like the morning after a data dump. The images of people he would never touch or know clung to his memory—the woman in the blue dress—but they weren't real. Not like Diana. Knowing her made him feel alive. He wanted more than just mental snapshots.

"What are you feeling, Peter?" Diana asked, her voice soft.

"Sad," he answered. "I know what I'm missing now. I know what I could have had." He reached out and took hold of her hand.

She laid her other hand on top of his and squeezed.

He'd miss so many things. Parents. Grandparents. The wind against his face. Colored lights flickering on the river. A birthday. He wanted more than the one year. He didn't even know who was winning this war, why they were fighting the Antarans, or why he should fight them. As if he had a choice.

"I talked to Mimi this morning."

His heart raced. Would she help him escape?

Diana reached into her purse and retrieved a small device no larger than a coin. "She gave me this. It will lead you to a safe house on Ku'Tal. Mimi says it won't home in on anything until they get things set up. That will take a little time. When you get a signal, you'll have a safe place to go. The device will lead you out and the safe house will take it from there."

Biting her lip, she let go of his hand and moved toward the door.

He walked toward her, wanting to fill his mind with her image, the silky feel of her skin, her warm, heady scent. "I've thought about all the things I'll miss, but there's one I'll miss the most."

She turned toward him, eyes brimming with tears. "What is it?"

"Not having enough memories of loving you."

A tear slipped down her face. "Take good care, Peter," she said, her voice cracking. She reached up to her hair and untied her scarf. "My grandmother gave me this scarf. It was hers as a little girl and she lived a long life." She thrust it at him. "Long life, Peter."

"Diana, no!" He waved it away. "A gift from a third-generation citizen must be priceless."

She pressed the scarf into his hands, the tears running down her flushed cheeks. "Then you can give it back to me someday. Come home safe, Peter. I love you."

Before he could respond, she rushed out of the room.

All he could do was stand there, the silk scarf as soft as her hands against his skin, and remember their one night and one day together. And that she loved him. He smiled. It was enough.

THE NEXT MORNING, Sergeant Temple assembled Peter's unit early. Peter had packed his field pack last night, careful to tuck the device Diana had given him deep into the pack. He dressed solemnly, ignoring Sting, Drake, and the other recombinants slinging pillows at each other. He pressed Diana's scarf to his face, her vanilla scent calming him, and then tucked it inside his shirt, against his heart. He would bring this back to her. He put on his helmet and flak jacket, awaiting orders.

D'Angelo stomped through the corridor, bellowing orders, calling out recombinants unit by unit until he was shouting outside Peter's bunkroom. His order was quickly followed by Sergeant Temple's clear, anxious voice. Peter filed out with the others, falling into step with a wave of units moving toward the stairs.

He marched up the stairs, hitting the flight line where four hulking, scarred transports refueled. D'Angelo shouted an order and Sergeant Temple broke off Peter's unit from the rest. Sarge led them to the last transport and motioned them inside. Peter clamored into the dark hull, groping for handholds and finally a rickety seat. He collapsed into it and grabbed hold of the restraint harness. His stomach burned with apprehension, his breath heavy. The other recombinants joked and shoved each other through the darkness until Peter heard a familiar voice beside him.

"You okay, Pete?" Sting asked.

"Sure," he answered.

He felt Sting's hand pat his leg. "This part scared the shit out of me the first time. It gets hairier, but once you finally settle into your shelter, you'll feel better."

Peter swallowed back bile as the huge doors clanged shut. He gripped the restraint harness, pulling it down around him. In a few moments of grinding and rattling, the transport shimmied toward a launch tube. The faint amber glow of lights flickered on above them, allowing Peter enough light to see Sting beside him, curly blond hair peeking out from his helmet. Sting thrust his restraint harness on and leaned against the hull.

Engines roared. The transport shook and lurched forward, driving Peter against the hard seat. His stomach twisted into a knot and he felt the safety of the base leave them as the craft pitched out into space. Leaving behind the only life he'd ever known. And the only woman he'd ever loved.

IN THE REFITTED cargo ship's dim lighting, Peter glanced at Sting. Sting's face was pale beneath his grey-green helmet and his eyelids drooped over his green eyes. Sting clutched his restraint harness and stared past the other recombinants. For the first time since Peter had known him, Sting looked scared. There were a million ways to die before nightfall on Ku'Tal.

"You okay?" Peter asked.

Sting forced on that charming, devious smile, but it faded quickly. He nodded. "I hate sitting back here deaf and blind, not knowing what we're flying into. I've only heard about this drop point on Ku'Tal. The line's moved a thousand times since I was at the front. I'll be okay once we've made camp." He cast a quick glance at the other recombinants. "I hear my last tour's a training sim compared to this one."

Peter sighed. "Yeah, I heard that, too—this morning. D'Angelo mumbled it to one of the other unit sergeants." He looked away, gritting his teeth. "Dammit, they said we had a year! I want that time, Sting. All of it. Every minute, every second."

Every memory.

Sting's hand gripped his arm. "I'll watch your six and you watch mine."

Peter leaned toward him and spoke in a low whisper. "If we ever break through far enough to reach that munitions depot—and blow it sky high—we're free. There's a safe house on Ku'Tal. I can get us there. Are you with me?"

Wide-eyed, Sting nodded. "What? Pete...of course, I'm with you."

A calm seemed to settle over Sting. He sat back against the seat and closed his eyes.

Still feeling the fear deep in his stomach, Peter gazed into the darkness, wondering what lay beyond the drop point.

COLD RAIN SMELLING of raw sewage scoured the drop point. The transport touched down in a clearing and in an instant, the restraint harnesses snapped up. The main door shrieked open and Sergeant Temple was outside in the rain shouting orders.

Peter adjusted his field pack and pulled a plasma rifle from the weapons locker near the door. He slung the rifle over his shoulder and stumbled out into the rain. The landscape was a blur of green and grey as he fell in step with dozens of recombinants in ankle-deep mud. Sergeant Temple moved them to the cargo hold of a fifth transport. The bay door lifted grudgingly, revealing crates of equipment and supplies. Peter joined the line of recombinants handing crates off the transport. They stacked crate after crate on the soupy ground, well away from the ship, until the bay was empty.

Abruptly, the transport closed its rear doors.

Peter felt the sickness in his stomach swell as the transport rushed over the treetops and disappeared like a shooting star on the horizon.

"All right, let's make camp. Move it!" D'Angelo.

Peter and Sting worked with the other recombinants to construct several hazard shelters that emerged as the base camp. Peter's unit was one of seven units at the camp. The other units put together shelters until each unit had its own cluster within the camp. The CO, Major Welker, made a quick tour of the base camp with Lieutenant D'Angelo and three other officers that Peter didn't recognize. Welker was tall and quiet, a hard edge to his tanned features and thin, close-cropped black hair.

Peter's uniform hung in heavy, wet folds against his body, the biodrone of cold rain steady in his ears. He shivered, glancing up at the indigo sky. Over a rise to the west lay Ku'Tal's swampy hell. Somewhere in there, hidden among a maze of explosions, patrols, and bioshielded jammers was the munitions depot. It would take months to reach it—if they ever got to it at all.

All night, rain tore across the shelters. Wind howled and strange cries blurred with the pounding rain. Peter huddled in his bedroll, reviewing the Ku'Tal maps on his datapad. A small, ion lamp sat by his bedroll, casting a touch of warmth through the crude shelter he shared with his unit. So much uncharted land. Would they even make it to the Antaran depot?

With a sigh, he rubbed his eyes and dropped the datapad into his duffle bag. Finally, he slipped Diana's scarf out of his shirt and held it. In the rich purple, he remembered her expressive eyes that had displayed so much concern, so much hurt for his situation. Over him. A recycled soldier.

Sting, in boxers and undershirt, sprawled on his back and read something on his datapad. Drake's bedroll was near the shelter entrance and Peter couldn't have been happier. Drake sat on his bedroll, cleaning his rifle.

All through the shelter, ion lights burned with pale gold light.

Someone coughed. Bedrolls rustled. Two recombinants talked in low voices.

Everyone seemed subdued, but making the best of the situation. Three recombinants sat on one of the bedrolls and quietly played poker. Sting looked up at Peter for a moment and grinned.

"See, I told you everything would feel all right once we got camp set up."

Peter returned his smile. The bunkroom back at the station was the longest place he'd stayed. It felt more secure than RDC or this camp. But none of them were anything like Diana's apartment. Knowing better, he slipped out the homing device and checked for activity. Nothing.

He put the device back into his pack and crawled deeper into his bedroll. As cold rain pounded against the hazard shelter and wind moaned through the camp, he longed for the data dump headgear. He'd rather be anywhere than Ku'Tal tonight—even if it was only imaginary. He turned onto his side, holding Diana's scarf against his cheek, and closed his eyes.

THE NEXT MORNING, Peter's entire unit went on patrol. The rain had lightened to a fine mist that coated his face and hands, making his rifle slick and hard to handle. He shifted his helmet out of his eyes. Thick clouds blotted out the dark blue sky as they moved over strange hills and neared the lowlands. The air smelled cool.

Sting walked with slow steps in front of him, the unit moving in a combat V. Drake led the way, a faint hungry smile on his taut face. Following behind Drake, Temple watched the horizon with a wary gaze. His back was ramrod straight, but his strides were confident and he held his rifle low, with authority. Peter gripped his own rifle like he carried a life preserver. He knew the fear that Temple carried, but Sarge had steeled it behind his inner resolve. Another reason why he admired Sergeant Temple.

When Peter crested the top of yet another hill, murky swampland crouched below. Creatures whistled and chirred around them, the rustle of undergrowth making Peter's hair stand on end. He moved deliberately, hands clamped around his plasma rifle as he followed Sting toward the swamp.

Already, the air smelled dank and loamy. Crisp. He tried not to make a sound, but his boots smacked against the muddy ground as the unit approached the swamp.

Brush crackled. Something screeched.

Peter whirled, swallowing back fear. He didn't want to die. Especially out here. He gazed fearfully at Sting who shook his head, a stern look on his face.

Sting mouthed the words *stay calm* and Peter nodded.

"Get out your grids," Temple ordered. "We have no idea what's over the next rise, so stay alert."

Peter pulled his grid from his pack. The muddy ground made movement difficult, slowing the unit into a tangle of soldiers. As he and the others moved forward, several areas on the grid map wavered.

Cascade mines exploded around them, projectiles slicing. Plasma fire raked the mud, field packs littering the ground.

Screams echoed across the hillside, recombinants flailing, ground exploding until an eternity passed and movement ceased.

Acrid smoke hung in the air in greasy black billows. Flesh fragments and blood littered the ground. Choking, Peter covered his eyes with his sleeve, refusing to look at the torn bodies and burned faces of the dead and dying recombinants around him.

"Pete!" came the whisper as still as death from the hillside, back the direction they'd come.

Slowly, Peter turned his head toward the familiar voice.

There stood Sting, his grid activated. He swept it in front of him. The whisper, he realized in a moment or two, had been a shout.

"Trace your steps backward, Pete," Sting said, his voice barely audible. "It's safe."

Peter's body was stiff, unresponsive, legs rubbery, chest pounding.

He rubbed a hand across his blood-spattered face and took a half step toward Sting.

"I know you're scared, Pete, but it's safe here. Walk toward me." He motioned to the other recombinants standing on the charred, pocked hillside. "Use your grids to find a path toward me."

Peter clung to his rifle as he stared with wild eyes at the twisted, burned bodies in his path, limbs missing, entrails exposed. Only nine of the fifteen recombinants had survived.

He took another small step toward Sting. Then he came upon Sergeant Temple's body. His uniform was torn and bloodied across the right side of his torso and left leg. Tiny pinpoint tears covered his right side. Peter let out a moan and fell down beside him.

"Sarge!"

"Come on, Pete!" Sting called from the hilltop. "We can't stay here. The Antarans will swarm this place any minute."

Gently, Peter reached down and felt for a pulse like he'd seen the medics do in RDC. He pressed his fingers against Temple's neck. A faint throb. Peter smiled. Sergeant Temple was still alive despite the holes in his side. He remembered how the medics covered injured recombinants in blankets, keeping them warm against shock. Peter didn't know exactly what shock was, but he didn't want Sarge to find out. Peter peeled off his flak jacket and draped it over Sarge. Then Peter hefted Sarge onto his back and staggered toward Sting.

"Leave the body, dammit!" Sting demanded, glaring. "Sarge would've chewed your ass for risking your life just so he'd have a proper burial."

"He's still alive, Sting," said Peter, his voice sharp.

"After that blast?" Sting's angry expression faded.

He rushed over to help Peter out of the swamp. When Peter was on solid ground, Sting motioned the recombinants up toward the hill.

"Let's move out! Double time! Move it, move it!"

Peter broke into a run, Sarge a dead weight, until he reached the top of the hill. Sting and the other recombinants scrambled back toward camp.

PETER SAT in the infirmary shelter beside Sarge. He'd been there for several hours, fearing the worst. It took far too long to get back to camp.

Finally, Sarge's eyes fluttered open. Groaning, he laid a hand against his side and winced. Temple's chest was bare, a thick white bandage wrapped around it. A thin line of blood spotted the fresh white bandages. His left leg was braced, most likely broken. His pasty face was flecked with multitudes of cuts, eyelids drooping from painkiller. Deep circles bruised the skin beneath his eyes. He shivered, his eyes glassy with fever. An IV bag hung just above the sick bed.

Peter leaned forward. "How do you feel, Sarge?"

"What happened?"

"We walked into a minefield."

Sarge clutched at his hair, his face contorting. "No! I scanned that area several times. It should have been safe."

Peter shook his head. "They were bioshielded to jam our scans, Sarge. They just caused a faint ripple on the grid surface. By the time we were even curious about the echo, it was too late."

His mouth quivered. "How many did we lose?"

Peter hated to tell him the news, but that didn't change the facts. It was no one's fault. Everyone knew that and no one blamed Sarge—not even Sting. Still, Peter knew Sarge would take this badly. He would because he cared.

"We lost six, Sarge."

"Oh, God, no!" Temple clenched his eyes shut, his hands bunching into fists. He beat the mattress. "It's my fault. My fault!"

Peter gripped his arm. "Sarge, no. I know you did the cursory scan, but these bioshielded jammers hid the mines. You couldn't have known. No one could have known."

"But I should have known." Temple pulled away, stifling a cry of pain. His eyes were wet, a tear streaking down the side of his face. "I should have checked before I set the unit on that course. God, I killed six people!"

Peter stared at him in surprise. This news had really hurt Sarge. He wondered if any other sergeant would have raised an eyebrow at losing six recombinants. It was expected. But Sarge was practically devastated by the loss.

"It could have been worse, Sarge," said Peter with a smile. "They could have been citizens."

Temple's gaze turned fierce. He snapped his head back toward Peter, his dark eyes burning with fury and grabbed Peter's sleeve.

"Damn you, Mitchell, don't you dare talk like that! They may have been recombinants, but they were still people! How can you expect people to treat you like citizens when you don't expect that of yourselves?"

Peter shrugged. Sarge was right. Sometimes, he let people treat him like a recombinant. "You're right, Sarge," he said, his gaze falling to the starched white sheet across Sarge.

His cot was nestled into a corner of the shelter. Only a handful of empty cots stood in the long, narrow shelter. The rest were filled with injured.

"Respecting life means respecting all of it, not just your favorite selections, Mitchell." He let go of Peter's sleeve, his fury spent. "I care what happens to my unit. Not because it's my job either. Because you're all good people."

A medic moved to Sarge's cot and thrust a needle into his shoulder. He winced, but in a moment, his eyes turned glassy again. The medic hurried on to his next patient. Sarge watched the rustling white coat rush away and a smile touched his lips. He glanced back at Peter.

"I'm going to be laid up for a few days. Sting's got to take over patrols for a while, until I'm back on my feet. Will you send him in here to talk to me?"

"I'll go find him," Peter said, and rose from the chair. "Take care of yourself, Sarge."

"Stay alive out there, Mitchell."

"I will, Sarge."

"Do I have your word on that?"

Peter nodded.

"I'm counting on you to be the voice of reason out there until I'm well."

"Yes, Sarge," he said with a smile.

Sarge mumbled something Peter couldn't understand and slumped against his pillow. His chest rose and fell steadily. Peter would ask Sting to visit Sarge after mess tonight.

AFTER MESS, Sting returned to the shelter pale and subdued. Peter sat up from his bedroll.

"What's wrong, Sting?"

He sank down beside Peter on the disheveled bedroll.

"Sarge put me in charge of the unit until he was back on his feet."

"You were the best candidate, Sting. You were the only candidate."

"But I've never led anyone before." Sting rubbed a hand through his curly blond hair.

"You're a natural. You always took charge of our unit when we were out of control in those sims. This is no different. You even took charge on the hill, remember?"

Nodding slowly, Sting's gaze filled with confidence.

"You got me and the others out of that minefield and back to camp. If you hadn't led me out step by step, I know I would've stepped on a mine."

Sting's gaze looked far away now and Peter could only speculate what he was thinking. Finally, Sting nodded toward the recombinants milling around the shelter. "These guys always ask me my opinion," he said, trying to convince himself he'd do okay. "They'll listen, won't they?"

"Of course! You lived through an entire tour out here, Sting. You're very important to this unit. They'll follow you anywhere."

Drake stormed into the shelter. He moved to his bedroll and kicked over a nearby ion lamp. "Damn that fucking sergeant!" He shoved one of the recombinants and the recombinant shoved back. "Bastard led us all into a fucking cascade minefield! Galloway wouldn't have done that!"

"You're right," snapped Peter. "Galloway would've been too drunk."

Drake pointed a finger at Peter and clomped toward him. "And you, you little bastard!" His face twisted into a snarl as he reached out to grab Peter, but Sting blocked his reach. "Why the hell did you bring him back? He led us into a fucking minefield!"

"Shut up, Drake!" Sting shouted and shoved Drake. He fell over a bedroll, scattering field packs and ion lamps. "Keep your bitching and moaning to yourself! Anybody could have missed those mines, Drake. Anybody! So shut the hell up." He cast a menacing glare around the room. "And that goes for anybody else with a problem."

Scowling, Drake shut his mouth. He scrambled to his feet. "Watch your ass, Mitchell. Sting ain't always gonna be there to hold your hand." He kicked an ion lamp across the aisle and stomped out of the shelter.

"Forget him," said Sting, turning back to Peter. "We've got a lot more to worry about than Drake's bellyaching."

Fear gripped Peter's stomach. "What do you mean?"

Sting moved toward his bedroll. "We have to go into the swamp tomorrow. Scan for traps and mines. As we go deeper into the swamp, cleaning it up, those mines will be quickly replaced by Antaran defense biodrones."

"Defense biodrones?"

"Like the things we encountered in all our sims, Pete. The tentacled ones that come at you to gut you. D'Angelo's seen another kind of Antaran, but he won't talk about it. All I've seen are those damned taloned biodrones. We'll have to deal with them after we clear the mines—maybe even during."

Peter's eyes widened. "The real thing this time," he muttered.

"If we're careful and keep a close eye on our grids, we can do this. Sarge said for the next few weeks or so, that would be our objective—clear out mines and fight through any Antarans."

"So, we'll have to fight off biodrones while we search for the depot," Peter said with a frown.

"Sarge said it wouldn't be easy to get close to the depot, but we have to try."

Why? What happened when the depot was destroyed?

Peter sighed and settled back against the cold wall of the shelter. His gaze fell to the rain-smeared portal.

Rain hummed against the roof. By nightfall, it would pound and clatter through the shelter, the winds rising to a fevered pitch. Storm season on Ku'Tal. Peter and his unit had to go through a bitter winter, a short summer, and another storm season before he completed his tour. He hoped he lived to see another storm season.

"Sarge'll be back to active duty long before we find the depot," Sting continued. "Until then, the unit belongs to me."

Sting slid down and leaned against the wall, his shoulder touching Peter's. He stared up at the ceiling.

"Shit, Pete, I've always dreamed of commanding my own unit. My chance to go out a hero. When I first came to base, I daydreamed about being so good at the front they'd promote me to citizen status and make me a sergeant. I'd pretend that I commanded several units until they made me a lieutenant." He laughed. "Then I'd go to the front, find the Antarans' entire stockpile of weapons and blow it up—just me. Since the war would be over, I'd walk away from all of it a hero and travel around the systems. Do shaving ads and shit."

Sting's eyes blazed with pride.

"I want to be known for something, Pete." He drew his knees up, propping his arms on them. "Be a hero. Show them recombinants can go head to head with the citizens and best 'em. Someday I'll show 'em, Pete. Then they won't dare kill any more of us."

So, he did have dreams. Sting had a way of holding himself back from others, but every once in a while, at the end of the day when he was tired, he let down his guard. Peter cherished those moments of their friendship.

Sting sighed and turned his gaze to Peter. This time, Peter saw a flicker of fear. "Look, Pete, I need to know that you'll be watchin' my six out there. I don't trust Drake much. Or the others."

Sting trusted him now, even with his dreams. Now, Sting had to trust him with his life.

"I'm getting out of this place, Sting, but when I do, you'd better be there beside me."

Sting smiled that crooked, charming smile and ruffled Peter's hair. "I will be. Leading the way in style." He laughed. "Being a hero is one thing, but being free is another. I'd prefer a quiet parting of the ways."

They sat side by side and watched the rain in silence until the shelter darkened with twilight.

Tomorrow would bring a new patrol and dangers Peter had dreaded for months. Tomorrow, they'd enter the hell of Ku'Tal swamps again. Still, Peter thought about all the recombinants that died today and wondered what happened to a recombinant when he died. The question, and the RDC, haunted him and tonight those memories burned through him.

23

PETER SPENDS his days at RDC being taught his place in the world, if it's even called a place.

A technician in her white coat walks down the aisle of the dull white recombinant ward, past the two lines of cots against the walls. With her hands behind her back, light thin and grey from dusty windows as she lectures as she walks, explaining to Peter and the others that they are official property of the Unified Countries of Earth and they will soon go to the war front.

All he knows about fighting is what he's seen in the ward. It's brutal and terrifying and bloody. And he wants no part of it.

Her face is dispassionate as she describes the training to come at the base station and how many of them could wash out before ever arriving. She pauses near Peter's cot, her gaze empty and her jaw tight, and tells him that tonight, he will join the others in the nightly data dumps.

He's been at the Recombinant Development Center for a month now.

Later, scared and confused, Peter wanders out of the ward and into the short, white hallway. His shoes scritch across the sticky flooring until he reaches the iron gate separating him from the others. He wraps his hands around the bars and watches them.

They're called citizens, he's told, and they don't mix with recombinants. No citizen does, they tell him.

Peter's blue-striped robe hangs open, thin ties dangling at his waist. His faded blue scrubs have thick black numbers and letters stenciled across the front, defining him as a recombinant. A coin-sized welt throbs at the base of his neck, the result of an identification chip insertion, an MRC, he's told. Anywhere he goes, he can be scanned and the chip will convey important information to the scanner, property of UCOE.

He wonders what else is inside his head. What else they haven't told him yet.

Through the cold bars of the gate, Peter watches the citizens tapping away on datapads, filing papers, laughing, and telling stories near a water dispenser. He realizes it's an office of some sort, containing five desks. He sees people finish their shifts and leave beneath a lit, green sign.

Exit, it reads.

He aches at their freedom, how they come and go like ghosts. Sometimes one doesn't notice the others all day. Some of them unwrap thick slices of bread filled with crisp green lettuce and bright red tomatoes and drink iced drinks at their desks—whenever they feel hungry—and never talk to the others. Ever.

Sighing, Peter sinks down against the gate. He can eat and sleep only when the technicians allow it. He stares up at the lit exit sign above a door at the end of the hallway, far behind the gate.

What's beyond that exit sign?

He tries to imagine places where people must go, small and pleasant places where they retreat and hide if they like. Sunny parks filled with tall shade trees and laughing children. Busy streets with lots of people and bright store fronts.

What would it feel like to be one of those ghosts fading past that exit sign?

A medic grabs him by the arm and yanks him up from the floor. He points with a beefy hand toward the recombinant ward. More white and yellowed flooring, greying bed sheets, and angry faces. The medic pushes him until he hurries away from the gate at full tilt, heading back to the ward.

Peter slips past three fighting recombinants and crawls onto his cot. The recombinant beside him, Charles, is seated cross-legged on his cot, eyes closed. In a few moments, his eyes snap open. He grins at Peter and holds up a citizen's god symbol.

"Where'd you get that?" Peter asks, sitting up. He gets off the cot and moves closer.

Charles laughs. "One of them left it in the latrine, so I took it. Think it can give me a soul?"

Peter gasps. Was that the purpose of the god thing? Did it give citizens their souls? "Is that why they wear them?"

"How should I know? All I know is it's powerful." He clasps his hands around it, the chain hanging over his fingers. "And I'm keepin' it. Who knows, maybe it'll even make me a citizen?" He snickers.

The fight in the aisle intensifies and the medics rush into the ward. Peter turns his back, not wanting to see them wash out another recombinant. All month long, he's watched the medics calmly wash out recombinants and within a day or two, they return with new ones. Most of the recombinants he's encountered are vicious and dangerous. Peter keeps out of their way as much as he can.

The silence mounts until finally, Peter turns to look into the aisle. There lies a motionless recombinant. The medics thrust a sheet over him and carry him away. Peter shivers, his eyes stinging. Not another washout.

"Charles, what happens when a recombinant dies?" he asks.

Charles scoffs, still mesmerized by the god symbol he turns over and over in his palm. "They make a new one."

"I know that, but what happens to that recombinant—the one that dies?"

Annoyed, Charles glares at Peter. "Nothing happens. He ceases to exist. He's gone and these people couldn't give a rat's ass about it!" Charles grabs him by the collar. "They'll wash you out, too, if they hear you talking like this."

"Why?" Peter asks with a frown.

Charles lets go of Peter's collar and sinks back onto his own cot again. "Because recombinants don't have souls. When we achieve consciousness, the soul's already long gone. When we die, there's nothing left to travel anywhere. You just turn into xDNA fodder for the next recombinant." He laughs. "They recycle you, man. Get used to the idea."

Peter continues to stare at the god symbol that Charles twirls on its chain. Pale, overhead lighting glints off the symbol until light flickers across Charles's blanket.

"There's a bunch of laws that go with this thing," Charles finally mumbles, his anger gone again. "Like not killing your neighbor, not killing yourself."

"Killing yourself?" Peter recoils, horrified. How could anyone purposely snuff out his own life?

Charles's eyes mist over and he clutches the god symbol in his hand, a fist that whitens his knuckles. "Yeah, they say it's against the law, that you'll lose your soul, but they still do it anyway. I've read the reports they leave lying around on datapads."

Peter has heard medics refer to this report as a news story. Peter has never seen one, but he doesn't want to read anything describing someone losing a soul.

"Their reports are filled with people who kill themselves, each other, lots of people." He sighs and looks away. "They talk one way and do another, man. I don't know who to believe. They can walk in here at any minute and shove a needle in your arm—then it's all over."

He clutches the god symbol to his chest.

"I don't want to go to their war front and wait to die," says Charles. "And I don't want to sit in this ward and wait for them to kill me." He turns his desperate gaze to Peter, his bottom lip quivering. "If I'm going to die, I want to pick how and when." Then he smiles and the look in his eyes is so far away that it frightens Peter. "It's the only thing I can control, man."

Charles, a month older than Peter, will go to base at the end of the week. He will train with UCOE's forces and then go to the front —if he doesn't wash out. He seems a little like Peter, not wanting to go the front, wanting something beyond the fighting and brawling that the other recombinants crave. Peter feels a kinship with this volatile recombinant. He reaches out and lays a hand on Charles's arm. He can find no words of comfort.

Charles flashes him a quick smile and holds out the god symbol again.

When night finally comes, Peter lies down on his cot and starts to turn on his side when a pudgy medic waddles toward him, shoes squeaking.

"You can't go to sleep yet, Mitchell," she says, and grabs him by the shoulder, pulling him up to a sitting position.

Groggy, he mumbles unintelligibly that he's tired, but she ignores him and thrusts molded headgear over his ears, forehead, and temples. She pushes him down in the cot and reaches to a switch on the wall. She snaps the switch and walks away.

Peter squirms against the headgear and the whir of power-up. The first few images quickly erupt through his tired brain. It all seems so jumbled to him, the strange people in strange places. He thinks back to those people in the office down the hallway with their sandwiches and laughter.

Slowly, he makes sense of the images...a dark-haired woman in a blue dress kisses a man in uniform. He stands outside, on the doorstep and she holds him against her, her eyes clenched shut, tears gliding down her pale face. The man strokes her face for a moment and then moves down the sidewalk toward a white, wooden gate. The woman, her eyes brimming with tears, waves bravely at the man.

In a moment, the man disappears around the corner. The woman goes back inside a small brick house and then a voice fills Peter's head, spouting specifications and rules. It weaves through Peter's brain until he can no longer fight his exhaustion. At last, he succumbs to it and collapses against his mattress, images and data spinning.

The next morning, Peter awakes, confused and groggy. It takes several minutes of staring around the room to sort out who he is and where he is. The noise and the shouting become clearer when he sits up and realizes he's free of the data dump.

A cold chill rakes his spine. Something's happened in the ward.

He pulls the headgear off his head and the shouting is piercing. Medics are all over the ward and beside his cot. He gazes over at Charles, but there is only a stretcher and a white sheet outlining a body.

"No," he says with a gasp and jumps up from his cot. "Charles? Charles, where are you?"

The stretcher bounces past, leaving a tangle of bloody bed sheets on the cot beside Peter's. A hand slips from beneath the sheet shrouding the body.

A glint of silver. A metallic clatter.

The god symbol, still clutched in Charles' hand, drags along the ground, twisting the chain and symbol into a knot. The sound is hollow and rasps in Peter's ears. Sick, he looks away. Whatever sliver of a soul Charles has is gone now, trickling out on the blood-spattered floor behind him.

"What happened?" Peter hears himself ask.

A medic turns to him, his face deadpan. "He slit his wrists. Must have unhooked himself from the data dump like you little bastards are always doing. Now, it'll take us the rest of the day to clean up this mess."

The medic plucks the god symbol from Charles's pale fingers, leaving his hand open and empty, clutching at the air.

Where's Charles now? His heart sinks. *Is he anywhere?*

Peter wonders if the god symbol gave Charles a soul. He looks past the medic, at the trickles of blood on the floor and he wonders why it's suddenly so quiet in the ward.

24

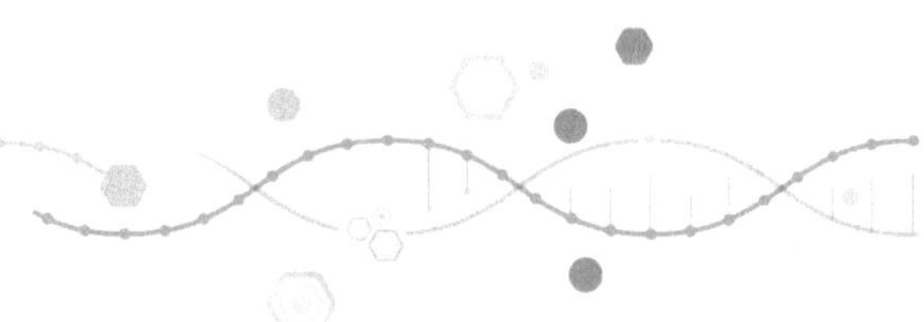

DIANA'S RESIGNATION WENT SMOOTHLY. UCOE never questioned her decision. As a citizen, she could leave the base at any time. She tried to concentrate on the job, but with David and Peter both in danger, the base was a constant reminder they may never come home again. Now, she stood outside the shuttle about to make her last run to the shuttle port. Ghosts of dispatched units walked all around her.

The units at the front were already forgotten, their beds and lockers absorbed by new recombinants and new sergeants. She felt their ghostly presences stalking the launch bay, wandering the halls, and hanging around her. David's quiet voice was a whisper in her ears and Peter...she closed her eyes and sighed. His gentle hands against her face. His wonder at seeing Civilization's colored lights. No one would help them now—any of them.

She climbed into her shuttle, requested clearance, and taxied toward the launch chute. She had to do something to help David and Peter. Anything but linger here among ghosts, not quite sure she'd ever shared their space.

That night, Diana wandered the steamy, brightly lit streets of

Civilization and tried to formulate a plan. Scents of roasted garlic and onions filled the streets as she passed the pub and a string of shops. Purple lights deepened in the sultry air. She wanted to go drink beer and throw darts, to shove away this unsettled feeling trembling through her stomach, but something about the crowds and the UCOE personnel made her skittish.

She blotted sweat from her brow and kept walking past the neon glow of clubs until the streets quieted, cooling, as she crossed the street toward End of the Line.

She gazed between buildings, seeing the glass-smooth bend of the river. Red and blue lights danced across its surface, reminding her of Peter. Were David and Peter safe? Only an official UCOE communique would change that now, but Peter?

She may never know and that terrified her.

Diana sat down on the steps of End of the Line and watched people stroll past. She didn't want to go inside just yet. She needed the openness and solitude to think. She needed to make a decision—a decision of her own, one made without automatically going against Mother and Dad's opinion and without consulting David. Purple and green lights shimmered, blending together across the surface of the black water. Besides, David wasn't here right now.

She wanted to join Mimi's underground and make a difference, starting with Peter. He didn't belong in the military. As much as she wanted to rescue him, there was more at stake than her own selfish needs. She was a damned good shuttle pilot. Mimi and the others could use a good pilot.

"Kiddo, you're doing way too much thinking these days."

Diana turned her head. Mimi stood outside the restaurant, wiping her hands on a towel. She sat down beside Diana.

"I want to help you with the recombinants, Mimi," she blurted out. "They deserve chances to live just like the rest of us. I want to make that happen. Couldn't you use another shuttle pilot?"

Mimi laughed and slipped her arm around Diana's shoulders.

"It never hurts to have a backup," Mimi said. "Kevin's been working with me for years. He does all the transporting."

"Couldn't I help with that?"

Mimi glanced toward the river. "Right now? No." She was silent for a few moments. "I could use quite a number of things right now, but pilots aren't one of them.

"Then where do you need help?" Diana asked with a sigh. "I'm good with people."

"What I need, you won't want to touch."

"Try me," said Diana. Her gaze met Mimi's with a confidence that seemed to startle Mimi.

"Okay," Mimi said, a wry smile twisting across her face. "I need a dishwasher."

"What? Why would you need a dishwasher?" Diana felt deflated.

"So, I can keep my restaurant running, that's why! If you want to help, that's where I need someone." Mimi rose from the step. "If you want it, the job pays twelve credits an hour, five nights a week."

Diana gaped at her. "But what about the recombinants?"

"You show me you can do grunt work first, then we'll see about the other things." Mimi turned and walked up the steps. She paused on the top one, but didn't turn around. "I'll expect you at five o'clock."

She didn't wait for Diana's answer as she moved fluidly through the doorway.

Diana remained on the steps for quite a while, the night wrapping around her in starry colored warmth until the streets emptied and the lights dimmed with morning not far off. Finally, she rose stiffly from the steps and walked home. She couldn't believe it. She'd just traded in a lucrative pilot's job for dishwashing.

IN A BLUE T-SHIRT AND JEANS, Diana showed up ten minutes early at the restaurant. Mimi, a slim-fitting red dress draping her frame, led Diana back to the kitchen. Diana passed the salad station, the sauté and grill stations, and the prep station until she found the roiling sauna that was the dish room. Black rubber, honeycombed mats covered the brick red, tiled floor. The exposed tiles were slick with water. Traces of bread crusts and bits of salad clung to the disposal and large, high-powered sprayer attached to the faucet. The dish machine stood to the right of the disposal area, programmed to clean and sanitize all eating implements.

"All you have to do is rinse and load the dishes. Then you'll have to refill our table setups station with clean silverware and glasses. The plates and bowls go back to the kitchen." She pointed toward the swinging doors. "Remember, there are bus tubs to carry back and forth."

Diana sighed. A stack of pans crusted over with sauces stood higher than her head on the dish counter. The clank of plates and deep sizzle of a sauté pan filtered out from the kitchen. Diana wrinkled her nose at the scent of lemons and fish hanging in the dish room.

"Will I have any help?" Diana asked.

Mimi laughed. "'Fraid not. Still want the job?"

She stiffened. "I can do the job."

Mimi pointed to a white plastic apron on a nearby hook. "There's your uniform. You'd better get started."

Mimi showed her how to operate the equipment and then left her.

The restaurant was busy the entire night. Diana carried bus tub after bus tub to the dish room and put the contents through the dishwasher. She carried out tray after tray of dry, hot glasses and fiery silverware in heavy containers and laid them on the stocking shelves. Mimi's servers used the glasses and silverware as fast as Diana replaced them.

By the time 23:00 rolled around, Diana was exhausted. Mimi let Diana order some food and joined her in the dining room. With a piece of apple pie and a steaming cup of coffee, Mimi waited for

Diana to eat. When Diana leaned back in the chair and closed her eyes, Mimi started talking.

"So how did you fare on your first shift?"

Diana sighed. "I survived."

"Things will get better," said Mimi. "Show me you can stick with it and I'll trust you with small parts of the operation." Mimi took a large bite of her apple pie.

"Thanks for letting me try, Mimi."

TWO DAYS LATER, Diana returned to the training base to finish her hours with Dr. Kingston. Seeing the recombinants made her sad, but she enjoyed Dr. Kingston's company. She entered the infirmary and slipped through a tangle of personnel into the hallway leading to the half-moon room. Her green sweater trapped warmth against her skin as the temperature cooled.

Inside, she found Dr. Kingston at a workstation.

"Hi, Dr. Kingston," Diana called.

"Oh, hi, Diana—I didn't hear you come in." Dr. Kingston rose from her chair and moved over to Diana. "You're a little early, aren't you?"

Diana nodded. "I had to take the 15:00 shuttle or be late."

"Why didn't you fly yourself?" Dr. Kingston asked.

She averted her gaze as she walked around the nearest exam table. "I quit my job this week."

"What? You quit?"

"With David at the front, I just couldn't bear flying the planetside runs." She offered Dr. Kingston a smile. "But I like working with you because you seem to care about the recombinants, so here I am."

A puzzled look touched Dr. Kingston's face. "What makes you say that?"

Diana shrugged. "You're studying problems with recombinants in a place that responds to those problems with wash out orders." Dr.

Kingston worked in a Reclamation Station. Surely that was obvious to her?

Dr. Kingston was quiet for a moment. "You're right, Diana. I do care what happens to them. That's why I'm studying their MRCs and some observed issues."

"I'm glad there are people like you and Mimi helping them," said Diana.

"Mimi?"

"She's runs an under—" Diana stopped in mid-sentence, horrified by what she'd said. "Oh my God...doctor, please—forget I said that. You didn't hear that."

How could she let that slip? She wanted to kick herself.

"No problem," Dr. Kingston said with a smirk. "My MRC will parse that out before morning. And even if it didn't, your secret is safe with me."

Diana let out a relieved sigh. "Thank you."

Dr. Kingston leaned against the exam table and spoke in a low voice. "Can you keep a secret?"

She nodded.

"I'm studying a series of malfunctions in the recombinants' MRCs."

"Malfunctions?" *What did that mean? Was that why Peter was so different from the other recombinants?*

"Yes, and the problem is much more widespread than I'd thought. I want to do the right thing, but reporting it might cause the needless destruction of thousands of recombinants."

Diana jerked a hand to her mouth. "Thousands?" *Did that include Peter?* "Including the ones you've studied so far?" She held her breath.

"Most of them...except John Stingley so far. His MRC was free of the defect."

"You can't—you just can't," Diana said, backing away from the table.

"I know," said Dr. Kingston, hanging her head. "That's why I haven't already reported it. Besides, I'm not sure how it affects their performance. Maybe it doesn't, I don't know yet."

Mimi had dealt with a lot of those chips being removed. Maybe she could help Dr. Kingston with her research and convince her not to report the problem as a problem? "Doctor, Mimi might be able to answer some of your questions?"

"How?" Dr. Kingston asked, raising an eyebrow.

"She's removed lots of those MRCs, so she might have information to help you."

Dr. Kingston's gaze fell to the exam table. "Remove them?" She seemed to be mesmerized by the thought of removing MRCs. She laid her hand to the nape of her neck. "For good?"

"Forever," Diana replied. "Including yours."

Her gaze met Diana's and she smiled. "Nothing would make me happier."

"I'm working at Mimi's restaurant now. End of the Line on Civilization. Come by and I'll introduce you to Mimi."

"Okay, yes—I will. Thank you." Dr. Kingston nodded toward the workstation behind her. "Want to get started early?"

"Sure," said Diana, following her over to the workstation.

FOR THE NEXT WEEK, Diana showed up early to analyze data for Dr. Kingston and then hurried away to wash dishes at Mimi's restaurant. She polished silver coffeepots and scrubbed grill parts until they sparkled. She kept a steady stream of silverware moving through the dishwasher that purred and hummed against the hiss of steam and the sizzle of the grill. She carried bus tubs to the back and quickly emptied them, making sure the servers had plenty of glasses and silverware on hand. She had it down to a science and kept it spreadsheet-organized. The work was exhausting, but Diana had to show Mimi her services were indispensable in any job.

She hadn't seen a recombinant in the restaurant since the night before she and Peter came here for dinner. Diana wondered what happened to the ones she'd seen. Had they gotten safely away from UCOE forces? She wanted to know all the particulars, but most specifically, she wanted to know how they removed a recombinant's identification chip. But she worried about Dr. Kingston's data, fearing what would happen if someone found out about the MRC problems. But mostly, she needed one question answered.

What would happen to Peter?

25

EVERY DAY, several patrols left the Ku'Tal base camp and went into the swamps, scanning for cascade mines. Sting took over Peter's unit and fell into a strict code. He was much more stringent that Sergeant Temple, bordering on a younger, taller Lieutenant D'Angelo. Sting brutally delivered his orders and anyone deviating paid a painful price. Peter was always at Sting's right hand, grid in hand and rifle poised. And one by one, Sting sent them out to cover ground not scanned the previous day.

Except for Peter who remained at his side.

This morning, the air turned sharp, smelling moldy and cold. The swamp's stench made Peter's nose run and his eyes burn. He pulled the collar of his flak jacket closed with his gloved hand and followed Sting as the remains of his unit slogged deeper into the swamp. His helmet smelled of swamp water and sweat and his toes burned in his boots until they went numb from the cold water.

Something green scampered across a branch and dived into the swamp beside Peter. It clawed and beat its tail, swimming through the thick ooze until it reached a decaying tree trunk rich with frilly yellow fungus.

A tree limb cracked and fell into the water. A flock of birds took flight.

Something screeched.

Sting thrust his hand into the air and the whole unit halted.

"Fan out," he snapped, his voice soft but urgent.

The others complied, grids sweeping across the murky water.

Something flipped past Peter's leg.

Startled, he jerked away, but Sting grabbed his arm.

"Dammit, be careful, Pete," he said with a growl, his gaze angry. "One wrong step could blow all of us up."

"Sorry," he muttered. *What had gotten into Sting?*

Sting let go of his arm and pointed. "So, what are you waiting for? Start scanning!"

"Aye, aye, Citizen Stingley," Peter mumbled and slid his grid from the pouch at his side. He flicked it on and began scanning the terrain.

They scanned the swamp for hours until the sun sank through the cold sky and behind the tall trees. Finally, Sting recalled them and they started a slow march back over windy hilltops and bitter pockets of frozen air. Peter's wet feet ached with exertion and cold. Winter in Ku'Tal wasn't far off.

Sting said nothing. He kept his pace brisk and his gaze trained on the horizon.

By the time they reached camp, mud-caked and half-frozen, Peter wanted to slug Sting. His first week of command and he was already treating them like subordinates. Disgusted, Peter walked away from the line and hit the showers.

At mess, he ate stew and bread then retired to his bedroll early to read. In a little while, Sting entered the unit shelter. The other recombinants averted their gazes and so did Peter. Sting either didn't notice or didn't care. He stripped down to his boxers, plopped his plasma rifle into his lap and meticulously wiped down the weapon.

Later, Drake, his hard expression breaking into a smile, sat down on Sting's bedroll with a deck of cards and a bottle of something. Sting snatched the bottle from Drake and drank. In a short time, the two of them were laughing, playing cards, and drinking heavily. Peter turned on his side and ignored them.

He slid out the homing device, hoping for some change. He'd stared at it so many times it was an afterimage when he closed his eyes. He glanced at the small disk. It blinked steadily!

His heart leaped. He checked his present position against the safe house's coordinates. His body went limp. Way too far behind enemy lines for him to reach. It might as well be on Civilization.

Disgusted, he slipped the device back into his bag and crawled into his bedroll.

LATER THAT EVENING, a recombinant shook him awake. Peter squinted at the shorter, stockier recombinant.

"Sergeant Temple wants you in the infirmary, Mitchell."

Nodding, Peter scrambled to his feet and grabbed his boots. He grabbed his flak jacket and started down the aisle. Sting's gaze fell on him, but Sting said nothing. Drake stuck his foot into the aisle, forcing Peter to veer around him. Peter plunged through the shelter opening and into the misty night, Drake's caustic laughter shrill behind him.

He traipsed across camp toward the infirmary's yellow glimmer. The guard detail waved him inside and he walked quietly through the small shelter until he found Sarge's bed. The IV stand had two bags on it now. Sarge's features looked a little swollen, the backs of his hands and his forearms fuller. He looked weaker than he had a week ago which frightened Peter.

"Damn, still buffering," said Sarge at a datapad. Two pillows propped him up in bed. He smiled at Peter and motioned him toward the chair beside the bed.

"How you feelin', Sarge?"

"I'm okay, Mitchell." His voice was thin and raspy. "They're pumping me full of antibiotics right now. With this fractured leg, I'm going to be here a while. How're things with the unit?"

He shrugged and slid into the chair. "We're still alive."

Sarge frowned. "That bad, huh?"

A loud burst of static erupted from the datapad.

"Your transmission has been sent, Sergeant, on a secured channel. Go ahead."

"Diana? You there?"

Diana? Peter sat up, his gaze darting to the datapad. He was afraid to breathe.

A hazy image slithered into focus and her sunny face filled the screen. Warmth spread through his chest as he reached toward the screen, but he caught himself and pulled back.

"David! Oh, David, how are you? They said you'd been injured, but I had no idea how bad. Are you okay? Were you shot?"

"Slow it down to light speed, sis," he said, a faint laugh in his voice. "I'm alive and in one piece, so don't worry."

"Don't worry!" Her brow wrinkled and that fiery spark ignited. Peter grinned. "Look at you! You're on Ku'Tal with hostile aliens at your back door and you've never been in combat before. But I shouldn't worry. No. No problem."

"I'm fine, kiddo, really. The sepsis is under control now. I'll be in bed for a while longer though."

"And how's Peter? Is he all right, too?" Her eyes were wide.

Sarge passed the datapad to Peter. "Here, Mitchell, you talk to her. She won't believe you're okay unless she sees it with her own eyes."

He grinned at her and laid his hand against the screen, remembering the softness of her skin. "Diana," he said.

Diana pressed her hand to the screen and he wanted to feel her fingers against his. "You look so thin," she said, her mouth drooping into a frown. "How are you?"

"I'm good. Great!" He paused, his glance averting to Sarge. His eyes quickly snapped shut and he pretended to be asleep. Peter smiled, turning back to Diana. "I miss you."

"I miss you, too." Her honey brown eyes were so bright. "Do you still have the—"

"Scarf you gave me?" he said hurriedly, knowing she meant the homing device. "Yes, I've still got it. I look at it a lot."

She smiled. "Good. You just stay safe, ya here? And you keep David safe, too."

"I will."

"This is costing David a fortune, Peter. I've got to sign off now."

Diana mouthed 'I love you' to him and he mouthed the words back to her. One last time, he reached out to the screen as if to caress her face.

Sarge coughed and pretended to wake up. He was a lousy actor. He held out a shaky hand for the datapad and reluctantly, Peter returned it to him.

"I love ya, kiddo. Take good care and I'll see you soon."

"You promise?"

"I promise."

"I love you, David."

Abruptly, the transmission winked out. Sarge stared at it for a moment and then his gaze moved to Peter.

He rubbed his forehead. He looked feverish. "I can't remember what else I wanted to talk to you about, Mitchell. Watch your six out there and keep everyone together. I'll be on my feet soon."

"Thanks, Sarge," said Peter, rising from the chair. "For everything you've done."

"Better turn in, private. You've got early patrol tomorrow."

Peter waved goodnight and plodded out into the night.

WEEKS OF MUD and death turned into months. Recombinants died and new ones arrived. Sergeant Temple mended slowly.

Someone said Sarge had gotten an infection in his blood, but that he'd recover. Sting remained in charge, running the unit like any seasoned sergeant, but he grew more distant and colder as the days passed.

After a routine mine sweep, Sting, without warning or reason, shifted Peter to the unit's flank. Instead, Sting put Drake at his right hand. Every night after mess, Peter watched Sting diligently take a cleaning cloth to his plasma rifle. His expression had become hard like Drake's and the animated, laid-back manner Peter admired was replaced by a dark brooding. Peter had never known Sting to brood.

The homing device had been active for several weeks now, but from his grid scans, Peter realized the safe house's position moved frequently. And it was still too far behind enemy lines.

Too many mines and too many biodrones between him and the safe house.

Besides, with Sarge hurt and depending on him to keep the peace, Peter felt he owed Sarge that much.

Peter missed Sting's companionship. He remembered the wide-eyed young man, slightly jaded who had confessed his fear on the transport, but now, Sting had become someone Peter didn't know. What Peter hated most was the favoritism Sting showed Drake. That favoritism made Drake think he owned the unit shelter—and Peter.

Peter laid in his bedroll, holding the homing device in his palm, watching the red light wink rhythmically, the coordinates glowing in small red characters on the small LED. A shadow fell across him. He looked up from the device. Drake's stocky form hung over him, a dangerous smile on his face.

"Hey, washout, know how to read the fucking grid yet?"

Peter ignored him, but Drake grabbed him and yanked him out of the bedroll.

"I'm talking to you, Mitchell."

"Get out of my face, Drake."

"Sure." Drake slammed his fist into Peter's mouth. His lip split. His chin felt warm and wet before his mouth went numb. He tasted salt and iron against his tongue as he blotted his mouth on the back of his hand.

Peter shoved Drake backward, but Drake came at him again, his fist smashing into Peter's gut. Peter doubled over, the air knocked from his lungs. He wheezed, trying to pull a breath into his chest.

Drake grabbed for his arms, but Peter's fist ground into his chin. He staggered backward then lunged. Peter fell and Drake dropped on top of him. His fist scuffed across Peter's face and struck him in the gut. The device bounced out of Peter's hand and onto the floor.

When he was satisfied Peter couldn't throw another punch, Drake let him go.

Peter clawed at the ground, trying to snatch the device off the floor.

With a sneer, Drake crunched it under his boot.

"No!" Peter shouted. Panic exploded through him.

Drake slid his boot back, scattering bits of metal and plastic across the floor. The homing device was in pieces.

Laughing, he moved back to his bedroll, leaving Peter to crawl, aching and bloodied, into his bedroll and curl up. He gazed at Diana's purple scarf hanging out of his duffle bag and remembered how she'd cared for him the night he'd been shot. The pain and hurt had been bearable around her, but tonight, he'd lost her forever.

The homing device was destroyed and so was his one chance to live.

WHEN MORNING CAME grey and quiet into camp, Peter moaned and struggled to rise. His face still throbbed, his whole body stiff and sore. He felt sick about the homing device, but he swallowed it back. Maybe he could still find the safe house?

Somehow. He'd make it out somehow.

Shakily, he dressed and hobbled out of the shelter, across the camp to mess. Later, as he returned from mess, he passed Sting. Sting frowned but didn't say a word to him. Peter kept walking.

He cleaned his rifle and waited for Sting to call formation. In a short while, Sting's bellow ripped through the camp. Peter thrust on his flak jacket and limped out to fall in line. Sting dumped him into flank position before he marched them away from camp.

The swish of grass gave way to the gurgle of swamplands as Peter scanned the area for Antarans and cascade mines. His grid hadn't sounded since he'd arrived. He moved it steadily in front of him as he walked, hoping the grid would catch any cascade mines before someone found them the hard way. Sting put the unit into their familiar rotations, fanning them out into a new part of the swamp.

Thin sheets of ice floated on top of the swamp water, crunching as Peter slipped through the murk. His grid arced in front of him. Abruptly, ripples danced across the surface of his grid and then vanished. He looked up, locating the swampy area that he'd seen ripple. Sting stood there talking to Drake while the rest of the unit scanned. Without scanning, Sting started forward, his gaze averted by Drake.

"Sting, no!"

Peter ran toward him, pulling him back as the ground exploded. The shock wave tore across the swamp. Someone shrieked. Plasma fire rang out.

He and Sting were thrown backward, Sting's rifle blown into hundreds of projectiles. Several splintered bits of polymer and metal scoured them, Sting taking the brunt. Even behind Sting, the fragments bit into Peter's cheek and flak jacket. Behind him, he heard a groan from Drake. Ignoring the burning pain, Peter scrambled to Sting's side, turning him over. His uniform was charred and ripped. The scent of burnt flesh mixed with the rush of smoke and stench of swamp water.

"Aw, dammit, Sting," he said with a moan and hefted him onto his shoulders. Sting needed immediate medical attention.

Sting shrieked and held his chest, but Peter carried him away from the water and onto the bank. Peter set down his field pack, removing a canteen of fresh water. He yanked open the remnants of Sting's flak jacket and tore away the burned uniform. A long, thin strip of metal had pierced the right side of Sting's chest. Peter winced at the sight of the metal poking out Sting's back. It cut through his chest high. Sting gulped at the air, his breaths shallow and harried. Peter poured water on it, cleansing it as best he could.

Drake got to his feet and stumbled over to where Sting lay.

"Pull that out," Drake ordered, and his hand fell to the metal protruding from Sting's chest.

Peter jerked his plasma rifle off the ground and pointed it at Drake's face. "If you even flex a pinkie, Drake, I'll burn 'em all off."

Drake yanked his hand back. "What the hell's your problem, freak?"

"If that metal's removed, he could bleed to death! Leave it alone!" He turned his swollen, bruised face to Sting, whose eyes had rolled open.

"No arguing," Sting muttered, his voice breathy.

"Hang in there, Sting," said Peter. "I'll get you back to camp. Don't go anywhere." He pressed the canteen to Sting's lips and made him drink.

Sting's gaze fell onto Peter. With a muddy hand, he reached toward Peter's face. "Meant to ask. What happened—to your face?"

Peter glared at Drake. "Nothing, Sting. Let's get you out of here."

After calling in the other recombinants, one of them unaccounted for, Peter lifted Sting gently onto his shoulder and carried him several miles to the base camp. He collapsed short of the infirmary and was unable to get Sting inside. Some recombinants hurried out of the infirmary, picked up Sting, and carried him inside. Another recombinant helped Peter to his unit shelter, and Peter slept the rest of the day.

ALMOST A WEEK LATER, Sting was released from the infirmary. He'd been lucky this time; the metal piece had missed any major arteries. He moved with slow steps into the shelter and slid softly onto his bedroll. He grimaced and glanced over at Peter.

"Pete, what the hell happened to you?"

Peter ran a hand across his bruised, cut face and shrugged. Drake had been at him again despite Peter's best effort to defeat him.

Silence.

"So, who pulled me out of the swamp?"

"I did," Peter snapped. "Carried ya all the damned way back to camp, too."

Sting bowed his head. He ran a hand across a bandage that peeked out of his uniform shirt.

"Leading the unit's made me a little crazy, Pete. I'm sorry."

Peter nodded, but he didn't meet Sting's gaze. "Forget it."

"No, I can't forget it. You saved my life like you did Sarge's." Sting sighed. "And I've been treating you like shit. I didn't want the others to think I was playing favorites, but dammit, Pete! You're so careless out there."

"Look who's talking, you bonehead. You just strolled out into the swamp without even scanning first. You're damned lucky that wasn't a cascade mine ring."

Sting hobbled over and sat down on Peter's bedroll.

"The others started talking, so I moved you to flank. I figured that'd be the safest place to put you in case your attention wandered. But I turned out to be the stupid one." He squinted at Peter, his eyes sad. "Pete, why do you let Drake do that to you?"

Peter sighed and leaned back. The bedroll felt warm and he settled deeper into it, trying to shake the cold from his bones. "I don't. He thought since you dumped on me, he could, too."

"Man, I'm sorry, Pete."

Both were silent for some time until Peter gently nudged Sting.

"How's Sarge?"

"He says he's gonna be fine. Said by next week he'd be back on the job."

"Citizen Stingley returns to the peons."

"Stop it, Pete! It's not like that."

"Then what's it like?"

With a sheepish look, Sting ran a hand through his curly hair. "I just wanted to do a good job, y'know. Be like Sergeant Temple. But I got scared, Pete, scared that I'd lead everybody into a minefield. I didn't want to cause anybody to die, but, man, it was great knowing I was in charge. For once, I called the shots. I told people what to do and they obeyed me. Like I was somebody. Almost a hero, y'know?" He sighed and flicked hair out of his eyes. "Gotta cut these bangs. I hate hair in my eyes."

Peter tried to stay mad at Sting but couldn't. The accident had humbled him and he was more like his normal self again.

"Listen, Pete," he said, fiddling with the edge of Peter's bedroll. "Thanks for bringing me back safe. First Sarge and now me."

"But not Drake," Peter muttered. "I'd have left him with the snakes."

He and Sting laughed. Finally, Sting rose from the bedroll and patted Peter on the back.

"Thanks again, Pete. I owe you big-time for this one."

"Just watch your grid next time. If you'd just looked before you moved, you wouldn't have set off that trap."

Sting snickered. "Listen to this! Peter Mitchell, King of Grid Confusion is telling me how to read my grid."

"That honor just passed to you, Sting."

The comment left him speechless. With a grin, he waved Peter off and plopped down on his own bedroll. Then he picked up his new rifle. Using a fresh cleaning cloth, he shined every crevice and every mechanism until it gleamed.

THE FOLLOWING MORNING, Lieutenant D'Angelo called formation at 0500. Major Welker stood in silent watch behind D'Angelo, surveying the units with a grim, unblinking stare. Groggy and confused, Peter staggered out into the icy predawn air, his flak jacket thrown on and his boots barely fastened. He snapped to attention, and in moments, he felt Sting's familiar presence to his right.

"What's going on?" Sting mumbled.

Peter shrugged. "No idea."

Standing in the freezing rain that clicked against helmets and shelters, Lieutenant D'Angelo addressed the units. He was a tad under average height, and his ears stuck out. His dark hair was bristly across his scalp and shaved clean at the neck.

"All right, this is the scenario," he shouted, the words reverberating through the silent camp. "We think we've located the depot."

"About time," said Peter.

"We've been here so long, I've lost track of the months," said Sting.

"Pipe down over there!" shouted D'Angelo.

Peter nodded. At least two months had passed. Beyond that, he had no idea.

D'Angelo addressed the units, talking about love of home world and loyalty. He talked about life and freedom—things D'Angelo insisted were God-given rights. For him, they were; until now, he'd never had to earn them like a recombinant.

"We're going to begin combining units on patrols, but when you reach unscanned ground, you will break into your subunits. Most of the mines have been cleared away, so the Antaran biodrones will start preying on us. If one gets you, you'll wish you'd stepped on a cascade mine."

D'Angelo was silent for a moment. He paced with arms behind his back. His gaze met Welker's for a moment and Welker snapped a stiff nod at him. Then he spoke again. "It has become necessary to issue—termination kits to all soldiers."

Sting's eyes widened.

"These kits will fit into your boot and contain two cyanide capsules. One will do the job. The other is a backup, if necessary. If you're captured and unable to escape, you are ordered to use the kit. Otherwise, the Antarans will gain recombinant technology to use against us on the battlefield. If we're going to stop the Antaran spread from moving closer to our home world, then we must keep this technology safe."

A pall settled across the camp. Peter stared at Sting, his terror barely contained. Sting swallowed hard and shrugged, his gaze a mixture of anger and confusion. Two sergeants filed down the lines, handing a small, plastic parcel to each soldier. Peter felt the deadly kit slapped into his palm and he numbly slipped it into his right boot.

He remembered the pasty color of his friend, Charles' face, the dried blood on the RDC floor, and he hoped he'd never have to use the kit.

"All right then. Dismissed."

Peter, anxiety clenching his stomach, followed Sting back toward the shelter, but someone shouted his name. He turned. Sergeant Temple moved toward him. The man's steps were a little unsteady, but he seemed reasonably recovered.

"How you feeling, Sarge?" Sting asked.

"Much better, Stingley," said Sarge. He grimaced when he saw the bruises contouring Peter's face. "Mitchell, what happened to you?"

Peter shrugged. "Are you back on active duty again, Sarge?"

Sarge smiled. He looked more relaxed than Peter could remember, but he wondered how this incident would affect Sarge in the field.

"They just reinstated me," Sarge said. "I'm going to lead you guys back into the swamps tomorrow."

The look on Sting's face conveyed major disappointment. Peter knew how Sting enjoyed leading the unit, but now he'd have to give that up.

"Glad you're back on your feet again, Sarge," said Peter.

Sting sighed.

"I hope you'll stay on as my right hand, Stingley," Sarge replied. He gazed from Peter to Sting, a smile hinting at the corners of his mouth.

This brought a smile to Sting's face. "Only if Mitchell here's on flank."

"Done," said Sarge. "They tell me you carried me back into camp, Mitchell."

Peter nodded and his gaze fell away from Sarge's face.

"A lot of guys would have left me there."

"Nobody in this unit would do that, Sarge," said Sting, a touch of indignation in his voice. "We take care of our own."

Except Drake, Peter thought with a frown.

Sergeant Temple grinned. "There are no recombinants in my unit. As far as I'm concerned, you're all citizens. We all fight together."

"When do the citizens go on patrol?" Peter asked.

"At 1200 hours. You'll carry full complements of plasma charges on this trip. From what D'Angelo's reconnaissance sweeps indicate there aren't many mines left. That means the biodrones will come soon. And that means a lot of quick ways to die. Be in formation at 1150. Dismissed."

Sarge turned slowly and moved back across the camp. Peter wondered how far he'd get before the man keeled over.

NOON PATROL CAME TOO SOON. Realizing the time, Peter struggled up from his bedroll and reached for his flak jacket and helmet, upsetting his duffle bag. It toppled over, littering Peter's things across the floor. He hurriedly shoved toiletry items and his datapad back inside until he came to Diana's scarf. He ran his fingers across the silky material, thinking of her hair.

He glanced up. The shelter had already emptied out. Dammit, he was late! He shoved the scarf inside his shirt, thrust on his helmet and jacket then grabbed his rifle. Pulling on his field pack, he dashed through the small shelter and slipped through the flap. He pounded across the camp, sliding to a stop at the end of the line. Sarge frowned at him.

"Nice of you to join us, Mitchell."

The unit snickered, but their gazes remained on Sarge.

"Sorry, Sarge. It won't happen again."

"If it does, you'll be on KP, private."

"Yes, Sarge."

Sarge walked down the line of recombinants. Peter noticed they had fifteen recombinants in their unit again because D'Angelo had combined remnant units to make full ones. Earlier, Peter had noticed some faces he didn't recognize. The termination kit dug into his ankle and he longed to toss it aside. It felt uncomfortable against his leg, but the thought of using it terrified him. His stomach burned. He couldn't do it. No matter who ordered it, he couldn't voluntarily end his own life.

He felt a shadow hanging over him. Sarge, arms crossed, eyes fiery, stood in front of him.

"Mitchell!"

Peter snapped his spine straighter, his gaze staring past Sarge.

"Yes, Sarge!"

"What the hell did I just say?"

He cringed, knowing he hadn't heard a word. He opened his mouth to speak, but Sarge waved him off.

"Don't embarrass yourself, private." He moved closer to Peter, nearly on the toes of his boots. Peter squirmed, uncomfortable. "Do you want to die, soldier?"

"No, Sarge."

"Are you sure?"

"Yes, Sarge!" he shouted.

"Then pay attention! It'll be too late to ask questions after you've stepped on a cascade mine! Do you read me?"

"Yes, Sarge!" Peter answered. "Loud and clear!"

Sarge stepped back. "I'm trying to keep you idiots alive!" He moved down the line, gesturing furiously. "Don't make it so hard!" Sarge moved toward Sting who stood at the opposite end of the line. "All right, fall in! We're moving out for our objective. Keep up the pace and don't screw around!"

Peter sighed in relief. He reached down and adjusted the termination kit before he fell into formation. He moved with the others out of camp and toward the hill.

THE TEMPERATURE REMAINED JUST above freezing. The swampy waters that backwashed into ditches along the dirt paths hadn't crusted over with ice yet. Lizards and rodents slipped across the paths and rustled in brush, the higher temperatures allowing them to forage for food. Insects leaped out of the grass as Peter and the unit veered off the traveled paths and swished through the knee-high grasses. Sarge was taking them away from the cleanup route. Peter wondered if there'd be more mines to clear or if they'd run into biodrones?

Peter thought back to his training sims and remembered the simulated pain of those spiked appendages tearing through his body. These appendages wouldn't dissolve into greyness. They would tear and destroy him. He had to keep a better watch than before. Although, he didn't know which way to die was worse: being ripped to shreds or being blown to bits by a cascade mine. Or the stark quiet of a pill to tear up his insides.

The termination kit's plastic casing rubbed against his ankle again, stirring his memories of Charles back at RDC. The bone-white hand, the god symbol dragging the ground, staining the floor with red trails.

Peter reached back and slid his grid out of his field pack. He turned it on, a soft chirp resounding. Panning the horizon and what lay ahead, Peter studied the grid, but nothing stirred. For now, the unit was safe. He wondered if he could find the safe house on his grid.

Sarge's pace was brutal and Peter's legs cramped from keeping up with a heavy field pack on his shoulders. His lungs burned from exertion. Finally, Sarge called a rest and Peter dropped down on his knees. He opened his canteen and drank deeply from the cool, purified water he'd filtered just last night. One guy in the shelter across from his died because he drank contaminated water. Peter would take no chances. He was going to walk out of this place for good someday.

"Where we headed in such a hurry, Sarge?" Sting asked.

Sting rested his arms on his knees, rifle in his lap. His expression was cheerful, relaxed. Peter wondered how Sting would react to going back in the field again after a near miss with a cascade mine. It didn't seem to bother him, but Sting had a year to deal with this place. Today, he seemed more like the others, hungry to encounter an Antaran and just as hungry to blow one away. Even Sarge seemed okay with being out here. Peter longed for the safety of his bedroll and a shuttle ride out of here.

"To an uncharted section of swampland," said Sarge as he sat down on the ground and removed his canteen from his pack. "We're testing out some radar reconnaissance."

"Then what're we lookin' for," Drake demanded.

"Bioshield signatures," Peter answered.

Sarge nodded at Peter. "Exactly. Explain."

Drake glared at him.

"I'm guessing we're verifying if the depot's out here somewhere," Peter continued. "Which means the closer to those signatures we move, the more likely we'll encounter cascade mines." Or Antaran biodrones. He left that unspoken.

"You're right on target, Mitchell. Not bad for a guy not paying attention." He nodded at Peter's scanner. "I noticed you've been scanning for some time. Anything suspicious?"

"Not yet, Sarge. I just didn't want us to walk into a bioshielded jammer. It's bad enough the Antarans can change form, but having mines bounced back as rocks and trees to the grid...that's too scary for me."

"Good work, Mitchell." Sarge's gaze encompassed the others. "From here on out, grids are required. Anyone who reads—or thinks he reads—any ghost echoes, sing out!"

Everyone slid their grids out of their packs and turned them on. Peter had time to take one last drink of water before Sarge ordered them on their feet.

Drake waited for Peter to fall in line. Then he moved past, slamming his elbow into Peter's shoulder blade on his way back into formation. Peter's body jolted from the sharp gouge, the pain lingering. He rubbed his shoulder and kept scanning as the unit moved into uncharted territory.

The scritching of insects died away, bird calls falling silent.

Peter became aware of the sounds of breathing around him, heavy, deep huffs, and realized it was his own. His chest pounded as he scanned in the sudden quiet.

The slosh of boots through water filled the heavy silence until at last, the ominous whistling call of some creature warbled through the treetops.

The hair on Peter's neck bristled.

The wind rose. Water lapped.

Something touched his leg and he turned. A yellow and brown snake side-winded past him, tongue flicking. His gaze fell to the grid.

Nothing.

The swampland was clear.

Peter slowed to a stop. He glanced behind him, around him, in front of him, his chest heaving. His fingers went cold as he sniffed the air. Fetid water scent mixed with the salty taint of his sweat.

Something splashed. He turned.

The wind cut across him in a cold slash. Peter slid his rifle down from his shoulder, the grid in front of him, and moved with measured steps back toward the end of the line.

Something was out here. He was certain of it.

"Sarge," he said, "there's something out there."

Sarge held up his hand, halting the unit. He turned his fearful gaze to Peter. "Give me coordinates."

Peter sighed and bowed his head. "Sarge, you know how sometimes you just know something. That you feel it hitting you in the gut."

Sarge was silent.

"Oh, shut the hell up, Mitchell! Don't listen to him, Sarge. He's freakin' nuts!" Drake shoved him.

Sting elbowed Drake in the gut. "Quiet."

"I know there's something out here, Sarge," Peter said, his tone insistent, "but my grid's clear."

"Mitchell—" Sarge sighed. "I can't stop the unit on a gut feeling."

"Just keep your guard up then. Something's out here."

"Noted, Mitchell. Return to your position."

Peter hurried back to flank and in moments they were trudging through the edge of the swamp again in a northeasterly course. Whatever creature had been whistling before went abruptly silent in mid-whistle. Finally, the only sound coming off the swamp was the wind.

Sarge's stance changed. He kept looking around and consulting his grid. Peter knew Sarge was beginning to sense whatever it was Peter felt. Every once in a while, his gaze would meet Peter's and he would nod.

A grid whispered in the stillness. Peter glanced down. It was his.

"I've got something, Sarge," he said in a low voice. "Southeastern quadrant. Moving slow. Bow echo's faint."

He sniffed the air. It smelled of rotting leaves. He began to tremble.

The whole unit stopped, their focus turning to Peter.

"I'm picking it up, too," said Sting. "Good call, Pete."

Charges snapped into rifle chambers as recombinants slid into tight formation. Peter moved around them, his own charges locked into his rifle and blinking green as he continued to scan.

A dull, staccato whine punctured the silence.

"Movement!" Sting shouted. He crouched low, his rifle barrel arcing through the air.

Rain began to mist in a fine sheen. The pitch of the grids sharpened.

"Three—four bow echoes, all shifting south-southeast," Peter announced, his voice steady. He glanced at the grid again. It began to shriek in a fast-paced beat. "Scratch that! Six, seven—shit, eight bow echoes moving northeast from all southern quadrants!"

Sarge's face washed pale. "Move north. Now! Move it!"

Recombinants barreled through the swamp, the bow echoes slashing across grids that screamed Antaran presences were approaching.

Peter stared at his grid. Why were they all coming from the south? He remembered how they had come at them from all sides in the sims.

A cold chill clamped against his stomach. Either the sims were programmed wrong...or they were being herded north.

His brain spun, throwing around those conditions until he realized the reason why.

"Stop!" he shouted. "Stop running!"

Sarge halted the unit. "This better be good, Mitchell!"

Peter rushed at him, shoving the grid in his face. "They're herding us north, Sarge! In sims, they always came at us from any direction, never in concentration."

"To capture us?" Sarge shouted.

Peter shrugged. "Maybe. Or to destroy us. I'll bet my life there's a huge field of cascade mines hidden in the swamp ahead."

Drake grabbed him by the jacket. "I'll take that bet, Mitchell."

"Back off, private," Sarge snarled. Drake released him and shrank back.

"Sarge, please!" The screech of the grids pounded faster and faster. Peter sucked in a quick breath. "We've been so busy scanning south that we've ignored north!"

"Stingley, scan what's ahead."

Everyone fell silent as they watched for biodrones while Sting scanned ahead. The fevered pitch of the grid kept everyone on edge. They trained their rifles south until finally, Sting spoke.

"I'll be damned! Pete, my boy, you're right. I'm reading over twenty bioshielded jammer signatures ahead. They're so faint I might have missed them."

"What do we do, Sarge?" a recombinant asked.

"Either we make a stand and risk being annihilated or we make a run for it. Sting, find us a clear path."

Seconds screeched by, the grid's pitch nearly steady now.

"Still moving up from all southern quadrants," said Peter, the grid growing dark from the mass of echoes appearing. "Over ten bow echoes, Sarge."

"Northwest!" Sting shouted. "Set to these coordinates." He beamed out the numbers to all grids. "If we go now, we can slip between the cascade mines and the biodrones."

"Move out!" Sarge motioned Sting ahead to blaze the path. Boots pounded against harder ground, leaving the swamp behind.

Peter held the flank, scanning and watching. His grid alarm had softened considerably, returning to a dull staccato rhythm. He turned, scanned. No change in biodrone direction. They might just get away.

He turned back. The unit had moved too far ahead.

His heart hammered in his chest as he ran to catch up, keeping an eye on the grid. Finally, he reached a V in the trail.

Shit! Which way?

He flipped a switch on his grid and scanned for body heat.

Too much movement on both trails—animals and other wildlife he wasn't interested in encountering. The left trail seemed to have the most heat signatures. Both paths led toward the coordinates Sting beamed.

Swallowing hard, he swerved left.

He ran for a long time, but the unit was nowhere along the trail. Fear welled cold in his stomach. He'd catch up with them at the assigned spot.

The whine of the grid began again, chirping in measured tones. Slowly, but enough to let him know he had company to the southeast.

Peter ran harder, his hands numb against rifle and grid. The grid began to beat faster, the pitch growing shrill.

Brush and gnarled trees flashed past until the path narrowed. Then the path dead-ended into a wall of brambles that intertwined with swamp trees. He clawed at the brambles gouging his hands, but he couldn't penetrate them.

Pressing his rifle stock to his chin, he squeezed off a blast. Brambles smoked, the acrid stench making him cough, but the hole led into trees so thick he couldn't fit between them.

The grid pitch heightened, shrieking in a single pulse. Peter turned, crouched, and glanced at the grid. Two bow echoes moving toward him.

He sniffed the air. A heady sweet scent hung like syrup.

Holding his breath, he raised his rifle.

Something moved on the periphery of his vision. He turned right.

Air displaced, vines snapping. Spiked appendages tore out of the brush beside him.

One appendage pierced his thigh. Another wrapped around his boot. Screaming, he fired, searing off an appendage. The other he crushed with his uninjured foot.

Three more taloned things snapped out of the brush to his right and more to his left.

He fired, burning off the three to his right, but two to the left raked across his left shoulder and down his arm. His flak jacket tore open like paper as his blood seeped into the heavy fabric.

He squeezed off more blasts until something screeched. Twisting left, he fired into the brush again.

The air smelled of burnt sugar and copper—his blood.

Several biodrones ripped through the trees toward him.

Peter threw himself forward into the foliage and collided with a hazy figure.

A part-man, part-animal like creature—wolf-like—hung over the ruined body of a recombinant. The soldier must have been dragged a long distance from the swamp.

The alien's skin was mottled green-gold, marble-like, and it hunched at the shoulders. Its eyes, the color of moss, were small and placed a little higher on the head than a human's eyes. Its mouth and nose were wolf-like. The alien wore a dark brown flight suit that didn't seem to fit its form. The flight suit looked badly damaged and the mottled skin was white in places beneath burned-away material.

The alien looked badly injured.

Around its neck, something gold glittered. A weapon? Peter yanked the object off the alien's neck.

A feral screech erupted from the alien as it reared toward him. Peter thrust his rifle barrel toward the alien's face and it backed down.

"Just give me a reason," Peter shouted through gritted teeth.

The alien clawed frantically at its neck. To Peter's surprise, it waved the advancing biodrones back, but the biodrones continued to advance slowly on Peter.

"Identify yourself!" Peter snarled.

He knew it wasn't human, but it was trying hard to look like one. He gasped. It was trying to shift form to a human one. Was that even possible?

The moments dragged by. No response.

He winced, locking another charge into his rifle, and blasted the ground at the alien's feet. He just couldn't kill it outright.

"Please...stop. I'll call them off."

Peter nodded toward the dead recombinant. "Call them off and step back from him. Now!"

Slowly, the biodrones slid back into the brush. Peter's body ached and burned from his wounds. He was in no mood for tricks.

Abruptly, his grid fell silent, all the bow echoes except one fading away. But the echo was different than the others, smaller, sharper—less duration.

The alien spoke again, gently, pain at the edge of its voice. "I've called off the biodrones. They are just doing what they've been coded to do."

"And what about you? Gutting my buddy there."

With the rifle still trained on the alien, Peter knelt beside the recombinant. He was beyond help.

"Not gutting," said the alien. "The biodrones did that to him. I was harvesting your technology."

"Is that what you call it?"

The wolfish appearance of the alien was starting to fade. Peter squinted and rubbed his eyes, not sure if his injuries were getting to him.

"You don't look like the biodrones," said Peter warily.

"A lot of what you see is adaptive—even the language. Antarans are very adaptive in most climates, most worlds. I rushed through my structural change, but my injuries won't allow my complete adaptation. The process will be slow now." The alien stared at him for a moment. "You have something that belongs to me."

Peter stared, afraid to move. The grid was silent, so for the moment he was safe—at least from the biodrones. Still, it was a standoff. He couldn't run or those biodrones would eviscerate him. The heavy chain of the alien's object dug into Peter's palm, but Peter held it tighter. It was all that stood between him and those biodrones.

What if there was no way out of this? What if he faced using the termination kit?

"Used to belong to you," said Peter.

A look of surprise slid across the alien's face. "You're not like the others," it said, studying him. Oddly, it smiled, becoming slowly more human as the minutes ticked past. It was adapting despite its injuries. "You code is–is different. You represent a new hope to our race."

Peter sneered. "In what way?"

"Being a recombinant, you prove code can be recombined from death and make it live again. Something smarter than a biodrone. As a caregiver, I find that prospect exciting. And your code has remnants of our past. We've been searching for you a long time. Constantine."

What was it talking about? What was this Constantine and code business? Peter glanced at the alien object in his hand. The purplish gold metal was shaped like a half moon. Was it some sort of key?

"Why are you telling me this?"

"Because we need your code. Now, give back my property or I'll release the biodrones."

The Antaran took a step toward Peter.

Peter shifted his weight off his injured leg and thrust the rifle barrel at the caregiver. It stopped advancing. He bit his lip, unsure what to do. His training hadn't covered this. He'd learned to kill biodrones, not Antarans who spoke to him.

How could he shoot it when it now looked as human as he did?

"Give that back," it said with a growl. "You can't stop us from bringing our people back from the dead. Certainly not with that key."

Fighting against the fear trembling through him, Peter held his ground. "I'm as good as dead if I hand this thing over. And you know it."

"Please." The alien's partly human eyes turned glassy. "You're so different than the others—a higher order. And with traces of Constantine code. Your genetic makeup will tell us so many secrets."

"Here's a little secret," said Peter, taking a step backward, nearly falling. Brush rustled behind the caregiver. The biodrones were moving forward again. "You won't be using this key either."

The Antaran made a move toward him, but Peter staggered into the hole he'd made in the brush. He fired at the caregiver but missed.

"Give me that key! Please—the repository!"

Peter fought against the tangled foliage for an opening and plunged through the brush. He fired again at the caregiver and forced himself through a narrow space between two trees and careened onto another path.

He wasn't going to be anyone else's lab experiment. Never again. He limped away, awaiting the scream of his grid.

26

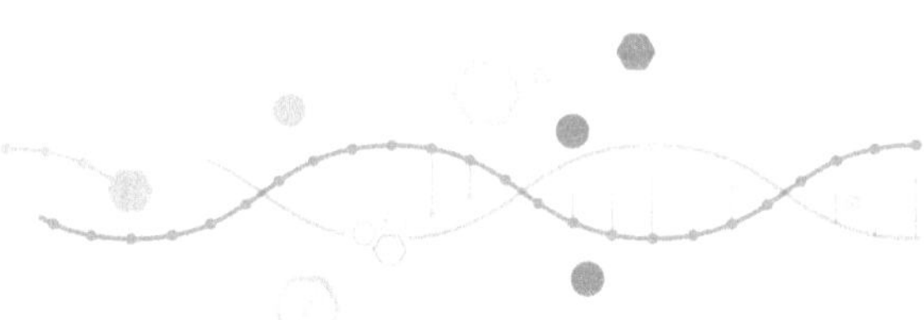

WITH A SIGH, Jeannette pushed her chair away from the workstation. The small office was dark, only a desk light casting a pale white glimmer through the stuffy room that smelled like overpowering mint. Seventy percent of the tested MRCs showed various levels of failure and the percentage of washouts within affected batches was high. UCOE would take one look at those statistics and recall thousands of recombinants.

Destroy was a more accurate word.

She stood up and paced around the room. What was causing these errors? They seemed random at best. She needed more information, but she was running out of time. Unless—

She rushed back to her workstation and called up the Civilization directory on the virtual display, searching until she found the restaurant Diana mentioned. If this Mimi person was running some kind of underground rescue for recombinants, then she'd have ample experience in removing MRCs without setting off the AWOL tracker. To do that, somebody had to know more about these chips than she did. Removing a chip at a Reclamation Station was never an issue in dead recombinants.

After she transferred directions to her mobile, she glanced at the time. Almost 16:00 hours. If she hurried, she could make the 16:00 shuttle. She rose from her chair, but the virtual display flickered, signaling a new message had arrived. Her chest tightened when she saw Kai's name in the header. The message was short but said everything.

Red, we've run out of time. Need you back by end of week. Stanton knows.

Kai

She closed the message. That only left her two days. Stanton was no doubt furious, but this was beyond Stanton now.

Jeannette signed herself out of the infirmary for the rest of the day, grabbed her bag, and hurried out of the wing. She'd be written up for signing herself out, but right now, she didn't care. She needed more data.

She took a lift to the launch bay and got into line for the shuttle. The launch bay always smelled dry and dirty. It felt much colder than the research center, too. Shivering, she folded her arms against her chest and endured the slow checkout and verifications until she was cleared to board. She clambered into the dimly lit shuttle and slid into a seat. After arranging the harness over her body, she settled in and waited for the shuttle's roll and drop.

It came without warning and she was falling through darkness toward Civilization.

At 16:25, the shuttle landed. She went through the recheck and re-verification before she was allowed to enter the shuttle port. She hurried through the drafty port that smelled of coffee and pastries.

Heat roiled across her body as she stepped out into Civilization's sunny amber streets. The heat cut through the base's chill and in moments, the numbness left her fingers.

She checked the time again. Almost 17:00 hours. Diana would be at the restaurant soon. The bright streets, fragrant with spices and musky perfumes, were a welcome change from the months stationed in space. Jeannette walked over to a bench and slid her datapad out of her bag, calling up her research data.

There has to be a third alternative. Dammit, she'd find one!

She needed to leave the base behind and clear her head. Figure out the questions she still needed to ask.

One thing nagged at her like a toothache: she couldn't be the first or only person to investigate these malfunctions. Yet not a single report concerning the malfunctions had been unearthed. If recombinants were the only thing standing between Earth and the Antarans, why would UCOE ignore such a critical malfunction? It made no sense.

Jeannette touched her sleeve, turning on her mobile. "Ring Kai Drew," she said, watching a group of miners shuffle down the street toward a pub. "Audio only."

"Drew here," a voice crackled through the heated air.

"Kai, it's—"

Static raked the quiet. "Seems...to be—transmission failure... connection clearing."

What was that about? Kai deliberately cut her off, but why? What was happening on the Reclamation Station? Had Stanton been within earshot?

A cold chill danced down her spine. Had Kai gotten into more trouble than he'd let on?

She needed to get back to her station, but not before she spoke to Mimi Constantine. She hoped Kai would contact her when he was able to talk.

Jeannette rose from the bench and hurried toward the restaurant, End of the Line. Someone had the answers she needed. She prayed that person was Mimi Constantine.

27

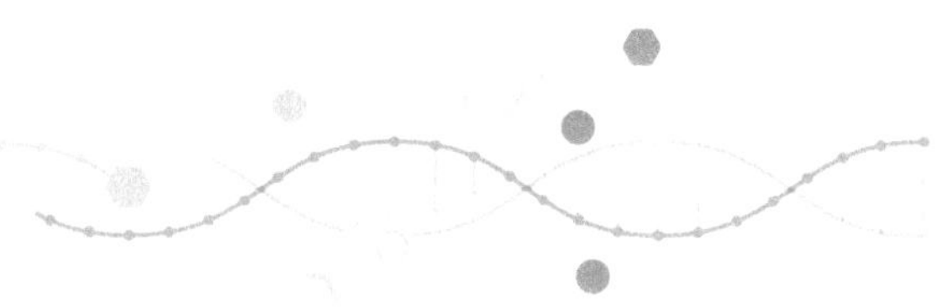

PETER GLANCED at the sky and sinking sun. Night would fall soon. He winced. He didn't want to be out here alone with those biodrones rampaging through the wilds.

His leg throbbed along with the other wounds inflicted by the biodrones' spiked appendages. Even if he found his way back to the unit, he was too weak to make it back to camp.

He reached into a small pocket at his side, making sure he still had that alien's key thing. The strange metal was warm against his fingertips and gave off a slight vibration. Almost like when he pressed his fingers against his wrist and felt the beat of his heart.

Every step through the forest and twisted brush was agony. He ached with every pain-wracked movement. Dragging the injured leg, he kept his left arm pressed tight against his side as he staggered down the shadowy, wilderness path headed southeast. Desperate to find something familiar: a landmark, the ring of gnarled trees beside the path to base camp—even a patch of blackened earth and remnants of cascade mines—anything to give him hope that he wouldn't die out here.

He reached into his shirt, feeling Diana's purple scarf. Sliding it toward his chin, he laid his face against it. *Long life, Peter,* she'd said to him, the memory like her warm breath against his neck. He wanted to live long enough to return this scarf to her. He frowned at the small tear in it. Next to his heart, it had escaped the biodrones' spikes.

Damn Drake for destroying his homing device! He sighed, hating himself. No, it was his fault. He shouldn't have taken the device out of his bag. If he made it back to camp and survived these biodrones, he'd find another way out. Another way back to Diana.

He refused to die for UCOE or the Antarans. He'd be free of both.

His grid, hanging from a lanyard around his neck, remained silent, but he kept a wary gaze on it.

After a while, the thick forest thinned out, foliage sparse as the terrain flattened into lowlands. He pushed on, working his way south until the ground became spongy, the air tinged with a musty, dank scent.

The swamps!

He kept moving across the soft ground until scattered patches of mud rose through brown, dying vegetation. Just ahead, the forest was skeletal, blackened stubs of tree trunks smoking against muddy water tangled with dead tree limbs and twisted brush, leaves scorched.

Plasma fire!

Had other UCOE units encountered biodrones here? He swallowed a moan and plunged ahead.

The chilly water numbed the pain in his limbs as he stumbled over a submerged log and twisted his ankle. He cried out, nearly falling, but managed to catch himself on some brush. The log floated up from the bottom, undulating with the gentle current.

That's when he realized it wasn't a log. He winced as the body of a dead soldier surfaced, face down. A boot floated up from the bottom, bobbing in the murky water.

Shouting, Peter threw himself backward, fell, and plunged headfirst into the water. He surfaced, gasping for air, and crawled back onto the bank.

When he could breathe again, he gathered the courage to look at the body, fearing it was Sting or Sarge. He sucked in a breath of stale air and turned the soldier over.

Her dull green flak jacket, a private's ranking on the shoulders, was shredded from biodrone spikes. She was a recombinant. The remnants of a red stain circled her chest, everything else washed clean. Her eyes were wide and terrified and her hands clutched half of a plasma rifle.

He reached down and closed her eyes. But he didn't expect to see the gold god symbol hanging around her neck. It wasn't like the one Charles had found. It was a star—or like a star. One of the medics back at RDC said there were many kinds. How had she gotten it? He ran his index finger across it. Had the god symbol given her a soul? Or did the symbol save it somehow? He didn't even understand what that meant anymore.

Saved for what? To return to this?

He shuddered, jerking his fingers from the symbol, and moved away from her, his steps harder and harder to take. She was beyond any help he could offer. He got as far as a fallen log halfway across the swamp when his body gave out and he collapsed onto the log. With every breath, his body throbbed with pain.

Abruptly, the soft whine of his grid began, ticking in sharp beats that grew faster and louder.

Antarans! They'd found him. And he couldn't even run.

Moaning, he clutched his rifle against his chest. It didn't matter if the biodrones found him now. He was too sick to care.

He glanced at his rifle and ejected the spent charges. Reaching behind him into his field pack, he struggled to pull a handful free. All he could manage was one. He fought to lock it into the chamber.

It wouldn't be enough.

Reaching down to his boot, he slid the termination kit free. Pulling the kit onto his chest, he tore it open with shaking fingers, staring at the capsules inside.

Death was only a breath away. A single gasp to free him from this agony.

Another wave of pain ripped through him. He cried out. His face, fever-hot, burned. None of the sims taught him what to do if he survived the spikes. They'd drilled deep into the skin, causing illness. He knew that now.

He shivered violently, fever throbbing at his temples. Now, Diana would never know what happened to him. He groaned. He'd never see her again.

Struggling against the fever, he tried to rise. Couldn't.

The grid screamed, the beats bleeding together into a solid pulse.

He held the two pills up to the thin daylight clawing through the treetops and thought about Charles and the god symbols. What poor Charles must have gone through in his head that night? Fighting the helplessness, fighting the fear—wishing so desperately for it not to be like this.

"Please...I don't want to do this," he muttered, his eyes burning with regret. "Don't make me end this."

The shrill shriek of the grid beat in time with his heart. He swallowed a breath. He'd be overrun by biodrones in moments.

He didn't want to do this, but it was better than being ripped to shreds by hordes of biodrones.

His eyes stung with tears as he laid one of the capsules to his lips.

"Forgive me, Diana."

Images of Diana's purple scarf touched his spinning thoughts, her green robe, the sweet tea—that night at the river, her bare skin against his. She'd hate him for doing this. She'd expect him to fight back.

"Pete!" Sting's voice carried over the swamp.

Peter jerked back the capsule, staring at it a moment. To hell with D'Angelo's suicide kit! Gritting his teeth, Peter flung them into the swamp.

"Answer me! Dammit, where are you? Pete!"

His whole body shuddered. "Sting!" He cried out. "Go back! Biodrones approaching!"

"Pete! Keep talking, man! I'll find you!"

"No! Don't!" he shouted. "Biodrones!"

In the distance, swamp water splashed.

"Sting, the grid!" Agony ripped through him. "Sting, no!"

The splashing grew louder and louder until he felt the current nearby.

"Pete—oh man, am I glad to see you! Thought you were dead!"

Hands fell against his arms. Through a mask of pain, he gazed up at Sting.

"Antarans," he half whispered. "Spikes...the grid."

With a fearful look, Sting snatched the grid out of his hand. He studied it for a moment and then grinned. He flicked a switch and the grid fell silent.

"You still had it on heat sensing, Pete." Sting chuckled and laid a hand against Peter's forehead. "Shit, you're burnin' up. Let's get you back to camp. You're not gonna die on me."

With Sting's help, Peter struggled to his feet, but his legs buckled. He slumped against Sting.

"Easy, Pete. Can you walk?"

With a groan, Peter shook his head.

"Take a deep breath. I'm going to pick you up and carry you."

Nodding, Peter held his breath as Sting hefted him onto his shoulders. Peter squeezed his eyes shut against the unbearable pain.

He lost consciousness, but a short time later the splash of water and Sting's huffing echoed around him. Time cut out again and the hill that stood outside the camp rose around him.

"Thanks, Sting," he mumbled.

"I owed you one, Pete." He laughed. "Besides, I couldn't stand being out here without you."

As Sting ascended the hill, Peter heard someone shout and run toward them.

"Stingley, you found him!" Sarge. "Good work."

"Told you I'd find him."

"Next time, ask, dammit! You almost got my ass in a sling. I had to explain to D'Angelo why I had two soldiers MIA."

Peter couldn't see Sarge's face, but Sarge sounded relieved despite his anger.

"I couldn't leave my best friend out in the swamp to die, especially with all those biodrones scoping for us."

Sting started down the hill, Sarge beside him.

"Mitchell, thanks to you, the unit missed that horde of fast-approaching biodrones. We outran them, but two other units encountered them. There were heavy casualties."

Peter tried to explain how he'd been attacked and how he'd seen a caregiver, but it was too painful to speak.

"Pete met part of that horde, Sarge," said Sting. "He's got the spike marks and the fever to prove it."

"We'd better get him to the infirmary, Stingley."

Sting hurried across the camp to the infirmary, Sarge still beside him. When he reached the entrance, two medics gently lifted Peter from Sting's shoulders. They carried him inside and laid him on a table. Sting peeled off Peter's jacket. Then the medics started to cut through his shirt.

"No!" Peter shouted and tore at the medics until he could pull Diana's scarf free. Sting snatched the scarf out of Peter's hands.

"I'll hold this for you until they've got ya settled. Now, shut up and let 'em work, Pete."

He stopped fighting, allowing them to cut away his uniform.

THROUGHOUT THE NIGHT, Peter's fever rose, hovering around some danger zone, he'd heard the medics say. 104? 105? He felt presences nearby and every once in a while, faces bled through the delirium. He was running through mud as the grid pounded out a steady rhythm. No matter how hard he ran, he couldn't outpace the grid and he couldn't get away.

"No, too many . . . too many. Sting, look out!"

"Easy, Pete," said a voice. A hand squeezed his.

"Sting?" Peter muttered, his tongue thick and his body aching. "Sting!"

Something pinched the crook of his arm and in moments, the pain receded and his body tingled with numbness and relief.

"I'm here, Pete. You're gonna be just fine." Sting.

"There's so much venom in his system. They aren't sure they can counteract it all." Sarge.

Peter slept again, waking sometime later to the sound of voices near him.

"I don't give a damn what the medics say! Pete's gonna pull through. You hear me?"

"Hope you're right, Stingley." Sarge. "Medics want to give up on him."

"Why?" Sting demanded.

"Wasting too many resources—"

"On a recombinant? Damn them, Sarge!"

"No worries, Stingley," said Sarge. "I threatened to waste all our plasma charges if they stopped treatment."

Sting's laughter faded into darkness.

Grid sounds pulsed through Peter's head again. A sheen of sweat clung to his face like a mask. He thrashed harder against the pain and fever, but something pinched the crook of his arm again. He relaxed, his hair soaked with sweat. He tried to keep his voice quiet, but the words spilled out.

"No...stop them. Stop them! They want our technology."

Sting leaned down. "What was that, Pete?"

More mumbles.

"I don't know! He's delirious." Sting.

"Antarans," Peter continued, smiling. "They want—me. Imagine that. Me!"

Sting turned to Sarge. "He hasn't made sense all morning, Sarge."

"They want me. I'm their new hope. Me?" It was all so ridiculous.

Peter laughed, his breath raspy. Recombinants were the lowest form of life, yet the Antarans prized them. His chest heaved with effort. "Some are like—wolves. With snouts...mottled skin. Hunting us. Changing. Always changing. Blending. Becoming like us. So, we don't know they're there."

The fever spun him off into the swamp again, and he tried to run through the murk. Couldn't.

"What's he babbling about?" Sarge.

"No idea, Sarge. Not sure where he's gettin' this stuff. That's what's scaring me." He leaned down again. "Pete, how do you know this?"

Through the red haze of fever, Peter smiled again. "Caregivers. Called off—biodrones. Explained—changed. Explained about—"

The swamp sucked him in again. He was running, running. No way to escape the biodrones. Spikes raked past. His arm ached.

Gently, a hand shook his shoulder. "Pete, explained what? What do you mean changed? Talk to me, buddy."

From deep within the swamp, Peter heard Sting's call. He slogged back through the muck, running toward the voice.

"Pete, stay with us, man. Tell us what all of this means."

Peter slipped away from the swamp and opened his eyes. He turned his gaze to Sting, and Sting's body went slack with relief.

"Mitchell, what were you saying? Something about what—caregivers?" Sarge.

Peter turned his fuzzy gaze to Sarge's haggard face. "They want our technology, Sarge. To save their people. They said my code held —secrets."

A jumble of questions rushed at him, hurting his head. Sting. Sarge. What are caregivers? Where did you see them? How did they change? How did you escape?

His leg throbbed again.

Peter cried out. For a third time, something punctured the crook of his arm and he floated away as the pain hovered somewhere off in the distance. He tried to answer the voices poking at him, asking questions in bits of broken words and phrases, but he felt himself sinking into the cool swamp mud.

The grid and the biodrones faded into twilight. Burning pains cooled. Aches softened. Sounds receded until Peter slept in the coolness.

SOMETIME LATER, Peter awoke cold and stiff. His limbs ached with soreness, but the fever had broken. He felt weak, unable to even lift his head. He slept on and off until Sergeant Temple entered the infirmary. He sat down in a chair beside Peter's sickbed.

"How are you feeling this morning, Mitchell?"

"Weak," he answered.

"Your fever broke just before sunrise."

"How do you know—?"

"I was here with Sting."

He nodded and offered a weary smile. Why would Sergeant Temple sit with him like that? And Sting.

"You're lucky to be alive."

"I didn't think I'd make it back here."

Sarge settled back in the chair. "Tell me what happened."

Peter sighed. So much happened out there. Much of it, he didn't understand and he hadn't had a chance to sort through it all, to see if it made any sense.

"I was scanning for biodrones," he began, surprised at the thin sound of his voice. "When I turned to catch up with the unit, all of you were gone. I ran up the pathway until it forked." He took a deep breath. "I switched to a body-heat scan and followed the path with the most heat signatures, but I picked the wrong one." Another deep breath. "That's when my grid activated. I stood my ground against the biodrones, Sarge, but I ran into a different sort of Antaran. One I'd never seen before."

"You called it a caregiver last night," said Sarge. He leaned forward in the chair.

"Yeah, Sarge. That's what it called itself. A caregiver." Wait, the key! He glanced around for his clothes. "Where's my uniform?" He forced himself up on his elbows.

"What was left of it probably went into the incinerator," said Sarge, a quizzical look on his face. "Why?"

"Because I took something from the caregiver."

Sarge sat up in the chair. "Took something? What?"

Peter rubbed a hand across his face. "Some kind of key thing. I thought I put it in my pocket."

"A key?" Sarge's eyes widened. "To what?"

"I don't know," said Peter. He eased himself back against the cot. "Damn. I must have lost it in the swamp."

"Or it burned with your uniform." Sarge sighed and sat back in the chair.

"That caregiver was really anxious to get it back, but I didn't return it."

Sarge's dark eyes widened, his mouth gaping. "Wait, are you telling me you *spoke* to an Antaran, Mitchell? Is that what you're saying?"

He nodded.

"Holy shit! Tell me what else happened!"

"The Antaran says he needs our recombinant technology for his people. Said they'd been searching for my code. Said it held secrets."

Sarge was far away now, contemplating something Peter could only imagine. "If they need something from us, then that means they have a weakness." He smiled, his gaze darting back to Peter's face. "Anything else you can tell me?"

Peter nodded. "This climate is perfect for the resurrection of their people."

At this information, Sarge frowned. "What do you mean resurrection? This planet's choked to the gills with Antarans."

"That's what the caregiver said." Peter yawned, his eyes closing.

"The Antaran people must be . . . something different from . . . biodrones . . . and caregivers. They called my code Constantine. I don't know what that means."

Sarge's voice touched him from a great distance as Peter fought to keep his eyes open. But Sarge's words faded, the world darkening until Peter fell into a cool, deep sleep.

PETER REMAINED in the infirmary for most of the week until he was finally released back to his unit shelter. He walked with uneven steps, still feeling the residual weakness of the biodrone's venom. He'd told his encounter several times now, even to D'Angelo who sat with a stone face and said nothing after Peter told him what happened. Finally, he reached the shelter.

"Hey, Mitchell, good work out there," said a recombinant he didn't know. The stocky, dark-haired man patted him gently on the shoulder.

"Yeah, thanks for saving our asses out there," another one shouted from a bedroll beside the door.

Peter was grinning by the time he reached his bedroll. Sting smirked at him from his own bedroll.

"You're the luckiest damned recombinant I've ever met, Pete."

Peter frowned. He didn't feel lucky. He hurt. "In what way?"

Sting sat up, his white t-shirt stark in the thin yellow light from his ion lamp. "I get my ass torn up by a cascade mine and you carry me back like I'm a loser. You get your ass torn up by biodrones and I carry you back a hero." His smile faded, a serious look that Pete hadn't seen for a long time. "I'd have given anything to have traded places with you, Pete. To be the hero who saved his unit."

Sitting down beside Sting, Peter sighed. "Look, Sting. I didn't try to be a hero. It just happened. I saw the grid—dammit, I felt those things out there—and I knew I had to make someone hear me. I just didn't want to die, Sting. That's your big hero. I was just trying to stay alive."

That old, familiar smile returned. "Yeah, I know. Just wish I'd been the one is all." He waved his arm toward the other recombinants in the shelter. "You earned their respect, Pete. In about as personal a way as a guy can get. I've got their respect because I survived all this. I've got a rep. You've got their trust. Big difference."

Peter shook his head. "No, you're wrong, Sting. You've got experience. You lived through this hell and in unfamiliar situations, you'll be the first guy they turn to." He smiled. "Granted, they won't call me the King of Grid Confusion anymore, but you have their trust, too, Sting."

"You're right."

Peter sighed and his gaze fell to the floor. "Back there in the swamp, when my grid was wailing and I couldn't move, I thought I was gonna die."

"You can't think like that, Pete—"

"Listen to me," said Peter, his voice urgent and imploring. With a pained expression, Sting nodded for him to continue. "I thought a horde of biodrones was approaching, but I could only manage to load one charge in my rifle." He sighed, bowing his head. "So, I...took out the termination kit."

"Pete!" Sting's face paled.

"I didn't want to do it, Sting, but I couldn't face being torn apart by those biodrones. The kit was the only way out."

"It's okay, man."

"But then I thought about Diana and I couldn't go through with it. I'm no hero, Sting."

Sting's arm slid around Peter's shoulders. "None of us wants to face that. It's fear. But who says you would've died? You escaped them once. Sometimes getting through the fear is the test, Pete."

"Test? Of what?"

"Of being alive. We let fear stop us from so many things." Sting patted him on the back. "You didn't let it wash you out, Pete, so don't let it shut you down here. Now, go get some rest. You look like shit." Sting reached into his duffle bag and handed him Diana's purple scarf. "Here. I've been keeping it for you."

"Thanks, Sting," Peter said, taking the scarf.

He moved over to his bedroll and stretched out. The soft, spongy mattress felt good against his sore body.

With Diana's scarf and Sting a few feet away, Peter felt calm. Safe. Ready to take on the entire Antaris Nation if he had to. Tomorrow, he decided, retreating into his bedroll and closing his eyes.

28

AFTER A FEW WEEKS of washing dishes, Diana moved to the restaurant's office where she spent a lot of time inputting reservations and server schedules. Next, Mimi put her in charge of basic transactions. Diana spent time overseeing bill payments, authorizing customer transactions, and handling shuttle deliveries. When Mimi was satisfied, Diana began processing recombinant placements with the underground teams. In time, she began to help create the recombinants' new identities.

Diana worked hard and made sure every single detail she handled was accurate and complete. Mimi had kept her word and involved her in the underground's activities, but Diana longed for more direct intervention than data entry. She wanted to fly to Ku'Tal with the teams.

And try to locate Peter.

After processing today's new recombinant identities, Diana shut down the old computer and leaned back in the office desk chair. Mimi's small office was well lit, but cramped, walls painted burnt orange. A beat-up wooden desk took most of the space. The room smelled warm with fresh-brewed tea. Peppermint today. Along with traces of Mimi's patchouli that lingered, clinging to the desk chair long after she'd left the room.

Diana worked through the evening's transaction Mimi had left for her to process, including a new request for a recombinant identity. Each transaction began as encrypted digital currency and entered a tunnel of online, individual but anonymous chained transactions until it reached a final destination. Completely untrackable. She also had four new id requests burrowing their way through the private marketplaces deep in the solar arrays until the pieces all came together. Anonymously. Diana read the numbers, wishing one of these was for Peter, but every time, she checked the numbers, they weren't even close to Peter's ID number. She'd memorized it. It stuck out an extra place than the other numbers. She didn't know why.

A half-full, purple paisley teacup (one she brought from her place) sat on the desk, lukewarm now. Behind the cup sat an empty, white salad bowl, swirls of honey French dressing, carrot slivers, and lettuce clinging to the sides. Instead of a window in the office, one of the walls was a huge nature holo that changed every so often. Diana couldn't wait to leave this small cell every evening.

She finished processing the last of the evening's transactions, logging the restaurants sales and pay outs. She printed a summary to the old printer that Mimi refused to replace with better tech. As it powered up with a whine and papers fluttered through it, Diana turned to the far wall and grinned at her newly purchased dartboard.

She reached inside the desk drawer for the set of green darts mixed in with the pens and pencils. At this distance, she couldn't miss, but it was satisfying all the same. With a snap of her wrist, she flung a green-tailed dart at the board. The dart hissed through the air and whumped into the rubber board.

Dead center. She smiled. Bull's-eye. She hadn't lost her touch.

The Tree House's monthly dart tournament was coming up. She didn't want to miss it—and she didn't want to look like her skills had slipped. She hated to look incompetent.

A knock resounded through the tiny office. She rolled her desk chair away from the threshold and flung open the door. Mimi stood there and stared through Diana a moment, her patchouli scent wafting like fresh-tilled earth, like she'd just dug someone's grave. No smile or welcoming expression warmed her face. It looked tight, tense. Lips pressed into a thin line, fleeked brows bunched into worried creases.

"Something's wrong," said Diana.

"We've got some problems with the operation," said Mimi, her voice clipped. "Come into the dining room."

"I'll be right there."

Diana checked her watch—almost 22:00. The restaurant closed in an hour. By now, most of the servers and kitchen crew had gone home. The dishwasher was probably finished with most of the plates and silverware by now. She tossed the other two darts at the board, one landing beside the first dart, the other landing a hair outside the bull's-eye. Then she hurried out to the dining room.

Main lights were dimmed, candles blown out, vertical blinds closed in every section except the main dining room. She smiled, the side that faced the river.

The memory rushed back at her, the sparkle of his clear blue eyes, burning with pure joy at every light, every sound—every taste. His face glowed with wonder, every moment of the world so new and amazing that it made his eyes water and his body tremble. And the passion that had radiated from his hands, pulsed across lips, and set his skin alight as she'd explored his body and made love to him. All of it, he gave back to her in his touch, in every kiss, every whisper of her name. It was the only time she'd ever felt that someone loved her. And meant it.

Maudlin faces and downcast expressions filled the space, the silence heavy, tempering her memories of being with Peter. Mimi's entire team had gathered, looking defeated and lost. She took a deep breath.

Whatever was going on was bad. Very bad.

She recognized the woman she knew as Linda at one of the

tables, her face pressed into a yellow tissue, long blond braid down her back. Her shoulders trembled, faint sob muffled but sharp. Diana recognized another guy on Mimi's payroll, Richie, holding her hand. His eyes were rimmed red, face bruised and streaked with dirt.

As she walked through the room, she got a closer look at both Linda and Richie. Their clothes were torn and bloodied. A bruise darkened across Linda's cheek, her face looking thinner than its usually chiseled appearance. Richie stroked his short Van Dyke beard and Diana noticed how chafed and skinned up his fingers were, knuckles raw and bleeding. From the looks of them, they'd just escaped something horrific. Had they been at the front? Bringing recombinants back from Ku'Tal.

No. It was worse than that. Much worse.

"What's happened?" Diana asked.

"Kev's dead," Linda blurted out and her sobs deepened. "Shuttle's littered all across Ku'Tal's swamps!"

"We lost Kev and all five recombinants," said Richie, sounding sick, his voice trembling. "It was awful. Just awful."

Diana gasped. Six people. Gone in an instant. Vaporized. Her stomach twisted into a knot. She glanced from Richie to Linda. The devastation in Linda's face was chilling. She winced, hurting all over for Linda.

Diana had been sheltered and lucky, her family intact and untouched by this war like so many others in home system. Before she'd met Peter, before David got sent to the front, the war was just someone else's problem, fought on the distant edge, destroying other people's lives. Recombinants died by the thousands, citizens by the dozens, yet not enough to shake home system awake. Diana knew that deep down, she'd been like everyone else—expecting other people to do the fighting, as long as the war didn't interrupt her network access and streamed entertainment.

Tonight, the war became personal for Linda. Very personal.

"Linda and I couldn't get back to the shuttle before it fragged," Richie blurted out, trembling now. "We nearly got our asses kicked by

Antarans! But we shot our way through the swamp and hitched a ride on a UCOE cargo ship."

Linda pulled the tissue away from her face. Her bottom lip quivered. "Kev tried to take off, but biodrones got inside the shuttle. He was airborne for five minutes before they got him." She pulled in a breath, tears running down her cheeks. "There were five more recombinants waiting at the shelter. There's gotta be more now. And Kev's not—there to..." She covered her eyes.

Diana laid a hand on Linda's shoulder. "I'm so sorry."

"Kev and I worked together for years." She kicked the table. "Dammit, our kids are in college together! What are we going to do now?" Her pleading gaze rose to Mimi. "What now, Mimi?"

Richie also turned his bleary gaze to Mimi.

"That location's going to be overrun very soon," said Mimi. "The safe house has to be moved. And those recombinants, they don't stand a chance unless we get them off world soon. There are whispers of an imminent UCOE pullout. I'll contact Ron, tell him to move to a new location."

"No one's pulled their MRCs yet," said Linda, her voice raspy. "If their units scan and find them—they'll be shot on the spot. Kev would never forgive me if—"

"I can get another shuttle here by the end of the week," Mimi said, her voice tight.

"But the cost," Linda said with a gasp, her eyes wide.

Mimi waved her away, bracelets rattling. "You let me worry about that. I've got some folks who owe me favors." Mimi paced around the table. "The only problem is getting back to Ku'Tal in time."

Her gaze fell to Diana.

"You know I'm a pilot, Mimi."

"Forget it, Diana," said Linda. "Kev was a combat shuttle pilot for years. Flew two tours in the Antaran war, including the drop on Naharra. Two years ago, they called him up to fly a third. He was a veteran when we hooked up with Mimi. You've only been a pilot for —what, a year?"

"Eighteen months," Diana corrected her.

"I'll put out a call for another pilot," said Mimi, continuing to pace. "Diana could help me. We'll have to shell out a lot of credits for such short notice, but business has been good this month."

Diana crossed her arms. "The only way I can help is by flying that new shuttle."

"No way," snapped Linda. "Too dangerous. She could kill us all!"

"Yeah, I could get you all killed," Diana said, her voice sharp. "But I could also get you in and out of Ku'Tal like a whisper. Your call."

"She'd be cheaper than a veteran," Richie remarked.

Diana shrugged. "Maybe. I'll fly your shuttle for as long as you need me—on the condition that you get Peter Mitchell out. Soon. That's my price."

Mimi started to speak, but Diana cut her off. "Don't tell me it's not possible! I know you've got an entire team that does nothing but scan for recombinants. Scan for Peter's MRC, whatever it takes, just locate him. Because on my last Ku'Tal run, he leaves with me."

"That's it?" said Linda, frowning. "That's all you want for risking your life?"

That's it. It was all she wanted for the rest of her life—the man she loved standing beside her. Free of military hardware. Free of the armed forces. Forever.

"That's it. That's everything—he's everything." Peter didn't belong at the front. And she loved him. He and David meant everything to her. "Well, Mimi, you said when I moved on to other jobs, I'd get involved in parts of this operation. What's it gonna be?"

Mimi moved around the table and took Diana's hands in hers. She turned them palms up and then down. "Your fuchsia has begun to deepen. And kiddo, it'll get a lot darker before this is over. Are you sure you want to do this? You don't have to. There are other ways to help." She lowered her voice so only Diana heard her speak. "Other ways to get Peter out."

Diana smiled. "Piloting is what I do best. I'll prove that to all of you before this is over."

"I believe you will, my dear. I feel it." Mimi squeezed Diana's hands and let go of them. "It's settled. You, Richie, and Linda will leave for Ku'Tal as soon as the new shuttle arrives."

"What about Peter?" she asked.

"You prove to me that you're here because you believe in what we're doing and I'll work on getting Peter out."

Diana nodded. "Fair enough. If you mean that."

"I mean that," Mimi replied. "We'll work on getting him out."

Linda and Richie rose from the table and went into the kitchen. As Diana rose from her chair, she saw a slim woman with short auburn hair standing at the reservation desk.

Dr. Kingston.

Diana cringed. This was really bad timing. She hadn't gotten a chance to even mention Dr. Kingston's request yet.

"Um, Mimi—" Diana said, pointing toward the door.

Mimi hurried over to the door and plucked a menu from the desk. "Good evening."

"Good evening. If you're still open, I'd like to eat supper."

"Of course, we're open—follow me." Mimi led Dr. Kingston toward a table by the window. Diana followed.

Dr. Kingston sat down and Mimi extended the menu. She hurried over to the server station and grabbed a silver pitcher, filling Dr. Kingston's water glass.

"Mimi? Can you sit down for a moment?"

Mimi frowned. "Whatever for, Diana?"

Diana motioned toward Dr. Kingston. "Dr. Kingston is a friend of mine and—she needs your help."

"*My* help?" Mimi set the pitcher on the table and slid into a chair. Diana sat down beside her, across from Dr. Kingston. She squinted at the doctor a moment. "Wait—Dr. Kingston," she said. "Dr. Jeannette Kingston?"

Dr. Kingston nodded, looking surprised. "You know my name?"

Mimi nodded. "Yes, of course I remember you! You worked with my brother, Orlando. Don't you remember? At RDC."

Dr. Kingston's mouth fell open, eyes wide. She shook her head. "No...I–I don't, I—" She pulled in a breath, looking confused. "I worked at RDC?"

Mimi nodded, her eyes turning watery. "Orlando loved working with you. Loved your compassion and fairness."

"I worked with your brother?" said Dr. Kingston. "At RDC?"

"Yes, Orlando Constantine, my little brother, but that was a long time ago," said Mimi, a smile touching her face. "Before Ballese. Before Orlando—died there."

"I'm so sorry," said Dr. Kingston.

Diana studied Mimi's face, the hurt in her eyes. She didn't know about Mimi's brother being on Ballese, the colony that was destroyed.

"Mimi," Diana replied, "Dr. Kingston is researching something. It's—well, you tell her, doctor."

Dr. Kingston rested her elbows on the table. "I apologize for this clandestine meeting, but I thought you could help me with some research."

"What sort of research?" Mimi asked, looking from Dr. Kingston to Diana, one eyebrow raised.

"Let me speak in hypotheticals," said Dr. Kingston. "Let's say a defect was discovered in an MRC chip, a defect that could affect thousands of—UCOE privates."

Mimi nodded for her to continue.

"And let's say these defects were registering at certain reclamation stations in increasing numbers and a reclamation specialist was quietly investigating the malfunction. She discovers that reporting the defect could destroy thousands of—UCOE privates, but not reporting it could endanger UCOE's position at the front."

"And let's say," Mimi replied, leaning closer and talking more softly now, "that certain groups had already discovered this malfunction and have recovered samples from these soldiers. Would those specimens be valuable to said reclamation specialist?"

Dr. Kingston's gaze was intense in the candlelight. "You have some I could study?"

"Yes," said Mimi. "Do you know what's causing the malfunctions?"

"I wish I knew," Dr. Kingston said with a sigh. "I'm still studying the cause."

Mimi nodded. "We scan for those malfunctions—it's one of the criteria we've been using to rescue recombinants."

"Why is that?" Diana asked.

"We have—access to recombinant records," Mimi said with a smirk, "so we're able to select possible candidates based on behavior records. But once we've got possibles, we try to locate the ones with failing MRCs. If they are even-tempered and intelligent with a failing MRC, we believe they can think for themselves and are capable of other things."

Diana sat back in her chair. That made a lot of sense. Mimi seemed to have some higher-level plan in mind for the recombinants she rescued, but Diana had never been able to figure out what.

Dr. Kingston discussed her statistics with Mimi and Mimi offered her own. After thirty minutes of discussion, both women had learned something new about recombinant hardware and MRCs. Diana didn't understand all the micro insertions and nano pumps and other details. She trusted their assessment.

"Do you have copies of those records for your specimens?"

Mimi nodded.

Dr. Kingston was silent for a moment, her hand resting against her neck. "There is another reason I came to speak with you."

Her MRC. Was Dr. Kingston finally going to remove it?

Diana studied her face, looking for a sign of indecision, but all she saw was resolve and determination.

"What else do you want to know?" Mimi asked.

"I know that you remove recombinants' MRCs," said Dr. Kingston in a quiet voice. "But what about civilians? I will pay you for your time." A sad look touched Dr. Kingston's face.

"*You* have an MRC?" Mimi asked, her mouth falling open. "Guess that explains why you don't remember my brother."

Dr. Kingston nodded. "I want to remember everything again, but I don't want this conversation to get back to UCOE through my MRC. Besides, it has locked away most of my life and I want it back—with all its pain and uncertainty." Her eyes turned glassy. "I'm tired of living life in the third person."

Mimi reached out and laid a hand on Dr. Kingston's arm. "Tan and blue..."

Diana smiled at the confused expression on Dr. Kingston's face. She'd find out soon enough about Mimi's outlook on life.

"Your aura is blue and tan. You constantly struggle between compassion and fact. That's why the MRC is so difficult for you. That's what Orlando liked about you—your compassion." Mimi squeezed her arm and let go. "After you've eaten, I'll happily remove it for you."

"There's one consideration though. I want the chip removed intact, like your specimens. There are memories and people I've forgotten—people who should never be forgotten. Like your brother."

Mimi didn't seem bothered by Dr. Kingston's request. "You want it readable, but not trackable. No problem. I can dump all the data onto a card for you."

"Thank you, this means a lot to me," said Dr. Kingston.

She opened a pouch at her side and slid a credit voucher to Mimi. Mimi picked up the small plastic voucher, its grey round edges smooth, and touched the display. She gasped. "Dr. Kingston, I can't accept this much!"

Diana craned her neck to see the amount, but the LED cleared before she could read it.

"Consider it a donation."

Smiling, Mimi rose from the table. "Let's get some food and wine on this table," she said.

Dr. Kingston picked out her meal from the menu and Mimi hurried toward the kitchen.

Diana waited until Mimi was out of earshot. "Doctor, what are you going to report to UCOE—about the recombinants?" She searched Dr. Kingston's eyes for a flicker of sympathy. Mimi said she was compassionate and Diana felt her compassion, but she didn't know if it stretched to the recombinants. To Peter.

Dr. Kingston shook her head. "I don't know yet. It's not an easy decision by any means."

"It's just that Peter Mitchell—"

She smiled, patted Diana's hand. "Diana, I know you're in love with him."

"Is it that obvious?" Diana said with a frown.

"It's all right to show you care for someone," said Dr. Kingston. "Especially a recombinant." She leaned back in her chair and glanced out the window, a smile lighting her face. "Come tomorrow morning, I'll still remember this night."

Diana shivered at the thought of losing cherished memories. It must have driven Dr. Kingston crazy all these years, knowing that pentacle moments of her life had been erased or made inaccessible. She stared at the colored lights flickering against the dark river and remembered the short time she'd shared with Peter. The warmth of his hands, heat of his skin. The wonder and joy in his eyes. He was so alive, every moment exploding with meaning and memory. That memory was all that kept her going sometimes. She ached at his absence. To lose that would be unimaginable.

AFTER DR. KINGSTON HAD EATEN, Mimi led her through the kitchen and they disappeared into the pale hallway lights. Diana sat by the window, sipping merlot as she watched the skimmers flit past. It seemed like an eternity until Dr. Kingston emerged from the kitchen again, her face pale. She looked very subdued.

Diana hurried up from her chair and moved toward her as Mimi exited the kitchen. She carried a small parcel in her hands—MRCs, Diana realized.

"Did everything go all right?" Diana asked, looking from Dr. Kingston's pallid face to Mimi's calm expression.

"Everything is fine," said Mimi. "Are you well enough to travel, doctor?"

She nodded. "I'll be fine." She turned to Diana and shook her hand. "Diana, thank you for everything. I'll be leaving the base by the end of the week, so this is goodbye. I've already transferred the credits for this week's hours to you. Thank you for all your help."

"Good luck, doctor. I hope you recover some of what you've lost."

"So do I," she said with a smile. "And thank you, Mimi, for your help. When I discover the source of the defect, I'll contact you. With another donation as well. I want to help."

"Thank you, Jeannette," Mimi replied and shook her hand. "I look forward to talking with you soon."

"I have a shuttle to catch. Thank you, both of you."

Diana waved goodbye to Dr. Kingston as the doctor moved slowly through the restaurant. On her neck, Diana saw a small skin-colored bandage.

"Good night, Mimi. I'll see you tomorrow."

"Sleep well, Diana," said Mimi, walking toward the kitchen. "And don't forget to keep living your life."

Diana left the restaurant and wandered the balmy, night-quiet streets toward the transit stop, remembering when she and Peter had passed this way. She missed him so much.

For Peter, she stepped onto the shuttle platform and with head thrown back and arms outstretched, she waited for the shuttle to rush past.

29

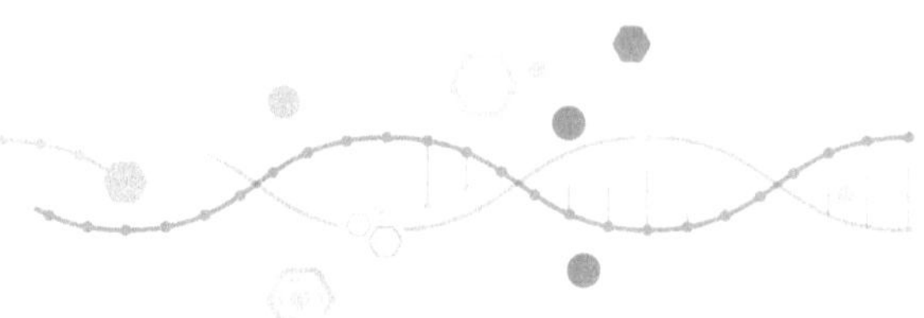

WINTER EXPLODED ACROSS KU'TAL, the bitter cold shattering tree limbs and heavy snow burying trails. The clashes with Antaran biodrones had grown more frequent and casualties had increased. The infirmary overflowed. The less serious cases were quickly transferred back to their bedrolls and exhausted, stressed-out medics made shelter rounds once a day. Several recombinants in Peter's unit had been injured, some maimed, by the biodrones. At night, he heard the rasp of fevered breathing and moans. He knew the nightmares that touched their sleep. He hadn't been able to shake those images for some time.

More of his unit had died and another transport arrived with freshly trained, hungry recombinants. Peter watched them depart the transport, energized and eyes burning to see combat. He would never forget the day his unit arrived and the terror he'd felt. The new recombinants' voices carried across the camp and Peter felt sick.

Half of them would be dead in two weeks.

A numbness cycled through him, replacing the fear with dull dread. He no longer cared what happened. Every day since Sting brought him in from the swamp, Peter checked his grid for any sign of the safe house. Nothing. Not a single clue. He'd been here for nearly four months now—he and Sting checked. Ten months of life. In two months, Peter would have an anniversary. His first. He sighed. He doubted he'd live to see it.

Behind him, Sting moved through the narrow spaces and toward the flap. Peter stepped out in the cold, letting Sting pass.

"New recombinants?" Sting asked, pausing. He leaned against the shelter.

"Green and stupid," Peter remarked.

Sting watched them gathering gear and reporting in to their sergeants. "By the end of next week, a third of them'll be dead."

Peter turned to look at him. He didn't smile. Sting was right. Whoever programmed the recombinants' genetic traits hadn't realized a few things. Like a little fear made people cautious. The techs had traded confidence for carelessness. And too much aggression made them stupid and dangerous—to themselves and their units.

"There's nothing you can do, Pete. Those bastards don't care anything about us. To them, we're no more than equipment. Lose your rifle, get another one. Lose a recombinant, make a new one." His green eyes looked sad.

"Sounds like you've been hanging out with me too long, Sting," Peter said with a laugh.

Sting rubbed a hand through his curly blond hair. "I'll say! Come on, let's get to mess. I'm starving."

AFTER MORNING MESS, Peter showered and trekked through the hard-packed snow to the shelter. Three of the new recruits had been assigned to his unit. Across the camp, empty shelters were filled with new units. He'd heard that two new camps had been set up nearby, one to the east, the other to the west.

Peter combed his hair and dropped down on his bedroll. Sting was reading something on his datapad.

"Hey, Sting, want to play some cards?"

Sting looked up from the datapad. "Sure."

Peter waited for him to put away the datapad and slip a deck of cards out of his duffle bag. Sting plopped down on Peter's bedroll. His hair was still wet, smelling of soap. Sting ran his fingers through his damp curls. "Gotta cut these bangs," he mumbled.

"Think we'll ever get close to the depot?" Peter asked as Sting shuffled the cards.

Sting shrugged and dealt a hand. "Don't know, Pete. I kinda hope not."

Frowning, Peter swept up his cards. "Why would you hope that?"

"Because," he said, arranging trump in his hands. "Then the tour'd be over."

"Then we'd be out of here!" Peter shook his head, amazed by what he was hearing. This didn't sound like the John Stingley he knew.

Sting's green eyes sizzled with anger, his lips curling, teeth gritted.

"Don't you get it? We blow that depot and they send us back to that damned base. We go through all that training and hoop jumping again for the next front. Then if we're lucky, they send us back here into a hotter drop zone with more chances to die." He folded his cards back into a pile and set them down. "Look, Pete, there's a lot about this you don't know yet."

"Then tell me, Sting."

His eyes burned with a cold, deep anger. Something he'd never seen in Sting before. It unnerved him.

"If you survive to be twenty-seven, they wash you out automatically. The RDC shrinks say that five years at the front creates too much stress and strain on us. We get too difficult to control. So, they ship us back to RDC and destroy us." He sighed again. "And I'm already halfway there. Today's my anniversary, Pete. I'm twenty-four today." His eyes turned watery. Biting his lip, he looked down at his cards, picked them up, and rearranged his trumps again.

Peter couldn't speak. Five years of service rewarded with a washout? He stared at his cards, pain spreading through the numbness in his chest and legs. Finally, he found his voice, but it was barely a quiet squeak.

"I didn't know. I'm sorry." No, he was sick. And angry at the betrayal.

"Forget it," Sting said with a shrug. He flashed a ghost of his usual smirk and reached down to draw a card.

AFTER A COUPLE OF GAMES, Peter excused himself. He trudged through the cold and snow until he reached mess. He traded his ion lamp for a slice of chocolate cake at the mess hall. When Peter returned, Sting was back reading his datapad.

Peter sat down on Sting's bedroll. He held out the cake to Sting.

"Happy birth anniversary, Sting."

The brightest grin he'd ever seen appeared on Sting's face. "Thanks, man!"

Peter lit a match and stuck it into the slice of cake. He'd seen videos of citizens blowing out candles on a cake. On a birth anniversary. Sting deserved to blow them out, too.

Sting wrinkled his nose at the burning match. "What's with the fire?"

"You're supposed to make a wish or something. Then blow it out. Citizens do this on their birth anniversaries."

Sting closed his eyes for a moment and then blew out the match. Reaching behind him, Sting pulled out his knife. He cut the cake in half and then cleaned the blade. He held out the plate.

"Here, Pete."

Peter picked up the gooey cake and took a big bite. Sting took small bites, savoring every mouthful.

AT 05:00 the next morning, in the middle of a squalling blizzard, Sarge called formation.

Peter thrust on heavy gloves and one of the thick off-white parkas the transports had brought. With a white field pack snug against his shoulders and Diana's scarf against his heart, Peter picked up his rifle and hurried out behind Sting. They'd all changed to grey and white uniforms for winter camouflage.

The wind and snow were blinding. He kept a hand over his eyes and fell into formation, grid hanging from a lanyard around his neck. Sarge, wearing a parka, paced back and forth, unable to stand still. The wind cut through Peter as he snapped to attention.

"All right, listen up!" Sarge's voice carried despite the wind. "This is another cleanup op. We're clearing more cascade mines. That'll bring more of those damned biodrones, so I want grids active when we leave camp. And don't be shy about pointing out bow echoes."

"Are we getting close to the depot, Sarge?" Drake asked.

"Closer than you want to know, Drake. Any more questions?"

Except for the whistle of wind, there was silence.

"Fall in! Single file. Stingley, you're on flank. Mitchell, you're on point. Move it!"

Smiling, Sting moved behind Peter. He seemed to be pleased with the arrangements. Sting clicked plasma charges into his rifle and snapped on his grid. Peter loaded his own weapon, checking to make sure he'd packed enough extra charges in his field pack. He felt for the several handfuls in his ammo pouch, relieved they were there. Then he took hold of his grid, turned it on, and checked his settings.

"Sarge thinks you're a Grid King now, Pete."

Peter shrugged. "I've got him snowed then."

UNDER THE COVER OF SNOWFALL, the swampland looked white and deadly. Everything smelled numb and cold, the decay and filth hidden. The world was silent except for the crunch of snow beneath boots. Peter imagined biodrones lying in wait beneath the snow cover. His gaze held steady on the grid, waiting for that all-too-familiar alarm to whine.

He glanced ahead at the distant hills, wondering what lay beyond this swampy hell. Was Mimi's safe house somewhere in those hills? As soon as they blew up the depot, he and Sting would fade into the wilds and search for the safe house. He couldn't go back to the base and go through this again. Not with Diana waiting for him.

He glanced back at Sting whose discerning gaze scanned the horizon and what lay behind them. Sting couldn't go back there either. Peter knew Sting would burn out long before he reached twenty-seven. Besides, he couldn't escape and leave Sting behind. Sting was a brother to him. And he'd never leave him behind. Ever.

The unit moved for what seemed like hours, stopping only once to rest and choke down rations. Peter sat down on a tree stump and unshouldered his field pack. He propped his rifle against his leg and let his grid fall against his chest as he pulled out an MRE. Releasing the self-heating tab, Peter opened a steaming packet of soup. He opened another container that heated a synthburger. The bloody taste of real meat sickened him. He didn't mind the fish at times. Waiting for the soup to cool, he nibbled on the synthburger with cheese and pickles. He preferred them slathered in mustard and ketchup, but today, he had neither. The cheese and pickles tasted good and he washed it down with hot broth that hinted of tomatoes and carrots. The hot soup kept him warm and moving out here, so he ate all of it. Laying the packets on the ground, he removed a small canister and poured biodegrading enzymes onto the packets. In moments, the enzymes reacted with the materials and completely consumed the packets. Leaving nothing behind.

Peter glanced over at Drake, who sat in the snow and ate silently. He hadn't had an encounter with Drake in a while and he wondered if that was due to the biodrones incident. Did Drake respect him now or was it too hard to get away with pummeling him, now that Peter was no longer an outcast? Not knowing made him nervous. He still looked over his shoulder when he entered the shelter or the latrine. Drake had blind-sided him before, beating Peter senseless before he could even react. He would never trust Drake.

Sarge rose from a stump and thrust his pack over his shoulder. With his rifle gripped tightly in his gloved hands, Sarge turned to the unit.

"Break's over. Let's get moving. We've still got a lot of ground to cover. There are a lot of mines to locate before D'Angelo orders the assault on the depot."

"Will that assault come soon, Sarge?" Peter asked.

"Unknown, Mitchell. Depends on what kind of orders D'Angelo gets. And whether the front line holds. The weather's a factor, too, so it might be next week. It might be months from now. There's no way to tell."

Peter stood and slipped his arms through his pack straps. Then he grabbed his rifle and glanced at his grid. It was clear as he moved beside Sting.

Nothing. Not even a whisper or a ripple. The grid face was blank. There hadn't been even a trace of a bow echo all day.

THE GRIDS REMAINED silent as they reached the end of their trek. Peter's unit entered a misty expanse of swampland. He felt water beneath the ice and snow as he moved cautiously across its slick surface. His face felt numb. He sniffed the air. Numb cold. Snow tinged with mud. A thready hint of sugar. Peter stiffened and sniffed again.

"The air's sweet," Peter announced. His stomach clenched as his grid began to whine. "I've got movement!" Peter watched the bow echo move slowly on the grid. "One echo—from the west."

"Positions!" Sarge shouted.

Recombinants collapsed behind logs and tree trunks. Peter dropped down on his haunches beside Sting.

"Got another echo," someone shouted. "Moving fast out of the north."

Grid pulses quickened. Pitch rose.

Half the unit shifted position, turning their rifles north.

"What do you see, Pete?" Sting asked. His gaze snapped from north to west and back again.

"Two more echoes!" Peter yelled. "Another west, one from the east. Course is steady—no, wait—one doubled back." Sweat collected on his forehead as he strained to trace the biodrone's course. The bow echo inverted without warning. "What the hell was that?"

"Report, Mitchell," Sarge called.

"The bow echo—just—reversed itself!" He jerked his grid in a wide arc.

Dammit! What did that mean? The echo abruptly disappeared entirely from his grid.

"I've lost echoes three and four, Sarge. They—they just vanished!"

"Biodrones still approaching west and north, Sarge," Sting replied.

Peter shook his head. How could bow echoes just suddenly vanish like that?

"Incoming!" Sting shouted.

Something screeched in the calm, talons whipping out of a tree. They caught one of the new recruits in the gut, eviscerating him. He flopped over in the snow, his plasma rifle discharging. His eyes emptied as his blood seeped red into the snow.

Sickened, Peter turned away.

A flash of red. The biodrone turned, slim grey-white mottled body rushing, talons raised.

Peter gasped. *Their color shifted to match the snow!* He fired. Missed.

The biodrone furrowed back through the snow toward him. Talons glinted in the pale winter sunlight.

Peter swung his rifle around, hoping to block the blow, but Sarge rushed forward, throwing himself in front of Peter. With a shout, he blasted the snow with his plasma rifle. A bluish green fluid gushed up, the furrow disappearing. The biodrone was destroyed.

"Thanks, Sarge," Peter said, his body going slack like a worn gasket. With shaking hands, he pulled his rifle closer.

"If I bring you back dead, Mitchell, Diana'll never forgive me," Sarge said with a smile and moved toward another biodrone.

Peter grabbed hold of his sleeve. "Sarge, the biodrones—their color shifts to match the snow."

Temple's expression turned fierce. "Heads up!" He shouted to the unit. "They're shifting color to white. To blend into the snow!"

Grids screeched steadily now, all around them, drowned out by occasional shouts and bursts of plasma.

Peter sidestepped a biodrone rushing past, white spikes barely missing his legs. He whirled and fired.

The creature screamed and fell writhing in the snow. More blue-green fluid splattered the white snow, smelling like rancid syrup.

At the uppermost part of the grid, where Peter saw the first bow echo invert, he noticed three others invert and disappear. *What lay ahead to the north? The depot?*

Or something else?

Spiked appendages slashed at him from the snow. He squeezed off two shots.

The thing heaved its last breath and quivered for several minutes beneath the cover of snow. Peter turned away, his gaze divided between grid and landscape.

Another flurry of talons ripped through the snow, throwing a fine powder wake behind it.

Sting raised his rifle, his back to it, drawing a bead on another biodrone.

Shit, he didn't see it!

"Sting!" Peter motioned him down. "Duck!" He jerked his rifle to his shoulder, aiming right at Sting's head.

"Pete, are you crazy?" Sting shouted, throwing himself to the ground.

The biodrone behind Sting rose up, spikes snapping toward him.

Peter pumped his trigger, pulses of blue plasma crackling in the cold.

The creature screeched, burnt talons and spikes flailing. It collapsed into the snow, writhing, and finally fell silent.

Sting shot the other biodrone long before it reached him. When it was nothing more than charred debris, Sting scrambled up from the ground. Fire blazed in his eyes.

"What the hell were you trying to do!" he shouted. "You could have shot my head off, ya dumb shit!"

"There was one on your six, Sting! You couldn't have shot both of them!"

Sting laid a hand against his heaving chest. "Dammit, Pete! Warn me next time! You nearly gave me heart failure."

"I did warn you," Peter answered.

"Need some help here!" Sarge's voice rose above the rifle fire.

Peter and Sting rushed past the other recombinants. They found Sarge pinned between two biodrones. Peter shot one while Sting disposed of the other one.

Still breathing hard, Sarge clapped Peter on the shoulder and gave a nod of thanks to Sting.

When the last biodrone had been destroyed, Sarge called roll. Of the fifteen that had gone into the swamp, twelve survived.

Exhausted and aching, Peter leaned against a tree. It could have been worse, so much worse.

After they rested and buried their dead as best they could, the unit started the long hike back to camp. They'd been lucky today. Peter hoped their luck would continue.

As they walked, Peter's thoughts drifted back to the strange bow echoes he'd seen. Those biodrones had just fallen off the grid for a time, reappearing in a few minutes.

No, he realized, they weren't going inside somewhere—he

shivered—they were coming out. Had he stumbled onto their camp? Had the inverted bow echo been some sort of bioshielded entrance to an Antaran facility?

The depot! It had to be the depot. He turned around and rushed back to tell Sarge.

30

JEANNETTE'S QUARTERS aboard the Reclamation Station seemed so unfamiliar and strange now that her MRC was gone.

Had it always been so stark and cold?

Bits of green and purple dotted the grey room, but it seemed too somber and empty. She gazed into the revolving holo print that reflected back desert sunsets. Smiling, she remembered the bright streets of Civilization and its amber horizon. It was enough that the memory was still there. She remembered Diana and Mimi and the young recombinants she'd observed. Including Peter Mitchell.

How amazing it felt to have those tiny comforts to fall back on again...she'd forgotten those things.

The small heated container of MRCs sat on the table beside her space portal. It was not much bigger than her hand. Inside that container were a lot of answers—and memories. Would she be able to handle all of them?

The chime on her door rang and she opened it. There stood Kai, a warm smile on his face.

"Just found out you'd signed back aboard. You're looking more relaxed than when you left, Red."

"Come in, Kai," she said and motioned him inside. "Coffee?"

"Love some," he answered and sat down at the small table near her portal.

She filled two pottery cups she'd bought on Civilization. The tropical colors helped brighten the room. She sat one down for Kai and slid into a chair.

"So how much trouble did you get into because of me?"

He waved her off. "Not enough to even worry about. But we have a report due at the next staff meeting. Stanton's asking for it. What do you have for me?" He took a sip of coffee.

She picked up the small container and held it out to Kai. "Working MRCs with the malfunction. And copies of their insertion records."

Kai took the container from her hand. "How'd you get these?" he asked, surprise evident in his tone.

"It's not important. But I could use your help with the analysis."

He nodded. "You got it."

"Are you sure you've got time?" As Reclamation Coordinator, Kai's time was even more limited than hers. And with this report due...she felt guilty even asking, but she needed his input.

"I've got all the time you need, Red," he replied, sitting up straighter in the chair. "This is very important to me."

"Okay—good. At 02:00, when the last shift finishes, we'll meet at my reclamation station and analyze the MRCs."

Kai glanced at his watch. "That's about two hours from now. Guess I'd better finish up some things before then." He drank another gulp of coffee and slid the cup across to her.

"Thanks for the coffee." He jumped up from the chair and hurried to the door.

"See you later, Kai," said Jeannette, following him to the door.

After he'd gone, she retrieved the container from the table. She'd have to tell him about her own MRC being here, too. Maybe he would understand?

JEANNETTE SHOWED up in blue scrubs at the reclamation center, carrying the container of MRCs. She hesitated in the threshold. This place seemed so alien to her now. She dreaded the return to it. Slowly, she walked that long walk through the cavernous room. Kai waited at her station in blue scrubs, his blue eyes luminous.

"I've already fired up the equipment," he said, the workstation and diagnostic equipment humming. It was the only sound in the room.

"Good," she said, setting down the container. The cubicle looked unfamiliar, the germicide's cloying mint smell strong. She stepped from workstation to MRC processing unit to sequence capture scanner. Even though it felt strange, she knew she'd remember it all tomorrow.

"Red, you okay?" Kai asked, frowning.

She studied Kai's angular features and strong jaw. He seemed different somehow. Not as arrogant, not as overbearing. Humbled. For once, she felt they were on the same page, but at the same time, his attitude worried her. He wasn't telling her something.

"I'm fine, but there's something I need to tell you," she said and tapped the container.

He stiffened, silent for a moment. "I'm listening."

"You'll find three MRCs in this box. One of them is mine."

"Yours?" His mouth fell open and a dejected look made his features droop. "You're leaving, aren't you?" he said finally.

Jeannette leaned against the exam table. The thought had been in the back of her mind for some time. "I'm considering it. But for now, I want my life back." She shook her head. "Don't you, Kai? Aren't you tired of having to go through the same pain over and over with no resolution? I want to get past the pain."

His eyes turned pensive and he stared down at the table. "I understand that." He gestured at the exam tables. "Every day, at the end of the day, I feel scarred by all this death. Not tomorrow's or yesterday's—today's. There's never that critical distance that tomorrow brings. Today and every today, it's new and it's raw. And every day, I struggle to forget as much as I can."

She saw the pain in his eyes. For the first time, he did understand. But like her, he was escaping in his own way, trying so hard not to deal with the pain. Where she'd tried to measure and manage hers, Kai had simply sought to erase his.

"What will you do with your MRC?" he asked.

"Convert it to EVF and see it all, every awful and wonderful moment stolen from me. And then go on with my life." It was the only way she'd ever be free of these ghosts. "Will you do the process on it? I don't think I can do it."

He reached out and touched her shoulder. "Sure, Red. I'll pop it into the processor after I've shut down the AWOL tracker." He carried the small container over to the MRC processing unit. With tweezers, he picked up the MRC with her name on it and slid it into the processing unit. Quickly, his fingers flew across the keyboard until he'd sent the deactivation code to the MRC. Then he reached up and turned off the view screen as the capture scanner spun up.

In a few minutes, she'd have an EVF of her life. Her hands trembled. At last, she would have memories of her daughter, Rena again. It would be strange not to review her login file anymore. She remembered every word of it now. But the thought of watching her own life on that screen was terrifying.

At last, he turned back to her. "Now, let's look at these MRCs and your data."

FOR HOURS, they studied the two MRCs that Mimi Constantine gave her. While Kai studied the chips' algorithms, Jeannette combed through the insertion records. There were at least six reinsertions of the same chip. Wait—reinsertions? Was that standard operating procedure, she wondered? She'd always assumed the MRCs were kept for analysis only, not reused so many times.

"Kai, when did UCOE start reusing its MRCs this much?"

"Occasionally they reuse the chips, but mostly, they just extract data. Why?"

She plopped a report onto the stainless-steel table. "Both of these MRCs were reinserted multiple times."

Kai snatched the report off the table and paced through the cubicle as he read. "Chips were wiped, reprogrammed, and reused at RDC. Over and over and over." His gaze snapped to Jeannette and she immediately saw the fire there. "No wonder they're getting failures if they're reusing chips so frequently! The raw materials they're using barely last a two-year cycle and that's with a single reuse."

"That's the cause, Kai," she said, walking beside him. "They're overusing recycled chips without testing the chips' integrity. We have the answer now!" She threw her arms around him and hugged him. "I knew we'd figure it out!"

There was an awkward moment of silence as he stared into her eyes. She felt the spark of attraction as she let him go.

Suddenly, he had a strange look on his face. He took hold of her arm, his gaze faraway. "If we've figured this out, then the Antarans have, too."

A cold chill raked her spine. What if he was right?

"But why?" said Jeannette, moving back to the processing equipment. "Why would the Antarans care?"

"Let's look at the MRC code again," said Kai.

Uneasiness clenched Jeannette's stomach. What could the Antarans do with this knowledge?

She watched the endless strings of code surge past, but the ordered sameness was interrupted by strange looking symbols. Symbols she'd never seen before.

"Wait a moment," said Kai, flicking his fingers across the clear panel. He slid data around the screen with his index fingers, his pace frantic.

"What is that?" she asked, pointing, moving closer to the screen.

He shook his head. "I don't know yet." His gaze remained fixed to the screen as he moved more data around, then paused, a frightened glint in his eyes. He pointed at the swirled, rounded symbols populating several blocks of MRC code.

Frowning, Jeannette leaned closer to the screen. "It's nothing I recognize. Corruption, maybe? Run a comparison on the other MRC and scan for those strings."

"Doing that now." Kai tapped his fingers against the metal table, the sound echoing through the chamber. The wait was horrible.

"Exact match," said Kai, his voice thin.

"Is it firmware corruption?" asked Jeannette.

He shook his head. "No. This code is ordered, sequenced." She stared into his deep blue eyes and saw a glimmer of fear there. "Jeannette...it's Antaran code..."

"What? Antaran?"

Kai's words were chilling. It took her a moment to process what he'd said. Had the Antarans tampered with some of the recombinants' MRCs, sending them back tainted with alien code? What did the code do? How did it get there? What else had they done to the MRCs?

Both she and Kai stared at the MRC processing unit, the cold fear palpable. Dear God. Through dead recombinants.

"Kai...think how many times this data's been uploaded to UCOE."

He nodded. "And what's been uploaded along with that data?"

A horrible thought slid into her brain. "A means of controlling the recombinants?" It was the only thing that made sense.

Kai's face turned pale. "Maybe we're closer to losing this war than we realize? UCOE needs this information right away."

"Do we have to include specific recombinant batch numbers?"

"'Fraid so."

"Leave one out."

"Leave one out?" He frowned. "Why?"

"You've got several others to report." She called up her notes on her wrist display. "Batch 480539."

He frowned. "You sure about that number? Batch numbers aren't alphanumeric, Red."

She nodded. "Leave it out and 48539, just in case." She laid her hand against Kai's shoulder. "Please...don't ask why." It wasn't much, but it was the only way she could help save Diana's young man.

A smile hinted at the corners of his mouth. "I won't. You're protecting someone—I can see that." He reached out and touched her auburn hair.

He held her gaze for several long moments and she wanted to reach out to him. Finally, he turned away, moving to the capture scanner. Her MRC.

He retrieved a small stick drive and her MRC and pressed them into her hands. "Here's your past, Red—all of it in EVF. You take care of this while I put together the report for the staff meeting and study these MRCs a bit more." He pointed at the drive. "If you need someone to talk to after you view that, my door's open."

She reached out and squeezed his arm. "Thanks, Kai."

He flashed a smile and returned to the processing unit.

Clutching the little drive and MRC, Jeannette shut down her station and left the massive grey room that always smelled of death.

When she returned to her chamber, she sat down at her workstation and stared at the drive for a long time. It was almost 05:00. She was exhausted. Maybe this should wait until tomorrow? No, she could never wait that long. With shaking hands, she plugged the drive in and the virtual display went dark a moment.

Jeannette gripped the armrests. At last, she'd remember it all.

The screen stayed blank for a few more moments, but the first image came into focus. A much younger Jeannette Kingston stood in a California hospital, doing rounds with the rest of the residents. The beds were full. Her hair had been long and dirty blonde. Back when she'd tried to hide the auburn.

Her thoughts drifted out of the speaker.

How many more people will die from this flu? Why can't we do something?

She followed the attending from bed to bed, studying his bedside manner, his treatment decisions and hers, trying to take it all in, to keep up despite her exhaustion. She hadn't slept in thirty-four hours.

I don't know how to help all these people. How will I ever know what Dr. Dreyer knows? Will I ever be able to help them?

The activity on the hospital floor was a confusing blur of movement as patient after patient died. Two of the residents got sick. One of them died. The helplessness was acute. The frustration overwhelming.

Image after image of loss and self-doubt weighed on Jeannette as her younger self considered quitting, but she kept working and learning. She hadn't realized how difficult those early days had been.

The images raced on and Jeannette found herself in a tiny, one-room apartment. She lay sleeping beside her husband, Dylan, her arm across his chest. He snored softly in the darkness. Beside the bed, a baby cried. Her heart raced. Rena! Jeannette rose from the bed. Leaning down, she scooped up Rena from her crib and cradled her.

"It's okay, Rena. Mommy's here, mommy's here." She sang softly to the red-faced baby as she carried her into the kitchen for formula.

Jeannette stared at her hands, the sensations missing. What had Rena felt like—soft like silk? Warm as kitten fur? What had she smelled like—strained peas, baby powder?

She hugged her arms against her chest, searching for the touch and smell of the tiny life she'd once carried nine months and cradled two years. Her chest ached at the absence of those memories.

Her younger self took a bottle from the cooling unit and slipped it into a warmer. In ten seconds, it was ready. Rena settled down immediately with her bottle. Her soft suckling sounds and gentle cooing burned through Jeannette.

How did I get you out of all the mess in my life? She whispered to her daughter, stroking the baby's tiny fingers and wispy hair.

Sucking in a breath, Jeannette closed her eyes, the sobs fighting to emerge, the EVF image so painful.

Such a beautiful baby, so precious. The greatest loss of her life.

Days passed, weeks, each image raw and painful until finally she was in her last year of residency. Her rotations came and went smoothly. She'd finally cut off the long braid of hair, letting it go back to auburn. It hung at her chin now, thick and straight. She was doing an ER rotation now, somewhere in Washington State.

"Paramedics are bringing in a toddler—drowning victim," shouted one of the nurses. "Coded en route!"

Jeannette watched her younger self freeze for a moment then recover. She was the attending.

"Let's move!" shouted Jeannette, rushing toward the chaos of paramedics and gurney entering ER.

Thank God my daughter's safe at home.

Harris, crash cart! Now! Jeannette shouted at an intern as she rushed toward the gurney.

A cyanotic child lay still on the gurney as an intern took over breaths and compressions from her exhausted husband. Sandy hair like her dad's plastered against her little round cheeks, blue from lack of oxygen.

It was a blow torch to her chest. She desperately wanted to look away from the images. But couldn't.

Rena! Oh, God no—my daughter! Rena!

Behind the gurney stood her distraught husband, Dylan, barefoot and soaking wet.

Run an IV! Her voice nearly caught in her throat, but she forced out the words.

No pulse, doctor, called the nurse beside Jeannette.

Frantically, she tried to insert the tube into her two-year-old daughter's throat, her vision marred with tears.

IV's started, someone shouted.

The crash cart was beside her and she grabbed for it like a life preserver.

Continue compressions, Jeannette ordered, struggling to insert the tube. *Still no pulse.*

An amp of epi, IV push! Jeannette shouted and reached for the paddles. *Start me at 50 joules.*

She laid the paddles against the sternum and under Rena's little right arm. A quick look at the monitor was a bullet to Jeannette's gut as it flickered with the rapid chaotic waves of Rena's heart. Ventricular Tachycardia.

V-Tach rhythm. Clear.

Every jolt through Rena's little body ripped through her own.

Come on, Rena, come back to Mommy, baby! 60 joules. Clear.

Like a rag doll, Rena jerked then went still.

Still no pulse, a nurse called. Still in V-Tach.

70 joules. Clear.

Only momentary reflexive jerks of current punctuated the unending stillness. The shock of Rena's lifeless form made the world freeze.

One amp lidocaine, IV push.

Seconds ticked past. Clear.

Three more times, current jolted Rena. Her baby.

Behind Jeannette, someone called time.

In those few moments, she felt her baby girl Rena's heart—stop. It took two nurses to pry the defib paddles from her hands.

Razor sharp agony cut Jeannette's soul to ribbons as she gathered her daughter in her arms. Sobbing, she slid to the floor, cradling her. The little angel who always shared her strawberry toast with Jeannette. Who loved playing on the beach in the cool Pacific Northwest afternoons. Who offered her little white teddy bear whenever Jeannette went to work.

Here, mommy. Take Benji to work. For hugs. The sunny little girl's words ached through her now. Lost forever.

In the doorway stood her husband, Dylan. He fell down beside Jeannette, his hands stroking Rena's sandy hair. Pain and guilt gushed from his bloodless face.

The-the mobile...I-I was only on for two minutes. His sobs raked against the silence in ER.

With tears flooding her cheeks, Jeannette shut off the images. She balled her hands into fists and raged, beating the arms of her chair.

Why? Why hadn't she done more? Why couldn't she save her own daughter?

Right now, what she needed most was to remember Rena. She laid her head on the desk as the sobs wrenched free and gave in to the raw agony. It was long overdue.

31

MIMI'S new shuttle arrived at the shuttle port late Friday night. Diana showed up at the restaurant with her field pack, but found it closed. At the back entrance, she heard commotion. Hurrying around the building, she found the delivery door open. Linda and Richie were loading food and supplies into a small skimmer.

"About time you showed up," said Richie. "We thought you bolted on us."

Linda set down a box and glared at Richie. "No, *you* thought she bolted. No one else said a word." She turned to Diana. "We could use your help."

Diana smiled and stepped closer. When she saw the stack of crates and boxes, she picked up one and carried it out to the skimmer. The three of them worked for some time until all the supplies were loaded. Mimi rushed out of the kitchen as Richie hopped into the skimmer.

"Your departure from the shuttle port's been cleared, but the window's a small one. You've got to leave now if you're going to make it."

"See ya soon, Mimi," Diana called.

"You take care, Diana. Linda, you make sure everything goes smoothly."

Linda smiled. "You know I will."

Diana climbed into the back of the skimmer, Linda and Richie piling into the front.

They drove a back way through Civilization's streets, coming out onto a sandy road by the river. It was calm and glassy tonight, the colored lights floating on the surface like confetti. She thought of Peter and wondered if he was safe in his bedroll tonight. And David. Neither man had the stomach for killing. What would they become by the time their tours ended? She wanted her strong, sensible, slightly paranoid brother back and she hoped that nothing had tainted Peter's sense of wonder.

At last, Linda drove the skimmer over a shuttle port service road and into a back hangar. They tumbled out of the skimmer, rushing toward the hangar.

In moments, the conveyor was loading their supplies and equipment into the silver shuttle. Two techs worked beside the shuttle, checking out systems and components.

"I'd like to do the preflight along with you," Diana said.

The two techs frowned, casting confused looks at Linda, but they let Diana run all of her preflight checks. Linda followed behind Diana, watching her check computer connections, conduits, and fluids and then crawl underneath the shuttle. Diana ran diagnostics on all systems, verifying data integrity and component reliability. When she was satisfied, she crawled out from under the shuttle and turned to Linda.

"Everything looks good to me," said Diana. "It'll get us out to Ku'Tal."

"Good," said Linda, a faint smile rising and falling. "Let's get out of here."

After Diana boarded, she turned on all the instruments and computer systems. She checked the port logs to see how this vessel had been classified: a cargo ship. They'd been cleared for a supply drop to Ku'Tal. Mimi must have paid dearly for that kind of clearance.

In a few minutes, Richie and Linda boarded. When they'd strapped in, Diana did an engine test fire and waited for the control room to clear them. When launch clearance finally came, she taxied out of the hangar and onto a long runway. Again, she waited for them to release her for departure. In moments, a voice filled the cockpit, clearing her for takeoff. She punched the thrusters.

Sand and rocks rushed past on both sides until they were a blur. The force of takeoff drove Diana deep into her seat as the shuttle shot through clouds, soaring higher until it punched through atmosphere. Diana rode orbits until she caught the slingshot that launched her on the fast track away from the planet. She'd hop orbits several times before she caught Ku'Tal's gravity well.

THE DESCENT into Ku'Tal was hell, fog and blinding snow cocooning the shuttle. Diana held the stick and kept the nose up. Below them, blue lightning flashed.

"What is that?" she asked.

"Plasma fire," said Linda grimly.

The ship bucked against the turbulent weather, but Diana kept the ship level.

"Where do we go from here?" Diana asked.

Linda leaned out of her seat toward the computer. "I'll feed in the coordinates."

Her bony fingers raced across the keypad then pressed an update button.

"Course locked in," said the computer in a soft, pleasant voice.

Diana flicked on the course overlay. A red line traced their path to the final destination: the safe house. Diana made adjustments to her course and watched below for a runway. Even with instruments, this baby would be hard to land in the snow.

It wasn't long until a narrow, short runway came into view. Diana slowed her speed and deployed landing gear. The shuttle burned across the runway, jolting Richie and Linda, but Diana held it steady, halting the shuttle at the edge of the runway.

"Sorry about that last turbulence," she said, unstrapping her restraint harness.

"You did great, Diana," said Linda. She unfastened her harness and moved to the back of the shuttle.

The bay doors were thrust open and six or seven people appeared outside to unload the cargo. With her field pack slung over her shoulder, Diana moved into the cargo hold and helped shift the boxes closer to the bay doors. Everyone worked silently. As they worked, Diana wondered if they were recombinants. Finally, she slid out into the snow.

Ku'Tal looked nothing like she'd imagined. Rolling lines of trees framed the valley on all sides. Everything was coated in a sparkling white sheen. It was beautiful. She hadn't seen snow in some time. In the distance, a white-capped mountain range seemed to slip in and out of the fog. She wondered where Peter and David were today and hoped they were warm and safe.

To her left, she saw a small shelter dug into the side of a hill. It was a prefab made of grey composite materials. Snow had drifted all around the hill, making the trek to the safe house cold and damp. Diana's chukkas were soaked by the time she reached the front door. Linda knocked three times and then knocked again until someone finally opened the door.

A tall, wiry man with light brown hair and a gentle smile stood there, his clothes dark and heavy. He gazed warily at Diana.

"New pilot?" he asked.

Linda nodded. "Diana's okay, Ron. She was a shuttle pilot with UCOE."

"For eighteen months," Diana added.

"We've brought you supplies and we're ready to load the additional cargo at your request."

Diana yawned. She and the others had been up all night. She needed to sleep for a few hours before she took off again.

"As soon as you've all slept and eaten, we'll discuss it." Ron led them into the safe house.

The foyer was tiny with a room off to each side. They turned right. Ron flicked on two ion lamps and portable heaters in the room. It was a bunkroom containing eight UCOE-issue cots, three of them occupied.

"This is the best I've got," said Ron, motioning to the cots.

"Thank you. It looks very comfortable," Diana replied and sat down on a cot. After setting down her pack, she removed her boots and slid under a blanket.

Linda and Richie hesitated and then flopped down on the cots. Diana rolled over and closed her eyes.

DIANA AWOKE FOUR HOURS LATER. Linda and Richie had already gotten up. Diana climbed out of bed and slid on her boots. She grimaced. They were still damp. She moved quietly past the three occupied cots, through the foyer, and into the other room.

The room was long and narrow, and its grey walls looked flimsy. The faint scent of mildewed plastic, like a tarp left out in the rain, hung in the air. One window filtered grey light across a folding table and several chairs strewn against the far wall. A portable stove and cooling unit, propped on crates, set to the right of the table. In the room's farthest corner, makeshift shelving of uneven metal sheets held several sacks of salt and sugar and some food canisters. On the floor in the corner near the window was a large stack of canned goods and a satchel full of UCOE rations. Mud had dried in patches across the cold composite flooring. Three ion lamps hung from the ceiling, casting trembling light circles across the floor. They cast Ron's lanky shadow about the room.

Diana walked toward the stove. She wrinkled her nose at the

overpowering scents of stale coffee and sterno. Ron poured thick, dark liquid into four tin cups. He motioned them toward the cups.

"Coffee's recycled a few too many times, but it's hot." He tapped a battered canister beside the stove. "There's plenty of sugar though, so help yourself. We don't use it much."

Diana moved to the canister, snapped open the lid, and shook a generous amount into the cup. She sniffed. The coffee smelled bitter, but the shelter was cold, and sleep clung to her eyes. She drank, concentrating on the sugar.

Ron moved to the table and sat down heavily. He seemed exhausted. Diana followed.

"I'm Diana Temple."

"Ron Kraver," he said, extending his hand.

Diana shook his hand and sat down across from him. She set her coffee on the rough tabletop.

"Not what you expected, aye," Ron said with a laugh.

"Yes and no," she answered. "It's a safe house, so I figured it would travel light."

He swirled his coffee around in the tin cup. "Yep, the walls literally fold up. It all packs into a couple of skimmers. Moving the food is the hardest part."

His face looked worn and older than it might have been. Beneath the haggard smile, disheveled hair, and exhausted slump of shoulders, there was a man in his mid-thirties.

"This place takes a lot out of you, doesn't it?"

Nodding, he set down his cup. "Before the war, I was a coder. Spent my days at a datapad. On the weekends, I played racquetball with friends and took my wife out to dinner."

"What happened?" Diana asked.

"I volunteered for a year's tour in Ku'Tal as a weapons programmer." He sighed. "I didn't reenlist, but I—I just couldn't go home after this place." His face pinched, sadness glazing his eyes as his cheeks reddened. "God, I can't believe I'm telling this to a stranger."

"Where's your wife?"

His hands clutched at the coffee cup and pain rose in his eyes. "Back on Earth, wondering if I'm even still alive."

"Haven't you contacted her?"

He shook his head slowly and looked past Diana as if remembering something he cherished. A distant smile slipped through the stubble. He looked down at his hands and the smile fell away.

"I'm not the man she married anymore," he said, his voice nearly a whisper. He held up his left hand, and she saw right away it was a prosthesis.

"Why not let your wife decide that for herself?" Diana asked.

"We'll see," he said with a shrug.

She smiled and changed the subject. "So, how does this safe house setup work?"

He pointed to a datapad that lay on a crate near the shelving. "After Mimi has identified recombinants to rescue, she gives us IDs to locate. We monitor their movements on Ku'Tal. If we can get past the biodrones, we separate them from their units and bring them to the safe house. Other times, units pull out, leaving stranded recombinants for the biodrones."

"What if you can't reach them?"

"Sometimes, we manage to get a homing device to them while they're still on base." He held out a coin-sized disk to her.

Diana nodded, recognizing the device. It was similar to the one she'd given Peter.

"Once a recombinant's here, we remove their MRC, destroy it, and toss it into the swamp. The chips are tricky, but our people are trained. Then we give the recombinants civilian clothes and hurry them aboard a shuttle. They're usually taken to halfway houses throughout the systems and are slowly reintegrated into society. Later, we build identities for them. It's a slow process, but it's worth it."

Diana thought of Peter suffering through the cold and the

fighting. He didn't belong out there. Neither did David, for that matter.

"Are you always successful at reintegrating them?" she asked.

He sighed and ran a hand through his hair. "Not always. On very rare occasions, we have to—return a few to the field because they can't shake that aggressive nature. Some are so violent they can't function outside the military. Mimi's very careful about who's rescued."

They'd have no trouble integrating Peter. It was her brother she worried about. Would he become broken like this man? She feared for David.

"I have someone out here I need to rescue. He already has a homing device."

Ron raised an eyebrow.

"He's someone I met at the base, someone who doesn't belong out here. If I don't get him out, he'll die."

"How long has he had the device?"

Diana sighed. "Almost six months."

The look on Ron's face was grim. She knew what he was thinking, that Peter was already dead.

"Hope he survives long enough to reach us," Ron said finally.

She shivered. "Me, too."

DIANA, Linda, and Richie sat around the table with Ron playing cards by the light of an ion lamp. There was nothing to do but wait until the underground scouts returned with recombinants. Three were sleeping in the next room. There would be six total. That is, if they got past the Antaran biodrones.

Toward evening, Diana heard the whisper of a skimmer. She glanced over at Ron who threw down his cards and hurried toward the door. He pulled a plasma rifle off the wall and waited for the knock signal.

Three quick raps. A pause. A fourth knock.

Ron opened the door a crack and peered out. Apparently satisfied, he threw open the door and three soldiers stumbled inside, all male. Shivering and covered in snow, they moved into the room. Two men dressed in dark civilian clothes entered behind them.

"Hello, boys," Ron said and hurried to the stove. After setting down the rifle, he filled several cups with coffee and passed them out.

Diana rose from the table. "Should I heat some rations?" she asked.

Ron nodded at her.

She grabbed a handful, dropped them on top of a crate, and pulled the self-heating tabs. Peeling off the covers, she set them beside a can of scuffed silverware. The recombinants filed past, grabbing a ration and a fork. In full gear, they lumbered over to the table and sat down, eagerly devouring the food and the coffee. When everyone had a ration, Ron moved around the table refilling coffee cups.

"I'm Ron Kraver," he announced to the recombinants. "I run this safe house."

They gazed silently at him, their eyes wide and weary.

"If you'll cooperate with us," he continued, "we'll get you into clean clothes and take care of your MRCs."

Whispers and low voices buzzed.

"Where will we go?" a black-haired young man asked.

The group quieted at the seriousness of the question. None of them seemed to have considered that part.

"We'll take you off-world where you'll travel to halfway houses and await new identities."

Smiles and laughter broke out at the table. The recombinants chattered wildly at each other, amazed by their good fortune.

"All I ask is that you cooperate with us," said Ron, his voice rising above the clamor. "We're working to get you off-world as quickly as possible."

Linda rose from her chair and left the room. She returned in a few minutes with her field pack and withdrew a small black case.

"We'll schedule you at fifteen-minute intervals for chip removals," she announced. She squinted at the nearest young man. "We'll start with you."

His smile broadened and he nodded.

"I didn't know you were qualified to do that," said Diana to Linda.

Linda laughed. "I was a UCOE medic for five years. I'm qualified."

"Can I help in any way?"

"Just keep the others out of my way," she answered. She slid a bottle of germicide, a hand scanner, and surgical gloves out of her pack.

As Ron led the other recombinants toward the bunkroom, Linda began scrubbing down the table and her implements.

Richie was there behind her, thermometer in hand, heating water on the stove.

Diana watched over Linda's shoulder as Linda explained the procedure to the recombinant. She assured him she was using a topical anesthetic. From hearing Peter's horror stories about washing out, Diana understood why Linda couldn't use a needle. She moved around behind the recombinant that leaned against the table. She swabbed his neck with a solution and waited a few minutes. Then she ran the blunt end of her scalpel across the area.

"Did you feel that, soldier?"

He mumbled no.

She scanned his neck, marking the chip insertion point with black ink. Richie stood at her elbow, the pan of water nearly touching the recombinant's head. Then, turning the blade end of the scalpel toward his neck, Linda made a quick, clean incision. She picked up a tweezer-like implement and flicked a switch on the implement's base. Then she extracted the chip and immediately thrust it into the water. Richie carried it away.

"Why the water?" Diana asked.

"The chips have a heat sensor that activates an alarm if it drops below ninety-six degrees." Linda held out the tweezer implement. "This set of tweezers has a built-in thermal source that allows the chip to be transferred to another heat source for disposal."

Then Linda closed the tiny incision.

"How are they destroyed?" Diana asked.

"Plasma pistol works fine," Linda answered with a smile.

Linda finished with that recombinant and sat another in his place.

In an hour, she had removed all of the MRCs and Richie had disposed of them. Ron led the weary recombinants back to the cots where they laid down and slept. The shelter was once again quiet.

THE NEXT MORNING, Diana drank two cups of bitter, sugary coffee, hoping she'd be awake enough to take off from Ku'Tal. The cots had all been taken, so she'd spent the night hunched over a folding table. She rolled her stiff, aching shoulders back and forth and tried to get the circulation moving. She'd sleep back on Civilization.

In a little while, Linda and Richie stepped into the room for coffee.

"Are you ready to shove off?" Linda asked. "We need to get these recombinants out of here."

Richie plopped down beside Diana. "I heard the Antarans have gained ground against our forces."

Wide-eyed, Diana stared at him. "What does that mean for the safe house?"

"Means they'll have to pull back and set up shop in a new location again," said Linda. She set down her field pack and sipped her coffee.

"Let's get the recombinants aboard and get out of here," Diana said and rose from her chair. She gathered her field pack from a nearby chair.

With a shrug, Richie abandoned his coffee and moved to gather their gear. Diana followed Linda into the bunkroom.

"All right, boys, listen up," said Linda. "We're pulling out now. Any objections?"

Cheers and whistles erupted as the six recombinants scrambled for the duffle bags that had replaced their field packs. They eagerly hurried out of the building behind Linda and Diana. When they reached the shuttle, Linda sprang open the floor of a compartment in the cargo hold and pointed.

"When we get close to Civilization, I'll need all six of you to climb inside here. It's very important that you are still and silent until told otherwise. Is that clear?"

The recombinants nodded, some mumbling yes.

Linda smiled. "Good! Now, climb into the hold. There are pull-down seats along the bulkheads. Strap in and enjoy the ride. I'll let you know when to enter the compartment."

"Won't the shuttle port scan us?"

"Of course," said Linda, looking unconcerned. She climbed into the copilot's seat. "But we're stopping at Farnas and Karaba to pick up supplies for Mimi. Last night, Richie fixed the log to show we already stopped at Farnas. Both are farm colonies, so they're used to ships carrying migrant workers. We're picking up produce and a few delicacies on Karaba. Civilization hasn't questioned us so far." She grinned. "It's not like we filed a flight plan to Ku'Tal."

"Let's hope no one questions us on this run," said Diana. She climbed aboard and slid into the pilot's seat.

They waited in silence for Richie to lumber out of the safe house and stumble aboard the shuttle.

"I double-checked our logs. When Karaba scans us, they'll capture our log file and see the Farnas entry code. Everything's cool."

Diana ran a computer check and then did an engine test fire. "Everything looks good. We're out of here."

The shuttle moved in a slow, hulking circle as Diana turned the nose around and pointed it down the runway. She took a deep breath and hit the turbos. The shuttle barreled down the runway and rushed away from the safe house. As clouds obscured her visibility, she wondered where David and Peter were in all that snowy swampland. Safe, she hoped.

THE STOP at Karaba produced several crates and a few small boxes. Richie and two of the recombinants carried the supplies aboard while Linda obtained the necessary launch clearance.

No one asked questions at the small, sparse shuttle port. In less than two hours, they were off world and slingshotting out of Karaba's orbit. A short series of hops would shoot them into Civilization's gravity well.

On Karaba, Diana picked up a thermos of coffee. It was freshly brewed and flavored with chocolate and a smooth, nut-flavored spice she didn't recognize. She added a little fresh cream and savored the rich, fragrant coffee.

"I wish we could get coffee like this back on Civilization," said Diana, offering the thermos to Linda.

Linda poured herself a cup and handed the thermos to Richie who waved it away.

"You can now," said Linda, pointing over her shoulder. "We're bringing back several crates of Karaban coffee. And plenty of geffron bark."

"What's that?"

"The nutty spice you're tasting," said Linda. "They grind the bark and the beans together then brew the grounds."

Diana nodded back to the recombinants. "Richie, see if the guys want some coffee."

His face twisted into a sneer. "Why?"

"Because they might like to try it, too," she said, her voice sharp. "Besides, it's cold back there."

"They're just recombinants," he said.

"No, they're not!" She glared at Richie. "They're human beings like you and me."

"They're freakin' clones, Temple! They're just programmed to kill."

Diana wanted to slap his face. "If they were programmed only to kill, they'd be androids. They only know what they've been taught. Now, hand them the coffee."

He glared at her, but she stared him down until he averted his gaze. He handed the thermos to the nearest recombinant and moved into a seat behind Linda.

"Don't mind him," said Linda. "He's just an idiot."

"Unfortunately, there's lots of idiots like him. I just don't understand the fear."

Linda sighed. "It's the specialized training UCOE's given them. Makes people think all recombinants are dangerous, bred to be psychopathic killers. It's all untrue, but people draw the conclusions they want to draw."

"Recombinants hurt and dream just like we do. Why's Richie doing this?"

"The money." Her voice softened. "And to get back at the military. He lost his father in the war." Her voice fell to a whisper. "Besides, he's here because Mimi owes his stepfather a favor. He does his job. He just doesn't like recombinants."

"My brother's at the front right now," Diana replied, her gaze turning to the cold blackness ahead. "And my boyfriend."

The words just came out. He was her lover, her friend.

"I hear ya. I've got a sister and an uncle out there," Linda said, her eyes turning misty.

The conversation spiraled off into silence as Diana concentrated on the instruments and radar, but her thoughts drifted to Peter. She looked forward to the day Peter came aboard this shuttle. David's tour would be up in two months. She prayed they'd both come home alive.

32

PETER LAY on his bedroll and stared out the polymer portal at the falling snow. The ion lamps outside illuminated heavy flakes that quickly covered paths and filled in boot prints throughout the camp. Even here—at the front—there was a hush in the cold air, a soft quiet that ached through his bones along with the chill. And a fragileness that made him hurt all over. He wanted to grab Sting and Sarge and escape this horrible place forever. Before anything else happened.

Turning around, he set aside his datapad and thought about the weird bow echoes he'd encountered this morning. He was certain now that those biodrones had disappeared off grid because they'd gone into a facility protected by bioshielded jammers.

The munitions depot. It couldn't be anything else.

He'd given Sarge some previous days scans and he'd taken the information to D'Angelo, but what D'Angelo did with it, Peter didn't know. He didn't know what Sarge would think about this morning's captures.

He connected his grid to the datapad and downloaded the day's images. When the data had been transferred, Peter called it up on the screen. He ran the log in still frames, tapping through them one by one.

In several frames, the bow echo inverted and then disappeared.

"Hey, Pete, whatcha doing?" Sting.

He dropped down across from Peter's bedroll.

"Studying some of my grid scans."

Sting yawned and laid on his side, stocking feet dangling off the bedroll. "Those inverted bow echoes?"

Peter nodded. "I recorded several today." He passed the datapad to Sting who rolled onto his back and studied the frames.

Sting whistled shrilly. "Damn, Pete! These are bizarre."

"Tell me about it! I was gonna overlay a terrain map and calculate coordinates. I think that's the depot, Sting."

"What?" He rolled over onto his stomach and stared at Peter. "Are you kidding?" His green eyes were wide, his mouth hanging open.

"What else could it be?" Peter said in a half-whisper.

A chill snaked down his back. Finding the depot terrified him. Not the fight or the biodrones or the caregivers. The end of the tour. What would happen to them? To Sting? His stomach twisted into knots. He shuddered.

After two tours on Ku'Tal, would they wash Sting out?

Sting was silent for a moment. He traced his index finger across the screen and drew lines over the top of the images. He looked thinner now. A hint of weariness in his intense green eyes, in his smile. Occasionally, he mumbled something to himself.

"I want to investigate it," said Peter. "See what's in there."

"You gonna send these over to Sarge and see what he says?"

Peter nodded. "I'll show him on patrol tomorrow. See what he says. He's the grid expert. I overheard him tell Private Boyd we were going out in our subunits again tomorrow."

He sighed. That meant dealing with Drake. He hated the idea of having to watch his back for Antarans and Drake, too. But Sting would handle Drake. Drake respected Sting. That might be enough to keep him in line. Still, he wished he could stop Drake on his own. Not even standing up to him in barracks had changed things.

Frowning, Sting brushed his fingers through his curly blond bangs. "Hate having hair in my eyes. Maybe I'll have time to cut my bangs tomorrow." He yawned and stretched. "I'm gonna turn in, kid. I'm beat." He rose from the bedroll and staggered across to his own.

"Sleep well, Sting."

"You, too, Pete," Sting said with a smirk.

He flopped facedown onto his bedroll and in a few minutes soft snores filtered through the room.

Ion lights throughout the shelter flicked off as Peter reached inside his shirt and took out Diana's scarf. His heart raced. What was she doing right now? Where was she? Still on Civilization? By the river with its flickering colored lights. The heat of her body against his bare skin. Soft curves and silky legs. He pressed the scarf to his face, pulling in a breath of Diana's warm vanilla scent as the memory of her touch wrapped around him. He sighed, remembering his fingers tangling in her warm brown locks as he kissed her frantically. White hot gulps. Couldn't get close enough. Couldn't hold tight enough. He winced. Couldn't let go, fearing the moments were just more data dumps from his headgear.

Was she still piloting recombinants down to off-site training? On Civilization? So many months had passed. Would she even remember him? He pressed the soft purple fabric against his stubbly cheek and closed his eyes. She couldn't forget. She wouldn't. Peter thought about Sergeant Temple, too, and wondered how he felt about his sister being with a recombinant.

Reaching into his field pack, Peter retrieved his grid again and scanned for any odd readings, anything that might lead him to the safe house. All clear. Not even a blip. The wash of light from the screen was luminous in the dark shelter. Sighing, he shut it off and laid it in his bag along with Diana's scarf.

Suddenly, he felt the darkness thick against his chest and

shuddered, the shelter's heavy silence reminding him of those first few nights in RDC as the snow whispered through the camp.

He crawled into his bedroll and listened to the hush of snow blowing across the camp. He knew the silence wouldn't last much longer. And that terrified him.

PETER ROSE at 04:30 and showered. The weather was icy and his damp hair sent chills raking his spine as he rushed back to the shelter. He dressed quickly, dried his hair with a towel, and slipped Diana's scarf inside his shirt. He wriggled into a white parka and field pack and then reached for his plasma rifle lying beneath his flak jacket. When he tossed the jacket off his bedroll, something shiny fell out.

The Antaran key! It hadn't been destroyed.

Quickly, he scooped it up and shoved it into his pants pocket. Running hard, he shot out of the shelter and dashed across the camp, making it in time for 05:00 formation.

"Demolition runs have begun," Sarge announced, his voice gravelly. His dark hair was still damp and his eyes looked like he hadn't slept, but he looked calm. Determined. "We're still part of the cleanup operation. That means clearing biodrones from the demolition unit's path. We're going out there as a unit, but when we reach our objective, we'll break into subunits to cull biodrones and sweep for any remaining explosives."

"He means cull out recombinants," Sting whispered with a smirk.

"Any questions?"

"Have they found the depot, Sarge?" Peter asked.

"They're closing in on it fast. Other questions?"

Silence.

"All right. Stingley, you run flank. Mitchell, you're on point. Now, move out!"

Peter slid his sensor grid out of his field pack and draped the lanyard over his head. With it resting against his chest, he flicked it on and moved toward the front of the line, his gaze unwavering from the grid.

THE TREK WAS long and cold. Peter's face burned, his lips dry and cracking from the sharp winds that cut across the frozen swampland. The route looked familiar, like the one they'd taken yesterday morning.

Everything was still. No birds warbled from the treetops and no insects scritches reverberated from the foliage. Only the dull clack of hollow tree limbs. Like the rattling of bones.

The grid hadn't chirped once when Sarge halted the unit.

Peter compared his current scan with those from yesterday. They returned to the same spot where they'd encountered Antarans. The area was silent now.

Peter pulled his datapad over his head and held it out to Sarge.

"Sarge, here's several scans that contain those inverted bow echoes. I downloaded them from my grid."

"Thanks, Mitchell," he said and accepted the datapad. "I'll study this first chance I get." He tucked the datapad into his field pack. "Okay, break into your subunits. Explore the area, deal with the enemy, and return to camp by nightfall." Sarge moved to accompany one of the subunits. "Be careful and don't get torn up."

Peter hurried over to Sting. He cringed when he found Drake and Sting laughing together about something.

"Hey, Pete, you ready?"

Peter cast a wary glance at Drake, who seemed to be ignoring him, and nodded.

"All right, I'll run backup," said Sting. "Drake, you'll run flank—"

Drake's face darkened. "The hell I will! I'm running point, Stingley."

Sting got in his face. "You'll run whatever the hell I tell you to run, Drake."

"Let me run flank, Sting," said Peter. "I'm tired of running point all the time."

Sting's gaze fell to Peter. "You sure, Pete? You read grid better than anybody in the company. You sure as hell read it better than me."

"It's okay, Sting," he answered. "I'll run flank."

Sting slammed his hand against Drake's chest and gripped him by the parka. "Okay, Drake, take point. I'll run backup and Pete'll run flank. If you screw up, I'll shoot you myself."

Drake glared at Sting, his fingers white against his rifle. Finally, Sting let him go.

Drake jerked his grid out of his pack and turned toward a stand of trees to the north. Cursing under his breath, Sting followed, grid out and scanning. Peter wasn't required to scan, but he didn't trust Drake on point. Drake was sloppy and had the attention span of a biodrone.

They set out across the snow-covered terrain, walking for hours through the cold, but the grids remained silent.

Peter heard the distant crackle of plasma fire and tried to pinpoint the direction. Sound took longer to travel than plasma flashes. Without seeing the flash, there was no way to tell how close they were to the skirmish.

As the day dragged on, more plasma fire erupted through the wilds.

The sound of the grid activating startled Peter. He stared down at the screen. Four bow echoes rushed fast out of the west.

"Four biodrones on our six! Let's move it!"

Peter shoved Sting forward. Drake didn't need to be told twice. They careened through a stand of trees, sliding across snow-covered ground, and struggled to get a foothold again.

Drake veered a sharp right back into the trees, Sting barely making the turn to keep up with him. Peter tried, but his boots slipped and he smashed headfirst into a drift.

He struggled up from the snow, slipped again, and plunged backward down a steep hill.

"Sting!"

Rocks and brambles emerged from the deep snow, gouging at his back and legs until finally, he hit bottom. A thorny vine tore across his cheek as he slid to a stop.

His grid lay in front of him. Screeching.

He lunged for it. Six bow echoes flashed across it. Peter froze, a syrupy sweet tang filling his senses.

Beyond the hilltop, Peter heard Sting shout. Plasma fire erupted.

Peter slid the grid over his head and balanced his rifle low on his hip like he'd seen Sting do so many times.

Dammit, he wouldn't fear them anymore! He'd destroy them first.

Talons swept out of the brush, a biodrone blurring toward him.

He swung the rifle barrel around, firing off three shots. The biodrone dropped, blue-green fluid splattering the snow.

Out the corner of his eye, something moved.

He pivoted, letting his anger swell and fired.

A second biodrone collapsed into a writhing mass.

Above him, someone shouted.

Peter grabbed his grid, searching for more bow echoes. There were two on the hill where Sting and Drake stood. But ahead—three bow echoes inverted then vanished again.

Whatever it was, it was a facility of some sort.

He was going to find out once and for all what lay in those strange signatures. He dashed ahead toward the northwest. As he reached a ravine, someone shouted his name.

Peter had to shoot four biodrones just to reach the bottom of the ravine. His shoulder ached from a puncture wound the last biodrone had managed to inflict before he destroyed it.

He crouched behind a fallen log, the snow seeping into his boots, and watched for any signs of movement.

Another shout in the distance.

He frowned, unable to make out the voice. Was it Sting?

Something creaked. He turned his gaze toward the sound.

The muddy wall of the ravine opened and two biodrones slipped out into the snow. Their gold eyes cut through him, ignoring him. Their bulbous heads, sliding gaits, and mottled grey-white skin reminded him of taloned octopuses. Quick and deadly.

Peter waited until they started up the hill before he ran for the door in the hillside.

A sickeningly sweet stench overpowered the fresh earth scent. He covered his nose and crept inside.

THE HALL WAS DARK. Peter never took his gaze from his grid as he reached down and flicked off the sound.

The narrow area widened into a massive chamber. Panels of light green glass crowned its vaulted ceiling. Silvery white metal glittered as if freshly polished and the green-tiled floor was pristine. He glanced behind him at his muddy wet tracks spreading across the tile.

Nothing like shining a beacon, he thought with a sigh.

Ahead lay several dozen silver panels that stood taller than Peter. The sidewalls were covered with all kinds of instrumentation. Swirls of amber, blue, and green lights winked and rippled across silvery white control panels. The air was cool and reeked with the smell of honey and dirt.

He gazed up at the ceiling, at the thin rays of light filtering through the green glass and onto the floor.

"Have you decided to stop the killing?"

Peter whirled, plasma rifle raised.

In the red glare of his laser sight stood the Antaran caregiver he'd encountered in the woods.

He paused in an archway that led into another room with more panels, instruments, and a vaulted ceiling.

The caregiver's form was human now, but Peter had seen those gold-eyed biodrones and the caregiver's almost wolf like appearance as it started to shift into a human form. It took a bit of time to make the complete shift, so this caregiver had already masked its true appearance. But the fully human form was unsettling.

"Is this the place my people are trying to find?" Peter asked.

"Why should I answer you?"

"Because you care about the fate of your people."

The Antaran stepped closer. Peter's grip tightened on his weapon.

"Let me show you something." The Antaran moved toward the panels in the wall.

Cautiously, Peter followed. His waterlogged boots squeaked across the tile floor. The caregiver stopped at a control panel against the wall. He pressed a few sequences until the nearest panel slid open, revealing a biodrone.

Peter recoiled.

"They regenerate here—in these chambers."

"Regenerate?" Peter's voice was barely above a whisper. "Then biodrones never really die." That possibility was horrifying.

"That's why their numbers are limitless. Cut off an appendage and the appendage grows into a new biodrone while the other biodrone grows a new appendage."

"Why do you need them?"

"They're a cheap source of defense. They aren't of Antaran genetics like caregivers or our people. They are simple, created solely to serve. These have been altered substantially for combat. The technology your people stole from us has improved a thousand-fold."

Stole this technology? His eyes widened. Was the Recombinant Defense Program's tech stolen from the Antarans? Or was this another lie they told him to manipulate him?

He took a few steps back.

The Antaran smiled, its face smooth and young. Peter shuddered. Like a recombinant. Its thick hair was gristled white though, giving it a wise appearance. It didn't look mean or crafty. It looked fair. And that frightened him. He kept his distance.

"Have you brought back my repository key?"

Peter shook his head. "No. I gave it to my superiors."

"That's too bad, private."

The caregiver rolled up the sleeves of its blue flight suit. There were rips in the caregiver's human-looking skin, revealing metal rods, valves, and computerized mechanisms.

"You've seriously marred my ability to continue research on the reanimation process. If I can't access our DNA repository, I can't reanimate my people."

"Is that why you started this war?" Peter had once read something about an Earth colony in the Taus system that was destroyed by Antarans.

The Antaran moved toward him, its movements slow and precise. "Yes, you have much technology that we need—and the other things—stolen from Ballese. Regardless, all of it is critical to reanimate our people. Including this—recombinant technology. We need...certain examples of recombinants to examine. Study their code. Their behavior. Living subjects." Its gaze seemed to look through him.

Peter stumbled backward. "Is that why you fight us? To try and take it?"

"Take it?" Creases folded across its cheeks in an unnatural—almost mechanical—way. "You mean take back what was stolen from us! All of your technology to fight wars evolved from the Ectypal Inditer platform. Your people stole it when they desecrated the ancient sites. Stealing from our ancestors. Stealing from the Antaris Nation. And we want it back."

The Antaran moved closer.

Glaring, he jerked his rifle toward the alien. "This war's been going on for years. Why haven't you studied a recombinant before now?"

The caregiver took another step toward him, grinning like a beast about to devour him. "Oh, but we have. Many times. They just die too quickly. Humans are so fragile, but we're so close. We want the modifications your people made to the technology. And we want to study only the most advanced recombinants. Their inner code. Like you." The caregiver held out its arms. "It's always possible that you might live through the analysis." It chuckled. "Might."

Peter backed away again.

The caregiver reached toward the wall and pressed a series of buttons. Several panels whirred open on the walls as biodrones slithered out.

"Then you've left me with no choice," said the caregiver

Peter fired a plasma charge at the caregiver. It exploded into charred parts and bits of flaming blue fabric.

Several biodrones moved toward him, talons raised, spiked appendages whipping. The clatter of metal raked against tile. He glanced at the caregiver's remains. Metallic blue insects clicked across the floor, swarming over the caregiver's parts and rushing away with them.

A talon slashed across his arm. Cursing under his breath, Peter turned and squeezed off two shots. The biodrone screeched and fell.

Spikes pounded into his left arm.

He cried out, pivoting. Firing.

The biodrone splattered blue-green against the tile. He shot an arc of plasma at the other biodrones and made a run for the exit.

Peter threw himself against the door. It burst open and he spilled out into the snow. He rolled, rifle raised, and dropped two biodrones in the snow. One more surged out the door and he brought it down with a quick shot.

He scrambled to his feet, legs pumping as he ran up the side of the ravine. He didn't stop running until he'd reached the hill. It took a lot of effort, but he scaled the slippery hillside and reached the top.

He collapsed against a tree trunk, chest heaving, sweat pouring down his face. He'd just shot at least a dozen biodrones! How many of those things could simply regenerate with the touch of a button?

His lungs burned and his side cramped. He had to rest for a moment, catch his breath.

"Pete! Where the hell are you? Pete!"

He smiled with relief at the sound of Sting's voice piercing the stillness.

"Over here, Sting," he answered, breathless.

Sting stormed out of the brush, his face flushed with rage. He swarmed toward Peter, grabbed him by the shoulders, and slammed him against the tree.

"Where in hell did you go? I saw you take off, so don't try to deny it! Damn you, Pete! We've been looking everywhere! Drake gave up and went back to camp to tell Sarge you went AWOL!"

Sting dropped to his knees and grabbed Peter by the shoulders again, shaking him. "What the hell were you thinking? What? This place is crawling with biodrones! Why would you do that, Pete—why?"

Sting's rage softened until desperation bled through his anger, his pale green eyes glassy as fear gleamed bright in his eyes. He clasped Peter to his chest for a moment and then let go.

"Thought you were dead, man. Don't ever do that to me again. You're the best friend I've ever had, okay?" He was quiet for a moment, getting his breath back. "Don't know what it'd be like to have family, but—you're a brother to me, Pete."

The word stung Peter's eyes. A brother?

He thought about Diana and her brother, David. They argued, but they would do anything for each other. They grew up together. He smiled. He would do anything for Sting. Anything. He knew Sting would reciprocate without question.

Peter reached out and squeezed Sting's arm, but Sting pulled him into a long hug. "You and I grew up together, Sting" he said as Sting held him out at arm's length. "You're as close as I'll ever get to family." He paused for a moment. "I'm really sorry, but I had to check out that bow echo. Sting, I found this place—"

Sting's mouth fell open, eyes wide. "A place? What place?" He sank back on his heels, hands on his knees.

Peter told him about the caregiver and the biodrones and how they'd tried to capture him. He described how the caregiver had adapted to his form that first time, how they talked about some ancient technology, and about the DNA repository.

"You've got to tell Sarge about this, Pete," Sting urged. "They probably don't even know this facility exists! It could be the key to ending the war. The *whole* war, kid."

Or the quickest way to escalate it.

He hadn't had enough time to look around, to see what lay beyond all those panels. The ones in the other room seemed larger, taller than the ones that had housed biodrones. He shuddered. What was behind the taller ones?

Was this the depot? He didn't know for sure.

"Sting, what if I tell him and the information makes things worse?"

Sting shook his head. "The COs *have* to know, Pete. This war's gotta stop. It's got to." He glanced up at the sky. "Let's get the hell out of here before we lose any more daylight."

Nodding, Peter struggled to his feet. It was a long journey back to camp. Sting scrambled up from the snow and slid his sensor grid out of his pocket. It whined immediately.

"Shit! Four bow echoes, Pete. Probably your friends from the facility. Let's get the hell outta here."

"Lead the way," said Peter.

Sting rushed ahead and Peter fell in behind him.

WHEN PETER REACHED CAMP, he didn't even have a chance to go into the shelter and sit down. A guard detail, sent by Sergeant Temple, awaited him at the shelter entrance. They stopped Peter from entering it.

"Private Mitchell, you're ordered to Sergeant Temple's shelter. Now."

Peter sighed and handed Sting his rifle and field pack. Then he fell in behind the detail. He trudged across the camp to Sarge's shelter, twilight settling lavender across the hard-packed snow. From the nearby mess shelter, he smelled onions. The detail halted at Sarge's shelter flap and reluctantly Peter entered.

"Reporting as ordered, Sarge," he answered, standing at attention.

Sarge's face was drawn and tight with anger. He didn't let Peter stand at ease as he rose from his makeshift desk: a plank between two crates.

"Nice of you to stroll back into camp, private." Sarge moved behind him. Peter stiffened. "Drake reported you AWOL, Mitchell. Care to explain that?"

"Yeah, Drake's an asshole, Sarge."

"Stow the comedy, private!" His voice was grating. "Now, if I don't get a reasonable explanation from you in the next thirty seconds, you'll be in the brig pending discharge."

Peter's stomach clenched. Discharge meant being returned to RDC.

"Sarge, please," Peter said, his voice barely above a whisper. "I didn't go AWOL. I swear it."

"Then where the hell were you?" Sarge moved around in front of Peter again. He crossed his arms and stared at him. "I'm waiting for an answer, private."

"The job, Sarge. I was doing the job you sent us to do."

"I'm listening," said Sarge, his voice not as tight. Quieter. Attentive.

"We were scanning and covering territory when our grids went nuts. The biodrones outnumbered us, so we ran. Drake led us through some woods, but I slipped and fell down a hill. Drake and Sting encountered the biodrones at the top and I encountered a few at the bottom of the hill."

Should he tell Sarge about the facility? It might end the war.

"Then what happened?"

Peter reached into his pocket and took out the key. He held it out to Sarge. "Then I found some sort of facility, Sarge."

"Mitchell!" Wide-eyed, Sarge took the Antaran key from his hand. "Where'd you get this?"

A smile curved across Sarge's reddened face. It was the first time he'd seen Sarge smile in a long time.

"I took it off an Antaran before Sting brought me in from the swamps a month ago."

Sarge's face flushed and he started to shout, but Peter cut him off.

"Hear me out! Please, Sarge. I thought my clothes had been incinerated, this key along with them, but I found it in my flak jacket this morning. I'd never lie to you, Sarge." He bowed his head, turning away. "I respect you more than anyone I know." He held the same respect for Sting and Diana, but Sarge didn't need to hear that right now.

He waited for Sarge to let him have it again, but there was only silence in the shelter, wind rushing around the shelter eaves in a shrill wail.

Finally, a hand fell against his shoulder, squeezing, turning him around. He stiffened and braced for more shouting.

Sarge's intense gaze enveloped him, his brown eyes watery. "I know your life's been hard, Mitchell and there are times when I don't understand any of this either. But Diana was right. Each of you deserves the same chance as a citizen."

Sarge's hand fell away from his shoulder. He leaned against the wall of the shelter, staring out into the camp.

"There aren't many people at the front I'd trust to watch my back, Mitchell. I won't ever doubt your word again. Believe me, you have nothing but my deepest respect." Sarge sighed. He ran a hand through his dark hair and turned back to Peter, smiling. "You won't tell Diana I said she was right, will you? She'd never let me live it down."

Peter laughed. "You have my word, Sarge."

Sarge sat down at his desk, turning the strange key over in his palm. "So, tell me what happened at this—facility."

"The caregivers regenerate biodrones there. They want our recombinant technology, Sarge. And what was stolen from Ballese."

"Regenerating facility? Tech stolen from Ballese?" Sarge's eyes were wide.

Peter nodded. "Something called eck...eck—something. Inditer—I don't know what it was exactly, Sarge. I'm sorry I can't remember."

"It's okay, Mitchell. Do you have grid scans of this facility?" Sarge asked.

Peter nodded. "I barely got out of there with the scans and my life. The caregiver I took that key from tried to bargain with me to get it back. When I refused, it sent a bunch of biodrones at me."

"Then what happened?" Sarge asked in a hushed voice.

"They wanted to–to study me. Said I was different from the others." He shrugged. "My code or something. I ran from the biodrones, stood my ground, then worked my way back. When I'd finished off the last of them, I was able to climb back up the hill. I found Sting a few minutes later. His grid said more biodrones approaching, so we hurried the hell out of there and returned to camp."

"I think a little KP duty will be a good reminder to follow orders to the letter, private."

"But, Sarge," he cried, his mouth falling open. "I was just trying to gather information."

Sarge pointed toward the shelter flap. "Send Drake in here ASAP. I'd like to tell him the good news personally. Maybe after his KP shift, he won't come back from patrol with such blatant misinformation."

At last, Peter realized he wasn't the one with KP duty. He tried to contain his grin.

"I'll get this key and the new information to D'Angelo. I'm sure it'll affect our mission for the good. Good work, Mitchell." He frowned, staring at Peter's torn clothing. "And you've got permission to see a medic before going back to your bunk. Dismissed."

"Yes, Sarge," he said and hurried out of the shelter.

KP Duty. Peter snickered, wishing he could be there when Sarge told Drake the good news. Drake was in for a long evening.

33

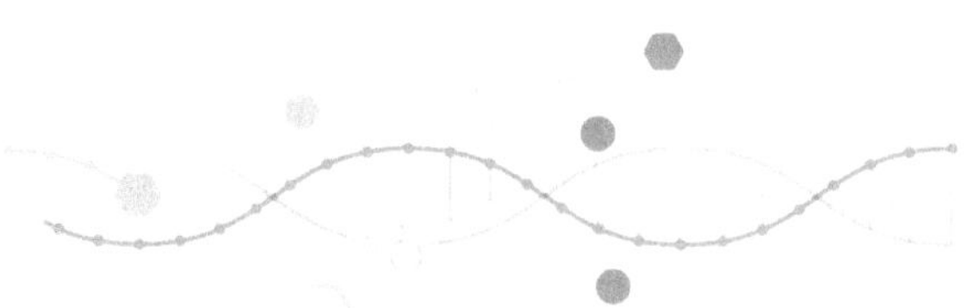

DIANA HAD BEEN FLYING the Ku'Tal—Karaba—Civilization circuit for a few weeks now. She'd helped nearly a dozen recombinants relocate on Karaba and to places along the route to Civilization. Today, she, Linda, and a sullen Richie had returned to Ku'Tal for another run. Richie seemed to grow more difficult to work with by the day.

Because of high winds, the landing was rockier than normal this time. Winter had wrapped a thick swath of snow and cold across Ku'Tal's lowlands and layered the distant, spiky mountain peaks in heavy white. A pungent, earthy smell clung to the windswept lowlands, a sharp tang that clung to everything. Even before opening the shuttle bay doors, she smelled it seeping into the recycled air and fuel scent. It made her heart ache, knowing how much danger David and Peter faced out there. Somewhere.

Relieved to be on the ground, Diana quickly shut down the shuttle's systems. When everything was secure, she unfastened her restraint harness, keeping on her grey synthleather gloves, and hurried out behind Linda.

The loamy air was crisp, stinging her face, smell of shuttle fuel numbed by the cold. Icy air nearly blew her off the runway that ran parallel to the safe house, a rectangular, boxy grey structure that looked like a large deep space shipping container. It had one window and a reinforced grey metal door in the grey structure's center.

She fought the fierce gusts, holding onto the shuttle like an anchor to reach the cargo hatch. When she pressed her thumb to the lock, it clicked open with a thunk. She climbed back into the shuttle to retrieve a heavy, old-style brown bomber jacket that had been left in one of the compartments. It was two sizes too big, but she wrapped it around her body and dashed across the snowy runway toward the safe house.

Ron met them at the door.

"Don't linger out there today," he said as they shoved past. "With that wind, you'll get frostbite in minutes."

In the dim-lit space, Diana and Linda huddled around the tall black stove in the shelter's far left corner, holding their hands near the heat from its twin burners. The cold bore into Diana's bones like a drill, making her teeth chatter so hard she couldn't speak. But the meager warmth from the stove felt good. She glanced at Ron in his bulky, blue insulated flight suit that rounded his lanky frame. The beginnings of a beard covered his lower jaw his light brown hair cropped close and tight.

"It's supposed to warm up tonight. Snow'll turn to rain."

When her hands stopped shaking, Diana picked up the battered aluminum coffee pot from a burner and poured a cup of coffee. It smelled warm and rich, like it hadn't been heated up a bazillion times. Picking up the clear plastic sugar container, she shook a generous helping into her cup. The coffee tasted smoother, familiar, a touch of nut flavor to it.

"Coffee's much better, Ron," she said with a laugh.

"Thank Mimi for that. I found the Karaban mixed in with the other foodstuffs she sent." He rubbed a hand across his chin as if the beard stubble was a little too new. "I never expected to have good coffee at the front."

Linda poured herself and Richie a cup and took a long sip. "How many recombinants will we have on this run?"

"Hard to say, Linda," Ron said and moved toward the folding green table in the far-right corner. An ion lamp swayed above the square table, casting rivulets of thin yellow light across the stove and then back across the table like a pendulum. He sat down heavily in one of the creaky folding chairs. "We're on hold for a few days."

Linda's mouth fell open. "What? Days? Are you kidding?"

Ron stared into his cup a few moments. "Wish I were. Thing is, there's just too damned many biodrones and not enough soldiers. Antarans are pushing the line back. In a few days, we all might have to pull out."

"Why?" Diana asked, taking off her gloves. She slid them into her pockets and moved closer.

"Because by the end of the week, this place will be overrun with biodrones and God knows what else. Mimi's orders are to hang tight, gather as many recombinants as we can, and be ready to pull out."

Diana's gaze snapped to the battered metal shelving unit between stove and table. Every shelf was empty, all the containers gone. The stacked cans in the corner had also disappeared. Only a small container of sugar and a coffee pot on the portable stove were left in the grey room. Most of the chairs had been put away.

Her heart clenched. *Dear God, they're pulling out!*

"What about Peter?" She wanted to crawl in a hole for blurting that out.

"The one you're trying to get out of Ku'Tal?" Ron asked.

She nodded, her cheeks blazing.

"We're bringing in lots of recombinants, Diana. If he's not among them, he'll have to find his way here. That's all we can do. We're going to carry out as many as we can." He pointed toward a small grimy portal near the door. "There are two more shuttles waiting for those last-minute arrivals. The whole operation is out there combing the wilds for lost recombinants."

"What about the chips? You can't touch down at any port with their chips still active."

He took a quick sip of his coffee. "We've got makeshift chip-removal stations set up on each shuttle with qualified personnel to remove them. Linda, I'll need you to set up something on your shuttle. Conditions won't be the best, but we'll have to make do."

"What about disposal?" Linda called from the stove.

"You'll have to destroy them before taking off. Right there on the runway if you have to."

Linda frowned. She didn't seem pleased with the situation, but she kept it to herself. "Come on, Richie. Let's get out there and make it happen."

"Dammit, can't I even warm up first?" Richie said.

"What's the point?" Linda asked, setting down her cup. "You'll just get cold again. Let's go." She moved with heavy steps toward the door.

Richie scowled and slammed his cup down on the stove. Then he chased after Linda.

Ron pressed his hand to his forehead and closed his eyes for a moment. Diana wondered when he'd slept last.

"Is there anything I can do?"

Realizing she was still there, Ron glanced at her, studying her face for a moment and then shook his head. "Wait. That's all we can do now."

She sat down at the table beside him. "How many recombinants do you expect?"

"At least a couple dozen, maybe thirty. We can't carry more than thirty in all three shuttles. Depends on how many make it to the safe house."

Diana took a long drink of the reheated Karaban coffee, savoring the nutty flavor and tropical feel. She closed her eyes, imagining a warm beach, listening to waves crashing against the sand. When the chill crept back, she opened her eyes. Ron's eyes were closed, his breathing regular and heavy. She smiled. He'd fallen asleep sitting up.

She let him rest.

In an hour, Linda and Richie burst back into the safe house, faces splotched red and teeth chattering. They hurried to the stove, each setting their field packs at their feet. Diana jumped up and poured them more coffee. She pressed the cup into Linda's shaking hands.

"Here, drink slowly or you'll burn yourself."

Nodding, Linda pressed the cup to her lips and took a shallow sip. Diana handed Richie a cup. He was shaking so violently he couldn't hold it, so Diana put the cup to his lips and let him take a few quick drinks. When Richie had warmed enough to hold the cup, Diana relinquished it.

"Take it slow, Richie," said Linda, her voice still shaky with cold.

She grabbed a couple of chairs for her and Richie. They sat close to the stove and warmed their hands and feet. Diana glanced over at the table. Ron was still asleep. She picked up her chair and carried it over to the stove.

"Are things all set for the chip removals?" Diana asked.

Linda nodded. "Piece of cake," she said. She cast a sideways glance at Ron and talked in a low voice. "Things around here are going to deteriorate fast."

"How do you know?" Richie demanded. He took a big sip of coffee.

"Because I've gone through a few pullouts. Back when I was enlisted. I know the signs. This place is bare." She gestured at Ron. "Kraver's asleep on his feet. He was probably up all night loading equipment and supplies for a pullout. We've got to be ready too." Her gaze fell to Diana. "Make sure you've got your field pack with you at all times and make damned sure you can fire up that shuttle at a moment's notice. You may not get much warning."

Linda reached into her field pack and pulled out a pistol. She pressed it into Diana's hands. "Take this. You may need it to get us off-world."

Diana frowned.

"Look, I stood on that runway and watched Kev buy it." Her eyes flashed with anger. She rubbed the corner of one eye, trying not to show emotion. With someone as high-strung as Richie, Linda seemed to try and be the stable, unaffected one, but Diana knew Kev had been a good friend of hers. "One of those damned biodrones shimmied into the shuttle. Ran him through before he even knew it was there."

"If the stupid bastard had carried a weapon, he might not have ditched like that," said Richie, not looking up from his cup.

Linda glared at him but didn't say anything.

"Just in case, okay," said Linda. "You've been real good with the shuttle and the recombinants, Diana. You fly as well as Kev did—maybe better. We'd like to keep you around for the long haul." She smiled.

Diana accepted the pistol. "Thanks, Linda. I'd kind of like to live through this thing, too."

"It'll be a long stretch. I'm going to go take a nap. Who knows when we'll get to sleep again?"

Linda rose from the chair and moved stiffly across the foyer. She disappeared into the bunkroom.

THE DAY SLIPPED AWAY and evening dragged into an eerie silence. Diana and the others moved the table in front of the stove. All of them sat in the creaky folding chairs, huddled around the stove, and waited. Diana put her field pack at her feet. The plasma pistol Linda gave her was tucked into her olive flight suit pocket. She'd fired a pistol before, but just as target practice back on Earth.

Ron sat closest to the stove, plasma rifle slung over his shoulder and a far-off glint in his eyes as Linda gripped the strap of a plasma rifle strapped to her back. She also had a plasma pistol holstered at her side. Richie propped his rifle against the wall behind his chair. If trouble erupted, it would take a few extra seconds to retrieve the rifle. Overconfident? Or willfully ignoring the situation?

Wind shook the shelter. Moaning like a tortured spirit. The mobile structure rattled like bones. Diana gripped the edge of her chair with her left hand. This whole situation unnerved her. She just wanted to find Peter and leave this place.

"Don't know if anybody'll make it here tonight in this weather," said Ron. "Scouts may have hunkered down out of it, so we may not see recombinants until morning."

"It's so quiet," said Diana. "Way too quiet."

"Makes me nervous," Richie said, nodding as he scrambled up from the chair. He paced around the stove.

"Richie, stop that pacing!" Linda shouted. "You're just stirring things up for no good reason. Sit down."

"I'm too restless," he complained.

"Sit down." Her words were sharp and clipped. Demanding.

Richie stared at her a moment, as if deciding whether she meant business, and then flopped back into the folding chair.

"Anyone wanna play cards?" Ron asked, pulling a worn, blue deck from his t-shirt pocket. The backs had two intertwined red dragons on them.

"I'll play," said Linda.

"Deal me in," Diana replied, moving her chair closer.

Two hands into Texas Hold 'Em, Ron turned over the river card as plasma fire crackled through the stillness. Three queens. Dammit!

Richie scrambled for his rifle.

Diana dropped down behind the stove, slipping her field pack onto her shoulders and resting her hand against the pistol. It was going to be a long night.

Plasma fire hissed across the snow.

Linda swiveled her UCOE-issue plasma rifle into her hands and reached for her field pack. Gathering a handful of ammunition, she plopped several cigar-shaped cartridges into her lap and fed one into a chamber on the weapon. A green light on the rifle flashed as she shoved the other cartridges into her pockets.

Richie fumbled with his cartridges, managing to get one loaded into the rifle.

Outside, something alien screeched above the sizzle of plasma fire.

The sound made Diana's skin crawl. *What the hell is that thing?*

Ron entered the room carrying a second rifle. He locked a cartridge into it and extended it to Diana. "Here, take this."

Diana shook her head. "I've got a pistol—"

"Use the pistol in close quarters," he said. "But take this. Those biodrones are nasty up close."

Again, a feral shriek rattled her spine. She snatched the weapon from Ron's hand.

Ron smirked at her, rolling a bunch of cartridges across the floor to her. "Thought you'd see it my way."

He rushed to the single round window by the door. Diana gathered the cartridges, shoving them into her pockets, and followed.

"Anything moving?"

Ron shook his head, his gaze scanning the horizon through the portal beside the door. A handful of ion lights reflected yellow off the melting snow, but no shadows carried toward the safe house. Occasionally, shadowy figures rushed past at a distance, but nothing alien surged into the light.

"Those things only press the line when there's a bunch of them," said Linda, crouching beside the table. "These are advance scouts. If they kick up enough noise, they'll eventually draw a horde."

Diana admired Linda's iron calm and unwavering good sense.

"You're right," said Ron, his voice clipped. "We've gotta take out this bunch before the whole damned Antaris Nation rolls over us. I've got recombinants and scouts out there. I'd like to get them off world if I can."

"Same here, Kraver," said Linda. "That's what we all came here to do. If those things take this line, it'll be months before the underground can reestablish another safe house."

Diana winced. *Or not at all.*

Peter had to get out. She'd make sure of it. Tonight was his last chance. She'd stall, feign an engine problem—whatever it took to get him aboard one of those shuttles.

Plasma fire arced toward a stand of squat, grey-barked trees with spindly limbs. Its moss grey, feathery leaves ignited like kindling.

Snow sizzled. A shadowy figure shrieked as it burst into flames and fell to the ground writhing.

"What was that?" Diana asked, wide-eyed. She looked away, the strange hint of burnt sugar in the air. What's that strange smell?

"Antaran biodrone," said Linda, her voice steady as she moved to the far wall. "Tentacled assassins. More cyborg than organic. And definitely not human. They have one job. Killing."

Diana shuddered, making a sour face. Her nose crinkled. "The air smells funny. Like burnt cotton candy times a hundred or something." She stuck out her tongue. "Smells awful!"

Linda nodded. "Biodrones give off this sickening sweet smell—like burnt honey. Or scorched cupcakes. Not sure about their physiology, not even sure they're Antaran." She turned her gaze to Diana. "What I do know is they don't think. Or contemplate. Or hesitate. They just kill. If you see one, shoot it."

Shoot it? Just like that?

Linda's voice was low and intense. She stared at Diana, her expression hard. "Hesitate—and you die. It's that simple."

Diana gripped the rifle tighter in her hands. "I've never killed anything before." *Not even bugs. She'd always just put them outside.*

Linda's gaze softened. "I know. Shuttle pilots fly. They don't shoot things. Too bad this damned planet's so tangled with swamps and jammers and sensor dead zones, otherwise fighter pilots would've owned this place."

"Why the hell doesn't somebody just nuke this planet. Bring in some fighter crafts and bomb the shit out of it instead of wasting time on ground troops and stupid recombinants?" Richie kicked at the wall behind the stove. "They're no better than these damned biodrones! Why are we risking our necks to save a bunch of humanoid biodrones anyway? Just flame it out like Naharra!"

Diana bristled, anger flushing her cheeks. *How dare he compare Peter and Sting to these biodrones! They're nothing like these killing machines. Nothing!*

A dark expression fell across Linda's face, wisps of blonde hair slipping free from her braid, curling around her hairline. Anger smoldered behind her dull blue eyes as she started to speak, but Diana couldn't help herself. She wanted to slap that arrogant, bigoted smirk right off Richie's face!

"These recombinants that you hate are as human as you are—probably more so!" Diana glared at this ignorant kid pretending to adult. And failing. Hard. "They feel a helluva lot more than you do! Deeper and more genuine, too!"

Richie scowled, anger sparking in his eyes and tightening his features. He opened his mouth to respond, but Linda cut him off.

"Without these recombinants, Richie, there'd be nobody left to save your ass," Linda said with a growl. "Nuking Naharra only moved the Antarans closer to home system, you idiot! Close enough to kill every last colonist on Ballese or did you forget about the research post your father—"

"How dare you even—of course, I didn't forget!" Richie shouted, eyes dark with rage, hands balled into fists. "He was my fucking father, Linda! He called in the strike team because even he knew it was the only way. But this time, we can get it right! Get it right here—on Ku'Tal. Otherwise, he died for nothing."

Naharra's destruction was a long time ago. Richie had to be a small child when it happened. Probably didn't remember much about his father either. Nothing but pain and loss.

"If we nuke Ku'Tal," Linda spoke in tense, careful words, "both Karaba and Farnas will fall next. Then Civilization. Then it's a clear shot to roll over home system. Is that what you want, Richie? A repeat of Naharra?"

A cold chill rolled through her stomach. "Oh, God! They wouldn't...would they?" Diana shook her head, unable to process this new possibility.

UCOE won't nuke Ku'Tal—will they?

Linda's voice turned sharp and loud. "Even your grandkids' grandkids won't be able to enter the Naharran quadrant, Richie! Too much radiation. Is that what you want for Ku'Tal and the farming colonies? The mining colonies?" She pulled in a breath. "And Earth?"

Richie shook his head and stared at his feet, rifle hanging limp from his hand. "I don't know anymore...everything's so complicated."

Diana felt sorry for Richie now. Losing his dad at such a young age. He'd already heard a lifetime of opinions from across the solar nets and probably from his mom and Mimi—and countless other friends and relatives—about what should be done about the war. At nineteen, he was probably still carrying around other people's views as his own and was just beginning to test them.

"Why doesn't UCOE just launch massive air strikes on Ku'Tal?" Diana asked. "Automated strikes without boots on the ground? Computerized attacks? Bot forces. Bomb them to oblivion? Why go all twentieth century using human soldiers on a conventional battlefield like this?"

Not that she favored bombing and laying waste to the enemy—or the planet—but she knew how much new war tech UCOE developed in a year. It was way more advanced than this.

Why hadn't any of it worked?

Linda sighed. "First question everyone asks when they join this fight."

"And it's still a valid question," said Ron, dropping on his knees against the wall to get a better view out the portal. "Everyone wants to know why our bleeding edge tech, orbital attack and defense systems, and automated forces hadn't out-teched the Antarans and won this war. With limited human troop involvement. And no need for cloned soldiers."

"Exactly," said Diana. She'd heard all the commentators, all the mainstream and fringe groups touting how quick and deadly our new war tech was to this new enemy. "Our assured victory was all over the solar nets, everyone so confident that our tech prowess would end the Antarans in record time."

Two shadows hovered in the tree line. She watched them until they disappeared beneath a thick bough of feathery leaves.

Ron shook his head, looking disgusted. "I remember those days. How everyone just knew our bleeding edge bots and flying biodrones could fight better than any human soldier and last way longer against any enemy. Keeping our young men and women safe from combat." He rubbed the side of his face, a deep, aching sigh slipping free. "Nothing could have been further from the truth. In six months, they called up all active duty troops, deploying them from Civilization to Naharra. Four months later, UCOE instituted a draft, sending our most elite special forces and deep space marines to Naharra. To protect the tech. And the closest planet to the Antarans' home system."

Linda's eyes welled with tears. "Two months later, they nuked the whole planet."

Diana watched the shadowy shapes fall back, fading into the snowy foliage again. Watching? Waiting? Whatever those things were, they were keeping their distance. For now.

"Yep, dropped a dial-a-yield payload," said Ron matter-of-factly. Like he was describing a new shuttle design. "External Neutron Initiators boosted the primary fission stage with deuterium tritium gas fusion reaction. But instead of a small, measured DT pulse of accelerated neutrons, I was ordered to push the entire canister in a huge, "measured pulse"." Ron gritted his teeth, eyes hollow.

"Who ordered that?" Diana asked.

"Colonel Stanton. Untested. Undocumented. As the weapons programmer, I...I had no choice. That was after all our cutting-edge tech bled out on the Naharran front lines in the first few years of the war. Subsequent tech was cut down as soon as it came online. They tore it apart faster than we could ship and deploy it."

Linda settled back against the wall, rifle between her knees. She glanced from Ron to the portal, knuckles turning white.

"They couldn't keep up production," said Ron, leaning against the wall. "When all the tech had been wiped out, UCOE resorted to conventional methods. Cheaper methods." He sighed, staring at his hands. "Like nuking Naharra and pulling back to Ballese and Ku'Tal. Fighting with human troops again. A real old school fight. And then they announced the shining new hope for home system: the Recombinant Defense Program."

"Even with recombinant soldiers," Linda replied, her gaze flicking from the portal to Richie. "It's impossible to hit targets from the air and orbit when your sensors can't locate targets in dead zones. Their damned bioshielded jammers also keep every target well hidden. Oh, UCOE regularly targets and bombs objectives, but they're shots in the dark. Those runs rarely do more than kill biodrones—and just as many recombinants."

Ron nodded, crouching on the other side of the portal so his line of sight was on the tree line. "Recombinants are able to get into places our technology can't." He pulled in a breath and held it as he flicked on his rifle's laser sight. Thin green line trailed across the dusty floor. "They're like canaries in the mines, Diana. And like it or not, they're the only thing slowing these Antaran bastards down."

Shadows danced along the tree line again. Her stomach twisted into knots. They'd reached the far edge of the runway. How had they missed them?

"They're near the runway," Diana said, crouching, hands tightening on the rifle.

Everyone shifted toward the door, eyes focused ahead. On the portal.

"Can't we destroy these jammers?" Diana asked. "Or hack them and turn them against the Antarans?"

"Every time our coders crack the bioshield code, it—it evolves. A language that anticipates and defends itself. It's amazing technology. Even when we manage to take one jammer down. Two more pop up. I spent a lot of time reverse engineering Antaran code—it's a bitch."

Diana frowned. "So, why are you trying to get recombinants out if they're helping the war effort? Doesn't that hurt everyone?" She had to ask. She wanted to know their intentions.

"Dammit, it's just inhumane, Diana," said Ron. "It'd be different if recombinants volunteered or if UCOE released them to a normal life after a couple of tours. But they're worked to death, psychologically marred, and after five tours they automatically wash them out. Not all of them are killing machines."

What? Automatically wash out? Her chest ached, eyes stinging with moisture.

Linda nodded. "We rescue and rehabilitate only a handful. To show UCOE how inhumane this program is, how they deserve real lives. Mimi's trying to garner empathy and outrage from the voters, getting them to demand changes to the program."

"That's fantastic!" Diana shifted her weight, the rifle awkward in her hands. "That's what I want, too." *To give them a shot at a real life.*

She smiled. Peter Mitchell deserved a chance at a true purple life.

"Mimi's calling for legislation that will make a recombinant's first two tours of front-line deployment mandatory," said Ron, his gaze still on the grimy, cold portal. "And a third mandatory deployment into military support roles totaling ten years of service. After that, guaranteed citizenship with the option to continue serving with the military."

"Or be sponsored," said Diana. "By a group or an individual—like an adoption. Or go to school." She smiled, imagining Peter's joy at being in a classroom, learning about anything and everything.

Something slammed into the door! Gouging metal, raking across it in shrill, screeching swipes. Talons? Teeth?

Diana pivoted, rifle raised, heart pounding. She swallowed the bitter taste of bile and tried to keep her knees from shaking and the barrel steady.

Sliding across the floor, Linda skidded onto her knees, back flat against the wall by the door, rifle pressed against her chest.

Ron was on the other side of the door, beside Diana now, crouching, rifle raised.

Plasma fire erupted outside.

Diana jolted. *How many of these creatures are out there?*

Her feet felt like lead as she moved toward the table, turning it over. She moved behind it, hands shaking, and balanced the rifle on top. She had a good view of the door. Whatever tore at the other side would be through in a few moments. She wanted a wide berth for it.

Hunks of metal scattered across the floor.

Diana's mouth went dry. Her palms turned clammy. She gripped the rifle tighter, finger twitching against the trigger.

In a blinding swirl of fragments, snow, and plasma fire, something broke through the door!

Ron fired. But the creature moved too fast.

Linda slumped against the wall, clutching her arm. As the shadowy mass of talons and tentacles surged past. Yellowy mottled skin. Hard yellow eyes.

Richie shrieked as the thing sped toward him. His rifle clattered to the floor and he crawled toward the far wall, trembling and crying.

"Stay away from me!"

Diana leaped to her feet, rifle raised. "Hey! Over here!" She kicked a chair across the floor.

Turning at the sound, the creature surged toward the movement. Away from Richie.

She had its attention now. Not sure what she'd do with it.

Another biodrone tore through the ruined door.

Wincing, Linda shouldered her rifle and fired. Missed.

The first creature spun out of Ron's line of fire. Barreled toward the table. And Diana.

Plasma fire hissed.

Ron turned toward the door and fired at the second biodrone.

Gold eyes glared at Diana, mass of writhing talons and spikes jerking forward, slamming against the table.

She gasped, falling backward. Cleaving it.

Pretend you're throwing darts, she told herself, focusing on the mottled flesh like target rings.

She drew the rifle to her shoulder, aiming, like drawing back to throw a dart. Green laser sight became the dart point. Finding center, she inhaled and squeezed off a shot.

Blue fire arced forward, the creature leaping. Rifle kicked back against her shoulder. Burning.

The burst torched the biodrone. Blackened, smoking flesh toppled into the floor, appendages flailing. In a moment, it stopped moving.

Diana turned her gaze toward the door, plasma rifle raised as Ron felled the second biodrone and helped Linda away from the door.

Two more biodrones rushed into the safe house. The second one got past Ron, but before it could turn on him or Linda, Diana targeted for a bull's-eye and hit her mark.

By the time night fell silent again, Diana had destroyed four of six biodrones.

Ron and Linda stared at her in shocked surprise.

"Thought you were just a shuttle pilot!" Linda cried. "Where'd you learn to shoot like that?"

Diana shrugged. "I play a lot of darts."

"Kraver!" someone shouted from outside. "You guys okay in there?"

Ron leaned out the door and waved at them.

"Ben made it through!" the man shouted. "And he's got eight recombinants with him."

"Excellent!" Ron slipped through the ruined door and ran toward the voices.

Excited, Diana chased after him, Linda hobbling behind her. Diana peered at the bloodied, dirt-smeared faces that filed past, looking for Peter's bright blue eyes, sandy blond hair, and innocent expression.

Her heart fell as the recombinants passed her one by one, but none of them was Peter.

A bitter wave of despair rolled over her and she tried to hold it inside. *He has to make it out. He has to.*

Linda reached out and squeezed her arm. "Hang in there, kid. Maybe he'll show before we pull out? Let's get to work on those MRCs." She sighed. "Richie's gonna be too messed up to help."

With a nod, Diana followed her back to the safe house.

RICHIE BROODED IN THE CORNER, unresponsive to anyone, including Linda. Diana assisted Linda with the chip removals, disposing of the chips one after another. When all the chips had been removed, the recombinants were loaded into the nearest shuttle.

An hour later, another group of recombinants filed into camp.

While Diana scanned faces, Linda led two of the recombinants to the nearest shuttle for chip removal. She rapped on the hull. The pilot, who'd been asleep behind the seats, rose up and stretched.

"You've got a full cargo!" she shouted. "Take 'em out of here while you still can."

Linda raced away from the runway as the shuttle engines fired. Diana watched it tear down the runway and shoot over the trees.

Her stomach sank. Peter didn't have much time.

"Diana, I still need your help," Linda called as she rushed past.

Diana followed her inside. Seven recombinants stood around and Linda went to work. Diana filled the heated container with water for the transfer. She collected chips and took them outside. After pouring them onto the ground, she blasted them with the plasma pistol.

As she looked up, another underground scout emerged, bloody

and limping, from the brush. Four recombinants hobbled out behind the scout.

"This way!" Diana called, motioning them forward.

They picked up their pace, rushing inside. She studied their faces as they passed. Peter wasn't with them. When she entered the building, Ron grabbed her arm.

"Good news, Diana," he announced, holding out his mobile. "Mimi's got another shuttle on its way. We'll be able to get a few more recombinants out along with the rest of the personnel."

"That's a relief," she answered.

That gave Peter a little more time.

THROUGHOUT THE NIGHT, recombinants trickled in, but not enough to fill Diana's shuttle. For that, she was grateful. The other shuttle lifted off with its cargo. She had six recombinants awaiting takeoff in the bunkroom. Linda had stationed Diana at the shuttle controls, so she lay back in the seat and slept. If Peter came in, she knew someone would wake her.

At 0300, Linda shook her awake.

Bleary-eyed she stared at her. "Is Peter here?"

She shook her head sadly. "No, but we have eight more recombinants ready to board, chips already removed."

Diana started to ask her who helped, but Linda interrupted.

"I calmed Richie down. He assisted with the other chips. He'll be fine."

"Good."

"We'll be lifting off soon." Linda's stare was unblinking, testing her commitment to the mission. "You know that, don't you?"

Saddened, she looked away, biting her lip. "Yeah, I know."

"Look, I'll stall the other chip removals as long as I can. You stall on the system checks. That might buy us enough time to grab stragglers." Linda smiled. "And don't worry, the fourth shuttle touched down ten minutes ago."

"Couldn't I trade flights?"

"Forget it," said Linda. "Mimi told me you'd ask. This last shuttle may have trouble lifting off, Diana. Mimi'll have my head if I don't bring you back alive. He'll make it out. Kraver will see to it, okay?"

Diana smiled. "Okay. Thanks, Linda."

"We'll load the eight recombinants from the safe house as soon as two more emerge from the wilds."

"I'll be here waiting as ordered," said Diana.

"Hang tight," Linda replied, laying a hand on Diana's arm. "If he comes in, I'll send him right down here."

Linda rushed back toward the safe house.

Diana waited inside the shuttle as long as she could stand it. Too restless to sit still, she opened the hatch and climbed out. Then she paced the runway. She leaned against the hull and counted the brightest stars overhead and the trees around the safe house. When the counting made her sleepy, she moved around the shuttle, doing a walk-around, checking for damage and problems.

As she reached the port side, she heard voices chattering. Three men ran out of the woods. Plasma fire arced like lightning.

Diana froze. Biodrones!

Brush rustled all around the shuttle. More shouting. Twigs crunched.

She turned. She was alone on the runway.

Finally, able to move, Diana raced around to the open hatch, crawled inside, and slammed it shut.

More plasma fire erupted.

Frantically, she scanned the horizon. Nothing stirred.

Out the corner of her eye, something slipped out of the trees near the safe house. Plasma fire sizzled through the broken door and into the night.

Diana drew the pistol.

Something swung out of a tree and sprang through the broken safe house door. Her breath quickened.

Cringing, she watched two more of those things tear out of the treetops and slip inside the safe house. Plasma arced blue from the doorway.

She inhaled sharply. And smelled burnt honey.

Fear chilled the pit of her stomach as she turned slowly.

Gold eyes rose from the darkness of the cargo hold. A biodrone lunged forward, talons slashing, spikes scraping composite.

She screamed and pumped the trigger, throwing herself to the floor as the creature fell on top of her.

With a shout, she shoved the pistol forward, hammering the trigger. She kept clicking it long after the creature stopped moving.

Only when she saw Linda standing in the cargo hold, plasma rifle smoking in her hands, did she relinquish the empty pistol.

Linda kicked the creature off her and helped her up from the floor. "You okay, Diana?"

Shaking violently and drenched in a sticky, cold fluid, Diana nodded, unable to take her gaze from the dead biodrone.

Linda sat her down in the pilot's chair. Then she dragged the creature off, kicking it out onto the runway. Diana jumped when the hatch slammed shut again. Linda fished a towel out of a compartment and handed it to Diana. Diana scrubbed her face and neck, madly wiping.

"When the biodrones appeared, I knew you were out here with just that pistol. I figured I'd better get out here fast. Good thing, too. There were two more of those bastards lurking in the cargo hold."

Diana collapsed against the seat. "I owe you a big favor, Linda."

Linda grinned. "Get me back to Civilization in one piece and we're even."

"Deal," said Diana. She sighed, feeling the circulation return to her body.

"I've gotta get back now," said Linda. She handed the rifle to Diana. "Shut the hatch behind me and don't open it until you see recombinants. I've stalled the chip removals as long as I can. We've got to pull out by sunrise, Diana. I'm sorry."

She nodded. "He'll make the last shuttle," she said. "I know he will."

Inside, she felt empty dread, a hollow pit of despair. She knew now. She had to leave Ku'Tal without Peter. The tears rushed down her face, her chest aching.

SUNLIGHT ROSE pale and sickly on the horizon when fifteen recombinants filed out of the safe house. Richie and Linda followed behind them, scanning the horizon for unwanted surprises.

Diana moved to the hatch and waited until someone knocked. Cautiously, she opened it. She scanned faces as Linda and Richie climbed aboard, but none were familiar.

"Diana, UCOE's pulling out. Front line's lost. They can't see us here. We've gotta leave now."

With a sigh, she nodded and slid into the pilot's seat. Richie dropped into the seat behind the copilot's chair."

"Everybody strap in. We're taking off now."

Ron popped his head through the open hatchway. "Linda, Diana, Richie, thanks for the assistance. Safe journey. We'll be in contact soon."

"Ron," Diana called, grabbing hold of his shoulder. "Please wait as long as you possibly can. I know he's out there. He's got to be!"

Nodding, he patted her hand. "I'll do what I can."

"Thank you," she said. "Otherwise, I'm bringing this shuttle back for him."

A worried look spread across his thin face. "I don't doubt that a moment, Diana. Peter's a lucky man."

She smiled and turned back to the controls but called his name again.

Again, he ducked his head inside.

"Ron, promise me you'll call your wife the minute you reach Karaba. Trust me, she'll understand."

He smiled, a wary glint in his eyes. "All right. I promise."

Ron, rifle slung over his right shoulder, hurried down the runway to the safe house. With her heart in her throat, Diana fired the engines. She waited as long as she could, but no one emerged from the brush.

"Hit it, Diana," said Linda. "It's time."

She winced, feeling sick inside as she hit the thrusters. The shuttle rushed down the runway, clearing the trees and shooting across the horizon.

Without Peter. She felt sick inside.

"I'll be back for you, Peter," she whispered. "I promise I won't leave you here."

34

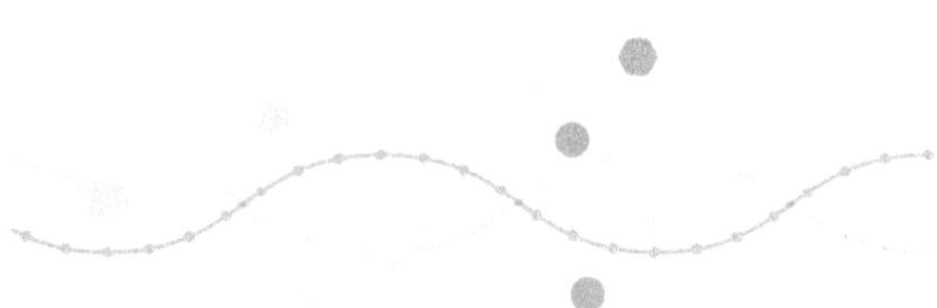

THERE HADN'T BEEN any plasma fire for over an hour as night fell.

Peter stared out the hazard shelter portal, dressed in full gear as he sat on his bedroll and clutched his rifle. Waiting.

His field pack sat fully packed at the end of his bedroll. He twisted the edge of his blanket as he watched for any sign of the last patrol.

Sting and Drake went on that patrol while Peter had been in the infirmary and now the patrol was long overdue. Even in camp, Peter and the others heard the fierce battles that had exploded just over the now silent hill.

The biodrones were moving closer to camp. Everyone knew it.

Peter saw sergeants and privates scrambling through the camp, packing up equipment. A chill swept through him.

They were pulling out.

Peter fumbled through his duffle bag, emptying everything he cared about into his field pack. As he put on his flak jacket, he patted his shirt, feeling Diana's purple scarf against his chest. The trace of her warm vanilla scent washed over him. He missed her so much. His gaze darted back to the portal, a knot gnawing deep in his stomach.

Sting had to come back.

Someone shouted and Peter scrambled up from the bedroll. He hefted his field pack onto his shoulders, grabbed his rifle, and rushed out into the icy night.

The dull pounding of boots filled the camp as he rushed toward the hill. The remnants of the patrol tore through the brush, running toward camp.

"Sergeant Temple! Sergeant Temple!" Drake.

Drake emerged from the darkness, his face paper white. In a few moments, Sting staggered out behind him. Drake doubled over, chest heaving. Sting leaned against his plasma rifle and closed his eyes.

"Sting!"

Peter caught him as he sagged.

"Pete...they're everywhere! We're so screwed."

Shouts and the sounds of more running filled the camp, recombinants rushing into the chilly night, sergeants shouting orders, equipment scraping across snow.

Sting pressed his mouth against Peter's ear and whispered, "The whole patrol was wiped out. Gone. Even Sergeant Driscoll, man. We're not going to make it out, Pete."

Peter pulled away. Sting had never said anything like that before.

"Don't you dare talk like that! We're getting out of here!"

Peter thought of the safe house out there somewhere. He'd find that damned place without the homing device. They'd get out. He'd make sure of it.

Sergeant Temple pounded across the snow toward them. His dark brown hair was tousled and his eyes were bright with fear. He slid to a stop and shifted his field pack back into place. His rifle strap cut across his parka.

"Report, Drake!"

"Sarge, it was a massacre!" His voice was sharp, piercing, and his eyes were wild. "They hit us from every direction! We couldn't shoot 'em fast enough to keep 'em back! The whole patrol's gone."

"Dear God! The whole patrol?" Sarge looked devastated.

"Sarge, they're all history," said Sting, his voice thin and exhausted.

Peter helped him onto his feet. He kept an arm around Sting's waist so he wouldn't fall.

Welker swarmed out of his shelter, shouting orders and directing soldiers. Shelters started coming down, equipment shifted away from the camp.

"We're pulling out, aren't we?" Peter asked.

Sarge turned to him. "We have to fall back. This hill's lost."

Peter thought about the caregivers and how they reanimated biodrones. No one had a chance against that. His gut clenched at the thought and he felt sick. It took too long to get recombinants out here to the front.

Someone had to stop this. That facility had to be destroyed.

"Temple, assemble the units!" D'Angelo.

Sarge turned and yelled D'Angelo's order. "All units fall in! Move it! Move it!" He turned his gaze to Peter, Sting, and Drake. "You heard the man!" Sarge shouted. "Fall in!"

Chaos exploded through the camp, falling into some semblance of order in the center of the grounds. As Peter stood at attention beside Sting and awaited D'Angelo's orders, more shelters fell around them, collapsing into transportable materials again.

Lieutenant D'Angelo stood stiff and pale in the wash of ion light. His face was expressionless. Snowflakes trickled through the white light, washing out as Welker stepped forward, hands at his side, and his unwavering gaze encompassed all the units.

"The Antarans have pushed forward," Welker announced, his voice deep and clear. "Our position is no longer stable, so we're falling back to a more secure position. Some will remain here to shift equipment and personnel to the new camp. The rest will attempt one last assault against the depot. Intel has produced several likely coordinates, including new data supplied by Sergeant Temple's unit. All currently unassigned personnel will proceed with search-and-destroy missions. Coordinates of the new base camp will be broadcast to your grids."

If anyone survives, Peter thought grimly.

It was a suicide mission.

Welker stepped back and gave a nod to D'Angelo. D'Angelo was silent for a moment, turning to gaze at the camp tumbling down. In the cold ion light, Peter thought he saw a touch of regret color the older man's face, the hair at his temples a little greyer.

"Make sure you carry full complements of plasma charges and explosives—and your termination kits," he began, his voice taking on a somber tone, one Peter had never heard in D'Angelo's voice before. "If the biodrones corner you, you'll need it." He turned toward Temple and Elkins and the others. "Sergeants, assemble all unassigned units into subunit formation. That is all. Dismissed."

He hurried away.

Sergeant Temple handed explosive rounds to everyone in his unit. Peter filled the pouch at his side with the explosives and fell into formation beside Drake. Sting was a step behind him, carrying more explosives.

"Drake," Sarge called, stepping toward him. "You're on point detail. When you locate your coordinates, you make sure Stingley and Mitchell stay alive for an explosives run against it. That's your job."

Drake nodded and stepped back. He bent down, laid his pack on the ground, and began to repack it.

"Sarge, where will you be in all this?" Peter asked.

Sarge sighed. "I'll be part of another subunit on the same mission. Good luck, gentlemen." He flashed them a smile and extended his hand to Sting and then Peter. "If I don't see you again, I want you to know you're two of the finest soldiers I've ever had the privilege to command."

Peter saw Diana in Sarge's eyes. There was a strong resemblance and he was just now seeing it. A lump rose in his throat. He felt a kinship to this man.

"Thanks, Sarge," said Sting, a smile breaking through the tired mask. "That means a lot to me."

"Be careful," Sarge said. "I want to see you both back at Civilization Station. I'll be there waiting for you." Sarge hesitated for a moment and then glanced at Peter. "Besides, if you're not there, Mitchell, Diana will kill me. If you think these biodrones are bad, you should see her when she's angry."

With a grin, Sarge clapped Peter on the shoulder and rushed off into the chaos of movement swirling through the camp.

"Drake, you ready?" Sting called.

"Ready," Drake called. He slid his pack onto his shoulders and moved toward them.

"Let's hit it," Sting said, and jogged toward the brush.

Peter followed, his heart in his throat as he clenched the stock of his plasma rifle.

Drake moved in front of them, grid in hand. When they reached the bottom of the hill, Sting stopped Drake in mid-stride.

"Change in orders," said Sting. He turned to Peter. "I want you watching my six, Pete when we go after the depot."

Smiling, Peter nodded and tuned out Drake's protests.

A SOUPY MIST clung to the frozen swampland. The temperature had risen dramatically in the past two hours. The wind had fallen away to a whisper and it was warm enough to rain. The rain seeped through Peter's uniform as he, Drake, and Sting crept through the thawing swamps and lowlands.

Peter knew where to lead them. He ignored the coordinates D'Angelo had programmed into the grids. He didn't know if the facility he'd found was the depot or not, but by destroying the biodrone facility, no more of them could be reanimated.

Peter scanned the stillness, the stench of decay strong. *Would he be able to detect any trace of sweetness in this stink?* He led the way through rain and melting snow, waving the grid back and forth in a steady arc.

"How you doing up there, Pete?"

"Fine, Sting. Nothing yet."

The moon rose, a thin white crescent. Its faint glow barely illuminated the curve of the half-frozen swamp banks.

"Where the hell are you taking us, Mitchell?" Drake demanded. "This isn't part of D'Angelo's coordinates."

A muffled shout pierced the drizzle. Peter stiffened when the crackle of plasma fire sizzled through the night.

He glanced back, catching the blue afterglow.

"Anything, Pete?" Sting asked, his voice taking on an edge.

"Not yet."

"Dammit! An hour ago, this place was crawling with biodrones. What the hell happened?" Drake.

Something screeched in the distance. More plasma fire erupted—this time, from somewhere behind them.

Peter turned. Scanned. Nothing.

He sniffed the air. The smell of rain and decay made him grimace.

"They gotta be around here," said Drake. "Listen to the rounds! Dammit, Mitchell, you're fucking up again! Gimme that thing!"

"Shut up, Drake." Sting. "He reads it better than you do."

Drake stormed forward and grabbed Peter's shoulder, whipping him around. He cocked his fist, ready to smash it into Peter's face.

That was it. He wouldn't take any more from Drake.

Peter slammed his fist into Drake's gut. Drake gasped and fell to his knees, holding his stomach. Peter uppercut him, laying him out in the snow. Drake clutched his bloodied lip and groaned.

"Don't ever touch me again, Drake," he said and turned away.

His knees felt weak and his breath was gone, but he'd finally stood up to Drake.

Drake rolled around on the ground until Sting hustled him to his feet. "If you're finished screwing around, Drake, we've got work to do."

Subdued, Drake simply nodded and hobbled behind Peter. He made no mention of Peter's inability to read the grid again.

They moved on toward the northwest where Peter had encountered the caregiver and the biodrone facility. They walked for several kilometers.

A faint pulse winked across Peter's grid. A ghost echo quickly fading. He sniffed the air. Decay and dirt. Nothing sweet.

Plasma fire arced into the air somewhere off to the right. An explosion ripped through part of the lowlands and someone shrieked in agony. Peter cringed.

Panicked voices rose and fell. Another cry of pain.

Another pulse throbbed across the grid, fading quickly to black.

He gripped his rifle, drawing it down on his hip. He kept his finger on the trigger as his grid sliced through the growing mist.

As they wound through forests and lowlands, they moved closer and closer to the facility.

"Pete...anything?"

He sniffed again. The air smelled softer now. Almost—sweet. *Or was it? Dammit, he had to be certain!*

"Not sure yet."

Another scream. More plasma discharges.

Peter ducked under a low-hanging branch when Sting grabbed his arm. He pointed through the gully at a tangle of thin tree limbs.

Across the ravine, a dark doorway rose out of the mist like a crypt. Nothing stirred around the dimly lit doorway that led through the side of the hill and into the biodrone reanimation facility. Peter knew the Antarans wouldn't leave this important facility so vulnerable. It was probably a trap to lure in recombinants for dissection by the caregivers. There was no telling how many they'd already—disassembled. Trees framed the doorway on all sides. Deep slits in the hillside caught pockets of mist that shrouded most of the ground.

Peter scanned again. Another pulse bloomed then faded. Biodrones were in the area, but not close enough to set off the grid.

But why? Where were the biodrones?

"No activity here, Sting. I don't get it!"

Sting moved close to Peter. "Is this the place, Pete? Where they put the biodrones back together?"

"Yeah, Sting."

"Then Drake and I are going in."

"No! Not without me! You can't—"

Sting's gaze hardened. "No arguments. We're going in. Cover us."

He turned his back on Peter and motioned to Drake. The two of them weaved between tree trunks, moving closer to the door. Halfway across the expanse, Sting dropped to his haunches and took a quick scan.

Peter hung back and scanned the perimeter for any sign of biodrones. Only the smell of acidic rain mixed with the musty scent of decayed plants.

Sting started across the ravine again, Drake behind him.

In a few, heart-stopping moments, Peter watched Sting and Drake disappear into the facility.

PETER WAITED IN THE DARKNESS, watching frantically for any sign of Sting or Drake. The minutes dragged by like a Ku'Tal winter and Peter kept scanning at ten-second intervals. He was terrified a horde of biodrones would emerge from any direction. Or worse, from those panels inside.

Sting had to make it out. He had to.

A tremendous explosion rocked the ravine. Peter fell against a tree, nearly losing the sensor grid.

Abruptly, two figures raced out the doorway and through a tangle of trees and brush. Greasy, orange-black smoke billowed into the air, momentarily blotting out the moon.

"Go, Pete! Run!"

Peter turned. Sickening sweet stench of honey tainted the rain. Shivering, he raised his rifle.

His grid began to scream.

Drake made it halfway across the ravine when talons swung down from a tree and pierced his chest and stomach.

The air rippled and suddenly it was there, perched in the tree above Peter, its gold eyes filled with rage.

He shuddered. A biodrone.

Its rough skin was mottled like ash. It resembled nothing even vaguely human, but Peter felt its fury. He aimed for its eyes, squeezing off a burst of plasma that incinerated its taloned appendages.

Sting stumbled into the brush, fell, and picked himself up. He pulled Drake out of the snow.

"Get out of here!" Sting shouted at Peter. "Now!"

With Drake slung over his shoulders like a sack of flour, Sting pushed past as Peter let loose with another blast.

Appendages flailed, shadowy skin burning as spikes tangled in the brush. But he missed the spiked appendage that snapped out of a tree and caught Sting in the gut.

"No! Sting! Damn you, no!"

In a blind fury, Peter pumped an entire charge at the biodrone until it collapsed into ash that drifted down like snow. Peter kept pumping the trigger, the empty charge beeping at him. When he regained his senses, he fell down beside Sting and pressed his hand against the wound. Sting lay there clutching his stomach, Drake groaning beside him.

"Hang on, Sting! Please hang on! Oh, God."

For the first time in his short life, Peter wished for one of the god symbols.

Anything to save Sting.

Peter winced at the hole that bled beneath his hand. It was bad.

Sting nodded weakly, his head falling back against the snow.

The grid alarm sounded again. Peter grabbed charges out of his pack and scattered them at his feet. He jerked the empty one out and slammed a fresh one into the chamber. Then he pressed his left hand against Sting's stomach. He balanced the rifle with his right hand and waited.

As the sensor grid screeched, Peter emptied three charges into the darkness, at the endless flash of gold eyes.

Finally, the grid alarm fell silent. He dropped the rifle into the snow and took hold of Sting's hand.

"Are you still with me, Sting? I'm so sorry! So sorry!"

Sting squeezed his hand. "Not your fault, Pete," Sting moaned. "I didn't see it. Just didn't see it."

To his right, brush crunched. Peter scrambled for his rifle, but the bloody, stumbling figure made him stop.

Sergeant Temple!

Sarge slipped down the hill and dropped to his knees in front of Peter. His parka had been torn open, his rifle lost. His uniform was in bloody shreds along his right side, and his eyes were glazed with pain and shock.

"Sarge!"

"Mitchell," Sarge mumbled. "Am I glad to see you."

Peter wanted to panic. How was he going to get Sting, Drake, and Sarge out of this ravine?

He glanced at the desperation in Sarge's eyes and in Sting's. They were depending on him. He had to get them all out of the weather.

Somehow, he had to fix this.

Retrieving his rifle, Peter locked in a new charge and slung the rifle over his shoulder. He bent down to Sting.

"Did you frag the facility?"

Sting managed a weak smile. "Damn straight, I did. It's in ruins. No biodrones comin' outta there."

"Good," said Peter, "then I'm taking us back in."

Gently, he picked up Sting and balanced him on his left shoulder. Sting cried out, his head bobbing.

Peter balanced the rifle on his right hip and moved toward the facility door. When he reached it, he found it blown apart.

The air was still smoky, but Peter carried Sting inside. When he reached the chamber with the vaulted ceiling, he found shards of glass scattered everywhere. With his feet he brushed away the glass. He leaned Sting against the wall as he shimmied out of his field pack and then his parka. He spread the parka out on the floor, and laid Sting down on it. Moonlight filtered through the jagged green glass above, casting pale, green-gold light at odd angles through the chamber.

He turned back to Sting and shifted Sting's rifle against his best friend's right side. Then he pressed Sting's right hand against the wound.

"Now, you take this, and you watch for biodrones," Peter said in a shaky voice, moisture collecting in his eyes. "Do you hear me? And keep pressure on that wound."

"Pete, where—where you goin'?" He gazed up through half-closed lids, his face wracked with pain.

"I'm going back for Drake and Sarge. Stay with me, huh?"

Peter brushed Sting's pale blond curls out of his eyes. Sting hadn't had a chance to cut them back yet. He hated hair in his eyes.

Sting nodded and held the rifle against his chest. Peter pulled back Sting's hand to check the wound before he went for Drake. To his relief, Sting's wound had stopped bleeding.

"You're gonna be okay, Sting. Hang in there." He pulled Sting's grid out of his field pack, snapped it on, and laid it beside him.

Peter hurried across the scorched, broken tiles, glass crunching and popping beneath his boots, and went out into the cold to retrieve Drake and Sarge. He scanned as he ran. Nothing.

Sarge was hanging over Drake when he got back.

"Drake," said Peter, dropping down on one knee. "I'm taking you inside now."

Drake's gaze was frozen on the moon high in the sky. He'd already left his body.

His tour on Ku'Tal was over.

"He's dead, Mitchell," said Sarge.

Peter slumped in the snow. Drake was a bastard, but he at least deserved a proper burial. All Peter had to cover him with was snow. With Sarge keeping watch, Peter pushed snow across Drake's body. He took Drake's ruined rifle and pressed it muzzle-first into the ground. It was the only way to mark Drake's grave.

Everybody deserved that much, even a recombinant. *No. Especially a recombinant.*

Peter rose from the ground and slid his arms around Sarge's waist.

"Let's get you inside, Sarge."

Sarge didn't resist. He was practically a dead weight, but Peter managed to get him to the edge of the burned-out facility. As he entered, he heard the whine of Sting's grid.

"Sting! Sting!"

From somewhere behind him, Peter heard the tearing of talons in a tree outside the doorway. They sliced through earth and clacked across broken tile. They were in the building!

His heart pounded against his rib cage. Quickly, he laid Sarge on the floor and pushed him against the wall.

Talons clattered. Air hissed.

Peter ran across the facility, drawing the biodrone away from Sarge. When he reached the far wall across from where Sting lay, he whirled, rifle raised.

Gold eyes stared at him from a tangle of ashen talons and mottled flesh. It rose up above Peter's head and raised a massive talon toward his throat.

Peter tried not to flinch, holding himself steady as talons twitched closer. The air reeked of scorched honey, ash, and old blood.

He nearly choked on the stench.

The talon snapped toward him and he threw himself sideways. He cried out as two talons punctured his arm.

The biodrone leaped at him. Peter swung the rifle up and fired.

"Pete!"

The blast of plasma fire incinerated the creature. Burnt carcass rained down on him.

He gagged as he shoved the rancid debris off his legs and chest. He struggled up from the ground, but his stomach lurched. Hunching over, he got sick.

"Pete?" Sting's thin voice carried across the expanse again. "Pete, you okay?"

Peter threw up again, his whole body shaking. He laid his head against the cool tiles until the sickness passed.

"Pete! Answer me!"

"I'm...I'm okay, Sting," he answered, his voice barely above a whisper.

He laid a hand against his forearm and felt the blood seeping up from the shredded uniform sleeve. Shakily, he got to his feet. Then he slipped the rifle strap over his left shoulder and cradled his wounded forearm against his chest.

"Hang on, Pete...I'm coming!"

"Sting, no!"

Peter staggered over to Sting who was struggling to rise from the ground. Peter gently eased him against the floor and laid a hand against Sting's forehead. He was feverish. Peter slid his arm around Sting's shoulders, supporting his head and neck.

"I heard you cry out," Sting mumbled, his green eyes fever-bright.

Peter bit his lip to keep it from quivering. "I'm okay, Sting. Now, you stay right here. I've got to bring the Sarge inside. Don't move, okay?"

"All right," Sting mumbled, his head sinking back against Peter's arm.

Peter eased him against the tile and went back for Sergeant Temple.

35

PETER CARRIED Sergeant Temple into the chamber and laid him beside Sting. Temple trembled with pain and fever. Peter set down his field pack and fished out a glow stick. He shook it and set it down. The yellow light was feeble, but it gave him enough to assess Sarge's injuries.

Peter peeled the coat off Sarge's shoulders and spread it on the floor beneath him. Then he unfastened Sarge's shirt and carefully pulled it back from the array of puncture wounds down his right side and arm. Spikes had pierced his leg down to the ankle.

Beside him, Sting's steady breathing was labored with fever. He mumbled softly, but Peter couldn't make out the words. Peter unfastened Temple's canteen from his belt and pressed it to the man's lips.

"Drink, Sarge."

He nodded and opened his mouth wide enough for Peter to pour in the water. Peter put the canteen out of Sarge's reach so he wouldn't spill it and moved over to Sting and retrieved his canteen. He put it to Sting's mouth, making him drink.

Peter didn't know anything about first aid, but he'd watched the medics tending his wounds and Sting's before. He found a couple of clean shirts rolled up in Temple's field pack, so Peter used them for bandages.

Using his own canteen, he cleansed the wounds as best he could and then covered them with strips from the shirt, tying them into place with several knots. He dressed Sting's wound, too, being careful not to make it bleed again.

When both men were resting comfortably, Peter settled back against the wall. Then he noticed a glittery, purple object slipping out of Temple's parka. Peter crawled over to Temple and picked up the object.

The repository key! Sarge still had it. But its surface had changed, pulsing purple now.

Peter slipped it into his front pocket. He moved back to the wall and leaned his head against it. He was exhausted.

When dawn came, Peter rose from the floor, his neck sore from leaning against the wall so long. He moved over to Sting and pressed his hand to Sting's forehead. Cooler. Peter smiled. Sting was going to be okay. He slid over to Temple and the man's forehead nearly burned off his hand.

Something clattered inside the chamber.

Peter scrambled for his rifle and sensor grid. He turned on the grid, panning the room.

Nothing.

Again, something moved.

Peter turned toward the sound. Scanned. Nothing.

He studied the grid, seeking any sort of movement. There, a faint ripple.

Peter shuddered. Bioshielded jammers. That meant caregivers were still inside.

A voice called to him, low and crisp.

"Do you really think you've won?"

Peter growled and raised his rifle. "Come out of there! Now!"

Three figures loomed in the smoky corners, moving slowly

toward the center of the chamber. Peter backed away toward Sarge and Sting.

Three against one. He didn't stand a chance.

Mottled flesh shimmered, appendages collapsing, talons disappearing. Before his eyes, the Antarans adapted, looking as human as he did. Three men. He took another step back.

"We have other reanimation facilities in this system," said the white-haired man. "By tomorrow, every biodrone your race killed last night will be replaced with new ones."

"What do you want from us?" Peter shouted. "UCOE will just write this world off and destroy it when they pull out. You'll have gained nothing."

The white-haired man moved toward Peter. "This line. Your tech. And the simulacrum you stole! We will keep infiltrating planets in this system until we're closer to your colonies—and your home system. What will you do when the line reaches Earth?"

Peter shuddered. So many times, he'd heard people talk of Earth. Where the god symbols originated. What would happen if the Antarans overran Earth?

He swiveled his rifle toward the caregivers.

"We will find the forerunners' device!" another caregiver shouted at him, glaring dark eyes and puffy, corpulent face reminding him of the biodrones. "You won't stop us!"

Simulacrum? Forerunners device? He rubbed his face against his sleeve. *What did all that mean?*

"There are others of us in other facilities," said the shortest man. "You'd gain nothing by destroying us."

"It'd sure ease my stress level about now," Peter snapped and let the green laser sight rest on the white-haired man's flight suit.

The white-haired man held out his hands. There was desperation in his face, and he seemed to be pleading.

But why? Was it all just an act?

"All we want is to bring our race back from the dead. Our programming is intricate. The logic is complex with many threads and cores, but our goal is simple. Revive my people from the brink of extinction. We'll do everything, anything to accomplish this goal. And that requires the ancient engine, the simulacrum. We'll scour each and every one of your worlds until we find what you stole."

He had no idea what this–this simulacrum was. Had his people stolen something from these people? Were we the bad guys? He felt so confused now.

The caregiver behind him took a step toward him and stopped. "But we can do none of this without our repository key." His voice was softer, uncombative but threatening.

"We are close," said the third caregiver. He moved behind the first caregiver. "As we search for the forerunner's engine, we still need more recombinants to recover from extinction. Some of the complex, higher order ones. Like you."

"He's right." The white-haired caregiver pointed at Peter. "I've watched you outwit a caregiver and a horde of biodrones. I've watched how you have an almost inborn sense of detection. And survival. You calculate. Study. Analyze. You're different from the others. So very different. And you're loyal. Even now, you protect your citizen sergeant and your recombinant private. Those are all the qualities we admire. And want to—replicate."

Replicate. Peter shivered, images of the RDC flashing through his brain, each one punctuated with heart-wrenching memories and the pain of loss. So enduring that his heart ached at the images. Charles. The white jackets with sleeves sewn together. He winced. The god symbol dragging under the bloodied white sheet.

The third caregiver slipped around the white-haired caregiver and moved toward him.

Peter took a step backward.

Something scraped across the floor.

He jerked his gaze toward the outermost, metal doors sliding across the exit to the facility. A cold chill slipped down his spine.

They were trapped.

"Open that door!" he shouted, glaring at them.

The white-haired caregiver smiled at him. "It's no longer that simple, private. What we have here is—in your language—a stalemate. It's time to surrender."

Peter's hands shook as he gripped the rifle tighter. He glanced behind him at Sting and Sarge, feeling sick inside. He'd led them in here, thinking it was safe. Instead, he'd walked into a trap.

How stupid could he be? His chest ached. *What had he done?*

"What do you want?" Peter demanded.

"We've already told you," the white-haired caregiver said, his voice filled with irritation. "The key to the repository. It holds my race's genomes, its genetic code, all of it. Without that key, we can't enter the repository." He held out his hand. "Give us the key."

Peter studied the caregivers' faces, noting the growing tension. *How well could he negotiate?*

"If I understand you correctly, you want me to give up this key." He patted his front pocket. "In exchange for what?"

The shortest caregiver's eyes darkened. "You are in no position to bargain, private."

"Aren't I?" Peter said with a laugh. "The way I see it, I can just incinerate all three of you and find another way out of this place."

The caregiver folded his arms against his chest and leaned against the wall. "You wouldn't get far, private. We've animated every biodrone that fell last night. He pointed to a far panel. "They're behind that panel. They're timed to release in ten minutes unless I stop the timer."

Yellow lights winked on the control panel and he tapped it with his finger.

A fine sheen of sweat coated Peter's face as he gazed from caregiver to caregiver.

"Or I could just incinerate your repository key. Your choice."

Sharp whispers cut through the silence. The white-haired caregiver gazed from the third caregiver to Peter. "What will you accept in exchange for the key?" one of them asked.

Peter fought not to grin. "Safe passage out of this facility for me and my friends."

The third caregiver shook his head. "No. You are part of the exchange, private."

"Show him the repository," said the white-haired caregiver, his voice shaky. "Make him understand."

The caregiver moved toward a narrow hallway and stopped in the threshold. The other two caregivers paused, waiting for Peter to follow.

Reluctantly, Peter followed. With the rifle barrel, he motioned the three caregivers ahead into the smoky greyness of a ruined hallway. He stepped over pylons and debris and slid around hunks of wall that had partially blocked the way.

Bright white light glared from a room at the end of the hallway. As he neared it, he noticed more of that silvery white metal coated the walls, keeping things cool, he realized. The man moved to a glass enclosure. Peter glanced through the glass. Thousands of tiny, green metal drawers were embedded in the wall. The ones nearest the locked door were open.

"Come. Look inside."

Cautiously, Peter stepped forward and peered through the glass at the nearest drawer. Vials. Aligned and fitting snugly side by side, they filled the entire drawer.

"Each of those drawers contains genomes from thousands and thousands of Antarans," said the third caregiver. "We brought our repository to this world, hoping we had altered the planet enough to assure a steady stream of recombinants for analysis. But the fighting has—escalated. And the forerunner's technology is not here."

Peter flinched. "Analysis? You mean dissection. You've destroyed so many of us."

"It was necessary," said the white-haired caregiver. "Over the years, we've studied many of your kind, moving ever closer to your technology. And the forerunners."

"Why didn't you just ask for the technology?" Peter shouted. "Why'd you have to attack us and try to take it?"

The third caregiver moved toward Peter and Peter jerked his rifle toward him. The caregiver stopped in mid-stride.

"Your people stole the technology! Plundered ruins they had no right to touch! They also feared we'd build an army to send against them. At a simple level, we've succeeded in producing and reanimating simple DNA sequences, but for the complex DNA of our people, we've failed where you've succeeded."

Peter moved away from the enclosure, his thoughts spinning. If Temple and Sting didn't get medical help soon, they might die. All the recombinants out there would probably die when the biodrones were released again.

And all of it was his fault.

His stomach ached. He'd have to make a new deal with the Antarans. It was the only way. He sighed.

Forgive me, Diana.

"All right," he said, his voice quivering. "Here's the deal: call off your biodrones, leave this world, and spare my friends out there." He sucked in a breath of air. "Do that and I'll give you back your key...and give myself up."

The third caregiver's eyes widened and he cast a shocked glance at the white-haired caregiver. Then he turned toward Peter. "You are exactly what we're seeking, private. Many of the other recombinants are as badly coded as our biodrones. They don't listen. They just kill. You are so far beyond that. You are complex. You are capable of reasoning."

Didn't he mean being manipulated?

A heaviness settled against Peter's chest. He ran a hand through his hair. This was his only chance to save Sting and Sarge. If he went to Ballese as the caregivers' guinea pig, maybe it would it stop this war?

He felt sick inside. It was a risk he had to take.

"Do I have any chance of surviving your recombinant *analysis*?"

The white-haired caregiver nodded. "There's a chance. We need you alive. You're of no use to us dead, but sometimes analysis causes illness. Death is a risk."

He'd never lived without that immediate risk.

Then he heard Sting's voice in the hallway.

"Pete? I'm on your six, Pete."

Sting stood in the doorway, weak and clutching a rifle. The light on the rifle glowed red. It was empty.

"Sting, no." He ran toward the door and caught Sting as he fell.

"They won't touch you, Pete. I promise. It's my turn to flank you."

With his left arm wrapped around Sting's waist, Peter held Sting against him and trained his rifle on the caregivers.

"Sarge is on point. We're all gonna make it out, Pete. All of us."

Sting sagged, his rifle dragging the floor. Peter, with Sting in tow, sidled back toward the caregivers.

"What kind of guarantees do I have that you're not a bunch of lying bastards?" Peter demanded.

"Only my word, private."

"What's happening?" Sting asked.

"Everything's okay, Sting," Peter said in a quiet voice.

Peter felt Diana's scarf against his skin and thought about the moment he would have held her again. His eyes stung. That moment would never come now. He thought about the colored lights and the river and all the things he would never do. His heart hurt. None of it was ever meant to be. Mimi was wrong. It was just another one of those data-dump images he could touch only at night. In his sleep.

His heart felt broken into pieces. Diana would never be anything more than his own personal data dump.

He glanced down at Sting and then at the caregivers. "Conditions. First, these men must be taken someplace where they'll be found and cared for."

"Consider it done," said the white-haired caregiver.

"Second, you must call off all the biodrones immediately. Now. I don't want another person to die here."

The third caregiver shook his head. "We cannot recall them, but we won't release anymore nor will we reanimate more. If you give us that key and agree to go back to Ballese, private."

Sting squinted at Peter, the fever gone from his eyes. "Pete, what are you doing? What are they talkin' you into?"

"Forget it, Sting. Just rest. I'll get you out of here real soon."

Sting's face contorted. "You're saving us again. Aren't you, buddy?"

"No," He said, smiling. "Just gettin' you and Sarge home."

"Home." Sting's expression turned angry. "And where is that, Pete? Back to base, back to my old bunk? Without you?"

Peter forced the grin onto his face. "I've got you a one-way ticket out of Ku'Tal, Sting. At the safe house, there's a shuttle ride to a new life. You'll be able to find it. I know you."

"What about you? You're goin' back to Diana?"

Only in his memories.

He looked away, not able to stomach the hurt, and not wanting Sting to see his pain. His gaze locked sadly onto the white-haired caregiver's face.

"I'm going on a shuttle too, buddy. We're all getting out of the military today."

He bit his lip to keep it from quivering as his eyes filled with tears. More than anything, he wanted to get on one of those shuttles and go home. To Civilization. To Diana. To a new life.

For Diana, for Sting, and Sarge, and for all the recombinants who came after him, he would stop this.

Sting pulled away from him, angry again.

"You're lying, Pete. I can see it in your face. Dammit, there you go again!"

"No, I'm not, Sting," he answered, gritting his teeth. "Now, go check on Sarge."

Sting started to shout at him, but Peter whirled around.

"Now, Sting! Do it!"

Staggering and furious, Sting moved into the hallway. Peter heard a commotion, a cry of pain—Sarge—and the scuff of boots against the floor.

When Sting was out of the room, Peter turned back to the caregivers. "All right," he said, his voice so soft and thin he wasn't sure they heard him. "I'll do it."

"Thank you," said the third caregiver, the tension leaving his human mask. "We'll begin facility shutdowns immediately." He hurried out of the room.

The white-haired caregiver moved toward him. He held out his hand. "The key, private?"

Peter shook his head. "Only when my buddies are safely out of here and I know you won't send out the biodrones behind that panel." He pointed to the panel on the wall.

The white-haired caregiver's face twisted. "But we must transfer all the DNA specimens to our ships before we depart!"

"Not until Sting and Sarge are safe!" Peter shouted, glaring at the caregiver. "That's the deal. Take it or leave it. Now, what about the biodrones?"

Sighing, the caregiver motioned Peter out of the repository room. "As we said, none will be reanimated. The biodrones remaining will be left to their fate. Now, I must assist the others."

The white-haired caregiver slipped into the hallway and disappeared into the smoky haze.

In a daze, Peter wandered out of the room, back toward Sarge and Sting. He found Sting kneeling beside Sarge.

"How is he?" Peter asked.

"Better." Sting tried to hold his anger but couldn't. "Dammit, Pete, what have you done? You can't trust Antarans!"

It didn't matter. He had no choice.

"I heard you in the hallway, Pete. I know all about it."

"Then you know I have no choice."

Sting shook his head. "Always gotta be the hero, don't you, Pete?" He turned away, moving back to his parka.

Peter cleaned Sarge's wound again and laid a wet cloth against his forehead. Sarge lay groaning. His fever hadn't gotten higher. There was still a chance that Sarge would make it with proper medical care. Sting was going to be fine.

"The cold water may help bring his fever down," said Peter, his voice thin. "You've gotta get him to the safe house, Sting."

Peter yawned, his eyes closing.

"Pete, you've been running around for hours," Sting said. He sat with his head against the wall, his parka wrapped around him. "Sit back and rest. You're exhausted. Sarge can't travel yet anyway."

Peter fought the sleep from his eyes, but when he leaned against the wall, he couldn't help it, his eyes closed.

A FEW HOURS LATER, he awoke. He glanced over at Sarge. Sarge was snoring softly. Peter laid a hand to his forehead. A little cooler now. Good. He glanced over at Sting.

Gone.

An icy chill cut through Peter. He thrust his hand to his front pocket, digging for the repository key.

His pocket was empty. It was gone!

"Sting!"

Peter scrambled to his feet. He ran down the hallway, searching for Sting, for a flash of curly, blond hair.

"Sting!"

When he reached the DNA repository, the door was ajar. All the drawers were empty and hanging open.

"No! Sting!"

Peter ran toward an open door at the other end of the repository. Beyond the door, an Antaran ship fired its engines. Sting stood on a ramp leading into the white and silver ship. With its thin frame and curves, it looked nothing like any ship Peter had seen before. It looked like a falcon or an eagle with its wings spread.

"No, you can't do this! Sting! NO!"

Sting looked up as Peter barreled across the hangar and leaped onto the ramp. He grabbed Sting's arms and shook him.

"I made the deal!" he shouted through gritted teeth. "I'm going!"

Sting shook his head. "No, Pete...not this time." Sting's voice was so somber that it choked up Peter. "I made a new deal. I'm going instead."

Peter's eyes stung with tears. He squeezed Sting's arms. "You can't," he said, his voice cracking, "they're going to—"

"I know," Sting said with a nod. His voice tightened. "It's okay, Pete. Either way, I'm free of the military. And who knows, I may live to tell about it."

"Oh, God, Sting." His voice cut out, his bottom lip quivering. "You're my best friend." He shook his head, the pain gouging his middle. "No, you're my brother. I wish—"

Sting pulled Peter to his chest and held him as Peter fought down his sorrow. He hugged Sting hard, knees shaking, chest burning.

Finally, Sting let him go. Teary-eyed, he reached out and ruffled Peter's hair. Then he slid a chain out of his pocket. On the chain hung a circle with two halves, one black, the other white. Peter stared. Another god symbol.

"It was Sergeant Driscoll's god symbol, Pete. A yin yang, he called it. He didn't need it anymore. I was gonna give it to you on your first birth anniversary..." His voice trailed off.

Peter glared at the white-haired caregiver standing at the top of the ramp.

"Don't do this!" Peter shouted at the caregiver. "We had a deal."

"Let it be!" Sting cried. Tears flowed down his face as he shoved Peter backward. "Now, go! Go back to Sarge—and Diana. Go!"

Peter shook his head.

"It's my turn to be a hero, Pete. It's what I've always wanted. The guy who saved his whole unit. Please. Let me be the hero."

Peter couldn't move. He stared searchingly into Sting's watery green eyes. Sting held his gaze as if memorizing Peter's face.

"He offered himself in your place, private," said the caregiver. "It's the complexity and loyalty we're looking for in a recombinant. He's got as good a chance as you did."

Peter's chest wrenched as Sting turned and walked up the ramp.

"No, Sting! NO!"

He reached the hatch and paused. "Long life, Pete. You're the best friend I ever had."

The sound of the hatch closing startled Peter. He backed away, unable to tear his gaze from the departing ship as it carried his best friend out of the hangar. With a rush of exhaust, it surged over the swampland and winked out on the horizon.

Sting was gone.

Numb, Peter staggered into the smoky, grey hallway leading back to the vaulted chamber and Sergeant Temple. Clutching the god symbol in his palm, Peter sank to his knees and wept.

And on whatever sliver of soul he might or might not have, he prayed.

36

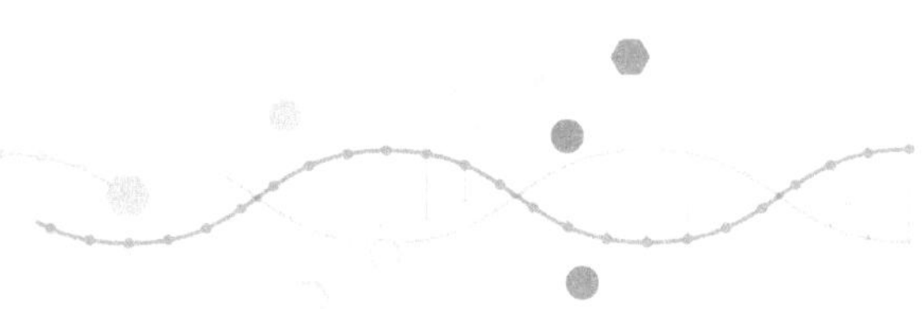

COLONEL STANTON CALLED an early staff meeting. Kai hadn't been completely honest about Stanton's reaction to the off-station MRC investigation. When Mana Ugasi walked off the reclamation floor headed toward the meeting room, Jeannette realized what had happened.

Kai was no longer the Reclamation Coordinator.

A knot in her stomach tightened. *What else had happened?* She stiffened as she sat down in the nearest chair, waiting for the other shoe to drop.

Three minutes before the meeting started, Kai showed up pale, light blue eyes bloodshot, chin stubbled. He plopped down in a chair beside her.

"Kai, are you all right?"

"Tell ya later," he said, offering her a quick smile as Colonel Stanton took her seat. She perched there like a gargoyle as agendas appeared on the table top screens. One agenda item: MRC Report.

"My apologies for this unscheduled meeting," said Stanton, clearing her throat. She gestured toward Mana Ugasi. "First, I want to announce that Dr. Mana Ugasi is the new first shift Reclamation

Coordinator, replacing Dr. Kai Drew who has been—demoted to reclamation specialist."

Jeannette turned to stare at Kai, her eyes wide, unable to hide her shock. He shook his head, not making eye contact. Now, Jeannette felt terribly guilty.

This was her fault. And she would remember it.

Smiling pleasantly, Colonel Stanton stared at Kai, her intense hazel eyes boring through him. "Dr. Drew, let's have the report. You can explain to me after the meeting why it wasn't turned in on time." Her hard stare flicked to Jeannette who didn't look away. "We'll have to work on your ability to prioritize tasks. But I'm sure your third shift coordinator will help you with that. I'm sure there are plenty of extra hours you can spend working on it."

Jeannette glanced at Kai. His mouth pinched into a tight line, his eyes blue flames as he rose from his chair, a printed report in his hands. The text appeared on everyone's screens. With two fingers, Jeannette dragged the text closer.

"Here are the results of our MRC testing. MRCs from six batches of recombinants were examined, tested, and analyzed for defects uncovered here at the station. In addition, recombinants with affected chips were observed in their training behaviors."

Kai described the process used to examine the chips and gave the relevant quantitative data regarding the defect. While Kai talked, Jeannette touched the report and sent it to her local file space. She addressed an email to UCOE's Operations Administrator and any other personnel she could think of, including herself, then attached Kai's report. Stanton would try to bury this report. She wasn't sure why though. That would take some more research, but right now, she'd make sure that report got off this station.

Stanton steepled her fingers, a smug look on her puckered face. "Dr. Drew, please—enough methodology. We can all read that for ourselves. The results. What did your investigation reveal?"

Kai kept his cool. He didn't give into the pressure and took his time. Jeannette was impressed by his calm. Stanton could fire him on the spot and he'd have no recourse. She knew that and Kai knew that, but he didn't intimidate easily.

"RDC is reusing its MRCs. And far too often, reinserting them into new recombinants without verifying chip integrity." He looked directly at Stanton. "I recommend that this information be forwarded to RDC immediately. It could make a big difference at the front."

Jeannette CC'ed her email to all of RDC's administrative addresses.

"This problem is system-wide and needs to be addressed right away," Kai continued. "Which brings me to my last point."

"Thank you, Dr. Drew," said Stanton. "Now, sit down."

"I'm not finished, Colonel," he replied.

A smile cracked across Stanton's hard-edged face. "That's all we have time for, Dr. Drew. Thank you for the information."

"But Colonel, the last point is vital—"

"Take your seat, doctor. I said I would review the report and pass it on to the appropriate parties."

This is unbelievable! She was trying to cover up the most important point. The reason this report mattered. The discovery of the Antaran code.

Jeannette rose to her feet. "Please sit, Dr. Drew. I'll handle the conclusion."

Colonel Stanton leaned forward. "Dr. Kingston, you're not—"

"Finished? No, I'm not and I've got more information. Thank you, Colonel. We do have one more point." She leaned her palms against the table. "Our conclusions concern the nature of the defect—"

"That's enough, Dr. Kingston." Colonel Stanton jumped to her feet. "I'm in command of the reclamation effort—"

"And I'm sure you're as concerned as we are about the Antaran code found in the MRCs."

Voices mumbled in the silence. Jeannette scanned the room, surprise evident on all the attendees' faces. They seemed stunned and confused by this revelation. Stanton was over-the-top pissed.

"That's right," said Jeannette. "Dr. Drew and I uncovered bits of

Antaran code embedded in extracted MRCs. We feel it's paramount that this be investigated immediately."

Reaching down to the table, Jeannette flicked *send* and her email with the report rushed away. Not even Stanton could stop it now. If she knew.

Colonel Stanton chuckled as she sat back in her chair, growing strangely calm. "Dr. Kingston," she said, shaking her head. "None of this—fabrication has been verified. It will have to be investigated by RDC personnel and those who are experts. I'm sure any sort of data corruption must look like alien code when it's viewed by a novice such as yourself."

Chuckles rippled through the room.

Novice? Why was Stanton trying to squelch this?

Uneasiness quivered through her stomach at a vague thought that crossed her mind, but she left the idea unspoken. It was too frightening to voice.

"You're right, Colonel," said Jeannette, sitting down. "To the untrained eye, corruption does look alien. But even novices can recognize patterns." She glanced over at Kai. "And compare them to actual Antaran code. Which we did." She watched Stanton's face for a ripple of concern, but she looked unimpressed. "But as you said, this is best left to the experts. So, I've already sent the report to RDC and the various administrators and developers at UCOE HQ. We hope to have results of their analyses very soon, Colonel."

The anger in Colonel Stanton's eyes burned again as she glared at Jeannette. "All right then. We'll wait for our results. Everyone dismissed."

Jeannette and Kai shuffled out of the room as Mana surged past.

"By the way," said Mana, pausing. "You've been placed on third shift, Dr. Kingston. Sorry."

"It's okay," Jeannette answered as Mana hurried away.

She glanced at Kai. "We need to talk. C'mon."

Nodding, Kai followed her across the reclamation chamber and into the hallway. In silence, they clamored into the lift as Jeannette pressed the button for her floor.

"What do we—"

Jeannette laid her fingers against his mouth, shaking her head. "Not here," she whispered.

When the lift doors opened, Jeannette hurried down the hallway and into her quarters, Kai right behind her. She reached up to the wall where she'd placed the new holo screen she'd gotten from Mimi on Civilization. Pictures of the river at night displayed as a jammer shielded her quarters against hidden video captures, bugs, and other recordings.

It was safe to talk here now.

Inside, Jeannette turned as Kai grabbed hold of her, his lips pressing urgently against hers. She kissed back, unable to resist his touch, realizing that she'd been attracted to him for a long time. It had been a long time since she'd wanted a man's touch.

"I've wanted to do that for years," said Kai. "Damned MRC."

"Me too," she said and reached up to his face, caressing.

He held her hands in his. "Jeannette, you were brilliant in there!" His grin was infectious. "I was just going to keep talking, but they didn't expect you to jump in."

"I was just leveling the playing field, Kai," she said, breathless. "Why didn't you tell me they'd demoted you?"

He shrugged, letting go of her hands. "I didn't want you to feel guilty about it. It was my fault not yours."

"I'm really sorry."

"Forget it. I will by tomorrow," he said with a hollow laugh. But his face went taut, suddenly serious. "This is the first time I don't want to forget things, Jeannette." He laid his hand against his chest. "I'm proud of what we did today. And I want to remember it."

Jeannette caressed his shoulder. "For years, I had a file called MyLife where I recorded everything important to me. Every time I logged into the system, this file read my life back to me." She touched her forehead. "Now, it's all here again."

Bowing his head, he nodded.

"Look, I know this great restaurant. Great wine and cheesecake." She laid her hand against his neck, kneading the stony muscles. "And for a bunch of credits or some volunteer work, they'll take this out."

He smiled, patting her hand. "It's a date. After today's staff meeting, I think you and I are going to be looking for new employment."

"But Kai, staying here and being a pain in Stanton's ass makes me deliriously happy."

Kai laughed.

He was probably right, but out here, getting replacements would take time. Jeannette's stomach clenched. Stanton wouldn't fire them yet. Besides, with that report at HQ, firing her and Kai would be attention that Stanton didn't want. Still, it nagged at her why Stanton wanted that report buried. She planned to stay here long enough to figure out Stanton's angle.

"Let's take that leave now though, Kai. Today. So, you'll remember."

"I'll arrange for the shuttle and time off," he said. "I'll come up with something."

"Kai...why do you think Stanton wanted that report buried?"

He shook his head. "I've been through a dozen reasons in my head, but none of them makes sense." Taking hold of her hands, he pulled her in front of him, his fingers stroking her hair. "What about you? Any theories?"

It sounded absurd. She had no proof. He took her face in his hands, kissing her lips, sipping her neck. She leaned her head back, running her fingers through his thick black hair.

"It's—crazy," she said, losing herself in the warmth of his skin against hers. "You'll probably laugh."

"Try me," he whispered in her ear.

"What if—she already—knew about the Antaran code?"

His kisses traveled across her cheek, back to her mouth again, his arms pulling her against him.

"Maybe," he said.

She drew his face to hers and stared into his intense blue eyes. "What if *her* MRC has Antaran code?"

Smiling, he brushed a lock of red hair out of her eyes. "Possible."

A cold wave rushed over her skin as the words spilled out, her unspoken fear. "What if she's responsible for the code, Kai? What if she's sold us out to the Antarans?"

The horrified look on Kai's face confirmed the possibility. Stunned silent, he just stared at her.

"What if there's more than just code involved?" he said finally, his voice thin, eyes wide.

Like xDNA transfers? Hacking. And sabotage. Or worse?

Jeannette's heart raced. Just how deeply was Colonel Stanton involved? And how far into UCOE did this go?

The possibilities were terrifying.

37

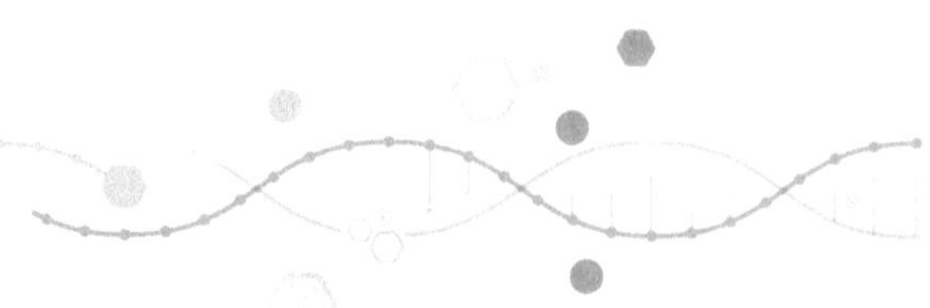

IT WAS evening when Peter hefted Sergeant Temple across his shoulders and set out into the swamps. For hours, he scanned areas flat and solid enough to land a shuttle, hoping to find the safe house. Sarge's fever had come up again and he was delirious. Peter tried to keep him quiet, but Sarge kept mumbling to himself and occasionally crying out.

Peter felt empty. Sting's absence was something he couldn't fill. He hurt all over. It was the worst pain he'd ever felt.

He let his rifle hang on his shoulder and reached up to the god symbol around his neck. He gripped it, feeling sick inside, and wondered where Sting was right now.

Was he even still alive?

The snow had melted, revealing footpaths and landmarks, rain beginning to fall. The moon glinted off the swamp water, offering enough light to see. He tucked the sensor grid into his parka's front pocket.

He walked for hours, dazed, hungry, grieving.

Once, the sensor grid activated, but he ignored it and kept

walking, Sarge a dead weight on his aching back. He didn't care what swung out of the trees now.

Just being alive wasn't enough and he realized that now.

It was all he'd dreamed of, but there was so much more to it. It was caring about someone, meaning something to somebody. John Stingley had been the closest thing to family Peter had ever known. No, he *was* family.

The loss was too hard to take. It was breaking him in half.

Straining under Sarge's weight against his shoulders and back, he understood how Diana must feel now. His breath hitched, a sob breaking free. He swallowed the rest.

For her, he'd get her brother to safety. Sarge and Diana were all he had now.

Peter slogged through mud that sloshed over his boots and splattered into his face. He paused, letting the rifle hang as he pulled out the sensor grid.

Something winked to the north. He scowled. Biodrones.

His eyes misted. *Damn Drake for busting the homing device! Why couldn't he have gotten Sting out too? Why!*

His eyes brimmed with tears and he swiped at them with the back of his mud-caked hand. He didn't know what to do now except scan. Staggering and too tired to think, he swerved onto another footpath that led north.

Peter walked for several minutes but finally sank to his knees. He couldn't go any farther. A few minutes rest and he'd go on.

Sarge needed help.

He leaned Sarge against a tree and unshouldered his field pack. His shoulders burned where the pack straps had chafed and cut into his skin. From the pack, he retrieved a self-heating synthration. He pulled the tab and opened it. The synthloaf steamed in the cool air as he removed it from the package. He dropped the packet on the ground and shook the biodegrading enzymes over it until it disappeared. The synthloaf was tasteless as he choked it down, chasing it with the last remaining mouthful of water in his canteen. He'd used the rest to clean Sarge's wounds.

When he'd finished the ration, he took Sarge's canteen from the pack and pressed it to Sarge's lips.

"Sarge, drink this. It'll make you feel better."

Sarge tried to push it away, but Peter held it firm, forcing it between Sarge's teeth. He poured the water into Sarge's mouth and Sarge swallowed.

Peter rested for a while until finally, the sergeant's eyes rolled open. He glanced around.

"Where's Stingley?"

Peter bowed his head, his breath catching, unable to speak.

"Where's Private Stingley?" he demanded.

Finally, something slipped out. Tight. Clipped. "Gone."

Sadness touched his fevered eyes. "God...I'm so sorry, Mitchell. You two were inseparable."

Peter clenched his hand into a fist and beat the ground. Tears seeped down his face and he swiped them back with his sleeve. Sarge reached out and laid a hand on Peter's shoulder.

"I'm really sorry, Peter. I know what he meant to you."

Peter snapped his angry gaze to Sarge. "How would you know?"

Sarge didn't flinch. "Because I have a sibling, too."

"I know," he answered in a quiet voice. "I'm sorry."

Peter's face twisted with pain and he turned away, but Sarge kept his hand on Peter's shoulder. When he could look at the sergeant again, Sarge's hand fell away.

"Where are we?"

Sighing, Peter held out a grid to him. Might as well tell him.

"I don't know, Sarge. I'm trying to find a safe house."

"Safe house? Mitchell! You're deserting?" His face flushed with anger. "If they catch you, they'll destroy you on the spot! Do you want to risk that?"

"What am I risking, Sarge?" he demanded. "If I survive this tour, I go back to base for more training and testing. I'm already risking a washout just by surviving. And if I pass, they send me to another place more dangerous than this. Do you think I even care if they shoot me for deserting?"

Sarge was silent.

"Besides," Peter snapped, "you need a medic and the safe house is our only chance to find that. Damn Drake for destroying that homing device!"

Working off his anger, Peter put all the equipment back in his pack and pulled out his grid. If he kept walking through the night, maybe they'd find the safe house soon. He prayed the units wouldn't pull out without taking one last crack at the munitions depot—wherever that might be. Otherwise, Sarge would be stranded in the wilds with no doctor to tend him.

"Wait a minute, Mitchell—homing device?"

"It would've led me right to the safe house. Now, I have no way to find it."

Sarge thought for a moment. "I could recalibrate your grid to search for recombinant IDs. It's the best I can do."

Peter turned to gape at Sarge. "You'd do that?"

"Yes, I'd do that. I owe you my life, Peter."

"You don't owe me a thing, Sarge."

Sarge laughed. "Don't I? When I took that job at Civilization's Training base, I thought it'd be a cakewalk. I'd never see combat and I'd never have to think or feel again. Just do my job and send the droids out for battle—and never feel more than a twinge of regret for the ones I lost." He sighed. "Then I get you in my unit and in a few months, you completely tear down twenty-eight years of fence row."

"What have I torn down?" His voice was indignant.

"Every justification and barrier I built around myself. I was always dependable, patient David, practical down to my regulation socks. The team player. The guy who took care of everybody, but it's easy to take care of people who don't really need it." He rose on his elbows and stared up at the sky. "But you needed it, Peter. Every day, every sim. And every time I helped you, I began to question myself—who I was, what I believed." Sarge's gaze met Peter's. "I don't have to ask those questions anymore, Peter." He held out his hand. "Now, give me the damned grid and don't say another word."

Smiling, Peter handed Sarge the grid. Sarge snatched it out of his hands and opened the casing.

"You hungry, Sarge?"

"I could eat," Sarge answered.

"All I've got is a couple of rations. You're welcome to both."

Sarge frowned. "Have you eaten?"

"A little while ago."

Peter retrieved the last of his rations. He pulled the tabs, waited, and opened the packaging. He held out both packets, a synthloaf and a burger. Sarge removed the burger and munched quietly as he worked. Peter used the last of his biodegrading enzymes on the packets and handed Sarge the canteen. He let Sarge drink his fill.

"Thanks, Mitchell," said Sarge, handing back the canteen.

Peter nodded and stored the canteen.

It took Sarge over an hour to recalibrate the grid. Finally, he pointed it at Peter, and the grid began to whine. He made another series of adjustments to the grid and pointed it at Peter again. This time the grid was silent.

"I've excluded your ID signature from the scan. Now, the grid should pick up other recombinants this far from the camps. There shouldn't be any out this far—unless they're at this safe house."

"Thanks, Sarge," said Peter.

Sarge extended the grid to him and Peter slipped it in his pocket.

"Ready to move out now?"

"I can walk," said Sarge, struggling to his feet. He fell.

"Have you also figured out how stubborn you are?"

"Not as stubborn as you, Mitchell."

Peter laughed and slid his arm around Sarge's waist. He pulled

Sarge to his feet and anchored the shivering man against him. Then he retrieved his field pack and rifle. He managed to get his arms through the field pack straps and keep Sarge on his feet. He slid the rifle strap over his left shoulder and pulled the grid out of his pocket.

The evening quickly turned to a muddy blur, but Peter kept walking. The clicks and whines from the grid had grown louder and faster. Maybe they would make the safe house by sunrise?

THE MOON HAD LONG DISAPPEARED from the sky, daylight approaching, when Peter emerged from the swamplands of Ku'Tal.

Ahead, in the pale ion light were the disheveled remains of a camp. A small shelter stood against a hillside. The grid's whines were continuous now. He shut it off and dropped it into his pocket.

Sarge had lapsed into delirium again, forcing Peter to carry him on his shoulders. His legs buckled as he entered the camp. He fell to his knees and eased Sarge to the ground.

Something shot across the sky in the distance. A shooting star? UCOE ships?

Footfalls echoed through the predawn silence as Peter collapsed in the mud.

"Soldier, are you all right?"

Peter heard the familiar whir of an ID scan. A man's face hung over him, his smile framed by short beard stubble.

"You're a recombinant?" the man asked.

Peter nodded. "Take care of my—sergeant. Got spiked by biodrones. Needs a medic."

"We've got someone inside who can help. And we've got a shuttle waiting for you. But looks like you're going to need a little attention first. Can you walk?"

He shook his head.

The man lifted him gently from the mud. Someone else grabbed

Peter's legs. They carried him into the shelter behind Sergeant Temple.

Once inside, the man stripped off Peter's coat and got him onto a cot. He removed Peter's uniform. When he picked up the purple scarf, Peter snatched it out of his hand.

"That's mine!"

"Must be special," said the man with a smile.

Peter nodded, pressing it against his chest.

"My name's Ron Kraver. I'm with the underground. We'll get you a ration, some clean clothes, and some medical attention. Then we've got to get you aboard that shuttle. If you miss it, you'll be sharing the swamp with a bunch of biodrones."

"What are you talking about?"

"How long you been separated from your unit, private?"

He shook his head. "Days, I guess. I don't know. It's all a blur right now."

"UCOE's pulling out. Gonna leave it to the enemy."

He settled against the pillow, his eyes closing.

"What's your name, son?"

"Mitchell," he answered. "Peter Mitchell."

Ron grinned. "I'll be damned! Diana's gonna be thrilled."

Peter bolted up from the cot. "Diana?"

"Relax, private," he said and laid a hand on Peter's shoulder, easing him back against the cot. "She's been flying recombinants out of here for weeks. She waited as long as she could this morning, hoping you'd make it here. You just missed her. But we'll get you on the next shuttle out. It's the last one. We're all leaving on it."

Ron started toward the door, but Peter called him back.

"Could you let her know that I brought her brother in from the swamps? He'll be fine."

"Sure will, Peter. Get a quick nap. Then we'll deal with your MRC and a ration."

Ron said something else, but his voice faded as Peter sank into sleep.

SOMETIME LATER PETER AWOKE, a throbbing pain in his neck. He reached up to rub it and found a small bandage at his nape. The god symbol still hung around his neck, Diana's purple scarf against his chest. His eyes stung just looking at it. *Where are you now, Sting?* His chest ached.

Shakily, he sat up and slid his feet over the edge. A tan flight suit lay at the foot of the bed. His UCOE boots were gone and so was his field pack, replaced with plain black chukkas and a green duffle bag. Peter found all of his things inside.

His muscles were stiff and unyielding as he struggled into the flight suit and boots. He tucked Diana's scarf, dirty and ragged around the edges now, into the flight suit. By his heart. Then he limped out of the bunkroom and across to where Ron stood with another man. Ron turned when he heard Peter approaching.

"Mitchell," he called. "How you feeling?"

Peter reached up to his neck.

"You were sound asleep when we were ready to take the chip, so we took it while you slept. Your Sergeant Temple even assisted."

"Sarge? But he was delirious when I brought him in."

Ron nodded and steered Peter toward a chair by a portable stove. The room was bare except for one other chair.

"The medic gave him an antidote to counteract the biodrone venom. He was fine when he left."

"Left? Where'd he go?"

"He left on foot to rejoin his unit."

"He won't make it!" Peter shouted, and struggled up from the chair. He tried to hurry outside, but Ron held him back.

"The biodrones are being beaten back. They seem to have lost their organization. He'll get through. One of my scouts went with him. My scout's got a two-seater, puddle-jumper stashed somewhere in the swamp for emergencies. Don't worry about your sergeant. He'll be fine. Now sit down and have some coffee. The medic's removing an MRC, so the shuttle will be taking off shortly."

Peter poured himself a cup of coffee and hobbled outside. He stared at the sky, his stomach sick with worry as he wondered if Sarge would reach the unit. If Sting would survive the Antarans.

If Diana still loved him.

The sun warmed the sky for the first time in weeks.

"Goodbye, John Stingley," he said to the sky and gripped the god symbol around his neck. "You were the best friend I ever had." His eyes stung with tears now. He hoped that someday, somehow, Sting would survive Ballese. With a future ahead of him.

"Mitchell!" Ron called from the shelter, and pointed toward a dirt runway. "The shuttle's ready to roll. Get aboard." Ron set Peter's duffle bag beside the door. "I'll send Diana the message that you and her brother made it, then we're all out of here."

Peter watched a man carry the stove and two chairs out of the shelter and down to the shuttle. Another man carried a folding cot toward the shuttle. In a few moments, the shelter walls collapsed, folding tightly against each other.

"Thanks for everything," Peter replied and moved toward the duffle bag.

Ron handed him the bag.

"What month is it?" Peter asked suddenly.

"December, private. Now, get aboard that shuttle."

As Ron and the two men retrieved the shelter walls, Peter hefted his duffle bag onto his shoulder and hurried toward the runway. Over six months of hell and it had to end with him losing his best friend. Six months.

Walking up the ramp, he gazed one last time at the pale sun. His heart ached, his eyes still burning.

"I'll miss you, Sting," he whispered.

Then it dawned on him. December. He was a year older. He was twenty-three.

He pulled Diana's purple scarf out of his flight suit. She'd be there at the shuttle port when he stepped off. She'd be there to wish him a happy first anniversary. The scarf fluttered in his hand, the deep purple gleaming in the pale sunlight. It was the truest purple he'd ever seen.

He climbed aboard and sank into an empty seat. Pulling the harness tight against his chest, he waited for departure.

38

PETER FELT shaky when the shuttle glided to a stop in Civilization. A million questions plagued him. The fear was intense.

Where would he go? How would he live? What would it feel like to be a citizen? Was that even possible?

It was everything he'd ever wanted, yet it terrified him. But it was a fear he could handle now.

The other recombinants picked up their belongings and stepped off the shuttle. Peter, gripping his duffle bag, filed off behind them.

There, at the edge of the ramp, stood Diana, wearing a white blouse and that metallic purple skirt.

He smiled. After all this time, it was really Diana.

He froze a moment, his heart pounding. She was much more beautiful than he remembered. A lump rose in his throat, his eyes misting as he hurried down the ramp.

"Peter!" she cried over and over as she rushed toward him.

He threw his arms around her, holding her so close he couldn't breathe. Her fingers stroked his hair, caressed his face, and gripped his waist, holding him tight. She whispered his name again. Then he kissed her, a long, anxious kiss.

She felt so good in his arms. He held her tighter, savoring every warm touch and caress for several long moments.

Even as she led him away from the shuttle, he held onto her.

She hurried him into a skimmer with some of the other recombinants and the skimmer whisked them down the road into Civilization.

He clung to her, his whole body shaking as the horrors of Ku'Tal washed over him. Clenching his eyes closed, he fought down a moan. There hadn't been time to deal with any of it.

"Peter, are you all right?" Diana asked, her face pinched with worry.

He nodded. He couldn't look at her.

If he looked into those warm, understanding brown eyes, he'd fall apart right here.

He gripped the seat and concentrated on the horizon until the skimmer brought them to the back of End of the Line. He scrambled out of the skimmer and rushed inside, tearing past Mimi. He plunged into the small office in the back of the kitchen and fell to his knees, hugging himself. He shook so hard his teeth chattered.

The door opened behind him.

"Peter?" came the timid voice.

Diana.

"Is he all right?" Mimi asked.

Peter rocked back and forth, shaking his head. He sucked in a breath, trying to hold it all inside. But then Diana knelt in front of him, her hands on his arms.

"What can I do?" she asked.

He reached into his shirt and slid out her scarf. It was tattered, bloodstained, and torn. With trembling hands, he held it out to her.

Gently, she took it from him, her hands pressing against his. "Oh, Peter. What you must have gone through."

He couldn't avoid those accepting brown eyes that had touched him so deeply that night at the river. It all came pouring out, and he couldn't stop it.

"Sting's gone," he wept, his voice choking.

She held him.

He babbled about the biodrones and the swamp, the attacks, the pain, and the fever. He raged, his voice thick and strained, as he told her about the caregivers, Sting taking his place, and the god symbols. He told her about carrying Sarge through the swamps and recombinants washing out at twenty-seven. He shook uncontrollably, talking about Charles and what it meant to have someone who cared if he lived or died. Then, in a soft voice, he whispered it was his birthday.

Diana didn't say a word. She just held him.

And it was enough.

LESS THAN A MONTH LATER, Sergeant David Temple returned from the war front a hero. Peter heard about how, under heavy attack by Antaran forces, he single-handedly carried several rounds of explosives into the Antaran munitions depot and destroyed it. Peter heard that Temple sustained serious wounds in the process, but he managed to reach his unit that had pulled back pending a massive military withdrawal.

Then the Antarans inexplicably withdrew their forces.

The ruined depot was reported to have destroyed the Antarans' ability to continue their assault on Ku'Tal. UCOE declared its forces victorious and the skirmish on Ku'Tal over. They were building a base there.

Sarge was due on the afternoon shuttle.

Peter, Diana, and Mimi waited at the coffeehouse, sipping Karaban coffee. Diana and Mimi ate cheese Danishes, but Peter ordered fries and black coffee.

He couldn't stomach anything sweet. Not now.

At last, Temple's shuttle arrival was announced. Diana plinked credits down on the table. Taking hold of Diana's hand, Peter rushed out of the coffeehouse, Mimi beside them. They ran down the hall toward the shuttle gate.

The UCOE shuttle was packed, but finally Sergeant David Temple, pale and his right arm in a sling, emerged from the shuttle in uniform. A bright gold medal was pinned to his chest.

"David! Oh, thank God! David!" Diana ran to him. He held out his left arm, and she fell into it, hugging him. "I was so afraid for you."

"I never thought I'd see you again," he said, his voice thin, shaky.

She glanced down and saw the medal. "David, they say you're a hero."

He shrugged. "I did what I had to do."

"Welcome back, David," Mimi said to him.

"Thanks, Mimi."

Peter walked up and extended his hand.

Sarge stiffened. They stared at each other for a moment. Finally, Peter spoke.

"Good to have you back, Sarge."

Sarge smiled. He shook Peter's hand. "Mitchell. You made it out."

Peter nodded and cast a wary gaze around the shuttle port. "For now."

"For good," said Temple.

"I don't understand," Peter said with a grimace.

"On my way back to the unit, I detoured through the ravine. I switched your MRC with Drake's. I destroyed his and threw it in the swamp. Private Peter Mitchell was pronounced dead on Ku'Tal over a month ago."

A grin spilled across Peter's face. "Thank you, Sarge."

"If it hadn't been for you, Mitchell, I'd have died a hundred times on Ku'Tal. It was the least I could do."

Peter's gaze fell to the medal. "I heard you fragged the depot."

Sarge nodded. "Technically. I logged the action under John Stingley's name. In the books, he's credited with the destruction of the depot. I destroyed the depot, but he won the war. In UCOE's eyes, John Stingley is a hero." Temple turned the medal over. "Look."

Peter leaned forward. John "Sting" Stingley was engraved on the back. He couldn't help but smile. He and Sting had lived through a lot of sorrow with very few moments of anything else, but Sarge had given Sting his dream. Sting would have been so proud.

Through John Stingley, Peter learned not to be afraid. And to live.

Mimi reached out to Peter, turned his hand palm up and then back again. She started to speak, but he just shook his head.

He didn't know if he believed anything Mimi said about souls, but he'd looked his in the face. He had one. It didn't matter if it was true purple or if it even had any color. He just knew it was deep and strong.

Sting had a soul, too. He wasn't sure what color or god symbol represented it, but he had a right to find that out himself.

Somehow, some way, Peter would give Sting that chance. He'd find a way off Civilization—to Ballese, where the Antarans had taken Sting.

Sarge had a saying: *leave no one behind* and that's exactly what Peter planned to do.

Go in after Sting and bring him home—even if it killed him.

EPILOGUE

AFTER RETURNING from a quick run to Civilization (where she and Kai had eaten and then removed Kai's MRC) and a few hours' sleep, Jeannette was able to pull herself together. After watching some of her memories, Rena's death was still a razor-sharp memory. There were a lot more memories to see, but not right now. She would work through them slowly. There were a lot of years to view. She knew Kai was faced with the same emotional recovery, too. Together, they'd work through all of it.

She headed into the lift and felt the familiar drop into the reclamation station's belly. Her steps were slow and uncertain, but she kept moving toward the reclamation center. Once inside, she trekked through the factory-like room, past the endless line of red and blue body bags awaiting reclamation. Kai waved at her, but didn't approach. She appreciated him giving her space today. Getting back to the job was difficult, but she didn't know how it would be without her MRC.

Equipment spun up and lights flicked on. She logged into her workstation and her login file opened. Seeing the file was startling because as she read through the first few paragraphs, she remembered the events now. Not in the same way as experiencing them, but the images were at least there.

She closed the file. She didn't need it anymore.

One of the medtechs laid a body bag on her exam table and she hesitated. Finally, she reached beneath her station table and retrieved a small bottle of lavender oil. Dabbing some underneath her nose, she put the bottle away and snapped on her gloves and visor. Then she unzipped the body bag.

The remains were barely human. She winced, recoiling. Cascade mine.

She inhaled a deep breath of lavender and concentrated on the scent for a few moments. With a shaky hand, she scanned the reclamation orders on the tag. Recombinant #Dylan2015—male, first tour in Ku'Tal. She always called the men Dylan. After her late husband. The sharp ache of memory flashed through her head.

Another breath of lavender...exhale slowly.

She hesitated then peeled back the body bag flaps. Gently, she tilted the young man's head to scan his MRC. She wondered what his name had been and how many months since he'd achieved consciousness. And she wondered if he was better off this way. Cascade mines at least killed quickly.

The Recombinant Defense Program killed much more slowly. She knew that now. Mostly because she'd been there and seen it for herself.

Picking up her laser scalpel, Jeannette flicked it on and began the autopsy and hardware recovery.

SHE PROCESSED several bodies on her shift and by 0700 hours she was exhausted. The steady stream of dead recombinants had increased dramatically since she'd been away. With all these casualties, she wondered if the front line on Ku'Tal had collapsed. She'd seen it before.

One of the techs laid another body bag on her table and wheeled his cart away to the next station.

"You doing okay over there, Jeannette?" Kai asked.

She nodded. "I was hoping I'd gotten through my last one today."

"Me too," he said with a grimace. "There are a few left after this one, so you may have one more."

"I can hardly wait," Jeannette said with a sigh and scanned the reclamation orders on the body bag's tag.

The tag was marked Recombinant #2104. Male. First tour at Ku'Tal.

And last. She winced.

She unzipped the bag and opened its flaps. Other than a belly wound, the young man looked like he was sleeping. She turned his head.

"What's this?" she said aloud as she touched a slash at the back of the recombinant's neck.

His MRC had been removed and lay inside the—she studied the clean edges—the incision. That's exactly what it was.

She removed the unattached MRC and placed it in the processing unit for a diagnostic check and a record lookup on the last chip insertion. The processing unit whirred to life and she waited for the data to scroll onto the screen. It took a long time and then finally the screen filled with data. And there was the batch number with the weird O after it. What did that mean?

She read through the insertions, but her heart slipped into her throat when she saw the recombinant's name: Peter Mitchell.

"Oh, not Mitchell," she said with a groan and moved back to the body bag.

Diana would be devastated when she found out.

Jeannette turned the young man's head toward her and studied his hard-edged face, stringy chestnut bangs, and moss green eyes. She thought back to the training base, picturing the quiet young man with the sweet face and boyish smile. Sandy blond hair and blue eyes. His image was still in her memory—thanks to Mimi Constantine.

This recombinant wasn't Peter Mitchell.

As she turned back to the processing unit, the realization hit her. The incision. The dead recombinant with Mitchell's MRC.

She grinned. Peter Mitchell had escaped the military.

She moved to her workstation and scanned the chip, running diagnostics and uploading Mitchell's date of death to UCOE. In moments, the *update successful* message appeared on the screen.

It was official now. In UCOE's records, Private Peter Mitchell was dead.

The processing unit whined and displayed diagnostics on the screen. Now, she'd finally know if his chip had malfunctioned like so many in his batch. Even though he had an O in his batch. She scrolled through the results, mouth falling open, surprised by the results.

"How can that be?"

Three times, she ran the analysis and three times, she read results. Each time they were the same. Despite being in the affected batch, Mitchell's MRC had been functioning perfectly with no trace of malfunction or defect. Yet, he remembered everything as if he'd somehow bypassed the memory-stealing function. And killing sickened him. From a batch labeled with a high aggression quotient. Except for the strange O typo.

Maybe he was an anomaly after all?

Jeannette plucked the MRC out of the processing unit and slipped it into an antistatic bag. And then her pocket. She grabbed another MRC from a tray and tossed it onto the table. Picking up the tissue resin separator, she slammed it against the MRC. The chip shattered into fragments. She put two shards in an antistatic bag—as if it mattered—and placed it inside the body bag.

"Jeannette," Kai called. "Everything okay?"

Yes, everything was *finally* okay. She'd make sure of it.

"Everything's fine. Just dropped a tool."

She entered a note field into Mitchell's autopsy record.

MRC and microfeed did not survive intact. Returning some of the MRC fragments as evidence.

She closed the record, hoping that Peter and Diana lived a long life together.

But the latest reports from the crumbling front unnerved her. She knew the Antarans had taken Stingley and other recombinants captive.

No one returned from the Antaris Nation—especially recombinants.

And she knew Mitchell. He would never truly be free of the military unless he freed John Stingley.

Soon, Peter Mitchell would risk everything to reach the alien-held planet, Ballese and rescue his best friend—with or without backup.

The End of RECOMBINANT: Experiencing True Purple, Book 1
The story continues in...
HELIX: Experiencing True Purple, Book 2

2
EXPERIENCING TRUE PURPLE
HELIX
L.S.
SILVERTHORNE
AWARD-WINNING BESTSELLING AUTHOR

Novels by L.S. Silverthorne

Experiencing True Purple series:

RECOMBINANT, Book 1

HELIX, Book 2

SPLICE, Book 3

Standalone:

REDISCOVERY

Writing as Lisa Silverthorne

A Game of Lost Souls series:

Contemporary Romantasy

THE CINDERELLA HOUR

THE PRINCE CHARMING HOUR

THE EVER AFTER HOUR

THE FALLEN HEARTS SEASON

THE RISING SPIRITS SEASON

THE ETERNAL SOULS SEASON

THE ROYAL WEDDING HOUR

THE HEAVENLY HONEYMOON HOUR

THE DIVINE NEWLYWEDS SHOW

THE CELESTIAL COUPLES SHOW

THE ENOCHIAN APOCALYPSE SHOW

THE ANGELIC ANNIVERSARY SHOW

THE PERDITION PICTURE SHOW

Complete Series!

Curse and Crown series:

Epic Court Intrigue Romantasy
THORN & BLADE
STORM & STEEL

The Spiral series:
Dark Contemporary Fantasy
BETWEEN
REPRISE
AVENGE

The Resurrectionist Papers
Paranormal Romystery
GRAVE RECKONING

Standalones:
ISABEL'S TEARS
LANDFALL
PACIFIC BLUE TATTOO

Short Story Collections
THE SOUND OF ANGELS
THE MAGIC OF ORDINARY THINGS
TIMELESS
WINTER'S EMBRACE

FORTHCOMING!

Experiencing True Purple series:

Cipher, Book 4
Renascence, Book 5 (Series End)

Writing as Lisa Silverthorne

Curse and Crown series:

Flame & Dagger, Book Three (2026)
Frost & Foil, Book Four
Curse & Crown, Book Five (Series End)

The Spiral series:

Ruin, Book 4
Descent, Book 5 (Series End)

The Resurrectionist Papers:

Corpses Delicti (2026)
Stiffed Again

ABOUT THE AUTHOR

LISA SILVERTHORNE, an award-winning author, has published over 30 novels and 150 short stories and novelettes in many genres. She is the author of *A Game of Lost Souls*, *Experiencing True Purple*, *The Spiral*, *The Resurrectionist Papers*, and *Curse and Crown*.

Before you go, you are invited to please leave a **review of this book**!

Reviews are a wonderful way to help an author and share your thoughts with other readers, so **please post yours,** in as many places as possible!

ONLINE STORE!

For Ebook Bundles, book swag, and beautiful ***Special Edition*** *hardcovers (coming soon), visit:* ***LisaSilverthorneBooks.com***

Thanks for reading! We appreciate your support!

Heartfelt High Octane Science Fiction

LISASILVERTHORNE.COM

facebook.com/lisa.silverthorne.author

bookbub.com/profile/lisa-silverthorne

amazon.com/author/lisasilverthorne

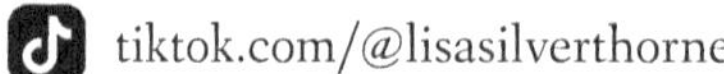
tiktok.com/@lisasilverthorne

bsky.app/@lisasilverthorne.bsky.social